CITY
OF
LIGHT

Across Time & Space series

The Eternity Stone
Mountain of Glass
Desert of Fire
Desert of Ice
The Hidden Door
Whiter Than Snow
City of Light

Fairytale Memoirs series
The Mostly Forgotten Memoirs of Rose Red
Viola Sends Her Regrets
Gifted

Standalone books
Breaking the Glass Slipper
Unshakeable
Tyger
Take Me Home

For information on new and upcoming books,
go to **mmarinanbooks.com**

CITY OF LIGHT

ACROSS TIME & SPACE BOOK 7

M. MARINAN

Silversmith PUBLISHING

First published in New Zealand in 2023
by Silversmith Publishing

A catalogue record for this book is available from the National Library of New Zealand

This paperback edition: ISBN 978-1-99-001430-7
Epub edition: ISBN 978-1-99-001433-8

Contents

Prologue

Erus city-state, 3004 AD

In the centre of Erus's temple district, streams of people came to pay their respects to the new Tiger statue. They disappeared into doors at its colossal, shining base, then reappeared some time later from different doors on the other side.

But now they wore dazed expressions as well as a tiny little mark right in the middle of their foreheads, shaped rather like a squiggly-legged starfish. The new physical mark served as a tracker, proof of loyalty…and a means of control.

Everyone in Erus had to pledge themselves to the Tiger in person. It didn't matter who they were already pledged to – they had five days to show up, or else.

Chairman Luca DeMannard, also known as Legion, watched sullenly from the nearby council office along with his Halfling mother Lilith. He'd had to get a Tiger mark as well to show his own allegiance. He'd managed to get it on his hand rather than his actual head, but he resented the intrusion. He was a Creature – mostly – and this was his body, damn it! Or Luke's, anyway. While Luca's true Creature body still lay safe and sleeping in the borderlands, he would be forced to put up with the desperately unwelcome mark.

"And after I destroyed the White Prince for him, too," he muttered to himself. "That was hard work, and dangerous. I could have died! And I sent him one of Gerak's old Princes of the Air too, not that he cares. So much for being allowed to rule on my own."

"Hush, Legion," Lilith said sharply from where she sat next to him, also overlooking the scene. Her mark was bold and black on her forehead, but noticeably smaller than those most wore. A perk of being one of the Tiger's semi-trusted people. "You are still the governor of Greater Erus, are you not? With control of Memrys and Dailan just as you always wanted. Stop complaining

2

about the Tiger and focus on thriving. He may be your father, but he has no parental affection for you, or anyone. Support his reign and you too will be supported."

Yes, that was right. Luca's parents were Lilith, daughter of the White Prince and currently the world's oldest Halfling, and the Tiger, the Other's original leader. Now the normal realm's official leader too, if from a distance. Full-blooded Creatures couldn't set a foot into the normal realm. They could only rule through their human or Halfling pledges.

But as Lilith had said, the Tiger held no fatherly feelings for Luca. He only cared about what Luca could do for him. And now Luca was as bound as any of these fools, unable to exercise his true independence and power over this new, combined city-state.

He looked past the statue to the glimmers of the Reamas river he could just see in the distance. He'd wanted so badly to bomb the Dailan side – to prove a point and because it would be amusing – but now he'd have to get the Tiger's permission to do so.

Hades. This was no fun.

Lilith stood abruptly. "I'm being called. You watch yourself, Legion – I won't always be here to do it for you."

Luca – or Legion the half-Halfling – was eighty-five years old. He did not need his *mother* watching over him...or watching him.

But because Luca was angry, not stupid, he kept his mouth shut.

Long may the Tiger reign.

Ha.

While humans pledged themselves en masse in the cities, something even more significant was taking place underground, right on the border between the Other and normal realms,

In a deep cave he'd visited many a time, the Tiger stood at the very edge of the Other realm, as far as its invisible barrier would allow him to go. Streams of power filtered into him from hundreds of thousands of new, more solid tattooed pledges, making his manlike form larger and stronger than ever before. The stripes and spots on his skin gleamed where his armour exposed it.

But his full, rather terrifying attention was fixed on a trio of humans directly on the other side of the barrier. They wore red cloaks, had marked foreheads, and were currently crouched around two sturdy, locked cases. He watched avidly as they carefully opened the first one, then withdrew a small wooden box, slightly battered by age. Then the second case was opened, and one human pulled out a tiny leather flask, the sort that hadn't been used in many centuries.

The spirit's blood. It was the last, missing piece of the Anima Chest, which for the Tiger was the most important object of power in the universe. He'd been searching for it for as long as he'd known it existed.

The red-cloaked humans moved as if to open the wooden chest, but he lifted a hand. ***"Not you."*** After what had happened the last time he'd tried to use the Anima Chest – exactly four hundred and six years earlier – he wouldn't risk this going wrong.

Then finally a new figure strode into view on the normal side of the barrier. Lilith wore a shiny, pretty face and body like a human would wear a coat, but the Tiger could clearly see straight through it to her real face. (Which by Creature standards was perfectly adequate.) She seemed a lot smaller than when he'd last seen her, but that was just an impression caused by the way he'd doubled in size.

"As the only free user of both realms, you are the one person I will allow to do this for me," he warned her. ***"But if you betray me, there will be no place you can run."***

He felt the flicker of her heartrate go up, but her expression didn't change. "Master, I have no need for the Anima Chest's power, and there is no one I fear more than you."

It was the right answer. But still, the Tiger pressed himself against the barrier as Lilith opened the chest directly on the other side, within inches of him. Inside were three neatly cut compartments, fizzing with alter-power. Two were already occupied with a fresh-looking flower and a mottled brown rock. The other was the right size for the missing flask, and Lilith barely paused before setting it in place.

For a moment nothing happened. The chest didn't look any different either, but suddenly he could feel a warmth where it pressed against the base of the barrier, right by his clawed foot.

And then when Lilith lifted the chest as high as she could reach, pressing it against the barrier, he pressed his hand against the other side…and grasped the box.

Then, buoyant with triumph at this long-awaited moment, the Tiger stepped through the barrier into the normal realm.

Mountain of Glass, time very relevant

Amaranthus stood in his Tapestry Room, studying the end of the tapestry that represented the whole of human history. More specifically, he was looking at one of the long, darkest grey threads that ran around the edge of the entire room.

Here, at the very end of the tapestry, the thread had abruptly moved away from its place at the border and into the middle amongst all the tiny threads signifying human lives. And everything it touched, it tainted.

Amaranthus didn't need to touch the thread to know who it was. The Tiger, his former Bright One, had escaped from his prison in the Other realm and was now making his way across the human landscape, searing a path into the soil as he went.

He'd seen this coming since the start. For while the Creatures had an imperfect, limited view of the future, his was as complete as it had ever been.

Then Amaranthus moved to the centre of the round room. Here, a fountain sprang from the centre of a gleaming, shimmering black rock – the Heart stone – then ran out to cover first the Mountain of Glass, then make its way as a river into the normal realm. Not just any river, *the* River.

Amaranthus set his hand against the stone's slick surface. Then connecting his mind with everyone who the River touched – from the immortal People to his human friends – he said, *"The countdown has started. Whatever you do next, make it count."*

1
Not Quite Home

Home. That's what this place was, but after all these months away – and the events before Maia had left – the word no longer seemed to fit.

Maia got out of her hire-vehicle, stopping with one hand on its low roof as she studied the view in the shallow valley below her. It had been a three-hour drive from the outskirts of Erus city; a long way despite the high speed even a tiny one-seater could reach. But that wasn't why she hadn't been back before now.

"Aren't you forgetting something?" the vehicle's auto-driver asked in a cheeky tone. The hire company programmed all their AI drivers to have personality, and Maia hadn't cared much either way. She might have even found the cheerful tone comforting, but its words made her panic for a moment.

Jayel. Had she forgotten the baby?!

But then a second later, her small backpack came hurtling out of the space underneath the seat and landed with a clunk on the grassy verge at her feet.

"Here's your luggage!" the auto-driver told her with just a little too much enthusiasm. *"Thank you for your custom, and have a nice day!"*

The vehicle's narrow door slammed shut, then it lifted into the air and pulled away.

Maia stood on the vehicle drop-off zone, rubbing her chest as if it would calm the sudden, unnecessary panic she'd felt. Of course Jayel wasn't with her, she scolded herself. She'd very intentionally saved her credits so that he could be cared for this morning, so that she could come home for a visit without the difficult questions – or without that particular awkward truth coming out.

It was just that ever since Jayel had been born six months earlier, she'd lived and breathed motherhood. Raising a child alone was no small task, made harder by the fact that she was only eighteen.

Maia took in another deep breath, then let it out slowly through her nose. It had all gone so badly, so quickly, and people she'd considered friends had abandoned her. They'd suddenly lost interest in spending time with her – in supporting her in any way. She still didn't understand why. Perhaps today she'd find out.

With another sigh, she began to walk down the sloping road into her hometown, her small bag hovering along behind her. After a few minutes it fell to the ground with a clunk, so she stopped to pick it up and carry it over her shoulder. There was a reason that the hire vehicle had left her so far out of town.

This town was right on the constantly moving borderlands, and everyone knew the borderlands were hellish on both technology and alter-power. No one tried to drive into them, because their vehicles would surely give out, probably at the most inconvenient time. And if anyone tried to use their alter-power gifts, they might find those too gave out randomly.

Everyone knew that if you wanted the strongest alter-power, you had to go right into the Other realm. That was why Maia had been brought up here. Her mother, Davinia, was a skilled practitioner of just about everything Other-related, and she proudly carried no pledges, but instead owed favours to and was owed favours by myriad Creatures.

Most of the people living in these kinds of towns were like Davinia. Power-seekers, hermits, loners, or people who wanted to unplug from the virtual life that pervaded everywhere away from the borderlands. That, or they had too much Creature blood to survive elsewhere.

After ten minutes walking towards the distant town, the scenery abruptly changed and Maia suddenly found herself right outside the nearest building. She paused, looking back over her shoulder in confusion. The vehicle drop-off now seemed quite close, a mere minute's walk. She shook her head then stepped into the town, knowing that the distance might have changed again by the time she was ready to leave.

She made her way into the town centre without any further interference. Unlike the massively built-up urban areas within Erus city-state, the buildings here were rarely more than three storeys high. They ranged from ultra-modern to pretentiously old-fashioned: for example, shaping plastimetal into antique white bricks.

As Maia walked, she saw a few people scattered around. One or two met her eyes then looked away. Even though she recognised a couple of them – Elsewhise having a shifting population of only around ten thousand – she didn't approach them. Her real destination was just up ahead: a narrow black door down a quiet alley, embroidered with red and gold designs and simple text. *Spellcaster. Curse-breaker.*

Well. It was easy to be a curse-breaker when you were the one who set the curses in the first place.

"Maia!"

Maia paused just outside the door, one hand raised to the old-fashioned door handle. They rarely used DNA scanners here, since if you meant harm, then you ended up cursed. It was a simple and widely used solution.

She glanced behind her to the source of the voice, and saw a slim woman, dressed all in black and wearing the strangest hat. It had a wide brim, and was shaped in a tall, pointed cone. Under the strange hat, the woman was young and pretty, with scrolling brown symbols shifting across the skin of her nose and cheekbones.

Maia did a double-take. Not because the woman was strange – there were all sorts of strange people here in Elsewhise – but because she finally recognised her. And she was a girl, not a woman; barely older than Maia herself. "Cahlie, is that you?"

The girl grinned, gesturing towards her face and outfit. "I'm surprised you recognised me. What do you think?"

"Ah…" Maia really had no answer. What was Cahlie supposed to be?

"I'm an old-fashioned spell-caster," Cahlie said proudly. "Or I'm dressed as one, anyway. It gets the tourists' attention, then they buy from me. Then I take it off at the end of the day. Come on, see my shop."

Maia followed her school friend into a nearby doorway, making approving noises about the carefully created (and somewhat overblown) interior, but inside she was wondering how her mother would have taken the competition. Elsewhise was a small town, but there were only a couple of spell-casters here, and the other lived right on the other side. Not here in the same alley, and not thirty years younger.

Cahlie showed Maia around the small shop, pointing out details in the décor, including a gigantic metal pot. "And here's my favourite bit," she said proudly, pointing to the wooden frame built over the pot. "It's actually a tiny doorway to the Other. Well, a partial doorway. I use it to identify curses so I can break them."

"Or make them," Maia pointed out.

Cahlie shrugged. "Sure. Do you want to see how it works?"

Maia moved closer to the wooden frame, studying it absently. Cahlie hadn't even said a proper hello or asked how she was, but then she'd always been self-absorbed. It was why they'd never been close. She was one of those who'd simply disappeared from Maia's life sometime around when she'd found out she was pregnant, and when everything had fallen apart.

Meanwhile, Cahlie was continuing her demonstration. She held up a tiny bottle, white with faint cracks from age. "This is an ordinary bottle. I ordered it as a pack of a hundred. But look what happens when I hold it under the Other frame."

She waved the bottle under the wooden frame over the cauldron, and a criss-crossing web of bright pink threads appeared over the bottle's surface. Maia caught a glimpse of multicoloured strands covering Cahlie's own hand before she pulled it away and the light disappeared.

"Did you see the pink?" Cahlie asked. "It means it's an alter-power blessing for whoever holds the bottle."

"I saw it," Maia replied, studying the framework curiously. Davinia had something like this, but quite a lot larger…and messier. "But I thought blessings were usually blue. Aren't curses red or orange?"

"It's pink, not red," Cahlie snapped, snatching the bottle away. "Just because your mother makes blessings blue, doesn't mean *all* blessings are." She shrugged a shoulder, her lip curling. "And maybe it's not entirely a blessing. It's a love potion, so it depends on who's using it."

A love potion which would influence someone to behave differently than normal. Not precisely Maia's idea of good. "Alright," she said mildly. "I didn't mean any offense."

"Of course you did. You're Davinia's daughter." Cahlie wore a hint of a sneer, and Maia was again reminded of why she didn't spend a lot of time with this girl, or mourn her loss as a friend. Her moods were mercurial, and she clearly disliked Maia's mother. (But then so did most people.)

"So I heard you moved away," Cahlie continued. "Did you have Luke DeMannard's kid after all?"

Maia froze, her own hand near the wooden frame. "I did have a baby," she replied evenly. "I didn't realise the rumours were that my little Jayel was Luke's." She'd also forgotten that Cahlie knew Luke. But then they moved in some of the same circles.

"Well, if you're going to argue with him in public, then announce you're pregnant, then he leaves for Dailan...it's not hard to figure out," Cahlie said. "Don't touch that!"

But Maia's hand was already on the edge of the wooden Other frame. And to her shock, her skin was lit up with a distinctive orange glow. Instead of listening, she pushed her hand in further. The glow became a distinctive curling mesh, all over her hand, then reaching up her arm.

Chaos. "I've been cursed?" Maia breathed in disbelief.

Cahlie abruptly pushed the wooden frame flat, and the telltale orange lights disappeared. "It looked pink to me. Something hereditary, maybe."

"It was definitely orange," Maia argued. "Chaos, Cahlie. Let me see it again!"

"Are you going to pay?"

Maia paused with her hand halfway back to the wooden frame. She'd spent all of her savings on this outing. She had no income beyond the base income given to all Erusians, and she certainly had nothing to spare. "I guess not."

"Then you see nothing. Get out."

Chaos again. That was rude. "Nice seeing an old friend," Maia told her sarcastically as she left the small building. She had somewhere to be, and the interaction had left her shaken. But she had to be grateful that she'd seen the curse. Her mother could help her remove it…unless she was the one who'd put it there.

Two minutes later, Maia was outside the same door she'd first been heading towards. This time she took a deep breath, straightened her shoulders as she mentally prepared, then opened the door.

She stepped through into a long, empty concrete hallway. Strips of lights showed it was empty through to its other end, where it disappeared suddenly into darkness. Even though she'd grown up in this area, she hadn't been inside this place more than a few times. She remembered the feeling of sudden heaviness, and the way the atmosphere would carry a thick smell, like something had died just out of sight.

Unlike Cahlie's place, this place needed no decoration. It was, in itself, a permanent doorway to the Other realm. Davinia always said that power should show itself, and she lived it.

She was terribly disappointed in Maia's choices.

At the other end of the hall, Maia stopped. The darkness was right in front of her, and she anxiously played with the jewellery on her wrist where it was hidden under the sleeve of her long top. She spared it a quick glance as if to reassure herself it was still there. It was thin and goldish-silver, an unknown metal that was incredibly lightweight and impossibly bendable.

She'd twisted it to wrap twice around her wrist, because it was actually a circlet rather than a bracelet, made to sit lightly over the head. Its thin, shining surface was inscribed with the same word over and over. *AMARANTHUS.*

She muttered under her breath, "Amaranthus, give me courage."

A wave of relief came over her at saying the familiar word of power. Not much, but just enough to keep her moving. She quickly hid the circlet again under her clothing, because she knew her mother hated that too.

Then she stepped through.

The interior of Davinia's workplace was dark. Pitch-black, lit with a series of ancient torches that flickered with green and blue flame, because technology wouldn't work here either. The air was icy cold. In the near distance, a figure bent over a long, flat platform. An altar. Alter-power sparks of different colours sprayed up and dissolved into the air, and the figure stood upright.

"You're interfering with my casting," Davinia said flatly. The torchlight revealed half her features: pale, smooth skin and hints of deepest red hair. Or was she paler than when Maia had last seen her? "What do you want?"

"Good to see you too, Mother," Maia said with forced cheerfulness. "Your grandchild is fine, thank you. I'm doing OK."

Davinia's expression didn't change. "I told you that if you were going to go through with the pregnancy, you wouldn't get any help from me. Don't expect me to make small talk. Why are you here?"

Maia's heart sank. She'd always known her mother could be a hard woman when she was crossed, but she'd never experienced that for herself. Anni, her older sister, had decided to settle for an ordinary life in the city, and when she'd left, Davinia had acted as if she no longer existed. But Maia had been the favourite – the talented one, almost in her mother's own image. Apparently that no longer mattered.

She dropped her original idea, which was that she could somehow rebuild the relationship and maybe even admit that not-so-little secret about Jayel's gender. Not today, clearly.

"I'm cursed," she blurted out instead. "I need to know how to break the curse."

Davinia paused briefly, then moved forward. "Come here."

She grabbed Maia's arm and pulled her back towards the altar, then pressed her hand down against its cold, sticky surface. Maia suppressed a shudder. She knew what her mother did to do her job well, and she'd be washing her arm as soon as she got out of here. But even now, she could see the faint outline of a flickering orange mesh over her hand and running up her arm.

Finally Davinia let her go and stepped away. "It's a strong one," she said flatly. "Who did you irritate so terribly, Maia?"

Maia paused. "Actually, I thought it might have been you."

"Not me." Her mother didn't even seem offended. "But it's a personal curse. Rejection or isolation, not sure which, with something else underneath it." She let out a bark of humourless laughter. "It makes you like a bad smell, so one wants to be near you."

Maia's heart sank, and with it came a pang of betrayal. She *had* been rejected and isolated from everyone she knew, from even before she'd known she was pregnant. And it had all happened so quickly. Somehow she'd gone from having a network of friends and acquaintances, to facing disapproval and just…absence.

And Luke…Luke had been the worst. He'd lost interest in her, and she hadn't even been able to find him in VR. She'd finally hunted him down to tell him he was going to be a father, and he'd emphatically – and publicly – rejected her. He'd even signed a document giving up any parenting rights, and then he'd disappeared for real. She had no idea where he was except that it was somewhere in the neighbouring city-state, Dailan. There was no record of him even in VR.

"So maybe you aren't really angry with me," Maia said in a low tone. "Maybe it's just the curse making you think you are." Because how could she have gone from being the apple of her mother's eye, to being nothing at all?

"Oh, I'm angry with you," Davinia replied coolly. "What a disappointment you've been. You have so much *potential…* not like your older sister. Nevertheless, you'll need to get the curse removed."

Oddly enough, that was almost a compliment, coming from this woman. "How can we do it?"

Davinia turned back to the altar and began moving the objects arranged on it. "It won't be easy. You'll need the help of a powerful Creature, or favours from several."

Maia waited quietly. Both of them knew she had no Creature links. She'd remained unpledged purposely, just like her mother, and just like many in this area. It was Davinia who could pull the favours.

"I'll call in those favours for you on one condition," Davinia continued. "Get rid of the girl, and come back to me. I'll allow you to start over."

It took Maia a few moments to realise what was being asked of her. Partly because Davinia was one of the few who thought Jayel was a baby girl rather than a boy – Maia having made up the lie in the desperate hope of pleasing her man-hating mother. "I won't give up my baby!" she exclaimed in dismay. "You shouldn't even ask!"

"Then you'd best be finding a powerful Creature. And you know they'll ask for a high price."

Maia went hot with anger. Her fists clenched at her sides, and she was trembling. "You're my *mother!*"

"And I've given my conditions," Davinia countered. She cast a glance at Maia's hands. "And get rid of that junk while you're at it. Two conditions now."

Maia looked down to see the Amaranthus circlet had slipped down her arm and into sight. It was glowing softly, the text standing out dark red against the fine surface. She'd picked it up from an open market eighteen months earlier. Something about it had caught her eye, and then it had proven to have some kind of effect in the Other. But Davinia and the others had scorned it, saying it was useless. Maia had disagreed, and their insults had made her grip onto it all the tighter.

But the Amaranthus circlet was nothing compared to Jayel. That Davinia would want to get rid of her own grandchild…

Maia went still, and in that moment she made a decision. She would never depend on her mother again.

She turned and headed for the door. It took longer than expected, since this room was in the Other realm. But finally when her hand rested on the doorhandle, she turned back towards Davinia. "I'll never fulfil those conditions," she said quietly. "And you – I guess you'll just be alone for the rest of your life."

Davinia didn't look up. "It's the Other. I'm never alone."

The reminder of this realm's unseen Creatures made Maia shudder, and the coldness of reply infuriated her. "And just so you know," she added forcefully, "Jayel's a boy, not a girl."

Davinia's stunned expression was the last thing Maia saw before she stomped through the door, back to the normal realm.

Several hours later, Maia stood outside the open door of an urban apartment. 42-G Eastern Way was a slightly aged residence in a slightly aged area, affordable and safe…enough. On the other side of the open door, a younger, darker version of Davinia stood, rocking Jayel in her arms as he sucked on one small, fat hand. His eyelids drooped, indicating sleep was close.

"Thank you again for taking him at such short notice, Anni," Maia said. "I wouldn't have asked unless I was desperate." She'd only been able to pay a carer for the morning as planned. Luckily her sister was so flexible.

"I know," Anni replied placidly. She gave Jayel a kiss on the cheek. "And I never mind helping my sister out, especially not with this gorgeous boy. I'm just sorry I've been so busy. Back by dinner time, you said?"

Maia nodded. She'd given few details along with Jayel's care items and Anni hadn't asked for any. Maia was just grateful that her older sister had been available.

They hadn't seen much of each other for years, not since Anni had moved into the city to live a 'normal life', but Maia was determined to change that. Just as soon as she could get rid of this rejection and isolation curse… Of *course* Anni had been too busy for her. But that wasn't either of their fault.

Having sorted out Jayel's care for the rest of the afternoon, Maia set off into the temple district. Her long trip back from Elsewhise had given her plenty of time to think, and there seemed to be only one clear solution. She needed to pledge herself to a Creature, one strong enough to break this curse, but disinterested enough to leave her to her own resources.

Through her mother, Maia had seen plenty of ways Creatures could misuse those pledged to them. She hadn't wanted to…but there seemed to be no other choice. Besides, the vast majority of citizens were pledged. Surely it would mean a better life for her, and for Jayel.

A new life.

Maia pressed one hand against her Amaranthus circlet, tracing her fingers over its familiar inscription. "Amaranthus, let this work," she said, feeling the faint tingle of alter-power being released into the atmosphere as she spoke the word written in the metal. "Let me be free. Pledged to a Creature, but as good as free."

Is this the best idea? Surely there must be another way.

No, there was no other way. She'd have to go ahead with this plan. *Let me be free. Pledged to a Creature, but as good as free.*

She murmured variations of that statement all the way to the first temple she'd chosen, a Creature known for strength and…well, unpopularity. Not having anyone to ask, she'd simply done a quick VR search for the number of people pledged per Creature, plus estimated strength.

The White Prince seemed the obvious solution as he had *no* known pledges, and was one of the few Creatures that could gift flight to humans. The informative VR session had described him as 'reclusive'. That was OK, right?

Except now that she was outside his – its? – mist-filled temple entrance, she wasn't so sure. There was a basic stone archway with a stylised stone carving of a butterfly. But apart from that, the place seemed deserted. With such a populated city, it was strange that even the surrounding buildings seemed to be windowless.

Maia paused outside the temple entrance, giving her circlet another quick pat. She felt uneasy, and as usual, there was that inner voice telling her not to go in, to find another way.

Her inner voice was always overly cautious. She ignored it, as usual.

Then taking a deep breath, she stepped through the entrance to the Other realm.

Later

Dark. It was dark. And warm – no, cold. No, warm again. The hum of voices filled her ears, the words unintelligible and strangely ticklish against her ears. More than that; something was tickling her *arms* – all around her.

Maia shivered, and suddenly she was fully awake. She lurched forward, utterly disoriented and surrounded by darkness. The ground was hard and cold underfoot, and all she could think was to *get out!* There was a hint of light *here*, and *here*, and she followed it blindly until she stumbled through a stone archway into brilliant sunlight.

Chaos, it was bright out here. The light was almost as blinding as the darkness had been, but Maia carried forward, propelled by the urgent sense that she had to get out of the place she'd just been.

A temple, she realised. That was right, she'd been in the Other realm, after going into a Creature temple.

The White Prince.

Maia stopped suddenly as the memories came trickling back. She'd gone in to break a curse, she reminded herself. But she couldn't remember exactly what had happened. There'd been a voice…

She shuddered, shaking herself. Cursed Creatures. Faithless Luke had been right in that at least – you couldn't trust them. Even now, she felt terribly disoriented, like she'd been asleep and had been suddenly woken. Which in hindsight, she probably had been.

Maia glanced at her surroundings. Now her eyes were adjusting to the light, she recognised a few major buildings, but everything else was unfamiliar. But then this was the first time she'd visited this part of town. In the end she programmed her directions into a hire scooter, then set off at pace.

But she couldn't shake that feeling of wrongness that had come from contact with a Creature. Even as she reached Anni's building and got into the liftpod for floor 42, everything just seemed a little…off. And in the hall, too. She didn't recall the walls being this particular shade of green.

It was lingering confusion from that visit, she told herself. A visit that had probably been a mistake, as she realised in dismay that she'd misplaced her Amaranthus circlet. She definitely wouldn't be going back for it, not until she remembered everything that had happened in there.

She huffed out a sigh, shivering in place once more. All she wanted now was a hot drink and to hug her baby. She'd worry about the curse some other time.

The doors opened to floor 42 and Maia stepped out into the hall. It was a short distance, with only two apartment doorways, and she walked briskly to the second one before pausing in confusion.

Had the neighbours always had such dark, muddy footprints outside their entrance? She would've thought the self-cleaning floors would deal with that. And had Anni's front door trim always been such a bright, shiny metal?

But she surely hadn't been paying that much attention in the first place.

Jayel. She just needed Jayel, and then everything would be alright.

She reached for the door.

Inside apartment 42-G

They were going to have to go into hiding. Jon hated to think it, after all the successes of the last few days, but it was indisputable. He sat in his adoptive mother Anni's living room along with half a dozen others, recovering from the aftermath of an explosion that had almost killed his neighbour Tarie and her family.

In the end it had only blown out a single wall of the neighbouring home. The person who'd surely set the explosive – their schoolmate Gavriel – was still out there, free and able to try again. He surely *would* try again.

"Right," Tarie announced loudly. She sat on the floor where she'd been for the last half hour, with her hair looking a bit mad from the force of the explosion and her eyes a little unfocused. She held a full drinking glass in one hand, and there was a bit of greenery stuck in her collar. "So let's address the real issue. Like Da said, we'll never be safe as long as we stay here, because someone's trying to kill us. Me. Us."

"We need to go to the authorities," Anni exclaimed. "It's not right that you'd have to leave!" She lifted a hand to her forehead where Jon knew her new mark rested unseen. "*We'll* have to leave, if the authorities don't help."

"The authorities like Luca?" Jon asked dryly. Never mind his carrier father's promise that they could dislike each other politely from a distance, like normal dysfunctional families. That had been broken the moment Luca tricked Jon into going to the White Prince – again – and Jon had no doubt that Luca would drop them all in a volcano if he could get away with it.

"Obviously not," Tarie answered. "But what do you do when someone tries to murder you?"

Bets put up her free hand, since the other was still tightly holding Jon's, as it had been for the last hour. He didn't feel inclined to let it go. "I typically leave the location," she declared, her green eyes earnest. "And the time period too, if at all possible."

"The time period?!" a couple of them echoed in unison.

"Are you saying you travel through time?" Tarren asked with one eyebrow raised. He looked very much like his daughter Tarie in that moment.

Bets nodded a little warily as if aware she may have said too much, then shot a glance at Jon. "Jon did too. 'Tis how we met."

Suddenly all eyes were on Jon again.

"Time travel?" Anni exclaimed. Her expression suggested she wanted to believe him, but wasn't sure if she could.

Jon opened his mouth to deny it out of habit – because only crazy people claimed they travelled through time – then realised that half the people around him had equally crazy lives and experiences. What was a little time travel compared to spontaneously growing and shrinking, or setting things on fire with your hands?

"You know how people can lose time in the Other realm?" he tried to explain. "They go in for what feels like a few hours, but come out and find that weeks have passed?"

Some of the others nodded.

"It's like that," Jon continued, "but with Amaranthus, it's not quite so…random. So yes, I've travelled through time. And a bit more, which I'll tell you about when we aren't planning to flee for our lives."

The others seemed to accept that, and Bets said, "What about Rokal-Max? Is he not still searching for a way to rescue Tarie even now? We should warn him of what happened here."

Jon made a scoffing noise under his breath. The idea of inviting his former worst enemy to flee the city-state with them seemed a bit much when he hadn't even received a proper apology, but he knew it was the right thing to do. "I suppose we can't leave him unaware of the danger," he said. "Not now that he'll be a target himself."

"He's not answering his comm," Tarie replied, holding up her own wrist device. "I'll try again later."

Then Tarie's little sister spoke up. "Never mind that. Look at this!" Lydia had been silent till now, but she lifted up her wrist comm, displaying a good-sized holographic view of the Erus city centre and the Big Three Creature temples. Those had recently merged so they were now just the Extra-Big *One's* temple, with a huge statue of creepy Audaline in her swirling robes and striped skin.

Even as they watched, the statue changed piece by piece. It grew until it was double the size, at least as tall as Jon's own apartment building if not taller, and resembled an enormous seated cat. Sharp teeth, shining gems set in its striped sides…and a head that turned to reveal one blue eye, one yellow.

"Oh dear," Bets squeaked. "That's horribly familiar."

"Get this," Lydia continued. "They're saying that Audaline is revealing herself – *itself* as some Creature called the Tiger. And it says that every major city now has one of these statues, and that every citizen has to come to the statue and pledge their allegiance within five days." She looked up at the others, her eyes wide and horrified. "It says that if you don't, then you're a traitor and you'll be…punished appropriately. What do you think they mean by that?"

"How about we don't hang around to find out?" Jon croaked. "Anyone got any credit chips? A vehicle?" It was rare to use physical credit chips instead of digital, but many people kept a small supply in case the power went out. Jon had never bothered to, since that hadn't happened in his lifetime.

"I've got a vehicle!" Tarren said. "A good solid one, right Tarie?"

Tarie just groaned and set her face in her hands.

Jon's earlier euphoria was gone. While whatever had happened with the White Prince was significant, it was nothing compared to this. They might have to leave their homes permanently, because there was no way any of them would be going near that Creature statue.

The door sensor chimed, breaking the heavy silence. "Hello?" a young woman's voice called, echoing through the speakers. "Anni, are you home?"

Jon looked across at his mother, who was sitting snugly against Tarren. Their neighbour's arm was around her shoulders in a rather friendly manner – but Jon didn't have the energy to be bothered by it. Good for them.

"Will you check who it is?" Anni asked Jon quietly. "Set the door to 'away' if you don't recognise them."

Jon moved to get up, then heard the door slide open.

A moment later a girl stuck her head into the room. She looked to be in her late teens: lean with long, straight auburn hair, fair skin and delicate features. "Oh. You've got company. Sorry to interrupt, but I really need to pick up Jayel. I didn't mean to leave him so long, but I think I was stuck in the Other realm…long story."

Pick up Jayel? Jon frowned, turning to look at his mother.

But Anni had frozen on the couch, her golden-brown skin draining into a pale, sallow shade. *"Maia?"* she whispered.

The girl's eyebrows shot up. "Anni. Wow…you really, *really* need a good sleep. And maybe a spa…and some makeup. You look *tired!* I guess my boy kept you up at night?" She frowned. "I guess it's been more than a night, huh?"

In the dead silence Jon could hear his own heartbeat pounding in his head. It couldn't be. It just couldn't.

The others in the room looked like toys with bobbing heads as they turned from the girl, to Jon, to Anni – then back to the girl. Only Lydia didn't seem to understand that something was wrong.

Then the girl – Maia – turned to Jon. Her young face showed only impatience and some curiosity, and she cocked her head as she studied him. "Hello there. You know, you really remind me of this guy I...*knew*, Luke DeMannard. Are you related?"

Jon forced himself to nod, but he couldn't speak.

Anni got up off the couch and walked over to the girl. She took her hands, staring into her face. "Maia, *where have you been?!*"

Maia half-smiled, pushing her sister away a little and glancing awkwardly at the others in the room. "I wasn't gone that long, surely? Come on, where's my little Jay-Jon? He must've been missing me, and I can't wait to see him."

In unison everyone turned to stare at Jon. But he just kept staring at the girl...who was his birth mother...who wasn't dead...

...and who thought he was still a baby.

"Maia," Anni said carefully. "You've been gone for seventeen years. Jayel is..." She turned to look at Jon where he was still half-crouched on the floor.

Maia slowly turned towards Jon too, and her expression of horror and confusion must have echoed his own. "*No,*" she breathed, and he mouthed the word along with her.

This couldn't be happening.

2
Tricky

Maia stared at the boy – or young man, rather, since he appeared to be her own age and stood half a head taller. He now stood an arm's length from her, looking horribly familiar for an absolute stranger. His olive skin was a shade or two darker than her own, and his dark brown hair curled over his forehead and around his ears, the colour matching his eyes. He looked like Luke, as if Luke had a brother.

He looked appalled.

Maia took a step back, her heart pounding double-time as she looked around at the room of unfamiliar faces. A dark-skinned, middle-aged man and two teenage girls who might have been his daughters. A dainty young woman, with unusually pale skin, brown hair and wide green eyes. And the boy who looked like Luke…

Maia fixed her gaze back on Anni, who at second glance still looked worn and lined and faded, as if seventeen years *had* passed instead of a mere few nights. But surely she'd been joking when she'd said that. People couldn't be stuck in the Other for such a long time without realising what had happened.

But these people didn't look like they were joking.

Maia forced out a laugh. "Ha. Ha ha, Anni. Good joke. Now where's my baby?"

Old Anni – because that's what she looked like now – glanced back towards the Luke-brother-looking guy. She looked stricken. "You were gone a very long time," she said hesitantly, and her voice cracked. "We thought you were *dead*."

"Where's Jayel, Anni?" Maia persisted. "Where is he?!"

"Um…" Anni bit her lip and looked again at that one boy.

"*I'm* Jayel Jonnamin," the boy burst out suddenly. His voice was deep, and even that reminded Maia of Luke. "But I go by Jon."

No. No. No. Just…*no.*

Maia spun on her heel and marched through the nearest doorway, into a neat, galley-style kitchen. There was no sign that any small child lived here, but she persistently moved through every single room, including the bathrooms, and made sure to check the closets.

She hadn't paid attention when she was last here, and Anni hadn't properly shown her around the apartment. But in the same way the exterior seemed different, everything here didn't seem quite right.

But when it was finally clear that she wasn't going to find Jayel here, she stomped back to the living area. Anni had been following along behind her like a ghost, her lined face creased in confusion, but the others were exactly where she'd left them.

"You all think you're so funny," Maia announced, setting her hands on her hips. She was shaking, yet somehow numb, and it seemed a miracle that she was holding it together. "You think you can play this kind of trick on me and that I'll fall for it, huh? That you'll get some kind of reaction? Well, the joke's on you, because I'm going to go shopping for a couple of hours, and you can keep watching my boy. And then when I come back to get him, I fully expect all of this to be sorted out."

She made sure to meet Anni's eyes, then the horrible Luke lookalike's, and even the tiny pale girl's. The last was watching her with an expression of absolute pity, and it made her gut twist in fear. (No, not fear, she quickly told herself. *Annoyance.*)

"I'm going out," she said again.

Then with nothing more to do, and no other way to fight, she left.

The girl stormed out of the apartment, and for several seconds, everyone inside just sat in silence.

"Was that…?" Tarren asked finally.

Jon leapt up and ran out after the girl who might be his

mother. His mind was spinning, because *it didn't make sense*, and even if it was her, how could she think he was a baby? Who could lose that many years?

But he was a time-traveller, he admitted to himself. Such odd things happened. Just…almost never.

He reached the hall in time to see the liftpod doors close. He couldn't wait for the next one. He turned and ran back into his apartment, then across the room towards the balcony. It took a bit of frustrated slapping and commands – the balcony's AI refusing to open the protective barrier because he was in an agitated state – until finally he overrode it. He leapt over into the air, barely letting the wind catch him before he zoomed around the building to where he'd be able to see her.

Jon came around the corner just in time to see the girl step out of the foyer. From up here, she was just a reddish-brown head with occasionally moving limbs, but he recognised her even from this height.

He flew a little lower, still making sure to stay out of sight, and followed along as she half-ran down the road. He wondered where she was going. With the tangled layers of buildings and roads, there was very little direct sunlight, but somehow he managed to fly through a patch of it. He saw his shadow fall over the girl, and she stopped, looking up.

Strange, because with all these vehicles moving around, what was one more shadow? But she *did* look up, and their eyes met even from this distance.

Then an extra-large vehicle pulled up beside her. A shiny, ostentatious vehicle that Jon recognised easily even from this distance. The door opened, the girl ducked down to get in, and the vehicle drove away into the twisting streets.

Jon didn't follow the vehicle after that. There was no point. Instead, he turned and went back inside – the long way using the liftpods, since his apartment balcony's protective barrier had automatically gone up again.

Bets was waiting in the hall when he returned, with Tarie just behind her. "What happened?"

He shook his head, moving back through the apartment door. Inside, Anni and Tarren appeared to be in conversation, with Tarie's younger sister Lydia nearby. "She got into Luca's vehicle," he said.

The room went silent.

"*Luca's* vehicle?" Anni echoed.

"Well, that's not suspicious," Tarie said with heavy sarcasm.

Tarie was exactly right, Jon thought. These people knew what Luca had done to Jon earlier today, how he'd tricked him into going straight into the Other realm – into the White Prince's temple. It all appeared to be a convoluted way of ensuring Jon destroyed that particular Creature, since he'd been prophesied as the first to ever do such a thing.

But it was clear that Luca – or the unknown Creature *running* Luke – didn't care whether Jon lived or died, and very much had his own agenda.

"Now I've had a chance to think about it, it seems unlikely that my long-lost birth mother should reappear, right after everything that happened with the White Prince," Jon said. "And right after that announcement by the Tiger." He glanced at his mother – his *adoptive* mother – warily. "And I didn't want to tell you earlier since everything was happening all at once, but I found something belonging to Maia in the Other, through the White Prince temple archway. I think…I had assumed she died."

There was a silence, and Anni's shoulders slumped. Suddenly she looked much, much older than before. "If you hadn't seen Luca's car, I might have believed a miracle had happened," she murmured. "But it's just another trick, isn't it?"

"It must be." And yet, Jon found he was disappointed.

"Better for it to be a trick," Bets said staunchly. "Imagine if 'twas true, and your poor mother was searching for a babe that no longer existed." She frowned. "I could feel the Creature influence on that girl, but I was too slow to use my flame. I wonder what she wanted?"

"What *Luca* wanted," Jon countered dully.

"The house," Tarie said suddenly. "She walked through the whole apartment and nobody thought to stop her. I certainly didn't see what she was doing."

There was a stunned silence. "Chaos," Jon muttered. "We better get out of here."

Just then he got the strongest sense. It was like a fist grabbing hold of his gut; not painful, but unmissable. *This time is important and limited. We must make it count.*

But before he could say something, Tarren spoke up. "I just have the strongest feeling that something important is about to happen. That…we have to make this time count."

It was almost word for word how Jon had been feeling, and he turned sharply to stare at Tarie's father.

"That's just what I was thinking!" Tarie and Bets said at the same time. They exchanged startled expressions.

Jon scrubbed a hand over his face. "Alright. If we're all thinking it, it must be true – it must be from Amaranthus. Now…what next?"

In the far north of Erus city-state, right at the point where the normal realm met the Other, a blackened trail began. It was as wide as two hover-vehicles and almost perfectly straight, as though someone had deliberately burned a path through the grassy plains that made up this area, taking care not to move outside that precise measurement.

The path smelled of sulphur and rot, but only those with power could see it. All would be able to smell it, though. And along its length, random doorways had opened into the darkness of the Other realm. It was, in fact, what happened when a real, solid Creature walked across the normal realm.

At the other end of the expanding trail, the Tiger moved step by unsteady step towards his goal. He still wore the two-legged form he'd taken on an infinity ago, when he'd been proving a point about his old enemy's precious little humans.

But two legs turned out to be a lot shakier than four when out in the physical realm, and the Tiger found himself longing for that original form. The beautiful one. The perfect one that he didn't yet have the strength to reclaim.

Behind him, a dozen of his red-cloaked human servants struggled to keep up, their small vehicles unable to match even this feeble pace. Their fear of him, and pride at their joint achievement of 'setting him free', was clear through the thick strands of power that tied them together.

As if they had anything to be proud of. They were pawns, nothing more, and soon he wouldn't need them at all. With that dismissive thought, and hatred filling his being, the Tiger put on a burst of speed as he headed towards the heart of the city. He left the weaklings far behind, but it still wasn't good enough.

Not yet.

Just behind the Tiger's red-clad servants and completely unseen by them, another figure followed the same path.

The young, redheaded woman trotted along the blackened grass, her steps silent, and her attention on the Other gateways that spotted the pathway. Each time she reached one, she'd pause. And then when she moved on, the gateway would either be different, or gone entirely.

When the last one was redirected towards a very special spot in the Mountain of Glass, the girl skipped in glee. This might be the end of the world, but it could be such fun!

Now, off to the next errand.

In Erus city

This wasn't a hire-vehicle. Maia had seen the open door and had flung herself inside, intending to get as far away from this hideous place as possible. But once she was inside and the door clicked shut behind her, it became clear that this wasn't any form of taxi. For starters, it was far too luxurious. The upholstery gleamed, and its incredible softness indicated its high cost.

And there was a massive VR screen along one wall…and a nutri-dispenser with an array of glasses and bottles…and the auto-driver hadn't yet asked her where she wanted to go. But the vehicle had already started moving, lifting off the ground and well away from this location.

"Where are we going?" Maia asked, fully expecting the auto-driver to answer. But there was silence in return.

"Stop the vehicle," she tried next, and was soundly ignored. The transparent walls (from this side) did turn opaque, though, leaving her completely unable to see their direction. "Chaos. Chaos." She slammed a hand against the door. "This is the worst day ever!"

Maia hunched over on her seat, pressing her hands over her eyes. She still felt horribly disoriented, and that ridiculous meeting with the aged Anni and the boy who was…who looked like Luke (and who'd flown after her!) hadn't helped at all. And now she was trapped in a random luxury vehicle, although to be fair, she'd put herself into this situation.

But it was nothing compared to the idea she might have lost seventeen years in the Other. That she might have lost her *baby*.

"This is so utterly, ridiculously bad," she said slowly to herself, "that it can't possibly be real."

Maia's heartrate settled at that thought, and her shoulders relaxed. Of course it wasn't real, she realised. Her last clear memory was going into the Other to request help from a notoriously difficult Creature, and after a jumble of confusion, she found herself in this nightmarish alternate reality?

Never.

She'd been warned about this kind of thing by her mother, that Creatures could create fantasies far more realistic than any VR session, with the intent of trapping people and draining their alter-power.

"The White Prince must feed off fear, or something," she continued aloud. "So all I need to do…is stop being afraid. Because it's not real." She paused, then added, "Amaranthus."

Just because she couldn't *see* the circlet didn't mean it wasn't there. Probably the Creature holding her prisoner had also hidden it.

Suddenly a man appeared on the seat opposite her. "It's a clever idea," he said brightly. "Shame it's wrong."

Maia jolted, startled at his abrupt appearance, but then forced herself to relax again. There was a faint shimmer to his appearance that suggested virtual reality, and he was sitting in front of that massive VR screen. Whoever he was, he wasn't really here. (Assuming *she* was also really here…) "And who are you supposed to be?"

The man cocked his head to one side, crossing his legs as if relaxing. "Don't you know?"

Maia considered him. He was startlingly handsome – as well as startling – with pale skin, shoulder-length black hair and bright blue-green eyes. His unlined skin and the distinct sense of

'Creature' emanating from him reminded Maia of her own mother. That meant he could be anywhere between eighteen and sixty. But his features were markedly familiar…

"I imagine you're supposed to be Luke DeMannard," she replied flatly. "You don't look much like him."

The odd, shiny version of Luke smiled, showing shining white teeth and transforming his entire face. (And that *was* Luke's smile, Maia thought.) "My, my, you have missed a lot. I'm no longer plain, pathetic Luke DeMannard. I'm Chairman Luca DeMannard of Greater Erus, and I was hoping for a chat with my son. *Our* son." He narrowed his eyes, studying her thoughtfully. "I didn't expect you to get into my vehicle, you know. I didn't expect to see you at all. I figured you were long-dead."

Ah, so in this version of reality, Luke did acknowledge paternity of Jayel. And he was a politician, and his name had changed. Why not. "Are you a carrier?"

Luke…*Luca* shrugged affirmation.

"Well, if whoever is running this nightmare knew Luke at all, they'd know he'd never get involved with a Creature. He hated them."

Luke's own father Mannard had more Creature links than anyone Maia had ever come across, and he was the most utterly unpleasant and miserable human being she had ever met. Luke had blamed the Creature links for his father's viciousness, and when he'd said he'd never take a pledge, she'd believed him.

"He did, yes," Luca agreed. "But as the years went by, he grew desperate enough to take a risk on one particular half-Halfling, who's not quite a Creature. And he found it was worth it."

Strangely enough, this silly conversation was helping Maia to calm down. "Why are you speaking about yourself in third person?"

"Because I'm not Luke. We share this body, but I mostly run it these days."

Ugh. If this had been real, Luke wouldn't have liked that at all. But still, she was curious. "Is there a reason you're keeping me in this vehicle?"

"It's not as if you have anywhere else to go," Luca countered. "And yes, there is a reason. It seems to me that you've lost some time. Just short of eighteen years, in fact, and I expect you want to get it back." He cocked his head to the side again. "Missing your little baby, are you?"

Maia's lip trembled. "This isn't true. *You're* not real." Even if it was the most realistic false environment she'd ever been in. With every minute that went past, the fog cleared from her head, and everything just felt…real.

"I'm afraid it is, dear Maia." He even sounded sympathetic. "You're not the first person to lose time in the Other, as I expect, but you'll be one of the last."

What could he mean by that?

"But even so, I believe we can help each other. You to jump back in time to the moment you were stolen, and me…well. There's a little something I want." He smiled again. "How about it?"

She knew deals with Creatures – even 'half-Halflings' – were never without strings attached. "Do I have a choice?"

The vehicle slid to an abrupt halt, and the walls turned transparent again so Maia could see their surroundings. They were in the upper levels of the city, with other vehicles skimming past beside and above them. To her left was a tidy sealed platform, with perfect green grass beyond it, and classically designed buildings beyond that. She recognised the city-state's council buildings.

"You can get out now if you like," VR Luca said. His image shimmered and wavered a little with the now-open door. "You can wander around for as long as it takes you to understand that this *is* real, and that time *has* passed. Then you can pledge yourself to the Tiger along with everyone else, watch our son die because he's made himself an enemy to the ruling Creature, and never get those eighteen years back." He shrugged. "Or, you can work with me."

"Who's the Tiger?" Maia cried. She gripped onto her seat, watching the smooth pavement as if it was lava. "And why would Jayel have made enemies of any Creature? And what do you *want*, Luke? Luca?"

The door slid shut again. "Now that's a long story," Luca replied smoothly, "but it's one I'm happy to tell. Say you'll come meet with me in person, and I'll explain everything. Oh, and as proof of my intentions, I'll remove this ugly little rejection curse you've been stuck with. How's that?"

He knew about the curse. That bloody curse that had started everything. She was *desperate* to get rid of it.

"Alright," Maia said. "You've got a deal."

Luca smiled.

It didn't take Tarie long to pack up her entire life – but then it wasn't the first time her family had had to do this. Her father had gone with Anni to get out as many credit chips as they could without setting off an alert, while Tarie and Lydia had focused on packing the essentials that could easily fit in their tiny vehicles. Life or death situations showed clearly what was important, and her entire wardrobe wasn't it.

Jon had gone to do something similar in his and Anni's apartment, and Bets had headed to the secret apartment at the end of the hall, the one with a direct entrance to the Other realm, intending to gain some wisdom. Tarie found it hard to line up this small, earnest person with someone who'd traversed centuries.

Tarie set the few items of clothing into her compression suitcase, watching as they shrank to one-third their usual size, then shut the lid. She sent the case off to the garage to attach to their vehicles.

"Tarie."

Tarie leapt in surprise at the sudden voice, and a stream of the Words spilled out of her mouth. A moment later she realised it was just Bets. She closed her eyes, breathing carefully and willing her heartrate to reduce. "I didn't see you there."

"Truly?" Bets beamed. "I'd thought my unnoticeability gift had failed, but clearly not." She perched herself on the small stool next to Tarie's now half-empty wardrobe. "Ooh look, 'tis a Word tree."

Tarie followed Bets' pointing finger to where the polished floors met the wall. A tiny red shoot was curling up from that miniscule gap, as small as Tarie's pinky finger but growing in size even as she watched.

"I'd vow you leave a trail of such things," Bets added.

Tarie stared at the still-growing shoot. "I didn't used to. Usually, I'd have to speak the Words for ages before a shoot would grow. I'd only grown a few saplings back home." But then back home, she hadn't had the issue where if she *didn't* speak the Words, she herself would grow in both size and strength until she got the chance to use that strength.

"Something's changed," she said abruptly. "My power is much stronger. Everything is…*more.*"

Bets seemed to pick up her serious tone. "Well, 'tis the end of the tapestry," she ventured. "One would expect changes. Everything has to…count."

They'd all had that same strong feeling earlier. That none of them should make casual decisions right now, and no time should be wasted. But Tarie frowned. "What tapestry?"

"In the Other realm," Bets explained with a hand wave. "'Tis a record of human history…but never mind. Of more import is that little hidden room. 'Tis shrinking."

"Pardon?"

"I went to check if the secret room would be of use to us now," Bets persisted. "But 'tis shrinking, and the door to the River of Life has vanished. We cannot use it." She shrugged. "I cannot find Fylax anywhere either, not even with Jon."

For a moment Tarie just stared. Why would they be shut out and cut off like this? She'd been considering the secret room as a last-resort hiding place, but clearly that wouldn't be possible. "Why are you not upset about this?"

"Difficulty of this kind is usually a hint of which direction to go. When the door closes, one must open a window."

Was that the saying? Tarie frowned. "Then…we're not supposed to use that room. We *do* have to leave."

"Mm." Bets moved over to the Word tree seedling, which was now growing another set of leaves. She glanced back at Tarie. "Mm…" she said again.

"You clearly want to say something else," Tarie said. "Spit it out."

Bets turned back to her. "Do you not feel as though we're making a mistake?" she asked quietly. "Fleeing in such a way."

"We almost died today twice over, by being driven insane in VR then by explosive in real life. Now we're supposed to show up in the Other and pledge to some crazed Creature. What other choice do we have besides running?"

Bets looked down.

"Although," Tarie continued thoughtfully, "my abilities *are* increasing, and I'm growing Word trees everywhere. And you can fight off anything Creature-based. And Jon can fly...*and* he destroyed a Creature today using a couple of objects of power." She frowned. Could that really be true? "And Jon still has the circlet, doesn't he? Shame we can't get more of those safekeeper things."

The two exchanged a long glance.

"*And* Rokal-Max is still missing," Bets pointed out. "Mayhap he is already in the borderlands beyond the reach of your comm, unaware you do not need freeing."

Yeah, that was still bothering Tarie too. The new and improved Rokal could be risking his life for no reason. They really should do something about that...

Just then Jon popped his head through the damaged doorway. "We're done, and Anni and Tarren are back. Are you ready to go?"

"Basically," Tarie replied. "Except we've got this idea..."

Bets and Tarie didn't want to flee with the others, they explained to Jon. They wanted to go after Rokal/Max, and take the chance to get more safekeepers if they could.

Jon didn't need convincing. He felt so strong today, like he was standing taller than he ever had before. Not literally, like Tarie, but on the inside.

Everything seemed to be for him, not against him. And if he could take down the White Prince, he felt like he could do anything.

Maybe even rescue his ex-worst enemy, although grudgingly. The chance to get more safekeepers appealed more. Then Rokal- ah, *Max* would *really* owe him.

Just then, Anni and Tarren came back. How would Jon tell them the plans had changed...?

"Random question," Jon said. "Do you know where we could find anything like a safekeeper? I mean an object that's an entrance to a pocket universe-"

"Mm, I know what they are," Anni replied thoughtfully. "You can get a nastier, cursed version called a soul-drinker, but you wouldn't want to meet the sort of people who make such things."

Jon stared at her in surprise, and she shrugged a shoulder. "I grew up in a border town. My mother made safekeepers on commission…and the other, nastier sort, too."

Anni's mother Davinia – Jon's grandmother. That reminded him of something he'd overheard right before he'd gone time-travelling, but hadn't had the chance to broach with Anni.

Davinia had died from a fall while trying to sacrifice baby Jayel (Jon) in exchange for his birth mother Maia's freedom from the Other realm. Now Jon knew about his life-long guardian-Person, Fylax, he wondered if that fall's timing had been more than good luck.

"What happened to your mother's things when she passed away?" Jon asked casually. "Wouldn't you inherit them? Maybe there are a few safekeepers still lying around."

"Things don't tend to just 'lie around' in those places," Anni replied. "But I suppose I might have inherited them, if there are any. Last I heard, the house was DNA-locked. Only descendants can get in, but I never bothered to follow it up." She looked at Jon sharply. "Why do you ask? You want to get more safekeepers, don't you?"

Descendants like Jon, maybe? He perked up, undaunted by her tone. "I do. It's the least Davinia can do for me after she tried to kill me as a baby, don't you think?"

Anni went silent, but he must have spoken quietly because the hum of conversation continued in the background. "Jay-Jon…"

"I overheard you telling Tarren about it before I…left." Jon smiled at her encouragingly, trying to show he didn't hold a grudge at her withholding the information. Well, not much, anyway. How would a mother share something like that with her child? "So what's the name of this border town?"

"You hear that your wicked grandmother tried to sacrifice you to Creatures, and you decide that you need to visit her house?" Anni exclaimed. "That isn't the right response, Jay-Jon."

Jon grinned. "After what I've been through, visiting an empty house isn't scary. We'll be careful-"

"We!?"

"Tarie, Bets and I. We're the best set up for it. And we'll stay out of VR to avoid being tracked, keep our faces covered where we can. Then afterwards we can meet you at the south-west border. It might even be safer travelling in two groups."

Anni was tight-lipped, but she glanced over to where Tarie appeared to be having a similar conversation with Tarren, then sighed. "Fine. I couldn't stop you going anyway. But be careful!"

"Ma, the town's name?"

"Elsewhise. It's Elsewhise."

Jon's eyebrows shot up, and he caught Bets' eye from across the room. She nodded once, showing that their conversation wasn't quite as quiet as he'd thought.

But when they knew Amaranthus was working in the background, a coincidence of this kind just confirmed they'd made the right choice.

Elsewhise it is.

By some miracle, Tarie's father didn't argue either. "You'll have to get that Max lad," he said, showing clearly that he had no idea of the unpleasant history between Rokal-Max and Jon. "But you be careful!"

They'd be careful! Jon was feeling brave, not suicidal. But they all agreed that unless told otherwise, they'd meet in two days in the south-west of Erus, just over the border.

Jon, Tarie, and Bets were going north. Anni's hometown of Elsewhise was a tiny place right on the border of Erus city-state and the Other realm where it overlapped the Baltane Sea. It was a mere three hours by vehicle, except that they'd have to stop well away from the borderlands or risk losing their vehicle's power. Jon would fly, because there was no way in Hades all three of them would fit in Tarie's tiny vehicle.

Jon gave his apartment a final glance before he left. It was a familiar place, almost home, and he couldn't accept that he wouldn't be coming back. So he didn't think about it.

Instead he focused on how excited he was about the possible safekeepers, and even about seeing his murderous grandmother's home that both Maia and Anni had grown up in. Less so about retrieving Max-Rokal, who he still had terribly mixed emotions about. Max was a victim…maybe. Rokal was a fiend.

"I vow 'tis most odd," Bets was chattering to Tarie as they entered the garage. "That you know so little of the surrounding nations, and that you do not even have free contact with them."

"Why is that strange?" Tarie replied. "I know about the Baltane city-states, and each city-state has a separate VR system. We don't need anything more."

"Except if you wish to flee to somewhere less tolerant of the Creatures," Bets pointed out. "As we do now. It seems to me that the rules of this land have kept everyone ignorant of the world, and therefore weak."

Jon looked at her in surprise. "We have better technology than any time before us," he argued. "No offense, but doesn't that make us strong?"

Bets tapped a finger. "Firstly, you may not use flying vehicles, which were in common use in the mid-millennium. Secondly, you may not contact those outside your city-state, which is the simplest of all technologies." She grinned cheekily. "I say this acknowledging that in my own time, we sent messages via pigeon. And thirdly, you may not *learn* about other city-states or nations. So is it not clear that something is amiss?"

Jon missed a step, realising she was right. This era surely had the technology to be more connected – freer – than any time before them. VR gave them the impression of unlimited freedom. But in reality, he'd experienced so little of the world outside Erus city-state. (Except for time-travel, of course.) That was why they'd agreed to meet Anni, Tarren and Lydia in person, and then travel over the south-west border together. They didn't have access to proper maps past the Erus border.

"Fine, you win," Tarie said to Bets. "But how would any leaders benefit from keeping their people clueless?"

"If you don't know what's going on, how can you complain about it?" Jon ventured. "Come on, let's go."

Bets gave Tarie's vehicle a flame treatment to deal with anything that had been attached to it. From Jon's perspective, that meant holding her hands up, palms out, as a faint silvery mist seemed to spray out.

He hadn't been able to see much of the cleansing fire gift until today. Now he knew for certain it was there, but could still only catch a glimpse of it. Funny to think that it could be powerful enough to break a Creature connection. But then powerful things often came in subtle packages.

They finally left. Tarie and Bets were in the vehicle, and Jon flew high above them, making sure to keep sight of that tiny, faded purple shape as it whizzed its way down the narrow urban streets. Then it slid onto one of the massive, slow-moving intersections where hundreds of vehicles would wait for their turn to move through. It seemed extra busy today, each vehicle looking as tiny as a toy car from up here, and each barely moving.

Jon slowed in the air, not wanting to lose sight of the other two, then began flying in wide, lazy circles when it became clear they'd be stuck for some time. Traffic jams weren't common, but they did still happen.

Feeling an odd sense of expectation, Jon flew over and around dozens of overpasses where they met with enormous, irregular blocky buildings, and up and down the many levels of the city. He went a little too close to the lower levels, then recoiled as the smell of sulphur, rot and stagnant water filled his nostrils, so shot straight back up again.

There were centuries upon centuries of city down here, and when the old levels became unusable as the upper ones blocked out their sunlight, they were abandoned, and in some cases, blocked up. Massive pillars were planted directly over and through ancient wrecked buildings, holding up the tonnes of stone, glass and plastimetal above them.

Jon came out into the bright light of the highest level, coughing as he tried to get free of that foul smell. Ugh, he could practically *taste* it. Had something died down there…?

But then he saw that he was right opposite Temple Square, which until recently had contained the temples of the 'Big Three' Creatures – Audaline, Gerak and Domitian. Those three buildings housed direct entrances into the dangerous, supernatural Other realm, and had been recently merged to house only one Creature. Formerly Audaline, now known as the Tiger.

Through Jon's whole life, he'd seen Audaline portrayed as a hooded, feminine being with long robes and a veiled face. Creepy, but able to gift Flight. A huge, moving hologram had projected up from the roof of her (its?) temple, so that it seemed like you were actually in the presence of a Creature ten times the size of any human being.

Fake, of course. The real Creatures *Jon* had seen were much smaller – maybe twice the size of a human at most.

Then Audaline had quietly pushed out Domitian, Erus city-state's ruling Creature. They'd just heard one day that all humans pledged to Domitian had been transferred to Audaline, who was now Erus's Patron Creature. Jon figured that would affect quite a few people, even fiendish Gavriel, who'd tried so hard to kill Tarie.

And then earlier today, it was announced that Audaline now owned ALL human pledges. Oh, and by the way…she (it?) was now going to be called the Tiger.

Jon had never heard of such a Creature, but neither had he heard of all pledges being taken over like this. He wondered if it was all across the world, or just here in these city-states they could get access to – Erus, Dailan, and Tarie's old home Memrys.

Bets was right. It was a big world out there, and they did have too little information outside their own tiny area.

And Jon hadn't been back to Temple Square since he'd time-travelled. He hadn't seen Audaline's updated image – the *Tiger's* updated image – even though it was surely splashed around VR by now.

Now, the shimmering hologram moved across his vision, seeming to glance at him as it did so. Jon pulled back automatically against the side of the nearest building, even though he was only one of thousands clustered in this area.

Audaline wasn't robed anymore. Instead of a tall, angular, seemingly feminine figure, the holographic figure straddling the three temples was decisively masculine. It was humanoid, with sharp features and a version of the same loose robe, but this time bound with ancient-style armour. Its long hair moved as if blown in the wind, with decorative objects through braided sections of it.

It had a symmetrical, semi-human face with bright eyes – one blue, one yellow. Clawed hands flexed under long, loose sleeves, the skin marked with faint stripes and spots like a wild cat. Those same markings stretched up the figure's neck and face where they were exposed by the holographic clothing.

The hologram was a spectacular fraud, Jon knew, because no Creature was so beautiful. So…fantastical.

It turned towards him once more, and he found himself lurching backwards, deeper into the hollow of the building behind him. *Gulp.* Real Creatures weren't out *here*, for starters!

Jon slid completely out of sight, his gaze fixed on that horrible hologram until he could no longer see it. Then he turned to leave, and realised he wasn't pressed up against an ordinary building. Instead it was a yellowish metallic surface, with the bump of a shiny, dinner plate-sized gemstone sticking out at about face level.

His gaze followed the surface downwards for a long stretch, until it hit the ground in this city level. People – so many people – milled around the base of the structure.

And then he looked up…and up…and up, and saw the underside of a sharp feline jaw, high above him.

Chaos. He hadn't tucked himself against a building at all. Instead, it was a statue the size of a skyscraper.

The Tiger.

3
Roadblock

Jon instinctively flung himself away from the statue's side so that he was hovering in the air. But all it did was give him a better view of Temple Square, with the nearby humanoid hologram.

It also gave him a better idea of the statue's size.

He'd first seen it displayed through VR, showing how it was in this very square, and he'd seen it was big. But it was bigger than many of the sky-scraping buildings around here, and probably twice the height of his own apartment building. Like the hologram, it was quite striking to look at, but it made the hairs stand up all over his body.

Jon *knew* what was inside.

He flew back slowly until he'd almost hit the building behind him, and he had a great view of this top-level area. Temple Square was an enormous space, big enough to fit twenty thousand people at a time. That wasn't much considering this was a city of ten million, but who left their house anyway?

Yet today, people were leaving their houses. The square was packed full of tiny figures milling around, split by dividers into winding queues that led into dozens of entrances into the statue's base. Further up, raised pathways allowed more queues to move from the surrounding buildings into more doors in the statue's side.

A light breeze brought a waft of that rank lower-level smell, and Jon pulled away in disgust. This was all so wrong. Those people down there didn't know what they were doing…

"Jon."

He jolted in fright, then realised the quiet voice was coming from his comm speakers, directly into his ears. He lifted his wrist.

(He could have had the speakers set permanently in his lips and ears, but who would want *that?* Talk about no privacy.) "Tarie. How are you doing?"

"We're just passing the city limits now. We've lost sight of you."

"Gah! Sorry, you were stuck in traffic and I got distracted in the city centre." Jon waved a hand in explanation, even though no one could see him, then pulled up their vehicle's location on his comm. "I'll catch up. If I go at full speed, I'll meet you in…oh. An hour."

He'd have to cut across the countryside too, since the road north curved to avoid some natural landmarks. Even a tiny old vehicle like Tarie's could get up real speed, and they'd have left him well behind. He'd save a bit of time going directly overhead.

So Jon rose up into the air, risking one last glance at the statue behind him, then at the circlet wrapped safely twice around his wrist. All going well, they'd find a bundle of safekeepers to use as weapons. Then maybe they could come right back here and see what was inside the statue…and if it was as defeatable as the White Prince had been.

He hadn't mentioned *that* to the others.

Jon shuddered with dread, then left.

Maia watched out the window as Luca's sleek, oversized vehicle skimmed through the city, making its way from the council buildings, along the higher levels. Then it finally came to the highest level, where they were surrounded by dazzling sunlight, with the whole city spread out below them.

The vehicle slowed as a semi-transparent barrier lifted, then a moment later they were through. They drove a little further, then the vehicle came to a halt and the door opened.

Maia stayed seated in the vehicle. She could see at a glance that she was in a fabulously wealthy property, and the vehicle was parked in an actual garden, with perfectly trimmed grass and topiary in geometric shapes. A nearby abstract sculpture sprayed shimmering light-blue water in an endless fountain.

Up ahead was an enormous, sharply modern residence with equally shining facades, probably made of the same substance as the vehicle's windows. The single property occupied enough space that it would surely block the sun from entire apartment buildings on levels below.

Her fingers tightened where they rested on her knees, and she didn't need to look behind her to see that the barrier had closed. Surely she'd be in here until her host chose to let her go.

Then a man came out of the house's entrance, walking down the perfectly straight path with long, loose strides. He was expensively clothed to match his surroundings, and his dark hair fluttered in the light breeze. Even from here Maia could see his grin – Luke's grin – and her heart skipped a beat.

Fool, she told herself. He'd rejected her and left her, just like everyone else. His looks didn't matter.

Except that he did look quite gorgeous, and surprisingly, just like the VR image from the vehicle. Most people looking nothing like their images in VR.

"Maia!" He bent down to look inside the vehicle. "Do you want to have the meeting in here? I've arranged for a lunch spread inside."

It was a smirk rather than a smile now, she decided, as if he thought she was too frightened to come out. She didn't like it. "Of course I'm coming," she replied coolly. "I want to see the house. How did you get yourself a place like this, Luke?"

"Luca," he corrected as she stepped out. "Remember who you're talking to."

Fury washed over Maia, and she fisted her hands at her sides. "I could hardly forget. I've woken up in crazy-town, and shiny new carrier Luke is here to greet me. Of *course* you've changed your name too."

"I'm here to help you, you mean. And you'll help me in return."

She followed him into the house, barely noticing the ornate, extravagant surroundings. Where had this anger come from? Her confusion and disorientation had faded upon seeing Luke's face all pale and handsome and far too confident, and now she was just furious.

They stopped in a large room edged in low, dark leather couches. A skylight in the ceiling lit up a table in the room's centre, covered in plates of perfectly arranged food.

Luca gestured at the food as he sprawled onto the nearest

couch. "Help yourself," he said, then popped something small and colourful into his mouth.

Maia stood at the edge of the room, her hands still in fists. "I don't want to eat. I want to speak to Luke."

Luca stopped with another blue cherry partway to his mouth. His nose screwed up. "Why would you want *that?*"

"I know Luke," she persisted, still unmoving. "If this is real, if you're real, then I want to talk to him."

Luca put down the cherry, his expression flattening. A moment later his colouring changed: his skin darkening to a deep olive, and his eyes and hair to a nondescript dark brown. Fine lines appeared around his eyes and mouth, and his shoulders curled inwards as if he was tired, or guilty, or both.

Yes, that was Luke, but so much older than when she'd seen him last.

"Maia. What do you need from me?"

His voice had changed too, she thought. Rougher, aged, just like his appearance. And suddenly this all felt terribly, tragically real. An image of that other young man flashed into her mind, the one at Anni's house who looked like a slightly fairer version of Luke. A little slimmer, too. But then that would be from her side…

"I…" She swallowed. "I haven't seen you since before Jayel was born. You rejected us, Luke. Both of us. You said the baby couldn't possibly be yours – even though he obviously was – and then you signed away your parental rights and took off. No one had any idea where you went. And now…now you're saying you know our son? How did you get back here, get your rights back?" She waved a hand. "How are you a *carrier?*"

Luke shuffled in place, and his eyes fell from hers. "It's harder to say what I feel when it's just me, and not *him* as well." He was surely referring to the Creature/half-Halfling that he carried. "But all those years ago, I left because I couldn't stand to be around you any longer."

Maia's jaw dropped.

"I can see now that it was the rejection curse you're carrying," he continued as if he hadn't just stabbed her in the heart. "But at the time it felt like it was you, just you. Like I'd been caught up messing around with someone who was just…*ugh.* And I was already unhappy anyway, you know that. When my uncle offered me a job in Dailan, I took it like a shot. And I signed away my parental rights because I didn't want you contacting me again." His shoulders hunched. "In my heart I knew the baby was mine – that's easy enough to prove. But I didn't care. I was only thinking about myself."

"I see." Maia's chest hurt, and her throat burned with unexpected hurt that quickly turned to anger. She'd known there was something terribly wrong, and his rejection had been clear. But she hadn't thought she'd hear it so bluntly, or that it would feel so awful when she did. "But it was the curse that's on me that you hated. Not *me*."

Luke shrugged, and his eyes met hers again. "I suppose so. I might have done things differently if not for that curse, but who knows? It was a long time ago now."

"Not for me it wasn't!" She glared down at him where he sat on the low couch. "We had a connection, Luke! Then you acted like I was a leper! I can't just forget that!"

Luke blinked, his brown eyes widening and an expression of panic coming over his face. Then suddenly his colouring changed again – skin smoothing out and becoming almost white, eyes to a bright blue-green, hair pitch-black. An unnaturally vivid version of the same man. But something in his expression changed too, and the hint of shame Maia thought she was seeing completely vanished, replaced by Luca's smirk.

"He can't handle dwelling on the past," he said in Luca the carrier's smooth, confident tones. "He bears so much shame over his failings that it overwhelms him. That's why he finally gave in and took me on; became a carrier."

"So he – Luke – regrets leaving me? Us?" A savage pulse leapt in Maia's chest. If she was hurt, then she wanted him to be as well.

Luca stared at her coolly. "You weren't the only girl he left behind. Certainly not his greatest regret."

Ohhh. "Then what was?!"

Luca sighed. "Where to start? Luke refused to pledge to any Creature so he wouldn't be like his horrible father, and was treated like he was worthless as a result. Then he messed around with a bored borderlands princess-"

"Hey!"

"...knocked her up, lost interest, signed away his parental rights, fled the city-state for a boring job in yet another borderlands town in Dailan, got involved with an even more bored and hard-to-please girl, wasted years on her while she cheated on him, expected very little of himself, was refused rights to his second son as well, got terribly depressed, came back to Erus, married his ex's sister so he could claim back those lost parental rights, then helped to raise an unpledged, rejected son who somehow managed to destroy a Creature."

Maia's jaw was hanging from the overload of dreadful information. Luke had another child? But one point stood out. "Did you say, married your ex's sister?"

Luca stared her right in the eye. "Maia, Anni adopted Jayel Jonnamin and raised him. When Luke came back to Erus wanting his parental rights back, she wouldn't agree unless he showed he was serious about sticking around. So they signed a marriage agreement." He paused. "A platonic one. Really, entirely platonic."

Anni and Luke? Maia's mouth was dry, and she wasn't sure whether to believe him about the platonic thing. "But...why did you say Jayel was unpledged and rejected? And how did he destroy-"

Luca sighed heavily. "I'm only going to go through this once, and I don't have time to dwell on a teenage girl's worries or injured feelings. And if we do this right, then none of the past will matter anyway. Because we'll send you right back to the time the rejection curse was laid, and you'll be free of it. Stay out of the Other realm afterwards, go challenge Luke again over his behaviour, and who knows? You *did* have a connection, so maybe he'll ask you to come with him to Dailan. Then he'll be free of most of his worst decisions, and you won't miss seventeen years' worth of time passing."

His last words held a distinct tinge of sarcasm, but Maia fell silent. "You can do that?" she whispered. It was getting back the lost time that mattered, of course. Getting her baby back. If she got another chance with Luke while she was at it... She didn't think she'd loved him, but she'd cared about him enough to go against her mother's ideas about males, and the way it had ended hurt so badly. Although from what Luke/Luca had just told her, he was no catch.

"Nope," Luca said with a pop on the 'p'. "But you can, if you do what I tell you."

Maia finally took a seat on the couch opposite to him. The food looked fantastic, and who knew how long it had been since she'd last eaten? But she didn't dare touch it. Her mother had taught her that to stop Creatures controlling *you,* never eat anything they gave you. Not ever.

"Assuming you can do what you're claiming, what do you get out of this? Out of helping me?"

Luca smiled, just a curve of the lips. "That, Maia, is my business. Suffice to say, while you get what you want, I'll also get what I want."

"I won't be a carrier for you," she warned.

"I don't need any more carriers," he shot back. "One is more than enough. I'm not a Creature, remember?"

A half-Halfling – only three-quarters Creature. Or so he said.

"So here's what I need…what *we* need." The nearest wall sparked into life, revealing another enormous VR screen. The image was extra-large, displaying what looked like a male wrist and forearm clad in white. A goldish, metallic band was wrapped twice around the unknown person's wrist. It had distinctive markings all around its circumference.

AMARANTHUS-AMARANTHUS-AMARANTHUS…

"Look familiar?" Luca asked with a grin.

Of course it looked familiar. It was *hers.*

He'd got her. The girl had been so wary up till now, seeming moments away from rejecting his proposal entirely. It had been easier when Luca had first found her, when she'd looked dazed and hadn't really argued with anything. Time in the Other realm would do that to a person. But as the minutes passed, her eyes had brightened and her gaze sharpened, and she'd looked more and more suspicious.

The rundown of my past sins didn't help, Luke commented from somewhere in the depths of their shared mind.

Ah, that was right. Luke's sleeping consciousness had been woken to greet the girl, and it would take a while before he slumbered again. And maybe the rundown of past sins hadn't helped, but revealing this object of power *had.* Maia had been carrying it around since Luke had first met her as a teenager.

"That's my Amaranthus circlet!" Maia exclaimed. "I lost it today…I mean, when I lost time. Whose wrist is that?"

Luca changed the image view until the whole figure was visible: a young, dark-haired man who looked rather like he himself used to, except in the distinctive white clothing of a Prince of the Air. His arm was loosely draped over what looked like a blur in the recording, but which Luca was certain was actually some kind of cloaked human, invisible to the apartment's cameras. Anni was just visible at the edge of the image, her faced lined with worry or unhappiness.

Always so unhappy. A bit stupid too, not to notice that for years Luca had been recording every last conversation that took place within that apartment. But if he hadn't, he wouldn't have known how the White Prince had been so easily destroyed – with that very circlet, and a basic alter-power safekeeper.

Maia's lips tightened into a flat line. "That boy stole it."

'That boy'. As if he wasn't her own son. Although to be fair, Luca himself wasn't terribly keen on the boy either.

"More likely he picked it up when he was visiting the White Prince," Luca countered. "I assume that's also where you lost it, hmm?" And what a stroke of luck that was. Not so much for the White Prince, but for Luca himself now.

"I find it hard to believe the circlet can turn back time," she said darkly. "I had enough trouble convincing anyone of its value back home in Elsewhise."

"That's because it's not exactly, ahem, 'Creature approved'. And it *is* more effective when used in certain circumstances, or at just the right time. So that's how we'll use it." Luca nodded at the scene where the circlet was now just one small feature on their son's wrist. He noticed Maia wasn't looking at it at all, as if she couldn't stand to see the person wearing it. "Something immensely important is going to happen in just over four days. Something that will affect the very fabric of time. And for one short moment, we'll have a golden opportunity to change our own realities. And *that* is when we'll use the circlet."

"How?"

"That's for me to know-"

Maia waved a hand dismissively. "Yes, yes. Keep your secrets. So, I suppose I have to go back to Anni's apartment to get the circlet off that boy. Will he hand it over?"

"I doubt it," Luca said cheerfully. "Not considering he thinks you're working with me, and he despises the carrier version of his father. And you *are* working with me, but not in the way he imagines." He added in a fake whisper, "I'm tracking him right now, and he's heading north. Guess where to?"

"Don't tell me," she replied flatly. "The borderlands?"

"Even better. Elsewhise." The town was on the edge of the borderlands, so assuming the boy made it, the timing was most convenient. Almost like it was meant to be.

She was silent, and he continued brightly, "Anyway, I'll set you up to follow his tracker. You tell me when you've got the circlet, then we'll meet in the borderlands. I'll tell you where."

"My curse," Maia countered. "You said you'd break it. Do that first, then we'll make plans."

Luca blinked. The girl really was moody today. Must be from waking up and finding a generation had gone by, but whatever. "Alright. I'll need some of your blood."

"I'm not giving you my blood." She sounded as appalled as if he'd asked for her kidney.

"Then I can't break the curse," he said matter-of-factly. "I've got some knowledge, and some ability with alter-power, but I didn't set that curse. I'm not a miracle worker."

Anyone raised in Elsewhise would know that unless you *were* a miracle worker, you couldn't properly break a curse someone else had set. Maia clearly knew this, because she huffed out a sigh and held out her wrist.

Luca got to work.

Even though he was here in the normal realm, if he squinted just right, he could make out the shape and colours of alter-power in use. Maia was wrapped like a mummy in faint strands of orange, from her fingertips to her forehead.

This close, Luca got a strong sense of the person who'd placed the curse; of the malevolence behind it. The pure spite. It had been terribly personal, this rejection curse, and far stronger than it needed to be.

He knew the one who'd laid it. They'd admitted it to him years ago. He understood the desire to chase what you wanted, but what they'd done was like squashing a mosquito with a boulder. Overkill.

He finished up, making sure to subtly add in some strands

of control and connection of his own. Not malicious, just smart, since the last person he'd tasked to collect an object of power for him had taken off and was never seen again.

This didn't make Maia a carrier, but she should be easy to keep track of, and somewhat controllable. Just like he needed.

The new wrapping of alter-power glowed deep red in his side vision, and he stood upright with a nod. "That's done. I couldn't get rid of the rejection curse, so I overlaid it with an intimidation one. It'll get you whatever you need. That, plus your own abilities. What were they again?"

Maia stood too, shaking herself a little as if she'd been in a trance. Although he could no longer see the new alter-power, he could sense it emanating off her; in her manner as well. The willowy girl's gentle nature had become noticeably harsh. "I didn't have any true abilities of my own."

"Yet you were the pride of your mother," Luca said jovially. "But I remember why that was. You *replicated*, didn't you? You echoed the abilities of those around you."

"My echoes were weaker," Maia admitted, and he knew his control was working over her. She wouldn't have spoken otherwise – and she hadn't questioned that he didn't remove the rejection curse. "They were nothing compared to the original gifts."

"Ah, well. We'll see how they go anyway. Make sure you get me what I've asked for, and we'll both get a fresh start." His tone dropped, and he let his own alter-power gift drift out. Intimidation was a natural part of who he was, of his real body, and it had taken Luke DeMannard from a worthless, miserable loser to the ruler of this region. "But if you don't...I won't give you a second chance."

She didn't meet his eyes, but he felt what she was thinking. *Bully.*

Wonderful! The control link was working even better than he'd expected. "Yes I am," he agreed aloud. "Now get going, Maia. We've got a circlet to catch."

Jon flew beyond the city limits, testing his speed (impressive) and trying not to get bugs in his face (impossible). He rose higher and higher, trying to avoid those pesky bugs, until the landscape was laid out in miniature below him. The road Tarie and Bets were taking was a thin white line out to the east, and he periodically checked his comm. It showed he was set to meet them in forty-five minutes.

He wasn't even tired.

Jon's comm flashed, along with a quiet verbal warning to readjust his direction, and he lowered his height accordingly.

Slow down, the comm warned. *Populated area.*

What? He was out in the middle of nowhere! There wasn't even a house-

Jon ducked to avoid a drone that seemed to come out of nowhere. He felt it clip his shoulder, ruffle his hair, and he spun a couple of times trying to right himself. Glancing over his shoulder, he saw the drone's lights flash as it wobbled in the air. A moment later gravity grabbed him, and he plunged downwards. It was as if his flying ability had suddenly vanished.

Panic! Jon tried to right himself, but ended up wobbling just as much as that drone. He rose a little, his heart pounding as he seemed to be alright again, but then once more, gravity grabbed him. Slower this time, so he was moving steadily downwards rather than in free fall, but there was no doubt he'd be landing in the foliage below.

A minute later Jon landed on the ground with a bump, then fell on his backside. There were trees all around, with lush undergrowth and a nearby stream partly overgrown with lilies, sheltered by the trees.

It was a charming scene, but Jon brushed himself off, scowling. His mind worked as he tried to figure out why he'd fallen. The drone had bumped him, but he was certain he hadn't been hit with another VR dart. This all felt too real. Lush growth plus fluctuations in alter-power. He'd almost think it was the borderlands, except that he should be hours from there still...

Jon frowned, taking another look around him. Just through the trees he could see the red roof of a small cottage; the stand-alone sort you'd only see in the smallest, most rural villages.

It was quiet, though. Not even the sound of birds, and his comm was also silent. He tapped at it once, then again, but couldn't get a response from the device even though the power still seemed active. It really did feel like the borderlands. A discomforting thought.

Jon let out a long breath through his nose, running one hand over the circlet around his other wrist, then headed for that nearby red-roofed cottage. Surely someone would know what was going on.

Except when Jon reached the edge of the forested area, suddenly he could see he wasn't in a flat area at all, and the cottage wasn't little. It was four storeys at least, with only its roof showing up here, and the unexpected drop from where he stood was dizzying. The village before him was set in a deep ravine – a kind of valley. Odd, since this part of the world was quite flat.

Jon took a deep breath and rose slightly into the air. Gravity pulled at him again, making him feel heavier than his flight ability should make him, but he was satisfied that he wouldn't plunge to his death.

Then he stepped over the edge.

Elspeth was riding along in Tarie's tiny vehicle, moving at exceptional speeds over a wide, long road that wound its way out of the city. First through the central areas highly stacked with buildings like a child's block game, then the lower-level suburbs that stretched on for miles, then an abrupt change to green countryside and fields. Unlike in many other time periods, this vehicle was self-driving, so they mostly just watched the scenery.

The thing about being perennially away from one's own time, Elspeth mused, was that everything was a surprise. But 'twas wearying being surprised all the time, so eventually *nothing* was a surprise.

Still, she found herself somewhat startled when Tarie announced, "Oh! I've just got a message from Rokal. I mean Max. He says he's on the train."

"The train?" Elspeth echoed in confusion. "Do you mean the same one we took to reach the borderlands museum?" The map displayed in front of them showed that very track was mere minutes away, running parallel to their current road, although just out of sight.

"Yeah…" Tarie frowned, clearly listening to something that didn't reach Elspeth's ears. "Huh. He's saying he was grabbed and put on the train, and there are others with him who don't have Creature pledge marks. He doesn't know where they're going, but..."

"What is it?!"

"That's it," Tarie replied flatly. She turned to look Elspeth in the eye, and her expression was sombre. "I looked up the train details after we came back from the museum that time. Did you know the train runs right through the borderlands? The details get sketchy after that. And this message from Max might be old, since the borderlands often mess up technology. It's kind of fuzzy as is."

The train ran through the borderlands? Did that not mean...into the Other? Elspeth was about to ask why Rokal-Max would be taken to such a place – although she was getting a bad feeling – when the vehicle began to slow. The road curved, and around that corner were flashing lights and a solid barrier, blocking the road ahead.

"Chaos," Tarie breathed. A smatter of unintelligible words followed, and she noticeably increased in height. A small, red-leafed plant appeared in the dashboard between them. "A checkpoint. Don't speak, OK? They might not even notice you're in here. I'll do the talking."

The vehicle stopped entirely. Elspeth could not see anyone outside, imagining that a 'checkpoint' must have people to do the checking. But then suddenly a bright, pinkish-orange light filled the windscreen and side windows. For a moment Elspeth saw a symbol appear on Tarie's forehead, something like a blotchy gold thumbprint or a smear of oil. She recognised it at once – here in this time, one's allegiances were displayed on one's forehead, visible either in virtual reality, or in the Other realm. The light must be some form of VR.

Then it disappeared, and a moment later there was a loud *clunk*. The vehicle shuddered, and then it was moving again. But not forward – sideways.

There was a long silence, broken by the faint *whirr* of whatever was above them, clasping the small vehicle. Elspeth looked out the window. The road was now far below them, to their left, and they were leaving it well behind as they moved along the length of the blockade.

Mayhap 'twas a detour...?

"Ought we be concerned about this?" Elspeth asked finally.

Tarie turned to look at her once more. Her dark eyes were too wide, the whites showing almost all around the irises, and she'd grown enough that she was hunching against the top of the tiny interior. A bunch of colourful vines trailed from her mass of curly hair, down onto her clothing. "Yes. Yes, we ought to be concerned."

As if motivated by her own words, Tarie suddenly grabbed the door handle and rattled it. But the door didn't move, which Elspeth considered a good thing. Looking out the window, they were rather high in the air, and neither of them could fly. And they were also locked inside a tiny vehicle, going who knew where.

"Shall we send Jon a message?" Elspeth asked.

"I already tried, and I can't get through. Whatever's grabbed us must be blocking my signal."

"*Oh.*"

Jon took a deep breath, then stepped over the edge of the cliff. But instead of a slow descent into the village below, he abruptly found himself on his knees on dry, unpaved ground. There was the slight sense of unease, like he'd walked through a thin layer of jelly to reach this space, which was much smaller and rougher than it had appeared.

And the village wasn't empty, either. A couple of people sat on a nearby cluster of boulders, and their conversation stopped dead when they saw him.

They'd been hidden by illusion. That was never a good sign. And these people didn't look precisely human…also not a good sign. Good thing he had Fylax with him. He felt so much safer with his giant, invisible protector around. Although, having Fylax with him hadn't always saved him from trouble and injury in the past…

"Uh…hi," Jon said with an awkward wave, surreptitiously looking around for exits as he did so. The multilevel cottage had been part of the illusion, he saw, since the real one was barely single storey, and looked like it had had a long, rough life. Behind him, there was a massive, flat barrier that shone dully in the bright light, partially obscuring the forest behind it. There was a similar barrier behind the people, as if it hid this small area from the rest of the world.

The people didn't respond; just stared at him wide-eyed. One of them was a teenage girl with long, very slender limbs and unusually pale colouring. Rather like a stretched version of Jon himself when he'd been carrier for the White Prince, except even from here, he could see her eyes were a deep lavender purple.

The other person was a similar age, androgynous enough that Jon couldn't pick their gender. By appearance, they might have been the girl's sibling, except their colouring was a solid beige. Hair, skin, and entire eyes: irises and sclera. It made their deep blue feet and hands stand out more obviously against their loose, plain clothing.

"You're Halflings," Jon blurted out in sudden realization. "I've never seen real Halflings before. Just holograms in VR. Well, there was this guy at school when I was a kid who said he was one quarter Creature, and he was really tall and had these kind of warped features – sorry – but no one knew if it was that or his parents doing too much genetic modification."

Jon snapped his mouth shut. He wasn't sure where that verbal explosion had come from. "Sorry," he said again. "I was flying over – 'cos I'm a Prince of the Air – and I fell suddenly. My comm isn't working either. This feels like the borderlands, but it can't be, can it? The Other is miles away, and I'm sure they don't extend this far."

The two Halflings exchanged a glance. "You can stop now, Elvan," the beige Halfling said in a distinctly masculine voice. "He's harmless."

Jon felt movement behind him just as someone moved into sight. It was a third Halfling; a man probably half Jon's own height, yet considerably wider. He had a curious flatness to his dark-haired head, as though someone had stepped on a clay figure while it was still wet and permanently changed its shape, but his black eyes were sharp. He held a small grey ball in each large hand.

"Second outsider in one day," Elvan said. He spat on the ground, just missing Jon's feet. "It's an infestation."

"Oh? Who was the first one? Where is this place? Is it the borderlands?" Jon knew he was talking too much, too fast, but couldn't seem to stop himself. "What are those balls you're holding?"

"Elvan, I said *stop*," the beige boy snapped.

Elvan shoved the balls into one pocket, and Jon's intense urge to blabber suddenly eased.

"Truth spheres," the purple-eyed girl explained to Jon. "We had to know why you were here. Most people never come into this place, and the last visitor wasn't exactly friendly. Although I suppose if you can fly, the cliff illusion won't do anything for you."

"Tiff, *you're* not using the truth spheres," the beige boy told her. "Don't tell him what he doesn't need to know."

Jon looked from the pale, purple-eyed girl – Tiff – to the unnamed beige boy, to the distinctly unfriendly flat-headed Elvan. Had he stumbled across something illegal? If so, he didn't want to know. "Don't know what you're doing here, don't care," he said lightly, raising both hands with palms outwards. "I'm heading up north and got pulled in here by accident. I want to get out before I'm any later than I already am."

The three exchanged glances, then the beige boy nodded, getting up off his seat on the boulder. "This way."

The exit turned out to be through the small village, which was a cluster of half a dozen structures all sitting very neatly between two low rocky cliffs. They walked silently along a dry path down the village's centre, and Jon noted with interest the difference between the outside of this place and its contents. Maybe it wasn't the borderlands after all. They were known to be wonderfully lush, and subject to night and day just like the normal realm. An abrupt contrast to the dry, everlasting night of most of the Other realm.

Jon didn't see anyone else in the village, but he heard slight noises indicating people were there, just out of sight.

The beige boy pointed at a random spot in the high, shimmering barrier blocking the end of the path. "There."

Surprisingly, Jon wasn't ready to go. Unlike most things Creature related, he didn't have any real sense of danger from this place, and he'd never seen such people before. He knew that Creatures didn't raise the children they created, instead abandoning them to their human mothers.

He'd love to ask more questions – get some real answers this time – even about the Halflings themselves. Did they have any special abilities? Did they age normally? Could they move freely in the normal realm? And who was the other outsider who'd come through today? But it wasn't the time for it, and he clearly wasn't welcome.

"Thank you," he said meekly, then stepped through the barrier.

4

Train Track

Chaos. Chaos. *Ohhh, chaos.*

Tarie pressed her hands against the shuddering roof of her vehicle, as if she could stop herself growing by sheer willpower. As if she could stop them being picked up and carried through the air, well away from the road they were meant to be taking.

She couldn't, of course.

Silvery mist filled her vision as it had for the last several minutes, and then Bets lowered her hands with a frown. "'Tis not an Otherly problem, this," she said thoughtfully. "Or 'twould have responded to my cleansing flame."

Tarie could have told her that. It seemed they'd been stopped by an official blockade, and were no doubt being taken to an official destination. (Possibly a horrible one, too, since the officials were usually carriers.) And while plenty of things – and people – were influenced by Creatures, most of the city-state ran on technology. Regular tech didn't respond to even the fiercest cleansing, alter-power-fuelled fire.

She said as much, and Bets let out a thoughtful huff. "Then 'tis odd that I was set as your guardian, for a simple rock to the head would have taken you out regardless of my alter-power gifts. But I expect that Amaranthus knew the threat to your life would be Otherly rather than ordinary weapons."

Tarie gave her a sidelong glance through the small thicket of red-leafed saplings now filling the car. Tarie herself had now grown a little too large for this small vehicle, and her head was forced on an angle by its low roof. "And what do you call this?"

"A new challenge?" Bets suggested brightly. "But we cannot

fight, and if worst comes to worst and it does end in death, never fear. My sister Anne assures me that death is not so bad, for 'tis a necessary step to reach immortality, and once attained, the memory of the pain fades." The edges of her mouth turned downwards. "All in all, I would rather avoid it, if I could."

Tarie would too! But her attention was caught by the claim of an immortal sibling, and for a moment she wondered if that would be their fate. "How did your sister, ah, die?"

"Burned at the stake as a heretic."

Tarie blanched and tapped at her comm. "That's terrible! Well, *I'm* not waiting for immortality. If it looks like we're in danger, I'm going to fight my way out!" She rapidly tried to message Jon again or even her father, but her comm still wasn't working.

"'Twas meant to be comfort in case of the worst-case scenario," Bets said apologetically. "Mayhap we are being taken to repledge, in which case we can fight our way out. Or mayhap 'twill be a mere inconvenience, for we shall miss meeting Jon."

It didn't feel like an inconvenience to Tarie. It felt like disaster. But she focused on her breathing, trying to relax as the vehicle seemed to grow ever smaller and they left the blockade well behind them. The view through the windows changed to show the low hills that ran up the mid-east of Erus. There was a faint gleaming line along their length, and she caught of a glimpse of a high, plain building against the brownish green hills. Then they were rushing up to it, up to a dark opening in its side.

Clunk. Their surroundings turned pitch-black, and the vehicle rocked madly for several moments, making Bets squeak. Tarie just closed her eyes and pushed her hands against the vehicle's vine-covered sides.

"What's going on?" Bets asked finally. "I cannot see a thing."

Tarie opened her eyes. A few cracks of light shone through gaps in the vines, but otherwise they may as well have been covered in a blanket. She tried to open one of the doors, but it was jammed shut. She pushed hard, then again, and finally it opened enough for her to give it a few good kicks.

Finally she sprawled out of the vehicle, feeling like she was being uncomfortably born again. The vines that had sprung up were thoroughly mixed with the Word trees, she saw, and they covered her little old vehicle more tightly than she could have imagined.

"What do you see?" Bets called from inside the vehicle.

"Hmm. A big room..." A warehouse, almost, but with dozens of vehicles lined up on multiple platforms, reaching up to the high ceiling. As she watched, a mechanical arm picked up one nearby and stacked it neatly with the others. The arm hung from the ceiling and was probably standard in factories, not that Tarie had seen many of those. Not far from that, a second arm pushed a struggling figure through a small door at the other side of the room.

Bets poked her head out of the partially open door just as a third arm came shooting down towards Tarie. Tarie swore and struck out, thinking she'd be crushed, but it just gripped her around the waist and lifted her into the air. She heard Bets' panicked tones somewhere beneath her, but the wash of silvery flame didn't make any impact.

Panicking just as much, Tarie grabbed the mechanical arm and tried to force it open. There was a massive *crack* and suddenly it fell open – in fact, one of the grippers fell to the ground. She fell with it, but only a short way. "Oof."

"Tarie!" Bets ran up to her, stumbling on the uneven ground. "Are you hurt?"

Tarie shook herself, baffled. "No. I'm fine." She looked down at Bets, then did a double-take. The other girl seemed to only come up to her chest. Then Tarie looked down at herself and saw that the smart fabric of her clothing had been stretched beyond its capabilities, exposing her forearms and ankles. But she couldn't blame it when she had to be what, seven feet tall?

She let out a startled huff, wiggling her fingers and staring at them in surprise. She could *feel* the alter-power moving through her, and the strength that came with it. She'd mentioned earlier that her powers had grown, but they'd done so more than even she'd imagined.

"I wonder how we shall go northwards now," Bets said, sounding disgruntled now her fear had faded. "Look at your poor vehicle, Tarie."

A second arm had come down to grab it, vines and all, and it carried it to the other end of the warehouse, next to that small exit she'd seen someone pushed through.

Tarie's attention was instantly caught. "I wonder where

they're taking people?" She thought she'd seen the train track. Imagine if they were putting people on that same train Rokal/Max had found himself on.

Tarie pushed her way towards the far door, ignoring the still-twitching mechanical arm she'd broken as if it was a dry twig. She spared a glance for her vehicle, then with a sigh, trotted over to where it had been stacked along with so many others. "Just the basics."

She grabbed her daypack with its essential items then jumped back down to where Bets stood on the warehouse floor, apparently invisible to any technology around here.

"What are we doing?" Bets raised her eyebrows quizzically. "'Tis clear that nobody has seen us. Shall we not work to free our vehicle?"

"Yeah…" Tarie crept towards the small, open door at the end of the warehouse. It seemed extra small now she was so oversized, but she ducked a little to poke her head through. On the other side was a wide passage with clear sides, leading to a familiar dark-sided shape. "It's the train," she said triumphantly. "I *knew* it-"

Something shoved hard against her back and side, and she stumbled out into the space on the other side of the door. There was a second push but this time she was ready, and she braced herself against the floor, feeling a pulse of alter-power as she did so.

It was the side of the passage, she realised. It was made of a series of clear, hard panels that pushed people towards the other end, into the train. Even as she thought that, the train's door opened – then closed – then opened again, as if the train's AI couldn't work out why she hadn't come in yet.

Then Bets was beside her. She grabbed at Tarie's arm, trying to help her up and push away the forceful panels, although clearly she didn't have the strength to do so.

And then suddenly the panels caught Bets. She flew with a shriek through the train's open doors and landed neatly inside the train. There was a soft *beep,* but the doors stayed open, and the panel's pressure on Tarie didn't ease. Clearly it hadn't even registered picking up Bets.

Inside the train, Bets clambered to her feet and moved towards the door. Then she paused, looking around to where Tarie couldn't see. "Oh! There are so many people in here, Tarie.

And all unpledged!"

Tarie made a snap decision. Pulling her daypack tightly into her chest, she relaxed and let herself be pushed onto the train.

Maia skimmed down the unfamiliar roads on her borrowed tri-wheeler powercycle. She'd expected the journey to take much longer, for more hold ups, but with the cycle belonging to Chairman Luca, she'd sped through every roadblock at uncomfortably high speeds.

She knew she was probably only travelling as fast as the average vehicle, but it felt so much more intense when there was just a clear, narrow safety barrier separating her from the ground, and even though she was strapped in as she straddled the silent tri-wheeler. Maybe that was why she felt so unsettled, so brittle: the nerves from this dangerous mode of travel. Or maybe it was just that she was heading north again, towards her hometown of Elsewhise.

Or maybe it was that she'd lost everything, and regaining it depended on this quest and her reliance on the unreliable carrier Luca. Maybe that was it – but she could barely bring herself to think about her circumstances.

She had to get the circlet. That was all.

Maia glanced down at her borrowed comm. Its holographic display showed the distance between her and her target: that boy who had her circlet. He'd blinked out of sight earlier for some time, only just reappearing on her screen, and in almost the same location. If he kept travelling in a straight line, she'd reach him in thirty minutes.

Maia brushed a hand over the small bag looped around her neck. Inside were several items that would help her catch him. Luca had spent quite some time discussing the possibilities and how to best bring the boy down, but in the end he'd recommended a basic paralytic dart. It'd make him sleep long enough for her to take what she needed, then leave him behind.

Maia felt a pang of unease at the idea of attacking someone in such a way, but she pushed it aside. There was no room for soft emotions. Her entire future – and Jayel's – rode on this.

Finally the tracker showed the boy was just ahead. He should be within sight now. Maia set the tri-wheeler into autodrive and squinted into the air. Just ahead she could make out a shape that wasn't a bird or a drone. It moved at great speed, far faster than she imagined a Prince of the Air could fly, but there was no doubt who it was.

He was also high in the air, as high as a three or four-storey building. Maia drove a little closer, then pulled out the preloaded dart gun and raised it into the air. He didn't seem to have noticed her, looking forward instead of behind. She gritted her teeth and locked onto her target. All it would take was a simple tap to lock the dart onto his tracker, then release it. He'd never get away.

Maia held the dart gun steady, the green light flashing to show she'd locked onto her target. She could see a tracery of red lines covering her hand and running down her arm, showing through her clothing, with a hint of orange visible through it. It was the alter-power 'gift' from Luca, plus the remnants of that nasty rejection curse underneath it.

She'd hardly been able to see it before, but Luca had. That meant she'd replicated his gift for seeing alter-power, at least to some degree. The new ability could last anywhere from a day to a month.

But while the gift-and-curse reminded her of why she was here, for some reason she didn't take the shot. She kept waiting and waiting…then finally lowered the dart gun.

The boy was too high up, Maia told herself. It wouldn't do much good for him to fall from such a height, since he could be seriously injured. Even though they were going to start over, and she couldn't stand to even look at him, she didn't want him hurt.

Back when Luca had been equipping her for this journey, he'd commented that he could have just sent a drone after that boy and shot him down that way, then followed along and picked up the circlet. He'd looked almost surprised at his own idea, and had mused that maybe he hadn't wanted to risk losing the circlet to someone else, if he was unable to collect it soon enough.

Maia thought it more likely that somewhere under that cold exterior, Luke still cared whether his offspring lived or died.

She trailed the boy for several minutes, careful to follow from far enough away to remain unnoticed. She kept one hand on the dart gun, but he never came lower to the ground.

And then suddenly he was gone, vanished into a bank of fog.

Maia blinked in shock. It was a clear day – *had been* a clear day – so where had the fog come from? But she had barely enough time to think that, when suddenly there was a terrible jolt, and she was in darkness. She was flung upwards from the tri-wheeler's seat, her grip on the handlebars the only thing keeping her attached. Its protective forcefield had failed.

But she was still moving, her gaze darting around and trying to make sense of what had happened. The cold of this dark place permeated through her borrowed jacket, making her bones ache, and she could see a faint orange glow in the distance.

Her lips tightened. It was just one thing after another! The tingling she felt told her she was clearly in the Other realm, but that didn't make sense. The borderlands were *hours* away, and she certainly hadn't crossed them!

The boy was nowhere to be seen.

But luckily Maia's borrowed tri-wheeler kept chugging along. Slower than before – though she'd have slowed anyway due to the darkness – until suddenly there was another jolt, and *pop*, she was back out in the light. The tri-wheeler's engine revved and it began to pick up speed, but Maia overrode the autodrive and slowed it right down. She turned back the way she'd come, then came to a halt.

The countryside around her looked much the same as it had before her odd little detour. She could faintly see the outline of Erus city on the horizon. Little boroughs and towns were scattered around in each direction, all built up within their precise town limits, while the land between them was made up of miles and miles of neatly tilled fields. Some were clearly ready for harvest, their crops fat and lush under their sheer protective coverings.

The strip of Other Maia had just gone through was nowhere to be seen. No cloud bank either, but she'd bet that if she drove back in that direction, she'd find it easily enough.

But wait. She scanned her surroundings once more, squinting a little as a pattern emerged. It took a touch of supernatural sight, but there was a faint line of darkness trailing past her, through the fields and back towards Erus city. It looked like a crop duster had left a trail of dark dust which hadn't settled or been caught by the wind.

Maia followed the faint trail with her gaze, back away from the city. It took a slight curve to the west, but then headed resolutely north once more. No mystery – it led towards the borderlands, and didn't look too far from Elsewhise.

For several minutes Maia just stared at it, looking from the north to the south and back again. The trail was clear now, or perhaps it was just that she knew where it was. She sniffed, wrinkling her nose when she got a whiff of sulphur.

But *what* was it?

She was a moment away from following the trail when she remembered her reason for being out here in the first place. Getting her life back. Chaos. She'd forgotten the boy in all this mess.

Worse still, he was nowhere in sight. Maia checked his tracker, but it just blinked aimlessly, clearly as uncertain as she was. She almost threw it down in disgust. But she knew what had happened, and she turned to look once more at the faint Otherly trail.

He must still be in *there*. But if she went back in herself, there was no guarantee where – or when – she'd get out again.

She clenched her fists and headed back in, leaving the vehicle behind.

Jon came to a halt in the frigid darkness. One moment he'd been speeding high above the Erusian countryside, determined to catch up to Tarie and Bets on schedule, and then there was a little jolt and he was here. He could tell he was high in the air, but the tingle of alter-power he felt also told him exactly where he was.

Chaos. He was in the Other realm again, not half an hour after he'd been caught in that odd little borderlands village, and less than two days after he'd last left the Mountain of Glass.

Why did this kind of thing happen to *him*?

Although at least he had Fylax, not that he could see his guardian Person right now.

"We're alright, aren't we, Fylax?" he said to the empty air.

Fylax didn't reply. But that was OK – he never did. Honestly, if Jon hadn't seen him those few times, he'd assume he wasn't even there.

But the thought of the Mountain cheered Jon, and he squinted around in the darkness, straining for a hint of glowing orange or anything that didn't seem to belong. A moment later it occurred to him to use his circlet. Unlooping it from his wrist and holding it up over his face, he said, "Amaranthus!"

Unlike the strong light beam from last time when he'd inadvertently destroyed the White Prince, this time a soft glow emitted from the circlet. Now he could see his surroundings clearly, as if it was early dusk. Every last detail of the barren landscape was in distinct detail, if somewhat dark.

He was also barely an arm's length from a solid rock mountainside. If he'd kept flying in the dark, Jon thought in dismay, he would have ended up with a flattened face.

But as he looked closer, he saw that the mountainside wasn't solid rock, nor solid darkness. It shimmered with a faint iridescent blue, as if it was glass in a dark room, just waiting for light to show its full beauty and substance.

Oh. Suddenly realising what he was seeing, Jon pushed eagerly towards the nearby rock, pressing one hand against the iridescent surface. For a moment it gleamed brightly, then *pop!* He tumbled right through.

This would only be Elspeth's second train ride in her entire life, but she had to say the first was more comfortable. The other train had gone on these very same tracks to a reeking museum that she'd eventually set on fire, but at least it had had seats!

This train had none. Instead, she stood in a narrow aisle between two walls of what looked like dark, shining glass. She pressed a hand experimentally against one surface and it gave slightly, rippling around her fingers. It felt like those safety barriers kept around high balconies and so forth. And was that the silhouette of a human behind it?

She pushed at it further, trying to see clearly what was on the other side, but it lit up intensely red.

"You are not authorized," a voice informed her. *"Wait for assistance."*

Elspeth glanced around in a panic, but beyond that somewhat scornful automated tone, no one appeared to have noticed her. She tried to move her hand away, but 'twas stuck fast.

Hmm. She tugged again and let out a little silver flame, but it made no difference, and with nothing to burn, the flame fizzled out.

Just then Tarie came hurtling through the nearby doorway, aided by those moving arms and barriers. She was bigger and taller than Elspeth had ever seen her – as tall as the roof of the train, in fact – and she hit the far side of the carriage with enough force to jolt the whole thing. The barrier arms moved as if trying to push her along, and a nearby section of dark glassy wall vanished, revealing a tiny chamber within. 'Twould be barely big enough to fit Tarie as she was now.

"I believe 'tis a form of prisoner transport," Elspeth told her. "But it does not respond to my gift. Mayhap do not allow yourself to be pushed- oh."

Tarie had planted her extra-large feet into the ground, pushing at the barrier arms which looked as weak as paper. She was muttering under her breath and reddish foliage was springing up all around her – from the manmade materials of the train itself, and even from her backpack. Elspeth had never seen anything like it.

"Also, I seem to be trapped," Elspeth added apologetically. "If you would be so good as to free my hand afore some form of guard comes... Thank you."

Tarie reached over and ripped Elspeth's hand free. The flexible glassy barrier flickered red then orange, and a truly horrid noise filled the air, screechy and loud enough to hurt her ears.

Suddenly all the dark glassy barriers turned clear, revealing well-lit chambers all the way down the train carriage's length. About half of them were occupied by people of all ages, shapes and sizes, squinting under the overly bright, shimmering VR light. Most were crouched in the small spaces, but they had certain things in common. All of them appeared to be most unhappy, and...

"They're unpledged," Elspeth breathed. Even under what was clearly VR light, each had a unmarked forehead.

Tarie kicked at a long, thick vine that appeared to be growing from her very shoe. Its leaves were crimson like the vines from the vehicle, and rather like the Word saplings Elspeth had seen here and there. But *those* had been small and apparently harmless. "Of course they are. And I've set off the Chaos-blighted alarm, haven't I?"

"Er…yes?"

The vine came free and set itself to climbing up the nearest wall. It quickly spread across the now-clear barrier, while the occupant, Tarie and Elspeth all stared at it in amazement. There was a cracking sound and the barrier began to disappear, while the red-leafed vine grew larger still. It looked almost as if 'twas-…consuming the barrier. Elspeth had never seen anything like that, either.

She very nearly missed what else had changed around her. The atmosphere felt different, and there was a faint whooshing sound from all around them. That, she did recognise.

"I do believe the train is moving," she said in surprise.

Tarie just groaned. "This day just keeps getting better."

BOOM. BOOM. BOOM. The sound of the explosions was impossible to miss, but somehow muted, considering the size of them and the light and shock waves they sent out. Luca was almost disappointed.

But then he *had* chosen these particular explosives because of the lack of fall-out, as well as the complete and utter annihilation they caused. It wouldn't be much good to destroy the most population-dense parts of what had been Dailan city-state, just over the Reamas river, if his own borrowed body was destroyed at the same time.

BOOM. BOOM. BOOM. With each explosion, a pulse of power shot into the small pale object he held cupped between his hands, and a triumphant smile curved his lips. It was going *so* well. Just another hour of this and he'd have everything he needed. Everything he'd planned for.

There wouldn't be much left of Dailan city-state or its people, but with what the Tiger had planned, some would say he was doing them a favour.

The explosions stopped. Luca waited expectantly for the next bomb to go off, both hands cupped around the precious object as he held it toward the old border between city-states. There were hundreds more set to go. But seconds, then minutes passed in silence, and his smile fell.

He put the object in his pocket, then picked up the hand-sized device that controlled all of the explosions. Even as the new governor over all Greater Erus, he didn't just have free control of all the city-state's weaponry. He'd had to actually go to a particular location – in real life, not in virtual reality – and pick up an actual physical controller.

Unfortunately, that also left room for physical breakages, and this thing looked as dead as a doornail. Its surface should have been lit up multicoloured and covered in scrolling text, but it was the plain, matte black of technology with no power.

Luca cursed, shaking it, then focused on examining it carefully. These things were meant to be self-sustaining, but where would he even start to fix it…?

"Legion."

Lilith's voice was sharp, cold…and in person.

Luca's lips tightened and he turned slowly, his borrowed body tense with anger. There she was, standing right behind him, her own expression as cold as he felt. "Mother," he bit out, stabbing a finger at the controller. "Did you do this?"

Her pale eyebrows shot up. "Did I stop your absolute idiocy? Yes, I did. You've already killed close to half a million people! Are you *trying* to get the Tiger to notice you?"

"It's only half a million," he argued sulkily. If he'd had it his way, it would have been three times that. "The Tiger killed sixteen billion people when he started the continental wars last century. Don't tell me he cares about their lives now he has a little more power."

"He doesn't!" Lilith snapped. "But he needs them *alive* and pledged, as many of them as possible. And for you to do something stupid like this when you can't even gather power from their deaths…" She paused. "Why *did* you do this?"

The precious object sat heavy in Luca's pocket. He wouldn't tell her the real reason, not when she'd come in and ruined things like this already. "I never liked the Dailanese. Do you know how much trouble they caused us over the Reamas city border? Ridiculous! They deserve a good bombing as punishment."

Lilith hissed out a disgusted breath. "Fine, don't tell me the real reason. She turned to leave, then paused, looking back over her shoulder. "I've put a lot of energy into keeping you alive these last decades, Legion. I'm not sure why I keep trying. But failed experiment or not, I will absolutely throw you to the Tiger before I allow myself to be tainted by your schemes. Is that clear?"

Luca bared his teeth in a semblance of a smile. "As always."

She finally left. She'd damaged his plan, but hadn't ruined it. There still might be time to make up for the losses before the Tiger completed his own plans…

But if things played out how Luca wanted them to, neither Lilith, nor the Tiger, nor anyone else would be able to touch him.

The centre of Erus city was close to the Reamas river geographically, but was so dense with buildings and sound and people that it may as well have been a world away. Not a hint of its neighbour's disaster reached it.

But then, its citizens had something else to occupy them. They still streamed into the doors covering the colossal Tiger statue, as ordered by their new patron Creature. And inside, they found the real Tiger, waiting on his brand-new throne.

Unprotected human minds were helpless against even ordinary Creatures, and the Tiger was far from ordinary. Within seconds he'd marked entire crowds, faster than they could even move through the space. Most exited out the other side of the statue, dazed and cranky and with no idea of what had truly just been done to them.

But a few, once marked, began to change. Those ones had already been close, had already such strong connections to the Creatures, such *resemblance* to the Creatures, that the Tiger's new mark tipped them over the edge.

And below their warping feet, the very ground began to blacken and swell…

In the depths of the dazed crowd, right inside the reeking Tiger statue, a single man moved with purpose. He was unseen by the others, certainly unseen by the Creatures, and on the side of his hand was a tattoo of a thorny crown. It was a cruel-looking thing, ugly and violent, and unfitting his otherwise gentle appearance. But that was the hand he used as he moved through the crowd, touching every human he passed.

And those he touched, he also marked. Not a mark like the Tiger left, which was a deeply etched, spidery shape. But a golden blob, like oil.

For some, the second marks sat loosely over their skin, unseen, yet still unwelcome. But for others, the marks sank inwards, to a place they couldn't identify yet needed so desperately.

And for those, a new connection was formed. The bold, strong connection to the Tiger remained, but now there was a second ribbon of power. Thin, almost invisible.

But stronger than death.

The Other realm

Jon burst eagerly through the wall of the Mountain of Glass. He was greeted by a wash of brilliant blue sky and green plants, sunlight with just the right amount of warmth from an unseen sun, and the smell of a lush, fragrant garden.

While from the outside the Mountain seemed to be yet another barren rock, from inside it was enormous, big enough to house a city that covered another smaller mountain shaped like a pyramid, which gleamed as if made of wet glass. Which of course it was. And streams of water ran down the sloped streets and over the walls, coming from the spring at the city-hill's apex.

Yes! Jon had been barely gone two days, yet he was still ecstatic to be back. Sure, Tarie and Bets were waiting for him. But he knew time didn't matter here. Chaos, he could stay here for months then get out in time to meet them as agreed…

"Most certainly not," someone said from right next to him. "There is no time to waste."

Jon startled a little – since he was floating in the air and hadn't expected company – but he recognised the voice. Lady Anne of Covington – or just 'Anne' these days – was Bets' older sister. Equally small and almost as pretty, but rather bossier and with bright orangey-red hair, and unlike her gentle sister, a permanent resident of the Mountain.

"No one is a permanent resident," she added. "This place is merely a resting point."

Jon's eyes widened at her words, then more as he realised he hadn't spoken aloud. "Excuse me?"

Anne pointed upwards. "We are readying ourselves."

Jon slowly turned his head upwards to where bright sunlight dazzled his vision. But it wasn't sunlight, he saw. And it wasn't the empty space he was used to seeing. Instead, dozens – hundreds – of human and inhuman figures floated up and into the light, while others in turn came back down. But they didn't come to rest in the garden or city. Instead they vanished before they even touched onto solid ground.

Jon watched in amazement for some time, enthralled by the appearances of the beings he saw moving in and out of the light. He'd known for some time that Amaranthus's People – the natives of this place – made themselves appear human, but were in fact something quite different. And *all* were different, he now saw. It reminded him of the Creatures – or what the Creatures wanted to be, perhaps. Hints of human and animal or something beyond any living being on Earth.

A fluttering blue ribbon caught his attention. It was the…fin? of a lovely *something* that reminded him of a tropical fish, perhaps, or a young girl wearing a very floaty dress. But Jon gaped as that being ascended into the light just like all the others. She seemed to wear the light as part of her clothing, and her appearance flickered and changed into that of an ordinary human woman. For a moment Jon's eyes met her yellow and blue ones, and she smiled, then vanished.

Not so ordinary after all.

"What's happening…?" he managed to squeak. "Where are they going?"

"Mm." Anne smiled, her gaze locked on that intense brightness as if she could see what it contained. "Home."

Jon frowned in confusion, then alarm as a familiar figure floated up into the light. This one was much larger than the surrounding ones, yet seemed to fit just fine in that too-small space. Huge forearms. Shaggy white fur, bright eyes under heavy brows.

Fylax.

Jon watched until his guardian vanished from sight, then waited…and waited. "He's coming back, right?"

Anne waved a hand dismissively then took him by the arm. "Mayhap. 'Twill matter little to you."

"He's my *guardian*," Jon retorted with more patience than the statement deserved as Anne tugged him away from the light show, down to the city. "He's kept me alive my entire life. So yes, it *does* matter to me that he comes back."

Anne might have said something in reply, but his attention was caught by the rapidly approaching city wall. In less time than it took to think 'are we going to hit that?' they'd hit the wall, then gone right through it.

Then finally they came to a halt. Jon hadn't been inside this part of the city. Most of the rooms and halls were spectacular while also somewhat ordinary, in that he knew what they were. But this place…

They were inside a golden tunnel that curved from his feet to just over his head. It curved sharply ahead so he couldn't see more than a short distance in either direction. But the walls and ceilings moved and flexed like a living thing, shining with flickering lights behind the translucent surface. Shapes, words, silhouettes moved across the surface faster than his eyes could follow, and the air was filled with what might have been incredibly slow music, the notes as drawn out as underwater whale calls.

Where *were* they?

Anne let go of his hand and moved on ahead of him around the corner. And she should have vanished from sight, but the tunnel seemed to be moving along with him…

Jon stumbled along behind her, the sense of movement making him want to fall even though it was solid enough underfoot. A shape behind the lit wall caught his attention. For a moment he thought it was his own reflection, as it was about the same size and outline, but then it lifted a hand as if waving. Jon hesitantly waved back, then shuffled closer, trying to see who – or what – it was. "Hey," he called out to Anne. "There's someone-ACK!"

A shining human hand darted out of the wall and grabbed at his wrist, pulling off the circlet, then drew it back through the wall.

He'd been robbed.

"Hey!" Jon shouted in distress. "HEY! Anne, they stole my—
oh."

The circlet was back on his wrist, or perhaps it had never left. On the other side of the shining golden wall – or perhaps *in* the wall – the silhouette just stood and waited. Two smaller outlines appeared on either side, and for a moment he imagined they were all staring at him. But then the outlines receded as if those on the other side were walking away, and the wall was back to just flickering text and unidentifiable images.

Jon stared at the now-empty wall, back down at the circlet safely wrapped twice around his wrist, then back at Anne. She'd finally stopped to pay attention, and her mouth was curved in a smirk as if she knew some joke that he didn't.

"That's not funny," Jon said indignantly. "Who was that, anyway? Where are we?"

"We are within the walls of the city," Anne replied. "And also technically in the space between gateways, outside of time. And also technically inside the tapestry itself, although not quite."

…Eh? And she hadn't answered his first question!

Then she stepped through the wall.

Jon stopped and stared at the place she'd gone through, then sighed and followed after her. Unlike some gateways, moving through this wall caused barely a tingle. But his new location was clear. They'd arrived in the Tapestry Room, and it seemed as if they'd stepped right out of the tapestry itself. The vast woven piece ran around the edge of a colossal round room, all in shades of darkest grey and white, and as big as a sports field.

Across the room, the small figure of Amaranthus focused on a section of the tapestry. He nodded at Jon, but didn't come over.

Well, he must have been brought here for a good reason, Jon mused. To be suddenly pulled into the Other realm like that, then to come across the Mountain of Glass? Of course, just yesterday he'd been drugged and dragged into the Other by Luca. Or had that been this morning?

Jon studied the tapestry closest to where he stood. A single thread seemed to stand out to him, one tiny white shape amongst the tangled dark-grey threads surrounding.

"'Tis your life's thread," Anne said casually.

Jon's eyebrows shot up and without thinking, he pressed his finger to the ultra-fine white thread at the very end of the tapestry.

He wondered if he ought to be touching this, but surely Anne would say something if he shouldn't?

Tiny text popped up where his finger touched. *Should I really be touching this? But surely Anne would say something if I shouldn't?*

Ooh! That's what I was just thinking! Ooh! That's what I'm thinking now! Ooh! That's what I'm thinking now! Ooh- heeeyy, *wait…if I just move my hand a little further…*

Amaranthus had been across the massive room, but suddenly he was by Jon's side, and he moved Jon's hand away from his life's thread with a gentle pat. "Few people can bear to know their own futures," he admonished, his expression kind yet firm. "But look above your thread. What do you see that is out of the ordinary?"

Jon blinked for a moment, since proximity to Amaranthus was always a little startling, and more so when he appeared without warning. Then he took a step back, trying to take in more of the complex – and chaotic – tapestry of tangled threads in shining white and darkest grey. And finally he realised what was different.

He'd been touching a spot right at the end of the fabric. No loose threads, not *near* the end, but right *at* the end. And if an entire human life was represented by a finger-length thread, then his days were numbered. But so were everyone else's…

"You must still be working on it," Jon thought aloud.

But Amaranthus just studied him, his expression solemn. "Must I?"

Then Jon noticed something else. The bottom of the colossal tapestry was a bold dark stripe, made of long, thick dark threads that ran the entire length of the piece. But right at the end, a single thick thread was making its way up into the finely woven fabric. It seemed to be cutting off the fabric, and was it moving…?

"I thought those long threads were meant to represent the Creatures," Jon commented, frowning. "And the edging repre-sented how they're confined to the Other realm, since the rest of the tapestry represents the normal realm full of humans. But then why is this thread at the end like this?"

And then he did something which in hindsight was very silly.

He reached up and touched that long dark thread.

5

The Prisoners

Tarie pushed her way down the train's centre aisle, trying to ignore the blaring alarm, flashing lights, and red-leafed foliage that sprung up everywhere she moved. She glanced into each clear-walled compartment, checking for familiar faces but instead seeing strangers. Most had bare foreheads even under the VR light, but a few showed Creature pledge marks. Not the new Tiger symbol, though.

Maybe the prisoners here had all tried to escape repledging to the Tiger. She was surprised, but couldn't blame them. But there were so many unpledged! She'd almost thought Jon had been the only unpledged person around, but of course in a city of ten million, there'd be more. And here they were.

She hadn't seen her family, though, nor Jon's mother Anni. The moment Tarie's vehicle had been stopped, she hadn't been able to get her mind off the others who'd been heading southwest, and had perhaps been stopped in much the same way. And to make it worse, her comm still wasn't working. She couldn't tell them where she was, nor hear from them.

Alongside Tarie, the red-leafed vines seemed to consume the clear barriers as they moved. She could hear absolute chaos behind her – people crying and shouting over the alarm, and hopefully not from fear of the vines. She was trying not to think about how the vines were acting so bizarrely aggressive, because she couldn't control them. And she definitely hadn't heard of Word trees acting in such a way...*ever.*

Amongst the chaos she heard a repetitive *pfft* sound, and something tapped at her chest and shoulder. She looked down to see dark marks appearing in her jacket as bright blue lights peppered the cloth. A moment later they flashed in her eyes, and a faint scorched smell filled the air.

"Am I being shot at?" Tarie wondered aloud. It didn't hurt…although it was certainly damaging her clothes. But weren't laser guns supposed to *kill*?

She pushed on, ignoring the pulsing lasers until finally they stopped. Then as

she reached the end of the carriage, a door slid open and a man spilled out. He was covered head to toe in some kind of armoured uniform, and he held out a short round shape she recognised as a weapon. "Put your-"

She smacked the weapon out of his hand before he could even finish his threat. It bounced on the ground, landing right between the two of them. They both looked down at it, then at each other, and it would have been a fight for supremacy except that the guard was suddenly enveloped in a silver fog.

His eyes widened, and he screamed…then turned and ran directly into the wall, smacking his head with an audible thud.

A moment later he was on the ground. Tarie looked down at him, then over her shoulder at Bets who stood with both hands raised, palms outwards. She'd clearly just blasted the guard. "My apologies," she said. "I'd vow he would have shot you."

Tarie looked down at her jacket again with all its scorch holes. "He certainly tried." But not a single one had hurt. In fact, she might have shrunk again, which implied she'd used power. The clothing's smart fabric didn't feel quite so tight, and Bets didn't seem so ridiculously tiny any longer.

She was also surrounded by a silvery mist that leapt higher and thicker as Tarie watched. "Bets," she said cautiously. "Have you set the train on fire?"

Bets' eyes widened, although she didn't seem overly worried. "Er…mayhap."

Tarie sighed. She put her head down and barrelled along, elbowing the barriers of each occupied cell as she reached them. "Sorry. Excuse me. Sorry." The clear barriers broke and collapsed as if they were made of paper, and Tarie decided not to focus on what was happening. She'd let herself thrill over her super-strength later, when it was safe to do so.

Tarie moved down the length of the train, smashing open each cell with barely a pause, barely any reduction in strength, and with Bets right behind her. The ever-moving red vines wound their way along with her, tangling around broken doorways and weaving through people's legs. And through all of it, the silvery mist/fire that marked Bets' gift in use. An occasional scream punctuated the chaos.

And then at the end of the long, winding train, Tarie came to one last cell. A large man sat inside on the floor, his dark head bent over a damaged comm as if he hadn't heard what was going on outside. Tarie recognised the former Rokal from his perfect profile alone. Even slightly battered and in a stained white flight suit, he was the most strikingly handsome man she'd ever met.

It was really irritating.

"Max." She tapped at the barrier. He didn't seem to notice, so she gave it a good hard rap, causing it to collapse inwards. "Hey."

His attention jerked upwards. "Tarie! You got my message-*ugh*." A red-leafed vine had snaked its way under the barrier and was tapping against his knee. "What's going on?"

"Train's on fire, sort of. Vines everywhere. We should probably find a way to stop it." She paused, then amended, "The train, not the vines. Or maybe both."

Bets poked her head around Tarie's shoulder, and waved. "Good day, Max."

Max scrambled to his feet, blinking at the sight. "Hi. Ah…how *do* we stop it?"

Great question!

The Tapestry Room

Jon touched that extra-long, extra-thick thread where it pushed into the finer surrounding threads. If he'd thought about it more, he might have realised it was a terrible idea, but he didn't think.

Then he was blasted with the most dreadful emotions. An overwhelming emptiness, fury, and the strong sense of a malevolent intelligence that somehow managed to be everywhere at once. **Nearly there,** it was thinking. **Three days and then I'll have it.** But that thought was overlaid with a thousand others, each dark and oppressive and overwhelming his senses until he could barely breathe-

Suddenly Jon's hand was jerked away, and the oppressive

darkness lifted. He was standing with his hand just over the tapestry, and Amaranthus was gripping his wrist once again, but tightly this time. "A mortal cannot touch the mind of a Creature without being tainted by it."

"Sorry. I didn't think." And Jon *was* sorry. That was probably the worst experience of his life, even though it only lasted three seconds. "But the thread's in the wrong place. It's not at the edge of the tapestry with the other Creatures; it's right in the centre of the weaving, with all the humans."

Amaranthus just looked at him. "Indeed."

Understanding hit. *Ohhh.* A Creature had escaped the Other realm, and Amaranthus had reflected that in this very tapestry that recorded the whole of human history.

But it was right…at the end…

Ohhhhh…

"This is why we have to make the time count," Jon said numbly. "Earlier today, we all had the same thought. That was a directive from here, wasn't it?"

Amaranthus nodded. Behind him, Anne's expression was solemn.

"And me suddenly coming into the Other when travelling across Erus," Jon continued. "Did you bring me here for a reason? Or was it just to say hello?"

Anne smirked at Jon, while Amaranthus turned back to the tapestry. He moved a couple of threads near that big, intrusive dark one, and said, "There's an Other trail cutting across the normal realm, but it isn't from the Mountain. It's for another reason that will soon become clear. But we did take advantage of your arrival, my friend. It's a good way to lose your pursuer and to catch up with your friends, mm?"

"Pursuer?" Jon echoed, startled. Who would Amaranthus be talking about? Luca was the usual problem, but since Jon had made himself notorious in the last couple of days, it really could be anyone. He blanched.

"Oh, cheer up," Anne said, patting him on the shoulder. "'Tis not so bad as all that. What is the worst that could happen?"

"I could die and all my friends and family along with me?"

"Death is not so bad. Afterwards, you forget the pain."

"That…" *Doesn't help*, Jon wanted to say, but then realised that actually, strangely, it did. The 'before' part still sounded dreadful. "So…am I going to die, then?"

Amaranthus tapped the end of the tapestry. "Of course. All mortals do – and many immortals also. But not yet. Jayel Jonnamin, how do you feel about returning to your friends by a direct route?"

"Ah…sure." That would save a bit of time, Jon supposed.

"Excellent! Anne?" Amaranthus nodded towards the centre of the room beside them.

Jon turned, curious, and caught a glimpse of something he hadn't seen before but had only heard about. The centre of the room usually appeared empty, but today, it contained an enormous fountain. Shining water flowed over smooth black stone and disappeared into nothing. But that didn't describe what he'd seen. It was the colour – shimmering through the water, through the black stone of the fountain, as if both substances were made of rainbows.

"Whoa," he said. He met Anne's eyes, his own wide.

"Good travels," she said. And then she gave him a good shove, right into the fountain.

In truth, Elspeth had not intended to set the train afire. 'Twas natural for her to use her gift against those covered in Creature darkness, especially when those were attempting to fill her and her friends with tiny laser-burn holes. And indeed, her gift could save some of them. It had for Rokal/Max.

But the silvery flame was not choosy in what it caught. It leapt eagerly from the guards to the ever-growing red vines to the train itself, until the whole vehicle seemed to be filled with a pale, glowing mist. The vines grew faster than Elspeth's eyes could follow, and she, Tarie and Max had to fight their way through the tangled masses to the back of the train.

Tarie stopped in front of a glasslike panel. She had shrunk significantly since arriving on the train – since while trapped in the vehicle, she'd grown to an exceptional size – but was still far taller than her true height, which was much like Elspeth's. Tarie punched a fist against the panel. There was a faint flash of light and a sizzling sound, and the panel crumbled. Behind it was a plain panel etched in an unreadable design.

Tarie studied it briefly then groaned.

"What is this?" Elspeth enquired. "The stop button?"

"It says that the train is controlled remotely," Max said from just behind Elspeth. He had no trouble seeing over her shoulder – he veritably *loomed.* "We can't stop it."

"Oh…"

"What are we going to do then?" Tarie asked, throwing a hand in the air. "Wait till we drive right on into the Other, then deal with whatever's waiting there? We *have* to get off!"

The train's metal body groaned around them, and they all cringed.

"If you could break a window, I could try flying people off," Max suggested.

Tarie's eyebrows shot up, and she pushed away a mass of rapidly growing vines that curled up the wall beside her. "There must be two hundred people on this train!"

"I'll try flying them off…fast?"

Tarie's reply was lost as the train made a shrieking sound, like metal scraping across stone. The machine shuddered underfoot, then seemed to settle for a moment. But the vines weren't settling. They grew faster, if anything, springing up by the second around the three of them and blocking the view. Elspeth felt their pressure against her legs under her loose breeches, but when she tried to kick the vines away, she fell sideways into a pile of them.

"Help!" Weren't these dreadful plants supposed to be from the Mountain of Glass?! Why weren't they *helping?* The vines would smother them all, if they didn't stop them!

Elspeth blasted them with fire at full force, but it only seemed to make them grow faster. Soon her sight was full of red leaves and flickering silver fog, and she couldn't *move-*

SCREEEEEEEEEEEEEEEEECH!

The train lurched sideways. Elspeth's scream was echoed by others as she tumbled onto her side, then partially upside-down…but the vines buffered her fall as if she was wrapped in padding. For long moments they rolled on, the carriage turning over and over, until finally the sound and movement came to an end.

The vines fell away from Elspeth's limbs and the fire-mist cleared, and she lay in a heap, stunned.

"Bets?" she heard Tarie call. "Rokal- I mean, Max? Are you OK?"

A moment later Tarie was in front of Elspeth, pulling away loosening tangles of red and green. She was sideways.

No, wait, *Elspeth* was sideways. Tarie grabbed her wrist and hauled her upright with startling force. "The train crashed," she said without preamble. "Are you hurt?"

Elspeth shook her head. Forsooth, she expected to feel the pain of a broken limb or at very least a bruise. But there was nothing, the vines and leaves having cushioned her as softly as swan's down.

And even now they were retreating; not shrinking, but moving to clear a path down the train's length.

Elspeth apologised to them in her head. Mayhap they were not so dreadful after all.

In the far west of Erus, in an area known for trees, rocks and not much else, there was a small village. Like a dozen others across the city-state, it was a cluster of ramshackle houses occupied by people who didn't want to be part of society, or didn't know how to be. They didn't even have basic virtual reality, and had no access to news networks. Drones were rare and often shot down. And that was why Gavriel had been ordered to go there in person.

His lip curled as he did one final round of the village, listening carefully for the telltale signs of anyone hiding. But there was nothing.

His eye fell upon a cluster of fallen figures of varying sizes, and a hint of guilt stabbed at his gut. He rapidly pushed it aside, because he had no time for that. Anyway, it was their fault.

Everyone had to pledge to the Tiger. Pledge, or die. Gavriel had explained that very clearly.

Unfortunately these villagers had chosen the second option. They'd turned him down flat, even when he'd clearly shown them the consequences of such bad choices.

Gavriel knew he didn't look like much. Good-looking, yes, but young enough that only those who looked closely would see the dark power that lived inside him. And those who didn't see it? Well, it was too late for them.

Gavriel. The feminine voice rang into his mind, an echo of its forceful origin some distance away.

Yes, Master? Lilith was female, but hated being called 'Mistress' as she thought it made her sound weak. Gavriel knew she was anything but.

I sensed use of my power. Did this lot not pledge either?

Use of her power, but also an influx of power, Gavriel knew. Lilith sounded utterly uncaring, and he knew her well enough that another dozen dead humans meant nothing. After all, that could just mean extra lifeforce for her to suck up via the vacuum cleaners of her men. Men like him.

They didn't pledge, he sent back, along with a brief mental image of the scene. *But they're gone now.* And it was so chaos-damned *wasteful.* He was happy to use his power to take out chosen targets, especially those who deserved it. But to use it indiscriminately… well. He wasn't a serial killer, nor did he want to be.

But Lilith must have picked up his mood over their mental connection, because her response came back sharply. *Dead or pledged, that's the instruction. We had five days. Now we have three, and the new men that've pledged to me don't know what they're doing yet. Don't fail me on this.*

Gavriel stood still in that quiet village, the instructions ringing through his head loud and clear. He didn't know what happened at the end of the five days – only the Tiger did – but he certainly didn't want to get between that Creature and its goals.

And when you're done there, Lilith added crisply, *I've got something new for you. There's a Word-speaker somewhere north-east of the city, in a crashed train.*

Gavriel perked up, reminded once more of that infuriating, apparently unkillable Tarie Filat. Could it be…?

Finally, someone worth killing.

Jon closed his eyes as he fell directly into the fountain of water. There was a moment of 'oh!' and feeling like he was caught in an exploding soap bubble, but then he was out in the countryside, hovering high above the green and brown hills. The light of day immediately told him he was back in the normal realm, but the atmosphere still felt heavy, more like it would in the power-rich Other realm.

Odd. Also odd was the way he'd been shoved out of the Mountain of Glass via the previously unseen fountain in the Tapestry Room's centre. Not the abruptness, because Jon was used to Amaranthus being abrupt. But the location.

A moment later Jon realised he was dripping with water that sparkled and tingled where it touched his skin. Water from the Mountain of Glass…from the River of Life. The droplets clung to his clothing although didn't soak in to the stainproof fabric.

A moment after that, he realised what was happening around him.

To one side, a long, dark path ran across the ground like a burn mark across the landscape, or like night had fallen just in that area. It ran from the north-west, where the borderlands provided access to the Other realm, past where Jon hovered, and disappeared behind him into the distant outline of Erus city.

He frowned at the path. He'd noticed it before, of course, but now it looked so much worse. He could almost feel the Creature taint from here. But now he'd seen the tapestry, he knew exactly what that path meant.

A Creature had left the Other, had walked right out of the borderlands, had gone to Erus city, and had left a supernatural scar on the landscape.

That wasn't good.

A sound from nearby caught Jon's attention. In the near distance was another line running almost parallel to the darkness. This one he vaguely recalled as some kind of transport – a train, was it? – that needed a permanent track in the ground.

But there was a faint silver shape just near the horizon, marked with red, and surrounded by tiny figures. It looked like a giant snake had spilled its guts all over the ground.

Jon sped towards it and it became clear as a train: a long serpentine vehicle covered in what looked like red and green vegetation. The train had come off its tracks and even appeared to have split in several places. Around it, people streamed out of multiple exits and disappeared into the hills. Puffs of silvery fog appeared around those exits and even on the people fleeing, and Jon's eyes widened. That silver looked familiar…

He quickly checked his comm to see that Tarie, and therefore

Bets, were showing as close. Very, very close.

Right...there, in fact. A trio of figures came tumbling out of the train a moment before there was an explosion of colour. Vines spilled out of the exit after a tall dark-haired man, a solid dark-skinned girl, and a tiny fair-skinned one.

Jon recognised his friends immediately, and tried to push back the pang of distaste he felt at seeing Rokal with them. Ugh.

No, *Max*. Jon had to think of the man as Max now, because Rokal had been a vicious brute who'd made Jon miserable, and that was when he'd been bound to a Creature. Max was a different person, just the same as Jon's father Luke was quite different from Luca, the name he used now he carried a Creature.

But the girls had found Max. That was probably a good thing, considering they *weren't where they were supposed to be!* And Jon coming out of the Other directly to their location was overly convenient, of course, but he'd clearly been sent right here.

"Thank you," he said under his breath, knowing someone could hear him. Then he shot downwards towards the others, landing hard enough that he left dents in the grass. "What...what happened to your vehicle?" he burst out. "Why were you on the train? Just...*why*?"

"Roadblock," Tarie replied succinctly. "We've left the vehicle somewhere back towards Erus city. I don't know where exactly, but we'll find it if we follow the train line." Her lips tightened. "Not sure it's the best idea, though. We might just get caught again."

"But look! We found Max," Bets added brightly, waving to the much larger man behind her as if Jon could have possibly missed him. "The train was heading directly into the Other realm, Jon, no doubt for nefarious purposes. But we stopped it!" She glanced over her shoulder, her fine brows wrinkling. "Although we do seem to leave a trail of destruction these days."

Jon slapped a hand over his face. One could say that, yes. "We have to be more discreet than this."

"Probably," Tarie agreed. She poked his sodden jacket, where droplets from the Mountain still clung like a blanket of diamonds. "Ugh. You're all wet."

"Sorry." Jon stepped away from the others, closer towards the train/pile of vines, and shook himself like a dog. Droplets went everywhere. "Oh, chaos. I had to tell you-"

About the escaped Creature in Erus and the end of time, he was about to say. But there was a groaning sound from the train behind him, and suddenly he was flung into the air. Something caught on the back of his jacket, and he felt himself yanked rapidly up, and up, and up, as the ground shrank below him. "Argh!"

For a moment Jon was taken back to that awful time some months ago, when Rokal had snatched up his jacket and taken him high into the air, high enough that Jon had thought he'd fall to his death. But this time Rokal/Max was far below, and Jon went crazy.

He thrashed and kicked and pulled as hard as he could, and after only a few seconds he found himself free, spinning in the air high above the ground. Over the pounding in his ears, he could hear screams and shouts from below, and he was shaking as he came to a stop mid-air.

But then Jon saw what had caught him. Not a Creature, not a drone, not another Prince of the Air.

It was a *tree*. And not just any tree. One the size of a skyscraper, with colossal branches covered in red and green leaves the size of Jon's outspread hands, extending from a gnarled brown trunk as broad across as Jon's bedroom back home.

And it was growing. As he watched, the nearest branch trembled and unfurled another cluster of red tipped leaves. Then it was finally still, as if it had finished the job.

Where had that come from?!

Jon looked down to the ground far below. The colossal trunk seemed to be coming straight out of the crushed train, with knotted roots wrapping around the train's metallic exterior and winding together with the smaller vines. The leaves looked quite similar to the vines, in fact.

Max drew up into the air slowly and pulled alongside Jon. "You alright?"

Jon didn't even flinch at his old enemy's closeness. He was too stunned by the monster-tree's appearance. "What just happened?"

Max smiled crookedly. "You weren't discreet, that's what."

He thought it was *Jon's* doing?!

"'Twas the water on your clothes," Bets declared shortly afterwards, once Jon had returned to the ground. "You shook it onto the vines, and they grew."

The four of them now stood in the shelter of the giant tree, which in spite of its unnatural and sudden appearance, was quite a pleasant place to be.

"Look," Tarie said. She poked at Jon's jacket. "You've still got droplets stuck to you. Where did you say you've been?"

"Uh…" The Mountain. It must've been because Anne pushed Jon into that fountain at the heart of the Tapestry Room – which of course hadn't been an accident. It never was, with the Mountain. Which meant that Amaranthus wanted Jon to be wearing this strange, clinging water which made things grow…

He quickly recounted the morning's events, ending with, "And I just realised what this tree reminds me of. It seems like something from the Mountain of Glass, don't you think, Bets?"

"Looks like a Word tree," Tarie said. "Except a hundred times bigger. And those vines, they've got the same type of leaves too, but they shouldn't *be* vines." She shrugged helplessly. "Nothing's normal."

Tarie herself was only slightly taller than she'd usually be, Jon had noted, which put her about a foot shorter than his own height. But he could feel the power buzzing from around her, and he suspected her smaller size wouldn't last.

Bets frowned. "Tarie is now growing vines rather than Word trees. Or vines that *grow* into colossal Word trees when touched with living water. But what role could such a tree have here, in the normal realm?"

Now that was the really bad news. "So it's not just the Mountain that's out in the normal…"

Tarie wrapped her arms around herself, feeling grim as she took in what Jon had told them, and what had just taken place.

A Creature out in the normal realm. Giant Word trees growing out of vines. *Tarie* still growing…

"And we don't even have my vehicle," she muttered under her breath. Sure, it was old, but at least it ran.

Next to her, Jon and Bets were debating forcefully about something called the Anima chest and how it might give a Creature access to the normal realm, and what that might have to do with the Tiger's sudden takeover and instructions for everyone to pledge. Apparently Bets' mysterious sister had told her about it.

"But what could the Tiger possibly want?"

She'd been speaking under her breath, but Max heard her. Moving up beside her, he said, "Power. To get out of the Other realm. To rule."

She glanced up at him – or at his jawline, rather, since he was currently much taller than her. "How would you know that?"

He shrugged his big shoulders. "When I was a carrier to Gerak, sometimes I'd hear his thoughts. Feel his feelings. And that's what Gerak wanted."

"But…to rule what?"

Max shrugged again, his palms upwards. "Everything."

Wonderful. Tarie ran a hand agitatedly through her frizzy hair, leaving a hank of it sticking straight up. "I can't handle this right now," she said under her breath. "Safekeepers. We were headed to Elsewhise to get safekeepers from Jon's dead grand-mother's house, then we were going to meet our family just south of the Erus border in two days."

"And I was hijacked when I was heading to Elsewhise," Max commented. He frowned. "I don't really remember what happened, which makes me think it might have been a tranq dart. Didn't you say Jon was hit with one yesterday?"

Tarie shrugged. Today, actually, but this felt like the world's longest day. She was exhausted, and it was barely lunchtime. "So we're being tracked."

"It's probably our comms," Jon said from nearby, showing that he was listening to both conversations. "We should probably get rid of them, and anything else like them."

"Mine hasn't been working anyway," Tarie pointed out. Although she supposed it still might be used for tracking, somehow.

"and without them, how will we find Tarie's family?" Bets asked.

Argh, that was true. "And Max has *nanites* in his hair," Tarie pointed out crossly. She looked up at him again, noting in annoyance that his dishevelment just made his silver-tipped dark hair look even more attractive, where hers would look like she'd been dragged through a hedge backwards. Life was so unfair.

"Nanites are meant to be for looks, but they're tiny programmable particles. What if they can be used to track people? What if *shoes* can?"

"What about the fact that we're standing next to a crashed train heading to the borderlands?" Max said evenly. "And we're *definitely* targets, even if we weren't sitting under a giant unnatural tree. I say we send a message to your families, get rid of all the comms, and head off into the hills. The sooner, the better."

Tarie hated the idea of losing contact with her family, but Max was right. They were sitting ducks here. Even the other train passengers had been smart enough to flee, the giant tree having scared most of them off rather than drawn them closer.

"Fine. But *how* are we going to get to Elsewhise?" Tarie asked, throwing her hands in the air.

Max's lips curled upwards, and he looked between Tarie, Jon and Bets. "Fly, of course."

"That's a brilliant idea," Tarie said sarcastically. "But you'll notice two of us can't fly."

He just smiled. "You two little ones. We'll carry you."

Jon's eyebrows shot up, but he didn't argue.

Tarie countered, "But you and Jon were both captured flying! And you want to put *all* of us in that situation right after you just escaped from it?"

She got murmurs of agreement to that, but Jon spoke up. "Do we have any better options?"

No. No, they didn't have any better options.

So five minutes later, even though the flying option had obvious risks, Tarie was being blasted by cold air and the occasional bug. She held Max's neck in a death grip, her legs wrapped around his waist as if they were the only thing holding her from a distinctive *splat* on the ground far below.

Because they *were* the only thing. She was hanging off his back like an oversized backpack as they rocketed along high above the green and brown hills of north-east Erus. Human beings shouldn't be able to move this fast!

"You're choking me again," Max said in a slightly strained voice. His hands gripped onto her knees. "I'm not going to drop you."

"That's all very well for you to say, Mr Antigravity, but I don't feel secure!"

He sighed. "Do you want me to carry you on the front, like the others?"

Tarie glanced to their left, where Jon sailed along, holding dainty Bets in his arms like a princess. She had her arms around his neck too, but even from here it looked less like a death grip and more like a friendly supportive hold. Tarie could see her mouth moving, but was too far away to make out the words.

"I wouldn't have thought you could carry me like that," Tarie said in reply. She might currently be short, but she was sturdy. "Your arms would get tired."

"Oh, I can. You'll notice I'm twice your size."

"For now," she shot back. "What happens when I panic and start growing?"

There was a silence. "You know," Max mused, "I think we'll be OK. Ever since I visited the River with Fylax, I've felt like no matter how bad things get, it'll all be alright somehow." Tarie felt him shrug underneath her, and saw a slight smile in his profile, which was mostly turned away from her. "Besides, you're so full of power these days that if I drop you, I'm sure you'll bounce."

Tarie let out a cry of dismay, then scowled. "Oh. You're joking." She hadn't realised he had a sense of humour. Until now he'd mostly seemed vaguely distressed, and before that, Rokal had had the sense of humour of a rock.

"I was. I wouldn't let you bounce. I'd catch you again." Max jiggled her a little, making her squeak. "And even if I didn't, we're only just above the ground. Look, that's what, two body-lengths?"

Tarie loosened her grip just enough to see they had dropped considerably lower, and were now following a narrow valley, close to the ground and out of sight of the roads. "Oh. I thought we were much higher up."

"I know," Max said cheerfully. "But don't worry. Friends don't let friends plummet to their deaths."

He seemed to have gained a personality in the last day or two, and she wasn't sure what to make of it. As Rokal, he'd been cold, angry and mocking. It seemed a little of that mocking wasn't the Creature he carried, but rather Max's own personality. Or perhaps teasing would be a better description. "Is that what we are? Friends?"

"Sure." Max paused. "Aren't we?"

"I don't know," Tarie said in surprise. "I...I suppose we might be." She'd wondered how much he remembered from his time as a carrier, since they certainly hadn't been on good terms before that. "We haven't known each other long."

Max glanced at her over his shoulder, but didn't argue. He tilted his head towards the other pair who'd moved just ahead of them in this narrower space. "So are they a couple or what?"

Rather than scolding him for being nosy, Tarie watched Bets and Jon for a while too. She could only see glimpses of their faces, but they looked so earnest. So intent on each other, even though if Jon lost his focus they'd both end up splattered against a grassy hill.

"I don't know," she replied finally. "But you've known Jon longer than I have."

Max scoffed. "I've only just met Bets, and that was when she set me on fire."

"Yeah. But you deserved it."

Tarie remembered how Bets had admitted to trying to trip Max/Rokal repeatedly, and smiled. She'd keep that one to herself for now, because Rokal had deserved it.

"I bet they *are* a couple," Max said decisively.

"Oh yeah?" Tarie studied them once more. She thought there might be something there, but it was on Bets' side only. "How much do you bet? Not money."

He glanced back at her with raised eyebrows. "A kiss?"

"No!" If she wasn't on his back, she would have punched him.

"Why not? It doesn't cost anything."

"Not money." And there was a cost, at least to Tarie. A casual kiss with someone she – well, she had to admit it – was strongly attracted to, but meant nothing to him? Not a good idea. "Choose something else." And it seemed that even more of Max's personality had been *him* and not just the Creature's influence. From when Tarie had first seen him, he'd always been surrounded by girls.

"A favour, then. I bet they're into each other. And if I'm right, you owe me a favour."

"You bet they're *together*," Tarie corrected. "And if they're not – if they say they're just friends – then you owe *me* a favour." She paused. "And nothing illegal or unethical."

"Done."

With that, Max looked back and grinned at her. It was the first time she'd ever seen him smile fully, because Rokal had worn a perpetual scowl, and this caught her off-guard even with his messy hair and the shadows under his eyes.

Tarie just stared, a little dazed, and he laughed.

She scowled. "Face forward! We're about to hit a cliff."

"No, we weren't." But he faced forward anyway.

No, they weren't, but she'd needed to take back control of the conversation. Why did some people have to have such a distractingly attractive shell? It wasn't fair, because it had nothing to do with who they were inside.

If only he was hit in the face with a frypan once or twice, that would solve the problem, Tarie mused.

Or maybe that could be arranged…

6
Memories

After untold hours in the darkness of the Other, Maia was regretting her choice to go back in. She'd left the tri-wheeler outside, not wanting to lose it in the unpredictability of this place, and she'd thought her own savvy abilities would be enough. But she hadn't seen that boy anywhere, and her comm locator was useless.

Worse, she was lost. She had to admit it. The dark patch – the Other trail leading from the borderlands – had been small the last time she'd gone in. In fact, she'd driven right through it that time. But this time it seemed to stretch out as large as the Other realm itself. Perhaps she'd somehow left this little area behind…?

She wasn't going to find the boy. She needed to find an exit before something else found *her*.

Quietly, lest she catch the attention of any wandering Creature, Maia crouched down low to the hard, cold ground. Gritting her teeth, she dug one nail into the side of her finger until a drop of blood welled up, then pressed it quickly against the metal-hard earth. "Give me a direct exit," she whispered, visualising a fine trail leading exactly where she needed to go.

She'd only done this once, a long time ago with her mother's guidance, so here was hoping it would work. Unless that was her mother's power too, not her own, and she couldn't replicate it. Or unless Luca's gift/curse somehow interfered…

The drop of blood marked the ground, seeming black against darkest grey, and for a moment Maia thought it glowed. But when ten seconds passed without effect, then a minute, she knew it wouldn't work. She slumped down to the ground, angry tears pricking at her eyes. She'd have to contact Luca through their connection. It was the last thing she wanted to do, because she'd owe him a favour, but how else would she get out of here?

She hissed out a wordless sound of frustration, but something else came out. *"Ks'atha!"*

A bright gold spark shot out of her mouth and landed on the ground. A moment later, a small seedling twisted its way out of the soil where the spark had hit. It glowed softly, just enough that she could make out its shape, and it waved softly as if in a gentle breeze. *Hello*, it seemed to say. *Would you like a way out of here?*

Maia stared at the seedling, one hand lifted to her mouth. That was…new. A strange word, causing random growth *here*? And possibly a talking plant – or more likely, her imagination and frustration.

She stared at it a moment longer, noting the slightly sweet, zesty scent noticeable from here. It got into her nostrils, and for a moment it seemed like the most beautiful thing she'd ever smelled. Then her skin began to itch, and the fine lines marking her curses/gifts lit up over her body and her hand where she was closest to the plant. And suddenly, the scent seemed over-whelming and repulsive.

It was from some sort of Creature, obviously, which meant she wasn't alone around here. Her attempt to divine a doorway had attracted that unwanted attention.

Maia sprang up and stepped away from the telltale seedling, hair standing up on the back of her neck. It had stopped moving, but still sat there glowing slightly and looking far too innocuous for what it was.

Nothing grew in the Other. Nothing, except this. Suddenly a memory popped up; one that had been forgotten till now. It felt like only yesterday, but of course it had been far longer. She'd been deep in the Other, outside the White Prince's temple. There'd been darkness, as dark as the Other always was, but with a distinct chill to the air that seemed somehow worse than usual. She'd been clutching the circlet, which had glowed as bright as a torch, lighting up the surroundings.

But all she'd seen was the path leading straight to this small, blocky building. It had a single high window which was black against the surrounding darkness, and it had felt *dangerous*. So much more so than she'd even expected, and everything in her had revolted against being in such a place.

But she'd reminded herself of why she was here – to remove this terrible rejection curse – and she'd called out for the White Prince.

And he'd come.

One moment she'd been alone; the next he'd been there. *It.* Creatures rarely ascribed to a gender; they only took one depending on the humans they were connected with. But this one had been twice her size. Pale white limbs, far too long for any human, and massive black eyes in a delicately beautiful face. Its wings had stretched up behind it, like a butterfly's with distinct black struts and each section filled with jewellike red, green and gold.

But in the next instant, the wings would seem to flutter and vanish. Maia had realised that they were just illusion – the Creature had no wings at all, but had wanted to appear like they did. She'd wondered why she could see past them.

Then the White Prince had spoken. He'd asked why she was there, and she'd told him about the rejection curse over her. She'd flattered him a little, saying that no one else was strong enough to break it, as if that could fool a Creature.

He'd been quiet for a while. Then he'd stretched out one bony white finger, pointing at her head. ***That,*** he'd said. ***That thing** is keeping me from seeing your curse. Take it off, and I will be able to help you.*

He'd been talking about her circlet. Maia remembered raising one hand to her head, and then-

…Then she didn't remember what she'd done. But she must've taken it off, right? Because now that boy had it. But she still didn't remember how she'd ended up missing seventeen Chaos-damned years of her life.

Maia blinked, fully back in the moment. She was in the Other, again, and she needed to get out. After remembering the last time she'd come into the Other – which felt like yesterday – she couldn't believe that she'd risked coming in here again. What if she'd lost more time?!

"Amaranthus," she muttered desolately, a throwback to when she'd worn the circlet with its word of power.

And then the little plant in front of her lit up as if hit by a spotlight. And behind it, in a perfect trail of lights, appeared a long row of matching plants. They trailed off into the distance, where a faint but distinct rectangular shape showed.

It looked like an open door.

Maia just stared. So the word 'Amaranthus' still had some power even without the circlet, did it? But she wasn't stupid enough to just walk through a doorway in the Other, not knowing where it led. You could end up in the worst parts of a Creature city that way.

The scent of the tiny plants wafted up to her nose, and she made a decision.

She'd just take a look. What harm could it do?

The Tapestry Room

'Twas a strange time, Anne thought. The point of the tapestry was that time *didn't* matter; that one could be anywhere one needed to be, any moment of any day.

Except now, Amaranthus had chosen to stay within the end of the tapestry. The point where it all went to custard – at least from her limited perspective – and yet where the tapestry's threads were denser, more tangled and more swathed in power than she'd seen before. He was giving it all of his considerable focus, and as a result, so were they all.

Anne had no idea what would happen next. And if she didn't know Amaranthus so well, she would've thought that he didn't either.

And then he crooked his finger at her. *Come have a look at this.*

She moved up beside him on the tapestry. Here at the end, four fine pale threads were woven tightly together, and she already knew who they belonged to.

"Our friends are short on time," he said aloud. "Let me show you a trick to save some…"

And then he pushed his finger into the threads, dragging them straight forward just a fraction of an inch. Golden light and images sprang up with his movement, and Anne's eyes lit up as she saw what was happening. She laughed, clapping her hands. "I love it!"

And so would they.

What a lovely view, Elspeth thought. The landscape of Erus skimmed past close below them, but her gaze was fixed elsewhere. Being carried in Jon's arms, with her arms around his neck and their faces so close, was like something out of a heroic tale. And while Elspeth knew she was smaller than most people of this time, her weight was not inconsiderable.

"I am not too heavy for you, am I?" she asked.

Jon glanced down at her, his face so very close from this angle. "Like I said last time, you're not heavy at all." He frowned. "Actually, I can hardly feel your weight, and that's weird. I'm not that strong. Can you fly, Bets?"

"Oh, no!" Elspeth could hear her embarrassment in her tone, but couldn't hold it back. "If I could, I would have said!" Rather than being carried like a child… or a princess in a folktale.

"Of course you would have," Jon murmured. "Turning a corner. Watch out."

She did no such thing, of course. Instead she kept her gaze fixed on his face. 'Twas not so perfect as she'd at first imagined, especially since she was close enough to see the fine pores in his skin. But she felt so much more affection for him now, even knowing his true struggles and his true self.

Jon glanced down and caught her staring. "What?"

Elspeth felt her cheeks heat. "Sleeper capsules." Rather than admit her true thoughts, she blurted out the first thing that came to mind.

"What?"

"'Tis part of the Mountain," she explained. "But not a part that we would usually visit. Anne told me about them – about the multitude who have not truly died, but who sleep outside of time. Waiting."

Now she had Jon's attention. "Waiting for what?"

"I do not rightly know," Elspeth admitted. "But 'tis for Amaranthus's purposes for sure. And with his instruction this morn, about making the time count…" She shrugged with difficulty. "Mayhap 'tis related."

"Sleepers," Jon murmured. "I wonder…" He sighed. "This all feels like we're on the edge of a colossal wave, and it's about to come crashing down. And I don't know what's next."

Elspeth wasn't quite sure, either. But she had an idea from what others had said. About those who died, but didn't quite die. Instead, they were transformed, and they left. But where to?

"Mayhap it does not matter," she suggested. "We must only make the most of this time, without regret."

"Hmm."

Elspeth searched his face, that little line between his eyebrows as he frowned, but his true feelings were as hidden from her as always. "Except," she said cautiously, "if one was to reveal a truth that was unwelcome, one would indeed feel regret. No matter how short the time might be. In fact, it could be quite awkward."

They swerved slightly, and the branches of a tree brushed just overhead as they skimmed by. Then Jon glanced at her sidelong. "By one, do you mean *you*? Or someone else?"

She hesitated a moment. "Me. 'Tis my truth, but I fear 'tis unwelcome."

There was an answering pause, then he looked away. "Is it something about...me? Because I think you revealed it this morning outside my apartment, if that's what you're worried about."

Elspeth's eyebrows shot up. "I did?" she squeaked. The day – these past days – had been so eventful that she'd forgotten details. Or she'd hoped that *he* had, because she did recall blurting out something of...love. "Was it...welcome?"

There was a terrible, painful pause where that line between Jon's eyebrows didn't budge. "I don't know if we're talking about the same thing."

"What do *you* think we are speaking of?"

Bets was in his arms, round-eyed and pink-cheeked. She looked as pretty as Jon had ever seen her, but perhaps that was influenced by the fact she was a cuddler. Not having cuddled a real human female before, he was finding it surprisingly pleasant. (Hugs with his mother or romantic programmes in VR didn't count.)

Jon was about to shoot back, "You started it, *you* admit it," then he sighed. "I know you like me, alright? You said as much this morning. Is that the truth you're talking about?"

She'd said a bit more than 'like', but he didn't want to make a fool of himself if she was reconsidering. After all, he was…him.

Bets bit her lip, then nodded.

Oh. She had meant it, then. Jon had always really known how she felt about him, or had strongly suspected, anyway. But he'd been so caught up in his misery and bizarre life that he hadn't really stopped to think about it. Or to think about what it could mean for them both, here at the end of the time tapestry.

No time to waste, maybe.

She'd said when he'd discovered her here in his time that knowing his struggles meant she was free to love him. Then she'd pretended she hadn't said it, and he'd let her. They had more to worry about in that moment. But now, when it was just them…

Jon looked over his shoulder to check the other two were out of sight. The valley they were flying low along had narrowed, becoming almost a ravine with narrow, high edges and the remnants of a stream at its base. For now, they were alone.

"That truth is welcome," he said, and as the words came out, he realised how true they were. "I…I feel the same way."

Bets' face lit up. "Wonderful!" Then she lunged at him.

Being headbutted by someone you're carrying is never welcome, and more so when you're having a tender moment. "*Owww…*"

"Sorry!" Bets loosened one hand from around his neck to gently pat at his cheek. "'Twas not at all what I intended."

"Then what *did* you intend?" Jon asked grumpily. She suddenly felt heavy, and the weight was straining his arms. Moment lost.

"Stop for a moment, and I will tell you."

"Why…?"

Bets' face flashed red, and she whispered, "I want to kiss you!"

Oh. Alright, then!

Jon found somewhere to stop, and was well into his first-ever real human kiss (since the VR ones or random Frencine ones also didn't count) when he heard a laugh from behind him, then a scoffing noise.

He looked over his shoulder to see both Tarie and Max standing behind them. Max was grinning widely, and Tarie looked disgusted. She was also a lot taller than when they'd taken off, almost looking Jon in the eye.

"You owe me a favour," Max told Tarie, nudging her with his elbow.

She rolled her eyes, but her next comment was clearly directed towards Jon and Bets. "You picked an interesting place to stop. You notice we're in the borderlands, right?"

Bets, whose face was flaming red, stepped out from between Jon and the handy rock wall they'd stopped next to. "The borderlands? Why do you say that?"

"Suddenly heavy," Max said. "I fell like a rock." To Tarie he added, "No, it wasn't you. I told you that already."

"Oh." He'd thought Bets' sudden weight was the headbutt she'd given him, but he now saw there was more to it. "But we should be hours away still," he mused. "We're not going *that* fast."

"There's a strip of Other right through the countryside," Max said. "You pointed it out yourself."

"Yeah…" Jon studied their surroundings with a frown. Now he thought on it, he did feel different. Kind of…light but heavy at the same time, and the air held a slight tingle to it. But he'd thought that was the kiss.

But were they really in the borderlands? Unlike other times he'd been there, this area wasn't unusually lush. The borderlands would generally be lush forest, dripping with greenery, as if the combined Other and normal realms would make double or triple the life in a small space of land.

Although he *did* feel too heavy… "We need to get back to the normal realm," he said. The borderlands were always bad news. They were gorgeous but creepy, right up to the point the gorgeousness disappeared and you realised you weren't alone.

Tarie wandered past, leaving a trail of red shoots coming up rapidly behind her. She didn't seem to notice. "Nothing's easy today, is it? Whatever direction we go, we should stay together. My comm's still not working, and neither's Max's."

"What about this?" Max asked. He waved at the steep, rocky hillside right next to him. "It's a straight path, by the looks of it."

Jon stared. "What are you talking about? That's a rock wall."

Max shook his head. "No, the path. It's hidden till you get right up to it."

Bets, who was nearer to him, moved a step closer with an expression of interest. Then her eyebrows shot up. "Ooh! 'Tis a path."

"That's what I said."

"Let me see," Jon said in unison with Tarie. They exchanged a startled glance, then stepped closer to the wall in almost perfect timing. And just as Max had said, as Jon drew closer to the rock wall, a gap appeared. It was about three feet wide and a little higher than Max's head, and its sides were perfectly smooth, as if carved. The ground was just as smooth, like well-packed dirt, and it shot into the distance in a perfectly straight line.

"It's more of a tunnel than a path," Jon pointed out. But he felt disconcerted. The tunnel/path was lit from inside, so he could see far, far into the distance – enough to see that the path went on for a very long way.

Next to him, Tarie had gone very still. Finally she spoke. "It's the Way."

"What? We don't know that," Jon scoffed. "We don't know where it goes, and I think it's suspicious that it just *happens* to be here, in this random patch of what might be borderlands, just when we're on a mission to possibly change the world."

"No, it's *the Way*," Tarie said again, emphasising the last two words. "You know, like I'm a follower of the Way? Like Amaranthus, the Unchanging One, the Eternal One type of Way?" The others just stared at her, uncomprehending, and she stomped a foot. Jon had never seen her so animated. "Back three thousand years ago, when the Way first started, this is what would happen!" she explained. "Pathways would appear, and they'd get the first Way followers out of the most dreadful situations. And as long as they stayed on the paths, they'd be safe."

Jon exchanged a glance with Bets, who shrugged. "Verily, it does not feel like a Creature thing."

"We should take the path," Tarie said firmly. "No doubt."

And then as if to prove her point, the delicate red and green vine that had been growing up beside her suddenly shot forward, growing down the wall of the tunnel/pathway at high speed. A flower bloomed at the entrance.

They all looked at it.

"Told you so," Tarie said.

Jon glanced at Bets, then at Max.

"It's not like I can carry Tarie now anyway," Max pointed out. "Look at her. She's huge."

Tarie looked back at him over her shoulder, scowling, then sighed. "True. I've been growing since we landed. I guess something's about to happen."

Jon had heard just enough about Tarie's incredible growth – and shrinking – to know what she meant. Right now, she'd passed his height by an inch or two, and looked like she could lift a boulder. "You're also leaving a trail of plants," he told her.

She sighed again. "Yeah. That's my life now, it appears. We'll have to work around that, or people will be able to find us just by the trail I'm leaving. So are we going onto the path or what?"

Jon's lips tightened, then he huffed a breath out of his nose. "My comm seems to be working, so we should contact the family, tell them not to wait for us. Who knows when we'll make it to the south border?"

"Then switch off the comm so we can't be traced," Tarie said.

"Then switch it off," he agreed.

And then they'd head into the tunnel, AKA the Way path. He'd just have to trust that they wouldn't be heading straight to a Creature city.

Sigh.

Ten minutes after they'd entered the tunnel, a light appeared at the other end. Soon enough, they'd walked through it, and ahead of them was an oddly familiar vista.

"I know this place," Max said in a tone of disbelief. "It's Elsewhise."

"What?!" several of them exclaimed.

Max turned and looked at each of them, his eyebrows raised in shock. "We've saved *hours.*"

Well. If that wasn't a sign that Amaranthus approved of their mission, then what was?

Taking a deep breath to steel herself, Maia stepped through the doorway. For a moment she was blinded by bright light, then her eyes adjusted and she could see her surroundings. She was back in the Erusian countryside, with brown grass underfoot, a lightly clouded sky, and her borrowed tri-wheeler parked not far to her left.

She had barely enough time to appreciate that the strange doorway *hadn't* been a trap before her comm went off madly, message after message, flashing lights and 'urgent' signs popping up from her wrist and lightly electrocuting her.

"Argh!" That was a strong one. She didn't remember granting the comm permission to use such measures – a simple alert was usually enough.

"Where are you, Maia?!"

She sighed. Luca's voice was recognisable, even faded by the comm's settings. "I'm here."

The call connected, and Luca's holographic image popped up in front of her, life-sized and flickering slightly. "Where in Hades have you been?" he demanded. "You've been offline for six hours!"

Six hours. That…could have been worse. You could lose *years* in the Other – Maia knew that well. "It wasn't my fault. There's a strip of Other right through the countryside, do you know that? And the boy disappeared into it. I was searching for him this whole time."

"And I assume you didn't find him and retrieve the circlet, or you wouldn't be standing here making excuses."

"You assume right," Maia snapped back. "I literally just got out. Now are you going to point me in the right direction, or would you rather waste time venting at me?"

Luca's hologram stared at her for several seconds, his expression unreadable. Eyes a little too wide, lips quirked into a slight smile. It was surprisingly intimidating considering his transparent nature, and she had to force herself not to cower.

"I'm done venting," he said lightly. "And as we *are* on the same side here, I'll tell you that the boy isn't alone. He's travelling with two or three others, and was spotted thirty minutes ago on the outskirts of Elsewhise." He let that sink in, then added, "While I have no drone visibility there, I have a fair idea where he's gone, and what he's looking for."

"What?"

Luca quirked an eyebrow. "According to your sister, any

direct family member will have access to your mother's house. A sort of inheritance, if you will. And considering that he destroyed the White Prince with an object of power, he's likely looking for more." He paused. "He's *definitely* looking for more. I heard him say so himself."

"But surely Mother's not going to just hand over objects of power," Maia said, frowning. "Or do they have a good relationship after all…?"

There was a pause, then Luca said delicately, "What an interesting question. I suppose you'll find out what your mother thinks of Jayel Jonnamin, *if* you get to him in time. Luckily, I have a shortcut."

Maia was still stuck on the idea of *that boy* intentionally visiting Davinia, but still, her heart sank. "Tell me your shortcut won't involve me going back into the Other."

"In fact, it *does* involve that! But if you'd rather break our agreement, pay the consequences *and* fail to get those seventeen years back, then please, just say so."

Her lips tightened into a thin line, and she thought about how lost she'd just been. The idea of going straight back into the Other, right now, felt like insanity. "Surely there must be another option!"

"There isn't." He cocked his head to the side. "But it's my shortcut, Maia, and it's good. I need you. I wouldn't risk losing you, not now."

Well, when he put it like that… Maia's shoulders slumped. "Just show me the damn shortcut."

You could lose time in the Other, Maia already knew that. What she hadn't known was that you could also skip across space. So, some undefined time later, she was back in the Other, even though it was the last thing she'd wanted to do.

It seemed even darker than before, almost too dark to see the ground in front of her feet, but that made the thread of power stand out even brighter. Bright pink and orange, it led from her chest, almost like a harness, and shot off into the darkness.

Just follow the thread, he'd said. She was doing as he'd said, but she felt like she was blithely wandering off to her doom. A stupid fly following the spiderweb to see what lay at its heart.

"Hurry up," Luca's voice echoed along the line of power.

"We're not the only ones in here, and not everyone is caught up in the Tiger's preparations."

The reminder of her danger wasn't helpful, but his comment caught her attention. "The Tiger," she whispered back. "You mentioned that Creature before. What preparations?"

There was a brief pause. *"Nothing that will affect either of us once we get that circlet."*

"But does it need to be a secret? Won't it help if I know what the...alternative is, if I fail?"

"Total domination. A plan that's been in the works for ten thousand years. And revenge. Not on you, precisely, but you'll definitely get caught up in it."

Maia stumbled, missing a step, and Luca's laughter echoed along the line. More than echoed – it sounded like dozens of voices, speaking in unison. "That's not funny," she muttered. And now she had no idea whether to believe him.

"Just hurry up, and you'll never need to know."

Maia followed the thread, walking as fast as she dared in the darkness. Then abruptly the bright thread disappeared into deeper darkness.

A cave or doorway of some kind.

"What's this? I'm not walking straight into a Creature city..."

"Don't be ssilly," Luca scolded, his words holding a distinctive hiss. *"It's just the back way into your old house. Your mother used it frequently."*

He could be lying, but it sounded reasonable. A flashback of that filthy altar came to mind, and with the memory came the way Maia had always felt when she'd had to go near it. She'd always known that the Other was beyond the structure that housed the altar, and she wasn't sure how Davinia would feel about her suddenly showing up through the back door. She might take it quite badly, in fact.

Although what did he mean by 'used'...? Did Davinia no longer use this route into the Other? That didn't make Maia feel any safer right now. But she pushed back her fear and stepped inside.

Several more steps, and she was still in darkness. Here, it seemed even worse, and there was a distinctive stench in the air. She knew the altar was nearby purely from that smell – metallic, rank, sickly sweet. No lights though – Davinia must be out. Or perhaps she used a different altar these days.

Then the thread veered sharply to the left. She turned towards it, and yellow lights blossomed in the darkness. No, not lights. *Eyes.* Dozens of them, tiny and round, speckled around a central larger pair.

Her breath caught in her throat.

"No need to look this way," Luca said, and this time she heard his voice in reality, not just as a whisper along the thread of power. And the echo – it was real, too. **"Leave the thread. Keep walking forward and you'll find the altar, then the back entrance to your mother's house."**

Maia swallowed, then forcibly turned her gaze away from those yellow lights. Luca had said that his true body, his almost-Creature body, was hidden somewhere in the borderlands. It seemed she'd just found it, and right by her mother's house. Was Davinia working with Luca all this time…?

"And Maia…"

This time the voice was too close. Right behind her, but she didn't dare turn around. Didn't dare stop.

"When you've got the circlet, bring it back here, to the altar. Then we'll *both* get what we want."

She nodded, still moving forward, and when the darkness turned to greyish light, indicating she'd entered the normal realm, she almost cried in relief.

She was safe, because he couldn't follow her here. Not in his real body.

And no matter what mood her mother was in, Maia did *not* want to come back.

Up ahead, a rectangle of light indicated the doorway marking Davinia's house. Maia picked up her pace until she stepped through into a long hallway. She slowed again, checking the sound of her footsteps, but couldn't hear anything inside the house.

No one. So *that boy* wasn't here yet, but neither was anyone else. Her mother must be out, and she wouldn't be pleased that Maia was showing up through the back door without warning. Or maybe she would be pleased – after all, it had been many years. Surely Davinia wouldn't hold a grudge for that long.

Maia paused at the end of the hallway. The house seemed

too still, too quiet. "Hello?" she called out. "It's Maia."

There was no answer. She took another step into the adjoining room, a storage/work area full of stacks of jars, boxes and unlabelled vials. A high, wide workbench was scattered with more of the same, with one of Davinia's notebooks open on its surface.

Maia paused to study it. Davinia D'Endria was paranoid that someone else would steal her formulas, so she rarely wrote them down, and if she did, it was always on physical paper. No tech devices here – although tech was notoriously untrustworthy here in Elsewhise. Or she'd just put hints as reminders to herself that meant nothing on their own. Maia had long ago given up trying to interpret the scribbled notes.

But this time, the note made sense. Sort of.

Desperate times call for desperate measures. She will forgive me.

It was dated late 2987. That was six months after yesterday- no, after the date it *felt* like to Maia. After the date she'd left Jayel with Anni and headed to see the White Prince about a curse.

But who was the 'she' Davinia referred to?

Maia checked the room's crowded surfaces again, looking for anything more recent. But there was nothing, and the closer she looked, the more she noticed things like congealed liquids, dry potions and the dust that sat on every surface.

How long had it been since her mother had been here?

She thought of how that boy was coming here, and how Luca had been silent on Davinia's response. And he'd said she *used* that entrance from the Other; not that she *uses* it. Was it possible that...Davinia was gone...but he just hadn't said as much?

Maia froze, her hand poised over yet another dusty box. It had been a day full of disastrous news, and she couldn't handle anymore. But she had to know.

So she took a moment to put her settings into the house's lock system, then headed out through the front door into Elsewhise, quietly closing it behind her.

7
Safekeepers

Elsewhise was busy. Far more so than Tarie had expected. People headed in every direction, all seeming busy enough that they didn't look twice at her, Jon, Bets and Max. The four of them had decided it would look more suspicious to creep around than just to walk confidently towards their destination.

And that was assuming anyone could even *see* Bets. In Tarie's experience, people often looked right past the girl. It wasn't quite invisibility, but more…unnoticeability?

But not having a working comm turned out to be a real pain. The real Elsewhise was one of those strange border towns Tarie had heard of, the sort where technology was avoided because alter-power fluctuations made it unreliable. So unlike in the city, there was no convenient map kiosk or massive clock displayed for those few without comms. That meant some wandering.

And beyond the lack of maps, this town had been built thoughtlessly, with winding streets on no particular framework, random alleyways and overpasses, and signage in all different styles and locations. Even though it was tiny compared to the cities Tarie had grown up in, it would be awkward to navigate even without its busyness.

"Do you notice that a lot of these people are wearing red cloaks?" Max whispered, leaning in to Tarie.

"Do you notice that many of them are wearing *Creatures?*" Bets interjected. "Walk a little faster if you can, my friend."

Tarie didn't question how Bets knew about the Creatures. This whole place just felt a bit…off. It reminded her of yesterday's – whenever's – trap in virtual reality, when she'd been caught in an inescapable VR programme intended to drive her mad. It

107

hadn't worked (or she *thought* it hadn't worked) but she and Bets had ended up in a virtual version of this very town. Hard to believe they'd come straight back here on purpose.

"Here it is," Jon said. He was standing in front of a closed door in a narrow alley. A slightly battered sign read *Spellcaster. Curse-breaker.*

Tarie curled her lip. "Charming. Are we sure this place is empty? It looks the sort that'll lay a curse on anyone who breaks in."

Jon's lips were tight. "Only one way to find out."

Jon raised a hand to the flat keypad to the door's right. There was a sharp pain in the tip of his index finger, and the keypad flashed orange, then green. There was a *click*, and the door swung open.

Lucky. He pulled his hand away, shaking it ruefully. A spot of red marked his aching fingertip. "It was a bloodletting key. But at least it recognised me and let us in."

He'd heard of bloodletters – keys that would take a small blood sample rather than just a scan – but hadn't come across one till now.

"Better make it quick then," Max said from his place at the end of the alley. "Shall I stay on watch?"

Jon exchanged glances with the girls, then shook his head. "Better for all of us to be out of sight, right? And if we heard correctly, no one's been in this place in close to twenty years."

"And let us stay together," Bets added earnestly. "We cannot risk losing anyone."

Agreed!

They stepped inside the house into a narrow hall cluttered with boxes and shelves. Several doorways opened off it on either side, and its far end curved out of sight. Jon poked his head into one of the doorways and was surprised to see just another hall, wider this time, and full of more boxes and pieces of furniture. At the other end, it curved off out of sight yet again.

What an odd layout. No real rooms, no real doors, just…halls, full of junk.

But beyond the odd design and uninviting entrance, the house was ordinary. Cluttered and smelling of dust, but with nothing to indicate it belonged to a wicked, child-killing curse-maker.

"I just figured what's strange about this place," Max murmured to Tarie back in the entrance way. "There are no windows, no internal doors. Just rooms connected by halls. And you know what that means?"

"No...?"

"The owner was paranoid. No way to surprise attack, see?" He slapped a hand against the nearest wall.

There was a faint sound like *pfft*, and Jon turned just in time to see Tarie stick her hand out in front of Max. A tiny, spikey shape bounced off her palm and clattered to the floor.

"Chaos," Max swore. "This place is booby-trapped!"

Tarie carefully kicked the dart aside, bumping the small Word tree that was springing up beside her feet. "Maybe don't touch anything else."

"Then how are we supposed to find the safekeepers?" Jon muttered. "Grandma was a hoarder."

He turned away to follow Bets into the next space, but came face to face with a woman not an arm's length away from him. "Chaos!" he burst out. "Where did you come from?!"

The woman's cold expression didn't change. She was very pale-skinned with intense red hair in a sharply trimmed cut, and she wore a long, plain outfit in solid black. It took Jon only a moment longer to recognise her from Anni's old pictures, and his heart sank. This was only an image – VR, perhaps? – but they hadn't come in unseen at all.

She was supposed to be dead!

"This is my house," Davinia D'Endria said, her tone cold enough to match her expression. "Who gave you the right to enter?"

"Uh..." Jon swallowed. So this was his infamous grandmother. Funny, it wasn't a stretch to imagine her trading favours with Creatures or trying to commit infanticide. Her somewhat familiar features were attractive, but entirely unfriendly.

"It's just an old security screen," Max said over Jon's shoulder. "A basic recording with some basic instructions – nothing compared to what you'd find in the cities, because the tech doesn't work here."

"Oh." Jon slumped in relief. "How do we get rid of the

image?"

"This is my house," the figure said again. "Who gave you the right to enter?"

"Jayel Jonnamin DeLuca, who entered by bloodletting at the front door," Max told it. "He gave us the right to be here."

The figure stared cold-eyed at the two of them. "Then let any damages be on his head." And she vanished.

Great. 'Any damages on Jon's head', huh? "How did you know what to say?" he asked Max a little accusingly.

Tarie looked at Max too, raising an eyebrow.

"I've been to a place like this before." Max scratched at the back of his neck, looking uncomfortable. "When I was a carrier. They often have that kind of security."

"And what were you doing in a place like this?" Jon asked a little tersely.

Max shrugged. "I don't know. I don't remember. The time I was a carrier all blurs together."

Convenient. Jon studied him with narrowed eyes, reminded that till recently, Rokal/Max had been Jon's worst enemy. They'd taken it for granted that he'd changed, but what kind of history and secrets lay under that dishevelled exterior?

Tarie piped up suddenly, "What happens if you don't say the right answer?"

Max shrugged a shoulder. "Not sure. Just make sure you do have it – or that you're physically indestructible like you."

"I'll be your bodyguard, then," Tarie said.

"And I shall be your bodyguard, Jon," Bets said earnestly.

Jon gave her a startled smile. "Alright. Tarie, Max, we'll go left at this hall, you go right. But yell out if you're in trouble, OK?"

And that was that.

Left at the hall just led to another hall, then beyond that, another hall-room full to the brim with boxes, bottles and bags of all kinds. They were all full or half full, and Jon caught a glimpse of something organic in a murky bottle. He shuddered. "This place gives me the creeps." As did Rokal/Max's familiarity with it. Jon found that distinctly suspicious.

"'Tis the Creature influence everywhere," Bets whispered from behind him, making him jump. "'Twould be better off for a fire-cleansing, but I do not wish to bring down the building by mistake."

Creature influence. Feeling a bit foolish, Jon took off the circlet looped around his wrist, popped it out to full-size, then studied the room. Through the centre of the circlet, his surroundings appeared to be covered in a faint grey fog, interspersed with thin lines of colour that he knew indicated power at work.

"No Creatures," he said. "But keep your fire at the ready."

"Most certainly!"

"And, ah, any idea where the safekeepers might be?"

"None at all!"

He sighed. "We'd better start searching, and fast."

This version of Elsewhise wasn't like Maia's childhood home. It felt like a disturbing dream: nothing looked quite right, and it was full of strangers. Finally Maia started hijacking random people as they passed – "Excuse me, do you know Davinia D'Endria? The spellcaster?" – but always got head shakes in response.

The fifth person Maia stopped knew of Davinia. A middle-aged woman, small and a little hunched under a heavy cloak, barely paused in her brisk walk. "The one who lived on the corner of Bracas and Wester streets? I heard she died."

"What do you mean, she died?!"

Maia grabbed the woman by a shoulder, and she looked up with fear in her gaze. "I just heard she did, alright? No one's seen her in years! But that's all I know! If you want more, you'll have to ask someone else." The woman shook Maia off and disappeared at a trot around a corner.

Maia stood on the busy street, people passing her on every side. She couldn't breathe. Was that true, that people thought Davinia was dead? The woman had been difficult, cold when Maia had needed her support. But she'd also raised Maia. Praised her, encouraged her. Given her a form of love, right up till it was snatched away by that Chaos-damned curse.

She might just be in the Other, like Maia had been.

Her comm went off. *"Maia!"* came Luca's voice straight to her earpiece. *"What are you doing? He's in the house! Go get the circlet!"*

In that moment she was grateful for the interruption; to be reminded of why she was here. Of how this nightmare could be undone. Finally she forced her legs to move again and headed back towards the house.

Back at the front door, Maia stood numbly for a moment looking at the lock and blood-letting keypad. She'd added herself to the house's security settings on the way out, but hadn't realised it was this kind of lock. She hated needles.

"Hurry up!"

Chaos, she was getting sick of Luca's voice. Maybe when she changed things back to how they should be, she wouldn't follow up with Luke. It would be hard to forget how awful he ended up being, before and after becoming a carrier.

She pressed her finger against the keypad, lips tightening at the prick of pain, then sighed in relief as the door clicked open. But there was no time to relax. She thought back to her training, pulling a couple of 'don't see me' illusions over herself, then pulled out her dart gun and slipped inside the house.

Inside, no one was in sight, but voices echoed down the winding halls and open spaces that made up this house. Davinia had been so determined not to be caught out by her enemies that she'd designed her space so any visitors would be immediately known. And that was in addition to any other security features…

Maia moved forward on silent feet towards the sound of those voices. She braced herself as she passed the VR panel against one flat, narrow wall. As expected, her mother's image flicked into existence. Maia stopped to look at it, bracing herself. If the memory screen spoke, it would reveal Maia's own presence here to the intruders somewhere in these rooms. 'Don't see me' illusions only worked when you were dead silent, and she wasn't ready to be revealed yet.

But the flat image just stared silently. Finally Maia stepped forward. She whispered, "Cut off sound to this section," and a second later, the sound of voices stopped. Then to the image she said, "Where is my mother?"

"In the antechamber leading to the Other altar," the image replied without emotion.

What… Maia had come through there! And Luca the semi-Creature had been there by the altar, all those glowing eyes in the darkness…

Maia asked carefully, "How long has she been in the antechamber…?"

"Seventeen years, two months, twelve days and fourteen hours."

Ohhh… Her heart wrenched, and fury filled her.

Not bothering to turn the sound back on, Maia leapt for the hall that would lead to the antechamber. She moved through the sound barrier with a noticeable *pop,* then suddenly she was in an occupied space. The loud conversation stopped mid-sentence as *that boy* looked up, his hands buried in the contents of an open box. Just to his right, a tiny, pale-skinned girl shot to her feet, her hands lighting up silver.

Maia fired the dart gun without hesitation, and the girl lifted one hand an inch, then slumped to the ground. Maia swung the gun in the boy's direction. "Don't move!" she ordered, and her voice sounded harsh to her own ears.

That boy's lip trembled. This close, he looked so tremendously familiar, like seeing a twisted version of yourself in a warped mirror. Almost like he belonged here in this house he was ransacking. "Is she…d-dead?"

He obviously meant his little friend, but Maia's mind went straight to her mother. "I could ask you the same thing," she hissed. "Did you kill the owner of this house?"

"Ww-what?!" he stammered.

It made no sense, because the boy was too young to have anything to do with Davinia being in a single room for seventeen years. But Maia didn't care. "What are you doing here? This isn't your house!"

"I'm…" He straightened, glancing again at his friend with wide eyes. She moaned and twitched on the floor, and his lips tightened. Whatever he saw must have soothed him, because he turned back to Maia with a determined expression. "I entered by blood-letting. This is my grandmother's house, and my inheritance."

That was a mangled version of the verbal key this house required – who'd let you in, and who'd be responsible for any damage. But the last part…

"Inheritance!?" Maia spat. "You can't inherit anything if the owner is still alive!" *Was she alive? Was she?*

"Are we talking about the same person here?" The boy's gaze didn't move from the loaded dart gun. His hands rested by his sides, and a metallic loop shone just under one sleeve.

"Davinia D'Endria! This is her house – and if not hers, then it's mine!"

His eyes flicked from the weapon, to her face, then the weapon again. "I'm guessing Luca sent you. I don't know who you really are, but as far as I know, the owner of this house passed away years ago in an accident."

"What happened?" Maia choked out. The weapon trembled in her hands.

The boy's eyes widened. "Uh…I heard she fell and broke her neck while carrying out a…sacrifice."

A sacrifice? That wouldn't be out of the ordinary. But what kind of fall could break someone's neck?

This was all too much. Suddenly overwhelmed, Maia swallowed back a sob…and her finger knocked the trigger. The boy looked down to see the tiny end of a dart poking out of his chest. His mouth opened… then he slumped to the ground next to his little friend.

Shaking, Maia moved closer to him. Could it be that easy? He'd had no defences at all. No shield, nothing to deflect her attack. But seeing him like this, collapsed and semi-unconscious because of what *she'd* done, made her feel like a monster.

She'd shot her own son. Because he *was* her son, and she knew it. He just belonged to a future that had come too soon, and one without her in it.

She crouched next to him, her hand shaking as she pushed his sleeve back to expose the twisted circlet. "I'm going to fix this," she vowed as she tugged the circlet loose. "We're going to start over, and none of this will have happened. I'm…I'm so sorry."

Her son's eyes were still open and fixed on her, although he barely moved except to breathe. Swallowing back a sob, Maia slipped the circlet over her own wrist, doubling it around so it fit snugly. "Amaranthus," she whispered. "Protect him." Her gaze slid to the small girl next to him. "And her, I suppose."

Everything seemed so wrong. All of this, especially her part in it. And wearing the circlet, she could distinctly see the lines of power looping over her – the power from Luca, and the original curse – and from whatever Davinia had rigged in this room. And they all felt wrong too.

So she had to go back to Luca. Even though everything in her revolted at going back to his presence in that hideous room her mother used as an altar, she had to make it right.

Maia backed out of the room, but she was still shaken. She hit the narrowed hallway wall hard, knocking down an entire stack of round containers. They clattered to the floor and rolled in every direction. One hit the base of a tall, narrow pillar set against the wall. Maia recognised it vaguely, but had no idea what it did. Still, she watched in horror as it tipped sideways into another stack of boxes, which also fell over…

It was no surprise the house alarm went off. Suddenly there was an image of Davinia on every wall, her expression cold and black-eyed. *"Destruction. Let the damage be on your head. Destruction. Let the damage be on your head. Destruction-"*

Maia stumbled over the fallen boxes, running for the exit leading to the Other altar. She didn't know what her mother had set up in this house and she didn't want to find out. She'd just made it into the hall leading to the antechamber when a solid wall slammed down behind her, skimming her back as it came down.

A few more steps, and the darkness of the antechamber loomed up ahead. Oddly enough, the Other realm in this case would be a protection from whatever physical threats had been set up against intruders.

But the darkness wasn't complete. With the light at her back, she could make out the faint shape of something at the end of the hall, something just short of the line between the normal and Other realms.

The circlet shone faintly on Maia's wrist, but she didn't need its light to know what she was looking at. That shape – that mix of soft and hard lines, of tattered cloth and a patch of faded red threads – it could only be one thing.

Seventeen years in the antechamber.

She'd found Davinia…what was left of her.

"This house is a mess," Tarie muttered as she rummaged through yet another box. Although she was cautious of booby traps, she hadn't come across one since the first dart that had almost struck Max. "How are we going to find anything, I ask you?"

From the corner of her eye, she could see Max waiting nearby, tossing an item from hand to hand. "Tarie…" he began.

"No, I'm not going to trade that favour for a kiss," she said firmly without looking up. "And stop asking. Yes, we might die anytime, but we might not! And then we'd have to live with each other." And what was stupider was that she owed *him* the favour because she'd lost that bet about Jon and Bets. Why would he trade it for something momentary that wouldn't mean anything to him?

"But...I don't think you should owe me a favour. It's just..."

A small, shining shape at the back of a shelf caught Tarie's attention. "Oh! I think I've found one." She got hold of the object and held it up in the air, admiring it. "It's a seashell like the one Bets mentioned. And it's got some ancient script on it, too. But how can we tell?"

"Try putting something in it," Max suggested. He was still shuffling uncomfortably, but Tarie put it down to their dangerous situation.

"Um, alright." She spotted an old pen, the sort that left actual markings. "Pen, get into the safekeeper."

The pen didn't budge.

Her shoulders slumped. "Oh. I guess it's not one after all."

"Don't get rid of it," Max said quickly. He took it from her and put it in the small bag they'd brought with them. "Maybe it's the other sort."

Urgh. A soul-drinker, he meant. The sort that stole energy – life-force – instead of simply holding a physical object. "Sure." Tarie shrugged. "I guess we'll keep looking."

"Yeah. But Tarie..."

"Can you look as well as talk, please? We have limited time."

"Yeah. It's just that, Tarie, I don't know how to say this, but I've been remembering things from before. And I think that...um..."

Tarie lifted an aged piece of cloth and revealed an entire tray full of identical seashells, all glossy brown, cream or white, but without that script on them. "Ooh! How about these? Let's show them to Jon, shall we?" She began shoving them into the bag, figuring they could work it out later. This place made the hairs stand up on the back of her neck.

Max reached across and took a small handful, slipping them into his pocket. "Best not to have them all in one place."

She nodded.

"Destruction. Let the damage be on your head. Destruction. Let the damage be on your head. Destruction..."

Both Tarie and Max jolted upright as a horrible loud voice sounded all around them and a red haze filled the air.

"Chaos," Tarie swore. "We have to get out of here." She felt the Words bubble up at the back of her throat, and she let them out as strength coursed through her body. She grabbed the now half-full tray of seashell objects and dashed for the door, then paused briefly when Max didn't follow her.

She turned to look back at him and saw he was curled over, his face darkening and his arms wrapped around his waist. He'd dropped the bag, and he didn't seem to be breathing.

"Max!" Tarie dropped the tray and ran over to him, grabbing his arm and trying to pull him away. But he fought her, as though he couldn't or wouldn't move, and when she looked up at him, his eyes had turned blood red.

"CHAOS!" She sniffed at the air and noted a chemical tang – he was clearly being poisoned. Panicking, and with the Words seeming pointless, Tarie scrambled for something to do. Eyes stinging and one hand covering her own nose and mouth, she snatched up the nearest of the plain seashells, held it up towards Max, and shouted, "Max, get into the safekeeper!"

She didn't have more than a moment to worry that it *wasn't* a safekeeper before Max seemed to be rushing at her, red eyes and all, and then in an instant he'd vanished, and the object in her hand felt just a little warmer.

Her eyes were still stinging. Wrapping her long sleeve around her face, Tarie snatched up two or three more shells and shoved them in the small bag, then sprinted for the exit. Which way had they come in...? Was it left or right? Ugh, these halls all looked the same, and the alarm had stopped which somehow seemed worse because there was this red haze over everything...

But she'd only turned a couple of corners before she stumbled across two fallen figures. Jon and Bets were sprawled on the floor in a small room space, mere feet from each other, and Tarie barely paused before whipping out the safekeeper and sending them into it.

She'd have to check if they were alive at the other end.

Alive? Of course they'd be alive, she scolded herself as she ran through the house's myriad halls. She couldn't let it be any other way. But still the Words spilled out of her mouth as she ran, and dark shapes filled the edge of her vision even as she grew larger and stronger. Then finally she spotted the door up ahead – but it was closed!

Not for long. Tarie put her head down and shouldered her way right through. The door flew open with a bang, and it wasn't until she was out in the fresh air that she realised how stifling it had become in there, how dangerous. Red smoke spilled out of the door after her, and she reached back in long enough to drag the door shut. It caught on the red-leafed vines trailing along behind her before slamming closed – those were what she'd seen 'following her'.

So that was how some people provided security for their houses. Poison gas. Lovely.

PHOOF. A soft but emphatic sound came from behind the closed door, and the whole house shook. The door crumpled inwards, and the gap around it was suddenly full of vines.

Tarie's jaw dropped. So *that* was the security – kill everyone inside.

Tarie met the eyes of one of several bystanders and immediately ducked her head, moving away from the scene of the crime. She'd have to find somewhere quiet to free the others from the safekeeper.

Although, her pockets clanked as she walked. There had to be at least a dozen in that small bag.

So which one was Jon, Bets and Max inside?

8
Change is Coming

Under the most heavily populated parts of Erus city, in the deepest, darkest places underneath hundreds of ancient building layers, the Tiger sat like a spider in a web. Ties of power ran off in every direction imaginable, with infinite strings of power leading to infinite other bodies, carriers and conduits throughout the normal and Other realms.

He didn't regret that he'd made the effort of coming out of the Other realm only to live the exact same way in the normal realm. He wasn't done yet, not by a long shot, and freedom from the Other was just the starting point.

The Tiger watched patiently as swarms of mortal beings made their way into the massive cat-shaped conduits he'd set up across the globe. And each of them came out different – if they came out at all. And each of them meant more strings of power, all flowing inwards.

This was going so much better than expected. After brief consideration, the Tiger sent out a message to his direct subordinates – the few he didn't entirely distrust.

We won't wait the full five days. The change happens tomorrow.

The Mountain of Glass

Amaranthus stood in the Tapestry Room, watching the array of dark and light threads intently. They were already laid, of course. It had all been set out before he'd even set this whole thing into motion, but somehow everything felt so *intense* in the moment, even when he'd already seen the moment coming.

The end of the tapestry. The big change…right before the *biggest* change. Whatever happened next was entirely off the record.

But all of it, every last thread, was linked back to one single moment some distance back on the tapestry. A point that humans called 33AD.

And while Amaranthus had woven himself all through the tapestry, right to every last thread, that single point was where all the colour change began. Where the *pattern* of the tapestry became complete, and beautiful, and whole.

So in spite of the disaster being put into play by the Tiger at the very end of time, he tapped his fingers on his leg…and smiled.

Inside a safekeeper

So this was what the inside of a safekeeper was like. Somehow Max had thought it would be round, or at least reflect the shape of the seashell it resembled. But instead he found himself standing on the wide white steps of an ancient colosseum, a semi-circle ringed with seats all facing down towards a central stage with tall stone pillars. It was huge, and the space above it disappeared into grey mist.

Had someone really put an entire building structure into this thing? How brilliant. Maybe you could even fit a city into a safekeeper, if you had to. An interesting thought.

He rubbed at his face, remembering the stinging feeling that had overwhelmed him moments before he'd found himself in here. But it was out of memory only, because now he felt fine. A bit…disconnected, maybe? Numb? But otherwise as fit as normal. Not a bad place to stay then, as long as he didn't need to eat or drink.

Max sat down, pondering the memory that had sprung up when he'd been in that room with Tarie. Ever since he'd teasingly got her to owe him a favour – payment for that lost bet over Jon and Bets – he'd had this feeling that she shouldn't owe him.

No, it was more than that. That she *mustn't* owe him

anything, not even as simple as an undetermined favour. But he couldn't think of why. And then he'd remembered.

Gerak had collected favours, and Max – or Rocell as he'd been known – had been the vessel for collecting them. So many times he'd helped someone in genuine need (or had forced them into a corner in the first place), and then had said, *now you owe me a favour.* And once they agreed that they did, a bond was created. A link of power that chained that person to Gerak, no matter who else they were pledged to. And later, when Gerak wanted something from them, he'd get it – right to the last drop of blood.

Gerak had traded favours with Jon's grandmother, Max knew. He didn't know the details himself – he was far too young – but something about that place had felt so familiar, as though he'd shared Gerak's memories too. And he'd known about the bloodletting key…

Max shivered at the memory, feeling sick. Those words had come out of his mouth so easily with Tarie. *You'll owe me a favour.* He'd meant them as a joke, as a way to tease her, but it seemed that he wasn't as free from old habits as he'd thought he was.

And that might mean he wasn't as free from *Gerak* as he'd thought he was. He couldn't shake the thought that he'd chained Tarie by mistake.

She *mustn't* agree that she owed him anything at all.

Just then, movement caught Max's eye from across the colosseum. Something faint and human-shaped: he wasn't alone in here. He took a step towards the other person and almost tripped on a ball. It was strangely translucent and seemed to gain and lose solidity by the moment – that was why he hadn't seen it.

Strange. As he was about to kick it aside, his eyes met that of a child who'd been at his feet, bent down to fetch the ball. They were translucent too, like in the old stories about ghosts. Their eyes widened and they turned and dashed away, taking the ball with them.

That was when he realised he *really* wasn't alone. This place didn't have just one or two other figures, hiding away in corners. No, it was chock-full of them, dozens or even hundreds of human shapes, fading in and out of sight.

Inside another safekeeper

'Twasn't so bad, in truth. Elspeth felt half-awake, hovering in a grey fog. She could feel Jon at her side and knew that he was sleeping too, or almost sleeping, but she didn't try to speak to him. She was just resting here in this cosy space that was just about the right size for them and-

"You're out!" The cosy greyness vanished, and suddenly Tarie's worried face loomed overhead. "Can you talk? Can you move?"

"Ugh…" Elspeth wiggled her arms and legs, feeling them tingle as though she'd been lying still for too long. Ah, that was right – there'd been that woman in the house. Had she *shot* Elspeth? "I 'spose so. Where are we?"

"In the forest just south of Elsewhise," Tarie said. She moved away a little, turning towards Elspeth's right. "This was the soonest as I could get you out. I pulled darts out of your chests, too. How are you feeling, Jon?"

Elspeth struggled upright. Next to her, Jon was doing the same. He had shadows under his eyes and his movements were awkward. "She took the circlet," he said grimly, holding up his bare wrist, and Elspeth's heart sank.

If the circlet was gone, then their journey to this place had far less value. But then, they'd never found Amaranthus to ask for advice. They'd just assumed…

"Who?!" Tarie asked.

"The woman who came to my house today, pretending to be my birth mother. She showed up at Davinia's place too, acting like she had the right to be there and *I* was the intruder, then knocked both of us out." He scrubbed a hand over his face, his expression defeated. "She obviously wasn't my mother or she wouldn't have almost killed us all. And now she's taken the Amaranthus circlet, our trip to Elsewhise was pointless!"

There was a disappointed silence while they took that in (and Elspeth tried to get movement back into her toes), then Tarie said briskly, "Well, we got a bunch of safekeepers, plus what might be a soul-drinker. And even if we can't put Creatures in them then destroy them with the circlet, we sure can use them anyway."

"I suppose so," Elspeth murmured. "But where is Max?"

"Oh!" Tarie jolted upright, scrambling through a pile of shapes scattered on the grass. "I was working my way through the safekeepers, since I had to get out of the house so quickly and I wasn't sure which was which. Yours was the seventh I tried. There are just two more…"

She lifted up a dark brown glossy shape, quite a lot like the seashell object Elspeth had recently rescued from a borderlands museum, and which Jon had later used to destroy the White Prince. "Max, come out." Nothing happened, and Tarie sighed. "OK. It better be this last one."

She picked up the palest of the bunch, a spiral-shaped shell that was almost white. Next to her, Jon pointed at a light brown shape covered in scrolling text. "What about this one here?" he asked.

"We're pretty sure that's a soul-drinker," Tarie said. "It doesn't respond to instructions like the others do, and Max said there was one like it at the borderlands museum."

"Used to be one like it," Elspeth corrected. She held out a hand and Jon passed the item to her. A bit of silver flame and a moment later, the scrolling text had vanished and there was yet another safekeeper free to use.

"Huh," Tarie said. "Smart. But Max still isn't in that one."

He was in the white one, it turned out. He appeared suddenly in front of the item, almost knocking Tarie over, since she was holding it in her hand. His face was red and his eyes bloodshot, and his mouth moved briefly before he crumped to his knees.

"Can you help him?" Tarie asked urgently, but Elspeth was already moving. Silver flame streamed out from her hands, covering Max as he hunched in a ball on the grass, but it quickly fizzled out, leaving him in just as poor condition. Worse, even.

A moment later, Tarie ordered him back into the safekeeper, back into a suspended state. The three remaining exchanged horrified glances.

"The fumes got him at your grandmother's place," Tarie said desolately. "But I was shorter than him so they didn't reach me. And you two were on the floor, I suppose. But the safekeeper must have kept him safe, for he seemed the same as when I first sent him in."

"Then 'tis not a sickness of Creature origin," Elspeth mused.

Her shoulders slumped. "I see my cleansing flame has very limited uses here in the normal realm. In truth, I thought he was going to die right there in front of us."

Jon sighed, scrubbing a hand through his hair. "He should be fine inside the safekeeper, because if that poison had still been working on him since you left Elsewhise, he'd be dead or a lot more damaged by now. For us, it was like we were asleep – or mostly asleep, anyway. I guess we'll have to keep him in there till we get to the Mountain, or the River, or some place he can be healed."

Tarie looked melancholy, the pale safekeeper held tightly in her hand. "But he was carrying me, and my vehicle's way back down south."

There was a moment of dismayed silence. Elspeth didn't even think to suggest Jon carry them both, for 'twas clearly impossible even had Tarie been at her usual size.

"Then I guess we're going to walk," Jon said. "Who knows? Maybe that pathway will still be around."

Maia didn't know how long she waited by that pile of bone and rags. Her mind was in overload – too much had happened too quickly, and she couldn't take any more. Finally, clutching her Amaranthus circlet tightly in one fist, she forced herself away from her mother's body and into the darkness.

It didn't scare her as much now, heading straight for Luke's Creature in a place that swallowed all light, although she'd happily never go back. But she had to go, to keep her bargain with Luca, because this present reality was unbearable.

The darkness muffled her footsteps the further in she walked, and she felt the atmosphere shift as she left the normal realm and entered the borderlands edging the Other. The air was cold – then warm – then cold again, and she could hear the faint rustle of whatever monstrosity made up Luca somewhere nearby. The circlet emitted a distinct warmth the colder the air became, and it began to glow just as distinctly.

"You've got it."

Even though she'd known he was close, and she'd told herself she wasn't afraid, Maia was startled anyway. She cleared her throat, trying to push back the fear that threatened to overwhelm her. "Yes, I've got it. Now you give me what you promised – a way to go back, to stop all this happening."

"A way to change *your* past," the Luca-Creature corrected, his voice in person having a strange, unpleasant layer to it, like audio played too slowly. **"Bring the circlet here, and I'll give you what you asked for."**

A faint light appeared up ahead, spotlighting a small item on the ground. The item was small enough to fit in Maia's closed fist, shining pale and textured. It looked like a little ball, maybe slightly warped in shape. In the darkness behind it, Maia could just make out dozens of faint lights that she knew marked the Creature's location.

Strange, he didn't smell bad like so many Creatures did. (Perils of being immortal, apparently.) But Maia didn't want to go any closer. "Back away from the item," she said, "and I'll bring it to you."

There was the sound of shuffling – not like footsteps, more like something massive was being dragged – and the faint lights receded. **"I'm not interested in hurting you. Not while I need something from you. Place the circlet over that silver object on the ground."**

Maia took a step closer. "And my reward?"

Something tinkled on the ground to her right, and the light extended enough to show an item had been thrown her way. It was amber-coloured, a short chain of connected cubes like someone lost interest partway through creating a necklace. **"Do what I ask, and I'll tell you how to use it,"** the Luca-Creature said. **"Break your word, and you won't leave this place."**

Still gripping the circlet, Maia crouched down and picked up the chain with her free hand. It felt warm and a little soft, almost as if it truly was made of amber. She looked up ahead at the other spotlight which highlighted the silver object. It reminded her of a safekeeper like the sort her mother would make, except with additions, of course.

She had no idea what this semi-Creature intended to do with it, and she didn't really care. Not if she could get her life back.

In a moment, she weighed up the risk of getting too close; if he intended to harm her. Then she dismissed it. How could life get any worse?

Five steps later, she'd reached the object. She crouched down, holding the circlet suspended over it. This close, it was clearly a safekeeper, but its off-white colouring gave away its history as a soul-drinker. A couple of times, Davinia had turned a soul-drinker into a safekeeper, and they'd always take on a strange pale shade. Maia didn't know too much about them, just that they were never the same after being used as a soul-drinker...

The Amaranthus circlet hummed and tingled in Maia's hand. Its text lit up in red-gold: *AMARANTHUS-AMARAN-THUS-AMARANTHUS* all the way around its circumference, and for a moment she was certain she was making a terrible mistake.

You never did anything for me, she thought fiercely, and set the circlet down. She felt pressure as it settled over the safekeeper, almost like she had to force it to the ground, but then it just sat there. The space inside it was tinted red-gold now, as though it was a tiny circle of power, and the light tinted the safekeeper the same shade.

Against the light of the circlet, the darkness around them seemed even more complete. The Luca-Creature let out a heavy sigh that echoed in a dozen voices. **"We've done it."**

Maia stood up rapidly, her eyes wide on the circlet. She clenched her fingers around the new object of power that she'd attacked her own son for. (No, not her son! It didn't count if she was going to turn back time, did it?) *"I did it,"* she corrected, her voice barely trembling. "Now tell me how to use this thing."

"It's a time-chain: a time-travel device from the early third millennium," Luca replied, sounding much more relaxed now, and definitely less threatening. Even his voice had lost some of its strength. **"Back when such things were allowed, before their destructiveness became clear and people realized how pointless they were, when you can't even change the past."**

"What?! You said-"

"It's been improved with alter-power," he cut in irritably. **"Unlike traditional time-chains that only harnessed technology, this one will allow you to view windows into the past, and to select one – and only one – to step into. And you, and you alone, can make a new future for yourself from that window, is that clear?"**

"Alright," Maia began.

"Five windows," Luca spoke over her. **"Crush a single bead**

and focus on where you want to go. And for chaos' sake, I don't want to see you back here moaning about how you misused it. I don't have a replacement. This is it, and it was hard enough to get as it was."

"Alright," Maia said again. "Alright. I'll…go."

And it was a sign of how overwhelmed she was, that she actually turned her back on the semi-Creature and walked into the darkness.

⁕

In his cosy, quiet spot in the borderlands behind Davinia D'Andria's destroyed house, Luca curled his awkward, massive body around the symbol of his success, and smiled.

In the normal realm, in an apartment in Erus's capital city, Luca's human carrier smiled along with him. "It worked," both forms said in unison. "It *worked*."

And now there was just one more thing to do. Three days to go, and one last important thing before he'd set up the Kingdom of Luca, ready to go indefinitely.

"*Legion.*" The digital voice echoed across Luca's physical apartment as Lilith's face appeared on all four wall-screens, super-sized to show her bright yellow irises. "*I have news.*"

He barely held back a sigh. "Surprise me."

His mother's eyes narrowed. "*The Tiger has shortened the timeframe. Everything's going so well that the change will take place tomorrow instead of in three days' time.*"

Luca jolted upright, appalled. "What!? Tomorrow? That's not nearly enough time!"

"*Enough time for what, Son?*"

For some lightweight treason, of course! "To prepare myself for the new regime," he said testily instead. "Life will be different, as you well know. I'm making arrangements to ensure I'll be comfortable. It's not as if anyone else will."

There was a silence from the screens, the sort that could mean confusion or serious thought or more likely, Lilith trying to make him uncomfortable. Then she said, "*Don't do anything stupid.*"

"Do I ever?" Luca said sardonically, but she'd already gone.

Tomorrow. That was…too soon. Time to get desperate.

He turned to his comm unit, moving smoothly into VR and

connecting to that one person in Dailan province that he'd intentionally made contact with, just in case. "Darling!" he said with an enthusiasm he most certainly didn't feel. "How do you feel about coming to visit tonight?"

Luke's most recent ex expressed her excitement and asked about bringing a visitor.

"Our little boy?" Luca asked. "Oh yes. I wouldn't *dream* of leaving him behind."

Moving south from Elsewhise took hours, even though Jon was able to fly some of the time. He carried Bets for as long as he was able, at one point having her on his back like a backpack, but as afternoon stretched on, his arms felt like jelly.

Tarie had been steadily growing since they'd exited the safekeeper, so carrying her was out of the question, luckily. But her strange strength had also channelled into impressive speed and endurance, so she ran along the ground as Jon and Bets flew low just above her.

The trail of red-leafed plants she left behind her somewhat thwarted their attempt to remain unseen, but as she pointed out, it wasn't as if she could help it. Everything was…strange. Strange, and out of control.

But at least everyone was still alive.

The sun was low to the horizon when they entered a familiar area.

"This is where that hidden village is!" Jon exclaimed. "The one with all the unpledged Halflings! I wonder if they'd let us stay overnight?"

"I don't see anything," Tarie began, but still she let Jon take her by the shoulders and descend over the false cliff, a little too fast for comfort.

One of the girls let out a squeak of surprise, which turned into a gasp as the real village came into sight. Jon dropped to the ground, feeling oddly proud of the village, even though he'd had nothing to do with it, and it wasn't really that impressive.

Bets straightened her clothing, looking around curiously. "What an odd little place. Is that man sleeping?" She pointed at a small figure slumped over at the base of a boulder.

Jon recognised the thickset form, although couldn't recall the Halfling's name. He frowned. Something didn't seem right.

"Um," Tarie said from behind him. "We've got a dead girl here."

And they did, he confirmed soon enough. The pale girl he'd met this morning lay on her back, limbs askew and eyes blank. Her lips were an unnatural shade of grey.

"I thought you said they were unpledged," Bets whispered from beside him. She was tucked into his side, her eyes wide, and he wondered if she'd ever seen a dead body.

He hadn't. Had he? But he felt numb even as he noticed the dark shape embossed on the pale skin of the dead girl's forehead.

It was a familiar leggy shape, like a spider starfish.

The mark of the Tiger.

It didn't take long to confirm the other figure was in the same shape. It was the man Jon had also met this morning, and he was just as grey, just as dead, with a matching pledge mark on his forehead.

So were the other seven people they found lying around, as if they'd been left where they fell. There were no other marks on them.

"I'm guessing they didn't choose those pledge marks," Jon murmured desolately. "Do you think the marks killed them?"

"No," Bets said definitely. "They were killed by something like a soul-drinker. That's how one ends up so still and grey – when the life is rapidly stolen from a person." She frowned. "Or at least 'tis what Anne told me, and I wondered why she would share such a thing. Mayhap she saw this dreadful moment coming."

"Soul-drinker." Tarie looked down at her pack, which held half of their precious collection. "Does that mean they'll wake up if we can find that soul-drinker and get them out of it somehow?"

Bets shook her head. "Soul-drinkers are much different from safekeepers. They kill at once – or so I am told – leaving only power behind. The soul goes…elsewhere."

There was a solemn silence, which Tarie broke by shuddering. "Well, if they're beyond help, then I don't want to stay here another moment. What if the killer is still around? Jon, have you got it in you to take us back out?"

Jon didn't want to stay either. "You have to leave by a different entrance," he said.

He pointed in the direction he'd left by last time, and Tarie strode towards it, Bets barely trailing her. Jon moved to follow them, casting his gaze once more around the terrible scene.

How could it be so…clean, for a place of violence? How could people go from alive to dead so very rapidly? And why was death so…obvious? It was as if he could *feel* the life was gone, even though at a glance, they almost looked asleep.

Jon paused by the small figure at the boulder, and saw a couple of little grey balls half hidden in the rock's shade, as if they'd fallen from a pocket and been forgotten.

Truth spheres. That was what they were – and this man's name was Elvan. He'd had Jon spilling his guts about the stupidest things, because he hadn't been able to help it.

Without stopping to think, Jon bent down and scooped up the truth spheres from the ground, slipping them into his own pocket. "Sorry," he whispered to the dead man, feeling like a thief even though there was no one to miss these things now. "And thank you."

Then he quickly moved to catch up with the other two.

Maia had run all the way back down the hall to Davinia's house before she remembered she'd set off the alarm. The door leading to the main house was shut, somewhat bent, and red powder stained the minute gaps around its frame.

She looked over her shoulder, back at the darkness where the semi-Creature waited with her Amaranthus circlet, then back to where the hall led past the main house and out to the street. That door looked damaged too.

Maia sniffed at the air, noting the tang of something she'd rather not inhale, then sighed. She took three distinct steps back towards the Other – just far enough to escape the chemical alarm, but not far enough for Luca's Creature to reach her – then sat down, her back flat against the wall. If this worked how it was supposed to, her current location wouldn't matter.

If it worked? It *would* work! It had to, she told herself. But her fingers trembled as she crushed the first, smallest bead on the time-chain and focused on her destination.

"Back to when the curse was set," she said aloud. "Right when it was set, so I can see who did it."

For a moment nothing seemed to happen. But then suddenly, *splotch*! The bead burst in her hand, spilling sticky goo over her fingers. She caught the barest glimpse of a tiny metal shape inside it before just as suddenly, amber filled her vision.

It was like she was inside a golden bubble, just big enough to fit her crouched form. Through the viscous layer she could see a new environment around her. Inside a small, cluttered room, a girl crouched over a mass of glowing strings in fiery orange, red and purple. They were wrapped around what looked like a chicken's egg, and Maia knew in a moment that egg was meant to represent her. This was the curse being laid.

As for the person laying it…

"Cahlie?" Maia exclaimed in dismay, her words muffled by the bubble's wall, but feeling less surprised than she'd expected.

Cahlie. Maia's former schoolmate who she'd briefly spoken to yesterday- *ah*, the day before she was lost in the Other realm. The day she'd gone back to her hometown, Elsewhise, to visit her mother. Cahlie, who always seemed like she couldn't decide if Maia was her friend, or if she hated her.

Cahlie had laid that horrible rejection curse on Maia, and it had ruined her life. Luke had left her, and so had her mother, and everybody else who could have possibly helped her had seemed uninterested. Too busy.

Because of Cahlie. But *why?*

Maia mouthed a curse word that disappeared into the bubble's sticky wall. If only she could have walked in at that moment, when the curse was being laid, she'd have had something to say!

Just then, a new figure burst into the room. It was a version of Maia herself – as if that very thought had called her into being. The alternate Maia looked down at the curse-laden egg, and her face twisted with fury. She reached for it, but Cahlie was faster, snatching it away a moment before Maia could reach it.

The two exchanged nasty words, and the real Maia couldn't quite hear them, but somehow she knew what was being said. The alternate Maia-in-the-room switched between calling Cahlie terrible names and begging her for an explanation, for any reason why she'd do such a thing to a friend.

And Cahlie was saying with a face twisted in disgust that Maia *wasn't* her friend; she hated her; and here were the reasons why…

"Everybody likes you, Maia. You're so chaos-damned perfect and talented. Well, they won't see you as perfect for much longer! See how you like it when no one wants anything to do with you!"

"Maybe people like me because I'm nice to them!" the alternate Maia shot back. *"Maybe if you weren't such a nasty, sarcastic fiend, people would like you too!"*

Well, that didn't help. Cue a stream of venomous words that Maia never wanted to hear about herself. Jealousy. Bitterness. So, so much jealousy coming from this girl…

In the bubble, the real Maia sat frowning, her attention fixed on the scene. This conversation had never happened. She was being shown a past that *could* happen, if she wanted it to. This was what would happen if she was able to challenge her enemy the very moment the curse had been laid.

Well, actually she'd wanted to go back to *before* the curse was laid, and stop it happening, but in her haste she'd used the wrong words. But she was already watching, so she just waited to see how the scene would end.

Then it turned extra-nasty. Cahlie ended up on a bench, holding the glowing egg above her head. *"No, I won't take the curse off you,"* she was saying with a sneer. *"You won't tell anyone, or else you'll be sorry."*

"I'm already sorry!" the alternate Maia snapped back. She was taller than the other girl, but from the ground, the egg representing her was held well out of reach. *"I'm sorry I was ever polite to you. I'm sorry I never realised what a petty, pathetic, vindictive witch you are."* On her wrist the Amaranthus circlet gleamed as if trying to call attention to itself, but the alternate Maia didn't notice it.

And then Cahlie's expression twisted into a snarl, and she hurled the egg right at the alternate Maia. It hit her in the chest and she caught it with both hands, but it was clear something was wrong. A moment later she pulled her hands away, revealing shattered shell and splattered yolk. The glowing threads of red, orange and purple glittered through the mess, which then turned a deep red.

Cahlie's eyes widened, her mouth open and edges

downwards, as the alternate Maia collapsed to her knees. The threads of power sprung out from the shattered egg, latching around her chest like a maddened box jellyfish. They pulsed once, twice; then the alternate Maia's mouth opened just a touch, and she fell over sideways. The curse shone deep red a moment longer, then turned dark.

In her amber bubble, the real Maia jolted upright, her eyes wide. She looked down at the chain in her hand, which now showed one less bead, then again at the scene in front of her.

That was…terrible. It looked like if she went back to the moment the curse was laid and challenged Cahlie, she would die… and baby Jayel Jonnamin with her.

Maia swallowed and leaned away from the scene as much as the bubble would allow.

Nope. She wouldn't be choosing this particular option to relive her past – because that alternate past wouldn't last very long at all.

"*Before* the curse was laid," she said with a shaking voice, squeezing her fingers on a second segment. "A day before it was laid."

And this time, she'd challenge Cahlie and make sure it could never happen.

— ✴ —

Inside a safekeeper

The ghosts weren't going to hurt him, Max decided. They were everywhere within the safekeeper, from the centre of stone colosseum to the safekeeper's curving walls, but they rarely seemed to notice him or care about him. They faded in and out of sight, occasionally interacting with each other, and in washed out, pale shades. But whatever they were, they weren't going to hurt him.

Memories, a whisper came. *Soul-drinkers hold an echo of those whose lives they stole, but not the soul itself.*

Max jerked upright from where he sat slumped on a bench of the colosseum. The voice had been quiet but clear, and somehow familiar. But when he looked around, he saw just more of those ghosts, fading in and out of sight.

"I thought this was a safekeeper," he said cautiously, still

133

looking around for the speaker.

Soul-drinkers can become safekeepers once the curse over them is broken, but they retain echoes of what they once were.

And then a man's figure appeared amongst the wavering crowd. This one wavered too, from tall to short to medium height, with features seeming to blur and change until they clarified into an ordinary man of unknown ethnic origin, dark eyed, with an expression of absolute kindness. "For you," the man said aloud, "this place *is* safety."

Max breathed out a sigh/laugh of relief. "It's you!" He'd met this man – or whatever he was – when he'd gone through a supernatural doorway along with Jon's protector, Fylax. There'd been a river, and he'd drunk the water, and he'd felt so clean…

"Me," the man said, smiling.

"How did you get in here?" Max asked. "Are you alright? I mean, I'm not really sure how I got in here either…"

And then memories flooded into his head, of talking with Tarie in that filthy old house, and of an alarm being set off and something toxic flooding his lungs…

Oh. "But…I feel fine now," he said.

"That," the man said, "is why it's a *safe*keeper. You're safe as long as you're inside. But I'm not here to get you out, not yet."

He stepped closer, close enough till Max could see the incredible depths of his eyes, could see the power overlaying him so heavily. This was not an ordinary man.

And then he held up his hand, palm upwards. In his palm sat a little glass vial of liquid, and shining on its side was the word *Truthteller*.

"What's this for?" Max asked, unable to take his eyes off it.

"It's from the Mountain of Glass, a true treasure indeed. Drink it, and you will know the truth. Not the truth only as it applies to you, or a heartless truth that destroys even as it's told, but the purest truth that does not change, no matter the circumstances."

That sounded terrifying, but also irrelevant. Why would Max need this right now? It seemed that what he really needed was health, to get out of this safekeeper in one piece, and some way to break the connection he might have caused between Tarie and his old Creature Gerak. Also, why had this man even shown up now?

Isn't truth always worth having? But when you know the truth, you will be FREE.

Well, he did need to be free, Max realised. This offer, strange as it was, would have to do. After all, the man hadn't steered him wrong last time when they'd met at the River.

He picked up the vial and drank its contents. At first it tasted like nothing, just like water, but then it hit him as sharply as liquor. And with it came understanding.

Oh. *Ohh.* So *that* was the truth!

"I'm free," he said in amazement. "When the bond was broken between me and Gerak, I was freed completely. He has no grip on me. No way to hurt my friends through me. I've got some old habits that are still sitting there, ones I can choose to continue or to give up, but I'm free of him. And I won't be fooled into believing that I'm not."

"Very good," the man said. "Also, the liquid will keep you just healthy enough to survive once you're brought out of the safe-keeper. Try not to panic, will you?"

"Uh…?"

Max looked down at his hand to where the vial had now vanished, and when he looked up, the man was gone too.

Try not to panic?

9

Changing the Past

This time, when Maia crushed the second bead, she got the wording right. A day *before* the curse was laid on her. Then she'd be able to challenge Cahlie and make sure the curse never happened.

A new amber bubble sprang up, and Maia watched eagerly as a version of herself sought out Cahlie at a gathering on the edge of the town, where it turned to fields. Full of righteous fury and wearing the bright Amaranthus circlet around her wrist, this alternate Maia stormed up to Cahlie and let her have it.

"I know what you're doing, Cahlie, you jealous, backstabbing-" Oh, and Maia had forgotten she even knew that word… *"You're planning to curse me. Tomorrow. Well, I'm not going to let you do it."*

And then Cahlie, surrounded by dozens of familiar faces from all ages, looked up at the other Maia and smiled. *"Prove it,"* she said, and in that moment, Maia saw a Creature's smile reflected on her face.

Well. In the scene, the alternate Maia…couldn't prove it. She gave great detail about what had happened/would happen – a 'vision', she called it – and then described the curse itself in great detail too. But when Cahlie's workshop too proved to be empty – the curse clearly being a one-day creation – the alternate Maia threw up her hands in frustration.

"I know she's planning it," she exclaimed to another friend. *"I know it, but I can't prove it!"*

"Seems to me that proving it isn't the problem," the friend replied. They'd taken her statement in their stride – after all, this was Elsewhise, and Cahlie wasn't known for being sweetness and light. *"It's stopping her from doing it."*

136

Huh. Good point. And so this version of Maia followed Cahlie to her house, which was on the third level of one of the taller buildings. Cahlie stopped at the balcony entrance, and when the alternate Maia said, *"I'm not going to let you do this,"* Cahlie screamed, *"Stay away from me!"* and jabbed Maia with something she'd tucked up her sleeve.

Blue light sparked, and the alternate Maia clutched her stomach, her eyes wide. She stumbled backwards…and fell right over the balcony, whose protective barrier wasn't working that day.

Crunch.

In the darkening bubble, present-day Maia blanched. Well, now she knew what she looked like with a broken neck. She wouldn't be replaying that scenario, either. Who knew Cahlie was so violent? That was two different death scenarios in a row!

"But it could have gone differently," she mused aloud. "I was so up-front and forceful. What if I'd been sneaky and laid a curse on Cahlie like, a week earlier? Or months earlier?"

But her hand paused over the third bead. She'd used up two very quickly, and all she'd learned was that Cahlie was happy to kill her. *Kill* her, which was a fair bit worse than a rejection curse.

Chaos. Maybe she was going about this wrong. Maybe she should avoid Cahlie completely, and look for a solution a little later in her own past.

Maia's comm light blinked in the semi-darkness, and she glanced down to see that several hours had passed, even though it felt like far less. It was well into the evening. No wonder she was tired.

But she wasn't ready to stop yet. "One more," she told herself. "One more try, then I'll take a break."

The sun was just beginning to rise when Tarie spotted something in the distance. The Way path was gone, so they'd been travelling on and off all night, only taking a few hours at a time for rest. By their estimates, the train wreck should be close, but…

"Was that forest there before?" she called up to the other two. Erus was full of random patches of trees, ranging from countryside thickets to proper woods, but this one seemed…odd. The trees were much too large, even from here.

Up ahead, a sleepy-looking Jon carried Bets on his back. Her head rested on his shoulder, and she jolted upright at Tarie's words. "Forest?"

"Wasn't there just one tree…?" Jon queried.

Tarie put her head down and forced herself to continue. She was exhausted from running at a pace far faster than her usual abilities, but she knew she couldn't stop. She dreaded seeing the blisters that no doubt lurked on her aching feet, though. These shoes weren't made for extra-large feet running hours on end.

Closer up, as the sun rose, the 'forest' was revealed as a stand of enormous trees. Not just the one that Jon had shaken that power-filled water onto, but many, arranged all along the length of the mangled train, whose shining carcass was tangled in the tree roots.

There must have been a dozen of the giants, all packed close together enough for their branches to intertwine, and each as tall as her apartment building back in the city. Each one had the red leaves of a Word-tree.

Tarie stopped in amazement some distance from the trees, and from the corner of her eye, she saw Jon come to land next to her.

"By the rood," Bets whispered as she slipped down off Jon's back, then moved closer. "'Tis a miracle."

"We don't know what they are yet," Jon warned.

"Oh, piffle. They are no danger; I'm sure of it. See, Tarie has been leaving a trail of them behind her!"

Tarie *had* been leaving a trail, she had to admit. The few times they'd stopped to sleep, she'd woken to find herself surrounded by knee-high seedlings, and herself back to extra-large size. But the dark had prevented her from seeing what she had actually left behind. Now, when she turned, she could see a trail of greenery leading right across the countryside. The closest were perhaps waist-high, and in the distance, some seemed to be mature trees.

Chaos. Now *that* wasn't subtle.

"Actually," Tarie said, cutting into Jon and Bets' argument, "we do know what they are. They're Word trees, which always come along with my gift being used." She frowned, moving closer. "Supposedly their fruit is good for healing."

"They sound rather like the Mountain of Glass to me," Bets said a little smugly. "And look, there is fruit!" She pointed upwards, her face lit with excitement.

So there was. The branches grew low and thick with leaves, and nestled among the lush foliage were glimpses of purple, red and white.

"Well, I'll test it," Tarie announced. She reached for a purple fruit, which fell off into her hand as she touched it. It was a little smaller than her clenched fist, and had a soft firmness that reminded her of a giant grape. "Mm, it smells good."

Jon was hanging back, his face screwed up. "Doesn't it look like an organ to you?"

"What? No!" Tarie looked at the fruit sideways, but could only see grape. Or maybe plum. "That's just wrong. Why would you even suggest that?" She took a solid bite out of it to back up her statement.

Rich, sweet juice burst into her mouth and she moaned. "Oh, this is *good!*" She finished it within minutes, then stretched her limbs, wiggling her feet in her too-tight shoes. "Huh. My feet don't hurt anymore."

Clearly encouraged, Bets joined her, and a few moments later, so did Jon. For several minutes there was just the sound of chewing as the three of them sat under the nearest tree and had an impromptu but much-needed breakfast. They hadn't eaten properly since the day before.

Tarie stopped counting after her fourth fruit. Taking a bite of one last purple fruit, she asked Jon, "Why did you say it looked like an organ? What kind of organ grows on a tree?"

He smiled ruefully. "Flashback to the White Prince's temple. You don't want the details."

Actually, Tarie kind of did, but she didn't push. She changed the subject. "So I'm feeling great," she said. "I think this fruit really does heal. Shall we test it on Max?"

"How?" Jon asked. "Shove it in his mouth the moment he's out of the safekeeper and hope it works?"

"Yes...?"

Bets raised her eyebrows but didn't argue.

Jon's mouth opened then closed again. Finally he said, "Alright. But if it doesn't work, we'll tell him it was your idea."

Ten minutes later, they were helping a very startled, fruit-splattered Max sit up. The redness of his skin was receding, but he looked stunned. Probably from the fruit-attack he'd just endured.

He wiped a hand across his mush-covered face. "Whuh…?"

"Oh good, you can talk," Tarie said in relief. "That means you can breathe."

"Have some more fruit," Bets piped in. And she shoved another handful of pulp into his open mouth.

"Go easy," Jon said. "We don't want him to survive that toxin just to choke to death."

Max swallowed – probably because he had no other choice – then lifted a hand, fending them off. "What's going on?" His voice was raspy but understandable. "Ugh, my throat feels like fire."

"Eat some more fruit," Tarie ordered. "It's medicinal."

"Uh…OK." But Max ate the rest without complaint, and his reddened face and eyes quickly returned to normal colours. "Ah, that feels better. What happened?"

They summarised the events since he'd gone into the safe-keeper, and his eyebrows shot up. "It's been that long? It felt like minutes."

"Yes, but you were asleep, were you not?" Bets said. "Sleep always distorts my sense of time passing."

Max frowned, shaking his head. "Asleep? No, not at all. I was walking around this place that was…quite a bit like Last Man Standing, actually. You know the colosseum?"

Tarie recognised that virtual reality game they'd played at Centre – basically a free-for-all of virtual murder. The last survivor won. It had been one of catalysts to Max/Rokal's worst treatment of Jon, and by the expressions on both boys' faces, they knew it.

Max cleared his throat. "Anyway, there was a white stone colosseum in there which seemed solid enough. But there were also dozens of other people! But they were transparent, sometimes, and they didn't notice me much. The man from the

River said they were just echoes from when the safekeeper was used as a soul-drinker."

The other three stared at him.

"Man from what river?" Tarie asked, wrinkling her nose. She looked down at the pale safekeeper dubiously. "And what's this about the safekeeper being used as a soul-drinker?"

"It was," Max explained. "Not anymore."

She certainly hoped so!

"I would've thought the colosseum was more surprising," Jon said grumpily, showing he also noticed the reference to Last Man Standing. "Something that size fitting in a safekeeper? How much space is in those things?"

Bets shrugged. "But ours was so small, was it not, Jon? Just big enough for the two of us, and I was so drowsy." She frowned. "Oh, but we had been drugged, had we not? That would explain our sleepy state."

Jon grunted, but his gaze was fixed on Max. One hand was in his pocket. "A lot of things have gone wrong around you," he said coolly to the other boy. "Can we trust you?"

Max looked startled, then slumped. "I wish you could, but I'm not sure if you can. I've got some bad habits still, you see, of behaviour from when I was a carrier, and I can't guarantee they won't come out by mistake once in a while.

"I mean, I know I'm free of Gerak! I'd started to panic a little because I remembered some things from when I was a carrier, like how Gerak would always get me to help people or trick them into owing us favours, then they'd be tied into servitude because I never specified the favour, and then I found myself making a bet against Tarie and getting her to owe me a favour-"

What!? Tarie's eyebrows shot up, and she folded her arms as Max rattled on, speaking faster and more openly than she'd ever heard him before.

"...And I was so worried that I'd done something to Tarie, like tied her to Gerak somehow? Or that *I* was tied to Gerak still! So I tried to get her to cancel the favour. I'd wanted a kiss anyway, not a favour, but she wasn't interested. But then I drank the truthteller and I realised I was still acting like a carrier even if I feel free.

"I need to act free. I need to choose to believe it, keep choosing the free type of behaviour, but like I said, I've got those old habits. So I want you to trust me, but what if there's something I just haven't dealt with yet or don't know about?"

"Max," Tarie began, frowning. Why was he talking so much? And had he really wanted a kiss?

But he continued rapidly, "Like, what if my nanites *are* being used for tracking? Someone mentioned my hair, but I also have a massive nanite tattoo on my back that changes every ten minutes but I can't remove it without surgery, and..."

Jon held up a hand, sighing. "OK, OK, that's enough. I get it. Your heart's in the right place, although apparently your hair might not be."

Max's mouth closed, his eyes wide. He looked as shocked as Tarie felt. "I- I couldn't stop talking. What...what did you do to me?"

"Nothing bad," Jon said, shrugging. He pulled out of his pocket a couple of little balls, which shone faintly in the morning light. "Truth spheres. I had to find out if Max really could be trusted, since we're listening to his advice in what's a really dangerous situation."

"Truth again, huh?" Max said mournfully. "It's been the day for it. But you heard me. I want to get it right, but I don't even remember everything that happened. Even without the Creatures, there's a good chance I'll screw up."

"We heard that you're afraid," Tarie cut in sharply. "Your intentions are good, and that's all we can expect from you. Right, Jon?" And she'd like to know where he got those truth thingies, too!

Jon shrugged again, and the corner of his mouth turned upwards. "Right. Max. Although if the nanite tattoos are a problem, then I'm in trouble too. I've got a small one on my ankle."

"Truly?" Bets piped up. "Might I see it?"

"Can we go back to all that stuff that's trapped inside the safekeeper?" Max interrupted. He still had purple and red mush splattered over his face and formerly white clothing, which was terribly distracting considering the conversation. "The River guy said the people I saw were just echoes, and I believe him, but it was a huge space, and I didn't see most of it. What if it's valuable?"

"It could've just been someone's storage closet," Tarie

mused. She studied the innocent-looking object. "Although, maybe there's something useful in there. What do we do if it's all just junk and echoes?"

Max threw his hands in the air. "Put it back in again?"

Tarie sighed and held up the safekeeper. "Anything and anyone else in this safekeeper, come out…there." She focused on an empty space away from the train.

Whoomph. There was a feeling of air being displaced, and suddenly Tarie found herself sitting on the highest seats of what was, yes, a sizeable colosseum, made of white marble. On the other side was Max, and down in the circular arena stood Jon and Bets, their mouths open in 'o's of surprise.

Tarie squeaked, and a red seedling sprang up from the stone next to her.

She hadn't expected *this.* There wasn't enough space for it either; to her right, the colossal trees grew *through* the marble in a way that shouldn't have been possible, and the train's mangled remnants merged strangely with the stone. As she watched, part of it cracked and fell away.

Jon threw his hands in the air. "Brilliant. As if the mega-flora over there isn't catching enough attention, we've just magicked up an entire ancient structure. Shall we send it back into the safekeeper, Tarie?"

Well, it wasn't much good to them out here, was it? "Let's check if there's anything useful first." She looked around. "I don't see any of those people echoes you mentioned, Max."

"Maybe they only exist inside the safekeeper," Max called across, looking relieved at the idea. "And there are dozens of rooms under these seats."

Tarie was about to respond in agreement when the air took on a strange, tingling tension. As if in slow motion, a bright light enveloped the centre of the colosseum where Jon and Bets stood. Max cried out, and for a moment, dark, thin figures stood out against the brightness, scattered around them.

Then the force hit Tarie. She was thrown backwards against the higher stone seats, vines springing up to cushion her, and her ears ringing. And when she was finally able to take in the scene around her, she saw the colosseum filled with fast-moving dark shapes, Max sprawled on his stomach with red pooling under his head…

…and in the centre of the colosseum, Jon and Bets were nowhere to be seen.

Erus City

As the new day was dawning, Luca's visitors arrived in a small hired vehicle at the entrance of his recently acquired mansion. He was gritting his teeth at their lateness, but he put on a smile regardless and welcomed them in. No point getting them here only to scare them away with his bad temper.

Luke DeMannard's former lover was dressed to kill, with bold lipstick in vibrant purple, a small Tiger pledge mark on her forehead, and a streak of sunflower yellow in her upswept hair. The similarity to Lilith made Luca want to curl his lip, but he hid that too. (See? Smart!)

And holding her hand was a small figure dressed in slightly too-large clothing, his hair the same soft brown as his mother's, but his eyes almost identical in shape and colour to the ones Luca saw in the mirror. In this body, anyway.

Luca crouched down to the boy's level, smiling in what he hoped was a fatherly way, but the child leaned into his mother, eyes wide.

"It's been a long time," Cahlie said as if in apology. "He'll get used to you."

"Of course." It had been a long time because Cahlie had cut off contact between the boy and Luke as a means of control, and because she was an awful person. And she'd leapt to visit once she realised her ex was now a Very Important Man, which was convenient because Luca really did need her right now.

Or the boy, anyway. (What was his name again?)

Luca slapped on a blinding smile. "Please, come in."

In they came, and the doors closed behind them.

Shortly afterwards, Cahlie was sitting in the only parlour Luca had bothered to furnish, her hands cupped around a small, colourful glass as she brought it to her lips. To her left, the boy played on the floor with an antique model of the solar system, from back when people had thought there were only ten planets.

"So why now?" she asked coyly, lowering the glass. "You turned me down two months ago when I asked if we could get back together. Why did you invite me today? Why in such a hurry?"

"Well, I did invite you yesterday, technically," Luca said, watching as she took another small sip of that drink. "But you were late."

Her smile faltered. "I came as fast as I could. I was still all the way in Dailan, and there are roadblocks in place what with the ruling Creature changes, and the western regions are inaccessible for some reason-"

"Yes, yes." He waved a hand dismissively. "And you had to leave Xavier in a hurry, because you were with him till the last moment. Couldn't risk that relationship till you had a sure thing with me, could you?" Xavier was the latest man Cahlie had left Luke for, and one of the longer relationships she'd had, as far as he could find out.

Now Cahlie's smile was gone. "You used to be more polite."

"I used to be a lot of things," Luca agreed. "I used to be Luke, for starters. Couldn't resist a confident girl, because if someone like that went after me, it made me feel like I was worth something. And in contrast, if someone begged for my attention, I was as disgusted with them as I was with myself."

Cahlie sucked in a breath through her nose. "I'm not begging for your attention; I'm here to give you another chance to get to know your son. You claimed you wanted it so badly."

The boy was watching them warily now, one hand moving the miniature spheres as they orbited the model sun far too close for accuracy. Luca spared him a brief glance. "You know, when Maia was here yesterday, she was smart enough not to drink anything I offered her."

"Maia was here!? I thought she was-"

"Dead? No, oddly enough she was just trapped in the Other for all these years. Showed up at her sister's house looking for her baby, still looking like she's eighteen years old." Now he allowed himself a real smile. "Such a disappointment for her to find her baby is as old as she is. But don't worry; we had a good long chat, and I daresay she knows exactly who was responsible for that curse that ruined her life."

White lines marked the sides of Cahlie's mouth, and her eyes bulged. "Is she here? Is this some kind of bizarre face-off you've brought me for, all these years later, for something I did when I was young?"

"Oh, no, no," Luca soothed. "She's off in the north, trying to find a way to turn back time, and good luck to her. I'm just purposely making you uncomfortable because I enjoy it. I expect that my carrier's painful memories and emotions have worn off on me somehow." He cocked his head to the side, enjoying the confusion on her face. "And I notice you didn't seem to understand my comment about the drink. Or does that mean the drink's working?"

Cahlie looked down at the half-empty glass, her movements now slow and exaggerated. "What…did…you…do?"

"It's more like, what am I about to do?"

The child he might regret a little, Luca thought, although it would be necessary to achieve his goals. But for Cahlie – he wouldn't regret his actions at all.

It seemed his carrier's bad feelings *had* rubbed off on him after all.

Elsewhise

Maia sat in that hall as the third bubble faded around her and stared thoughtfully at the time-chain's two remaining beads. Two chances at reliving her past. Only two more.

Chaos knew that this third one hadn't done her any good. She'd decided to be smart this time – to arrive *after* the curse was laid, since she hadn't been able to stop Cahlie laying it (or hurting her in the attempt). And then she'd set out to try every single curse-breaking method she could think of.

She'd watched the alternate version of herself approach dozens of people for help, from a disinterested and unpleasant Luke, to her tutors from the small centre she'd attended, to her mother (again). The last had agreed to help, as long as Maia ended her pregnancy.

Worst. Mother. Ever. Outside the bubble, Maia had thought of Davinia's unburied body and didn't feel quite so bad about it after all.

But no one would or could help. A few of the methods seemed to shift the curse a little: one of them turned its power strands green, which gave the alternate Maia a permanent twitch as she walked; and another partly shifted the curse's orange strands, but that only revealed something nastier and redder underneath.

But in the alternate past, alternate Maia didn't give up. She went outside of Elsewhise and into the Other realm, dangerous as it was. Present-day Maia watched as the other version of herself stood outside the entrance to a Creature city and spoke with a small hunched figure in a hood, its face hidden from view, and then multiple coloured threads of power were thrown over her arms and neck, almost like leashes...or chains.

The orange threads of Cahlie's curse slid off only to become part of the other coloured ones, which slithered over her to cover the remnants of dull red which still covered her body. And the bright gold of the circlet wrapped around her wrist went unnoticed...

In reality, in the empty hall at her mother's house, Maia sat staring dully at the wall. She'd have been worse off if she'd gone to a Creature, she realised. Here, this showed clearly that whichever Creature she sold herself to would have just given her another form of bondage, and she didn't even know what. Still didn't know what the dull red power lines signified, either.

Why did nothing work? Why was there no way out of this? Maia could only think to never get involved with Luke in the first place, since he was proving to be the opposite of a prize. But then there'd be no Jayel Jonnamin, and her baby was the point of this whole effort.

Maia thought back over the steps she'd taken in real life. She'd gone to her mother for help – none there – then had lost touch with Luke completely, and had finally given up and gone to the White Prince, hoping for a breakthrough with that particular Creature.

And she still didn't know what had happened there. She just remembered walking inside the dark, decrepit temple entrance, holding the glowing circlet, and finding herself in the Other realm, in front of a small stone building. And then...

Who knew.

Maia looked down once more at the last two beads of the

time-chain. Two chances to relive her past and to avert this disaster. She could try one of them to replay whatever happened with the White Prince, but it seemed incredibly risky considering how badly the rest of the attempts had gone.

"I don't know what I'm doing wrong," she said aloud. "There must be some way."

Her lips went to form the word *Amaranthus* as they'd done so many times before. But then she remembered that she didn't have the circlet – she'd given it to Luca in exchange for the time-chain – and in fact, in all those alternate pasts, she hadn't once used it again. She'd carried it around, but she hadn't tried to use it in any way to break her curse. It was as if she'd thought it was useless.

Maybe that was the mistake.

"But it didn't save me from this disaster," she pointed out to no one in particular.

And yet Luca thought it important enough to trade a precious time-chain for. Why is that?

Hmm. That was a good point. Maia was increasingly feeling like she'd got the worse part of the deal. That Luca knew something she didn't about the circlet and even this time-chain too.

What was she talking about? Of *course* he knew something she didn't. Of *course* he was messing with her in some way. That was what Creatures did, even semi-Creatures like the one controlling her former lover.

Maia moved to get up and grimaced as pins and needles shot down both legs. She'd been sitting here far too long – all night, if her comm was to be believed. She was in desperate need of a bathroom, a drink and a nap, in that order.

And then Luca had some explaining to do.

Near the wrecked train

One moment Jon stood in the arena of an ancient colosseum that reminded him too much of Last Man Standing, the bitterness of that memory overtaking the sweet taste of fruit lingering in his mouth.

And the next moment, as if in slow motion, there was a buzzing sound and he was enveloped in white light. He felt something grab at his collar, and suddenly he was being pulled backwards into a hazy golden space. He could see Bets out of the corner of his eye, then intense sound filled his senses as he landed hard on his backside, then bounced.

In the aftermath, as his ears rang, he heard Bets exclaim, *Forsooth, that was a close one! I'd vow that was an explosive of some kind!*

Jon would have to agree. He picked himself up from the oddly bouncy ground, grimacing out of habit rather than any pain. They were inside another of those golden/amber tunnels, the sort he'd been briefly pulled into on his journey up to Elsewhise. But outside and above them, the bright white light obscured all view. *Oh. We're inside the tapestry again.*

And there was Anne, who it seemed had just pulled them in and rescued them in the nick of time.

I vow, what he meant was 'thank you', Bets said from beside him. She hugged her sister tightly, their dark and red hair contrasting as they embraced. *Thank you, thank you. For all you say that death is worth the trouble, I'm not quite ready for it.* To Jon she said, *Did you say 'inside the tapestry?'*

"Or a thread," Anne said aloud, showing that their previous conversation had in fact taken place telepathically. "Or within a gateway, depending on how one views it."

Jon's eyebrows shot up. Now that was a clever trick, that he and Bets had also been speaking with their minds. He wondered if all his thoughts transferred – Deias forbid – or just the very intentional ones? But to Anne he replied, "The Other is complicated."

"Or mayhap we are merely too simple to understand it," Bets commented, sounding unconcerned. She looked around her with wide, curious eyes. "Ooh. How far do these tunnels go, I wonder?"

"In the other direction? A very long way," Anne said. "Tis the length of the tapestry, and will take you back in time as far as time has existed."

Jon studied the curving form, feeling not the slightest urge to travel the length of history. He turned back to where she'd pulled them in through, which was still obscured by white light. "And this way?"

"That's frozen in a moment in time. Also, 'tis the end of the tapestry, so I know not what comes next."

Both Jon and Bets turned to stare at the redhead. "You don't know?" Bets queried. "What of Amaranthus?"

Anne shrugged, holding her hands up with palms outwards. "If he knows, he has not said. From here, 'tis a mystery to me."

So basically like everyone else's experience of living life, Jon thought. Across from him, Bets laughed as if she'd got the joke.

I did.

Oh, he was doing it again. Huh.

Bets smiled at him, and it was like he felt the smile rather than just saw it. Something about being inside this tunnel made him feel...alive. Alert. With every sense at full capacity, but without being overwhelmed.

Bets' smile widened until a faint dimple appeared in one cheek. Then setting her hands behind her back, she meandered across to the other side of the tunnel and down a bit, back towards...wherever this place led. She paused a little way down, squinting through the golden wall at something out of sight. "Look, 'tis you!"

"What?" 'Twas – er, *it was* him, Jon saw as he moved to stand beside her. Through the tunnel wall, he could clearly see another tunnel that almost intersected with this one. Inside was another Jon, looking tired and confused as he wandered along the length of it. Just past him was another Anne. Both mouths were moving, but Jon couldn't hear what they were saying.

'Tis your yesterday, Anne said from beside him. *Do you recall?*

Oh, yes, he recalled! It was when some jerk had given him a real fright through the tunnel wall, and he'd thought they'd stolen the circlet...

...Oh.

Yesterday's version of Jon wandered closer, squinting at the three of them as though he could only just make out their forms from his side of the wall. His mouth moved as though speaking.

Grinning widely, Jon reached out a hand to touch the tunnel wall. Yesterday's Jon's eyes widened and he lifted his own hand – the one with the circlet wrapped around his wrist – to meet Jon's fingers. The circlet seemed to glow, its text lit up in fiery orange.

Quick as a flash, Jon reached through and grabbed at the circlet. It slid off easily into his hand as he pulled it back through the wall into his own tunnel. On the other side, yesterday's Jon lurched back, horrified, and clutched at his own wrist. When he looked down to see the circlet was still there, he scowled at the wall and said something like, *That's not funny.*

Actually, it was hilarious! He'd just stolen a copy of the circlet from his past self, and now both of them had it! On this side of the wall, Jon and Bets burst into laughter.

And on the other side, yesterday's Anne looked right through the wall at today's Jon…and winked.

Max's nose hurt. Also, his head, and his shoulder, and one knee too. And why was he lying on this cold, hard surface? Bright lights flashed, filling the air in conjunction with soft, intense *pops* of sound, like gentle lightning.

He wiggled his arms and legs, confirming they all still worked, then pushed himself up to a sitting position. He'd fallen on the colosseum steps, he saw, and there was a sizeable patch of blood that seemed to have come from his nose…and maybe a split in his forehead. He touched one then the other gingerly, relieved when the damage didn't seem to be severe.

And the flashing lights that filled his vision were in fact weapon fire being rained down on a massive pile of red and green vines on the other side of the colosseum. The vines were moving and expanding like they were alive, and he'd bet his life that Tarie was underneath them.

Greenery. Weapon fire…? And where had Jon and Bets gone?

Max looked up to see a small hover-vehicle suspended high above the colosseum, open-topped and about the size of a regular two-seater. He could just make out two dark shapes in an armed vehicle that he hadn't seen outside of council facilities, the Creatures being strongly against ordinary people getting to do any form of flying. The two gunners seemed to have their attention fixed on the pile of vines and hadn't noticed Max was up.

His own gaze fixed on the hover-vehicle, he reached into his jacket pocket for a safekeeper. Sharp edges met his questing fingers, and he realised in dismay that two of the three he'd grabbed were broken.

Well. One would have to do. Holding the last remaining shell safekeeper up in the air, he focused on the hover-vehicle and its occupants. What was it Tarie had said? "You there, get into this safekeeper!"

Ugh. That sounded so stupid… For a fraction of a second the hover-vehicle seemed to blur towards him, and then it was gone. It had worked! But he'd already seen one figure leap off the vehicle and land lightly on the opposite side of the colosseum. The figure was wearing light armour including a face shield, and for a moment they seemed to look in his direction before they moved faster than he could think, blurring out of sight.

Max blinked – had that really just happened? Because he only knew one person who could really move that fast, and it was-

Suddenly the figure was right in front of him, and they hit his wrist where he held the safekeeper, sending it flying. It bounced down the stone steps and they lurched towards it, but he'd already got hold of them. They were fast, but he was strong, and he grabbed at the blurring figure's face shield and ripped it away.

"Gavriel."

Max had known it was him just by his speed, but his former friend looked different to when he'd last seen him. His good looks had turned sharp and predatory, with hollowed cheekbones and shadows under his too-dark eyes. A new pledge mark stood out against the skin of his forehead like a brand.

"You're not looking so good," Max blurted out.

Gavriel grinned – or was it a snarl? He gripped Max by the front of his torn jacket, and the grip made Max feel weak. "Speak for yourself, friend. You reek of blood and rotten fruit. I haven't ever seen you look so battered."

Fair, except for the bit about rotten fruit. But… "Why are you trying to kill us?!"

"I'm after the Word speaker, not you," Gavriel said. "But you've picked the wrong team. Poor choice, Rokky, poor choice."

Something twisted in Max's chest. He was feeling weak, so weak where Gavriel gripped him, like he couldn't get a proper breath. But he could still fly.

Gathering the rest of his strength, he shot upwards, straight into the air, and Gavriel went with him.

"Last man standing, is it?" Gavriel said through clenched teeth. "Let's see who wins when it really matters." Now he was also gripping onto Max around the neck, surely to prevent himself falling the now-considerable distance to the ground. It was closer than they'd ever been to each other, but they hadn't tried to kill each other before.

Chaos-damned last man standing. Max couldn't get away from that stupid game. "Fine," he gritted out. He pressed one hand against Gavriel's forehead, grabbing at his fair hair and trying to push him away. What was Gavriel *doing* to him? Max had never known the other boy's full powers, not even when Max had still been a carrier, but it seemed…to involve…sucking the life…out of people…

"If…I fall," Max managed to say, "then you…will fall…with me."

"Not such a problem as you might imagine," Gavriel panted. One eye was stretched and distorted by how tightly Max was pulling at his hair, but he still didn't let go. "And then I'll kill the Word-speaker. I'll do it. I really will."

He meant it. He really meant to kill Tarie. She'd said as much earlier, and Max had mostly believed her, but it was different hearing it from Gavriel himself, and knowing he meant it.

Briefly lost for words, Max said the first thing that came to mind. "I remember when we were twelve and you pissed yourself laughing."

He'd agreed never to raise that again since Gavriel had seemed so embarrassed, but…well, if not now, then when?

Gavriel snarled, and suddenly the breathlessness became acute. It felt like Gavriel was ripping something inside Max's chest. Spots flickered in Max's vision, and he felt his grip weakening. *Fly up, fly up,* he thought intently; *the higher we go, the better chance that Tarie will make it.*

Max's vision turned to grey, and Gavriel's face in front of him vanished as if in a fog, and-

Elspeth stood in the odd little gold tunnel, watching the white-filled entrance curiously. It had not changed – for of course 'twas but one moment in time – and yet she found herself insatiably curious about what lay beyond it. If they returned to the moment they'd left, would they be burned up in an instant or exploded into tiny pieces? And if so, would they feel it?

She should probably worry about what was happening to Tarie and Max too, but in this endless moment, it did not seem so very worrying.

Next to her, Jon stood with the pilfered circlet in one hand and a smile on his face, same as he'd had since he'd regained the circlet. *Maybe there can only be one circlet in any one time,* Elspeth could hear him thinking, *but because I'm not in time, I can also have this, even though the fake-birth-mother-person also stole it from me. Or do I now have it from her…?*

And then just past him, Anne wore an expression of deep concentration. *Ooh, ooh, ooh,* she was thinking. *It's about to happen! And then what comes next? Ooh, they'll want to see this…*

"Want to see what?" Elspeth asked her.

"The very moment," Anne said breathlessly. "The end of the tapestry and of time as we know it."

Elspeth was not sure if she liked that sound of that. "And when might this be?" she asked cautiously.

"Through the white light, just past where you came in." Anne paused. "You do not have to, but I vow you'll be glad that you did."

Elspeth looked up at Jon, who held out a hand. "Shall we?" he asked.

Whyever not?

Nearby

In the depths of Erus city, the Tiger sat on his throne like a spider in the midst of a massive web. Thousands of power strands ran from him to the Creatures he now controlled, and from them, to billions of mortal beings. The vast majority of them now wore the Tiger's pledge: the physical marks tying them to him on a supernatural level and granting him a power they could never have imagined.

The very earth below them had changed. The mortals them-selves were changing.

And now…the power was just…enough.

Finally.

I'm doing it. I'm reversing the Rift and taking back what was stolen, and more still.

It's all going to be MINE.

Beyond the Tiger, from somewhere that wasn't really a place, Amaranthus watched. And also from here… and here… and here. He wasn't limited by space *or* time, unlike the Creatures.

But what he knew that the Tiger didn't, was that the Rift couldn't be truly reversed. They could never get back what had been; not when everyone involved had changed so completely.

No, what came next would be completely…new.

10
The Great Reversal

Maia was in the hallway leading to the Other realm when it happened. She'd found a bathroom and a drink but was yet to have a nap, so the sudden, earthquake-like lurch just made her extra irritable.

There was a flash of light in the darkened hall, then everything took on a blueish quality. Or was it red? Either way, the air tingled like the most alter-power-saturated parts of the Other realm, even though she knew she must barely be in the borderlands. Suddenly she could see the curse strands covering her arms and legs – the orange and red that seemed so much thicker and heavier than it had before.

And from somewhere very close, a horrible voice roared in her head. **MINE! It's all MINE!**

Ugh. *Awful.* That hadn't sounded like Luca's Creature, which meant there was another one somewhere around here. Maia stumbled and landed hard on one hand, then climbed back to her feet, muttering in irritation. She'd have to take extra care to avoid whoever that was.

Stupid Creatures. Stupid Luca. Stupid *her.*

Her head hurt. Rubbing at it with a red-and-orange-striped arm, she set her jaw and moved onwards.

At the same time

Tarie was under a mountain of Word vines, muttering non-stop with her eyes tightly shut. She was being bombed, and it was a miracle she'd survived this long. The crashes and flashes kept going until suddenly the whole world lurched around her.

For a moment she seemed to be upside down, and then there was silence. The atmosphere was tingling with potential, alterpower so thick she could almost taste it, and then- *PHOOF!*

Everything around her exploded with growth – including her. She felt her feet explode out of her too-tight shoes as her smart clothes were stretched to their limit. The vines that enveloped her were now each as thick as her waist, with leaves as big as dinner plates.

She lay for long moments in the sudden silence, panting and eyes wide. But when the explosions didn't resume, and she didn't seem to grow any larger, she relaxed a little.

Shaking her head, she set one massive hand on the nearest vine/trunk and hauled herself to her feet.

Also at the same time

Max opened his eyes to find he was falling. He was somersaulting towards the rapidly approaching ground, and he just needed to stop-

Too late.

Crunch. Max landed on the stone of the colosseum with an audible crack, and he knew he'd broken something he'd needed to keep whole.

Oh…dear…

And the world changed around him.

Yep, at the same time too

Jon stepped through the white, mist-like light at the end of the tunnel with Bets' hand firmly in his. For a moment the light was intensely, painfully bright, and then they were back out in the colosseum where they'd last been. But now it was covered in vines, some of which were blackened and scorched.

Then Max landed with a *splat* on the stone directly in front of them. A few moments later, a dark figure blurred away in the opposite direction.

Bets gasped, and Jon forgot to breathe.

Bets' hand tightened on Jon's. *By the rood,* he heard her think. *Max looks dead.*

Max did look dead. *So* dead. Jon didn't question that he could still hear her thoughts even out here, because he could hardly take in anything except that Max…was splatted on the stone in a way he really oughtn't to be.

Chaos. They should try to help him, Jon thought slowly, except that it was obvious he was beyond help…

And just then, on the crux of that terrible thought, the world changed.

There was a rumble like an earthquake, then an abrupt lurch which made Jon shift his footing so he wasn't sent sprawling. Then alter-power rushed in thick as fog, making his skin tingle. Next to him, Bets looked radiant, like a light shone from under her skin.

The nearest hills vanished, and others rose up from the ground, dry and brown and cracked as though from centuries of drought. And up ahead, where there'd been a massive expanse of green, an ancient city appeared. It was made up of blocky stone shapes mixed with curved ones with turrets and outcroppings, some crudely built as if made by a child, others ornate and detailed. Tiny doors or windows spotted the city all over, with darkness visible within. Next to the city, the nearest giant Word trees almost looked normal-sized.

Oh. That looked like a Creature city from the Other…except it was out here in the Erus countryside…

And Max was dead, Jon thought again. His mind seemed to be working too slowly, and he felt numb to the insanity going on around him. Parts of the countryside were gone, replaced with desert and strange structures, and in some places, all mashed together. The very air felt wrong…

And he finally realised what had happened. It felt like he'd had double vision, seeing two entirely different scenes, but now he just saw one.

"I can't believe I'm saying this," Jon said carefully, "but I think the Other realm has merged with the normal, because I'd swear that's a Creature city right there."

And Max was dead. In this moment, that felt like the bigger

problem.

Bets didn't speak. She just clutched his hand more tightly.

To their left, the pile of now-enormous vines shifted, and out came an equally enormous Tarie. She must've been eight feet tall, and her clothing no longer reached her wrists and ankles. She pushed her mass of hair out of her face, looking around anxiously. "You two! I thought you were killed in that first bomb!"

Jon blinked, finally seeming to regain control of himself. "Ah...yes. I mean, no. We didn't die." Unlike someone else. His gaze slowly turned back to Max. "You think the Word fruit would heal...that?"

Tarie's face crumpled. "Oh no! What happened?" She rushed over to Max and crouched over his still form, her expression distraught. "He looks...he looks..."

"He fell," Bets said into the silence, her voice small. She moved to follow Tarie, setting a hand on the girl's massive shoulder. Next to Tarie's new size, Bets looked like a child. "We came too late to catch him. I am so dreadfully sorry."

Tarie was shaking her head. "But...but...this wasn't supposed to happen!"

Of course it wasn't meant to happen, Jon thought, still feeling numb. Their people weren't meant to die like this, were they? Not even one of his least favourite allies like Max. Gone in an instant. It all felt so unreal, and he felt so disconnected, that when something wet trickled over his foot, he looked down. An inch of water gleamed over the pale stone surface. It seemed to be rising.

"We're in a puddle," he remarked. "Where's that water coming from?"

"What?" Tarie looked up indignantly. "Max could be...*dead,* and you're talking about wet feet-"

And then the flood came.

It rushed up from under their feet and poured over the stained steps of the colosseum, moving up over every surface in defiance of gravity – except for the Creature city, which it noticeably missed.

It sparkled and shimmered and *burst* with alter-power life, and Jon couldn't help but laugh as it drenched him from head to toe, seeming to rush over him as if it was alive, but never getting more than a few inches deep on the stone they stood on.

"It's water of life from the Mountain of Glass!" he breathed in amazement.

"What does that even mean?!" Tarie shot back, pushing the water off her face with one hand. But she seemed calmer. "What in chaos is going on here?"

How was he supposed to know?!!

And then the water turned into mist, lifting away from the ground in a thick layer of gleaming droplets. In a matter of seconds, it passed over them, and as it covered Jon's eyes, it seemed unbearably bright. In that brightness, for the merest moment, Jon would swear he saw the Mountain of Glass.

Then the alter-power water moved past them, and he looked up to see it move higher and higher until it reached higher than the highest buildings. Then it settled, sitting there in a shimmering, reflective, silvery sheet as if marking the end of the atmosphere.

"Oh my," Bets breathed from beside him. "Whatever do you think that is?"

"I don't know." But something had occurred to Jon while the water was passing them by. "Bets...have you seen Fylax lately?"

"I have not."

Jon slumped. He'd seen his guardian Fylax on his brief visit to the Mountain the day before, and he'd been heading upwards into the light, along with many others. Jon had assumed the guardian would come back, because wasn't he always there? But Anne had never confirmed as much...

Chaos. Jon made so many courageous decisions in the last few days because he'd thought Fylax was invisibly backing him up, just as he had been Jon's whole life. But...what if once Jon destroyed the White Prince, Fylax went elsewhere?

Huh. He should probably be more upset about that, too, but apparently he was still in shock, because he felt...neutral. Also, they had bigger problems.

Then he looked at the stone where Max had been lying in that unnatural pose, red under his head. It was empty, gleaming as white as if it had just been cleaned.

Max was gone.

Tarie's mind buzzed with grief and confusion. Mountain of what? Fylax who? What was happening here? What was that place and those people, and why was she so fracking enormous? And who was attacking them *this* time?

And Tarie didn't want to even *think* about what might be happening to her father and Lydia.

And Max... Max... was gone.

Tarie sat down on the rapidly drying stone, straddling an oversized vine, and burst into tears.

"Don't panic," she heard Jon saying quietly to Bets, "but those Word trees are growing fast. Probably because they just got hit with water from the Mountain. Maybe we should move back, or...?"

'Or' turned out to be the vine Tarie was sitting on exploding in size. It shot out in every direction until it was as wide as a table, and rushed upwards. She fell backwards but was cushioned by more leaves, now also colossal, as the vine warped and grew into what seemed to be a branch of yet another vast tree.

She didn't panic. She'd hit her panic quota for the day, because enough bad things had happened that she just felt numb. Oh, a giant tree was forming directly underneath her? That was OK.

And when the vine/branch finally came to a halt, she found herself completely surrounded. The branch was wide and flat, and pressed right up against another similar branch, which was a little higher. Then another beyond that, then another. It was like an oversized spiral staircase, and the leaves were enclosing the whole space with red and green. She had no way of telling how high in the air she was.

She climbed to her feet and took a few careful steps up the staircase – leaps, really – and came to a ceiling. It shimmered and moved like water, if water could ever be a ceiling rather than a floor, and reflected with a full rainbow of colours.

Tarie just stared. She had no idea what was beyond it, but she certainly wasn't going to try to find out. Not after the day she'd had, with Max...

She couldn't get the image out of her head. Her pushing her way out of the pile of vines only to find Jon and Bets just standing and staring, and Max lying there in a bloodied heap...

She choked back a sob. If that could happen to him, when

they'd been so determined to make this time count and to do something amazing for the Unfading One, then why would she be safe? She wasn't so special.

Just then, a tiny twig grew out of the branch over her, blossomed into a little white flower, and then into a fruit which deepened to a rich purple.

Tarie blinked at it, and it shook a little on the branch as if trying to get her attention. Its beautiful fragrance tickled her nostrils, and her stomach rumbled.

She slumped, sighing heavily, then took the fruit. No sense being sad *and* hungry.

It was a good choice, she decided as she finished it in two mouthfuls. It tasted delicious, and her mood had even lifted a little along with her energy levels. "But I'm still *really upset!*" she muttered to no one in particular, looking around for another fruit. "Everything's going to chaos down there, and a nice fruit doesn't make up for losing a friend!"

She spotted another fruit nearby, clearly ready to eat, and picked it with an almost aggressive movement. "And another thing," she said through a mouthful. "I've grown so, fracking, HUGE! I can feel it, although I don't know exactly how big I am. And that feels threatening, because I only ever grow when there's some kind of challenge to face!"

And what kind of challenge would need her to be so huge? Nothing good!

Just then, there was a rustling sound from behind her. "You did notice that the Other and the normal realm have merged, right?" a male voice came clearly. "That's quite threatening to most people. Or the smart ones, anyway."

That sounded like Max. But it couldn't be, not when he'd seemed so *dead*…

Tarie turned slowly, afraid to even hope, but with her spirit lightening immeasurably. And there he was, poking his head through the thick leaves at the end of the nearest branch, a cautious smile on his face.

"I…thought you were dead," she stuttered. He had *looked* dead, lying there in a bloodied heap, but she hadn't had a chance to check his pulse…

"I thought I was too," he said frankly, climbing through the leaves to join her on the wide branch. "And then right after I fell, the water came. And now I feel fine. Great, actually- *oof.*"

Tarie had launched herself at him and was hugging him tightly. He seemed remarkably small compared to her unusually tall state, but he was solid and warm and healthy and unexpectedly clean now, and she was so relieved that she cried. "Are you really alright?"

"I'm alright! I'm fine!" Max sounded strained. "You don't need to squeeze me so hard..."

She loosened her grip and leaned back to examine him. She couldn't see any injuries – or even any marks on his clothing – but for some reason, that made her cry harder. "Don't do that again," she whispered through her tears. "No getting hurt like that, OK?"

The corner of his mouth quirked. "I'll do my best."

Tarie scowled. It wasn't funny! "And no letting me think you died! I thought Jon and Bets died too, in that explosion, but I didn't have time to think about it before I saw they were alright. But you, you I had time to cry over, and I didn't like it!"

"Me *and* Jon and Bets all at once, wow. What are the chances?"

He was still smiling. It really bothered Tarie that he was still smiling. She opened her mouth to tell him so – her relief easily slipping into anger – but he cut in.

"Now, do you want to go up or come down? As nice as this is, we should probably make a decision."

Tarie's eyes widened. "Up...like through that water stuff?"

Max nodded.

"What happens if we go up?"

"I...don't know. But I wouldn't mind finding out."

She let out a scoffing sound. Curiosity wasn't a good enough reason to risk going into what was clearly intense alter-power. The sort that could transform you...or turn you into dust. "So that's a *down* from me. Jon and Bets are still there, anyway, and we have to meet my family on the south-west border."

"Fair enough."

So down they headed, even though Max surely could have flown a lot faster. There was no way he'd be carrying her in her current state.

"I can't help thinking these trees are my fault," Tarie admitted. "They're a version of Word trees, although I lost control of the Word power days ago."

"Fault? That makes them sound like a problem."

She shot Max a sidelong glance. "What would you call them?"

He shrugged as he jauntily stepped down another enormous branch/stair. "An opportunity? I don't know, but this doesn't seem accidental. The normal and Other realms have merged, Tarie! And now these trees have appeared. They must have some purpose."

He had a point, she admitted to herself. Then another thought occurred. She'd been speaking the Words her whole life, on and off, sending little Word seedlings into the ground everywhere she'd visited. Assuming some of them had made it, that meant there'd be arboreal staircases all across this part of the country and in her birth state of Memrys.

That was a lot of giant trees!

"Huh," she said lightly, even though inside her, something leapt with joy. Had there been a greater purpose to her challenging 'gift'?

"I hate to rush things," Jon's voice came up the staircase, "but we've got a slight problem down here."

Luca was gone. Or Legion, or whatever the Creature with too many eyes was calling himself. In the strange blue/red light that persisted into where the Other began, Maia could clearly see that the cave where she'd left him was completely empty. There was a foot-wide chunk of rock missing from the ground where the circlet had been, like it had been glued down so he'd just taken the ground along with it.

Maia stared at the empty space, her lips a flat line and her fingers tightening around the last two beads of the time-chain.

She should have expected as much. It was like a too-slick virtual reality vendor who sold shoddy goods and then ceased to exist when you went back to complain. And Luca, or Legion, was the epitome of slick.

What was she going to do now?

Maia hung her head, and distinctive lines of orange and red caught her attention. There were two distinct threads leading from her chest, off into the semi-darkness. They led approximately in the same direction: one orange, one bright red.

She frowned. They were the alter-power manifestation of the curses and bindings affecting her, and she wouldn't normally see them outside the Other. If she knew her alter-power, they'd each lead to the person responsible.

She remembered the red one was Luca's – he'd laid intimidation over her so even though the orange rejection curse remained, she'd still get what she wanted from people.

But wasn't there a duller red one underneath too?

Maia studied herself once again, and yes, there *was* a distinctly different red one, underneath it all. But where was the power thread?

She eventually found it by looking over her shoulder. It led from her back, not her front like the other two, and it was misty, almost transparent, but very much there. And unlike the brighter two, it seemed to be made up of many fine threads.

Maia turned and followed the dull red line across the room…and to the pile of cloth and bone that she'd been distinctly *not* looking at. It was a lot easier to see now that everything was lighter in here.

"Mother," Maia groaned in intense disappointment. "What did you do to me?"

But of course there'd be no answer. Davinia was gone, and all that was left most certainly wouldn't be able to explain why Maia carried an old, old curse on her body – one that had gone unnoticed until now.

But now Maia had a clear line to Luca/Legion, and even to Cahlie, should she want it. But by the look of things, they were in the same direction.

She set her jaw and headed off after the Creature.

It didn't take long for Maia to realise that something was wrong with the world. The oddly coloured light, the extra-high levels of alter-power in the air – they carried on outside in Elsewhise too.

And the town looked different now. Some parts were missing, and other buildings had been replaced with ancient-looking stone structures that reeked like old outhouses. And the people – they wandered with their heads tucked down, muttering to themselves, and didn't seem to notice her.

But it was when she saw the Creatures that she realised something was really, really wrong.

The first one was mostly human-shaped and looked like a soldier wearing a bird-headed helmet. She hadn't thought anything of it, because Elsewhise was full of unusual folk.

The second one looked like a big human wearing a fur coat; also easy to ignore.

But Maia ran into the third Creature when she turned a corner, and hitting that thing full force was an entirely different experience. The leathery, discoloured skin; the dead eyes; the *smell* – she knew at once that she was meeting a real, true inhuman, and it was nothing like the stories. Not lovely. Not supernatural. Just...ugh.

It grabbed at her, and she shoved it away as a cloud of silvery fog came rushing out of her hands. The Creature screamed (that sound was a scream, right?) and lurched back, and she turned and sprinted for the outskirts of the town, not slowing until she'd left it all well behind.

She looked down at her hands, checking them front and back. They looked normal, without a hint of that silvery fog that had chased away the Creature. And when she tried to replicate it, nothing happened.

Maia sighed and dismissed it. Her replicating abilities meant she occasionally did strange things without explanation. This time, it had saved her. That was all that mattered.

But out here, where the land was open, Maia could see even more differences. The sky seemed too low, like there was a strange, dense cloud at about the level of the tallest buildings. And in the distance she could see the irregular clump that made up Erus city. It should be hours away by vehicle, but when she squinted at it, it seemed somehow...close? Like she could reach it quickly if she tried.

And where had those super-sized trees come from? She didn't know trees could get that large. These ones were every-where, oddly shaped, and emanating alter-power she could feel even from here. She shivered.

"The world is turning upside-down," she said aloud, "but I just need to get back to my past. Then all of this can be forgotten like the nightmare it is."

She looked down at the bright red thread that would lead

her to Luca. It was almost perfectly intertwined with the orange thread that was Cahlie's curse, and both of them shot off in the direction of Erus city. Now why might that be?

Maia checked the precious time-chain beads were still her pocket, then set off.

Jon waited at the base of the tree that grew directly from the stone of the colosseum. From here, its trunk and tightly knit branches looked remarkably like a spiral staircase.

A few minutes later, Max came into view, walking down the oversized branches/stairs.

Jon had heard Max talking with Tarie, so seeing him wasn't a surprise. He looked incredibly healthy for someone who'd seemed dead only ten minutes earlier.

Jon knew he ought to be shocked by all of this. Like he ought to be horrified at the damage Max had taken, and thrilled at Max's sudden return. And he *was* thrilled. But he wasn't surprised. He still felt strangely disconnected from everything happening around him, and all he could think was: *Of course. Of course Max is fine. That's what the water of life is for!*

And seeing Max now made it so clear how different this Max was from his carrier self as Rokal, and the last of Jon's resentment against his old enemy finally fell away.

Thanks, Max said. *I'm not mad at you either, anymore.*

Oh! Max was doing the telepathy thing now, too. Somehow that didn't overly surprise Jon either. But... *Why would you be mad at me?*

Because you broke my legs that one time.

It hadn't even occurred to Jon that Max would have any reason to hold a grudge. It didn't seem fair that he would after all the times he'd hurt Jon without consequence, but then humans weren't always fair.

Max shrugged, smiling crookedly. *That's true. Fresh start?*

Jon thought about it. *Alright.*

Then Tarie followed Max into view.

Whoa. Tarie was giant! Like, possibly a record-breaking size right now. Jon had better not say anything because she was probably sensitive about it, but it was a miracle she hadn't busted right out of her clothes like some kind of…Incredible Bulk.

Bets gave him a sidelong stare from where she waited beside him, but it held amusement rather than censure. Then to Tarie she announced, "Do not be alarmed, but some form of villain is hiding in the colosseum and we've been unable to catch him thus far, even with my flame or a safekeeper. He moves dreadfully fast, but does not approach the trees." She patted the trunk as if in confirmation. "Thus far I have been able to hold him off with my flame, but every time we step out from the tree, he attacks us."

In the short time since the trees had grown (again), taking Tarie with them, and Max had leapt up suddenly from the ground and flown up into the tree as well, a dark shadow had appeared half a dozen times. It had come near to striking Jon, but Bets had frightened it off with her flame. But it was too fast to spot, too fast to speak into the safekeeper Jon still held…

"Gavriel," Max said. "I guess he survived the fall after all. Chaos, he's hardy."

"Gavriel!" Tarie looked around, suddenly tense. "Are you sure it's him?"

"Unfortunately, yes. I had a run-in with him while you were buried by vines, Tarie, and the other two exploded-"

"We did not explode," Bets said indignantly. "We are all in one piece, are we not?"

"Yes, yes, you were saying something about a run-in?" Tarie continued impatiently. "Is that why you were lying on the ground like you were dead?"

"I suppose it was." Max frowned. "I've got a bad record with falling, which is ironic, huh?"

Jon thought so, too. Not too long ago, Max had almost dropped Jon to his death – back when Max went by Rokal, and Jon couldn't fly.

Max continued, "Anyway, there were two people on a hover-vehicle, and they were firing like mad at the vines. Left me alone for some reason. I managed to get the vehicle into a safekeeper along with one of the people, but the other charged at me." He smiled sheepishly. "I've also lost the safekeeper somewhere around here…"

"Never mind that!" Tarie cut in. "Attacker. Somewhere around here. Gavriel again?"

Max quickly explained what had happened to him while Jon

and Bets had been 'away' – actually inside the time-tunnel. It sounded brief and violent, and Jon thought that if the water hadn't come when it did, Max would be dead for sure.

"Why is it always bloody Gavriel?" Tarie burst out. "What's he got against me that he has to be so Chaos-damned relentless? That's it! I'm not putting up with it any longer!" She took her safe-keeper and stormed out from under the shelter of the tree. "Gavriel!" she shouted. "Get over here!"

A shadowy figure blurred into sight, and for the briefest moment Jon recognised Golden Gavriel, wearing dark armour and with a strangely hollow, thin face. But he looked…awful. Blue bruises marked under his eyes, which shone an odd yellowish orange…

He rushed at Tarie…and vanished into the safekeeper she held up. It didn't even rattle.

There was a long, shocked silence. Jon couldn't believe that had actually worked!

"Good riddance," Tarie said finally, but she looked shaken too.

"What an anticlimax," Jon muttered. "*We* could have done that, if we'd known who he was."

"We do have the circlet," Bets encouraged him. "We could still dispose of him, should my flame fail to separate him from his Creature."

"Circlet?" Max and Tarie said in unison. Tarie added, "I thought you lost that yesterday!"

"Long story," Jon said sheepishly.

It wasn't that long, Jon found once he recounted it. Quite quick, actually. But while he answered questions, Bets wandered up to the highest steps of the colosseum where it was hemmed in by a ring of oversized Word-trees, and peered through a gap.

Jon, she thought at him a few moments later. *We have another problem.*

Don't say it's another super-fast assassin?

Er…mayhap worse?

"What are you two miming at each other about?" Tarie asked impatiently, because of course she wasn't in on their silent conversation.

"Do not be alarmed," Bets called down, "but we are

surrounded by Creatures, and more approach by the moment."

Tarie's jaw dropped, and Bets added quickly, "I did say not to be alarmed."

"Why would we not be alarmed?!" Tarie hissed, her eyes wide enough to show whites all the way around the iris. "That's alarming! And why are you all so relaxed about this, huh?"

Jon wouldn't say he was relaxed, precisely. But he still felt that strange peace that he'd had since finding himself in the time-tunnel with Bets. He didn't know what to think of it except that it was really useful right now, when they needed clear heads.

He broke the awkward silence that followed. "Near-death experiences? The normal and Other realms having merged? Having reached the end of time? Panicking seems pointless now, don't you think?"

Tarie put her face in her hands. "I thought I'd lost my panic," she mumbled to herself, "but I've found it again."

Max raised his hand. "I also had a near-death experience." He frowned. "It really does seem to help with the panic, right?" *Also, I could fly away from here if I needed to. But I won't say anything to Tarie, because I wouldn't leave her behind, and I can't carry her now. Huh. I wonder if we could startle her into shrinking again...maybe throw her at the Creatures?*

Jon and Bets both gave Max incredulous stares. *You do know we can hear you, right?* Jon thought at him.

Oh. Max paused. *That's new, right?*

To us, indeed it is, came from Bets. *But 'tis no new thing in the Mountain of Glass. In fact, 'tis the usual manner of communicati-*

"Can we stop with the weird silent conversation?" Tarie cut in. "I don't know what the shrugs and the eyebrow wiggles mean, or why you're all suddenly doing them. But what are we going to do about our current situation? I assume we've all still got safe-keepers."

Jon held up the one he'd tried to use to capture Gavriel. (And which surely would have worked, if only Jon had known it was Gavriel!) "I've got mine."

"I've got two!" Bets chimed in.

"I've got one left," Max said, looking around him at the remains of the colosseum, rock broken up by colossal trees. "But like I said, I lost it somewhere around here. It also has someone in it, and one of those hover-vehicles the council uses."

"Have my spare." Bets handed over one of her two.

"And I've still got mine," Tarie said, pulling a small shape out of her jacket and waving it around. "Shall we have a go?"

May as well make this moment count, as much as they could.

Maia followed the glowing red and orange threads of power all the way into a vastly different Erus city. On the surface it was the same, massively built-up with levels upon winding levels of buildings created over thousands of years, but same as Elsewhise, there were terrible differences.

Too much alter-power. Parts of the city vanished, and new (old?) reeking buildings having appeared. A colossal statue of a seated cat, shining with alter-power. People acting…strange. And more Creatures.

Maia avoided the last as she made her way to the highest parts of the city, back to a familiar mansion she'd visited only the day before. This time, the security barrier was down, and she opened the manual gates with only a light push.

Inside the gates, the tall structure and its perfect garden seemed somehow threatening. Too quiet. Darker even than the distorted city, but with a strange power to it that she couldn't quite place. She paused outside the front door, watching the orange and red threads that led directly through it, then shrugged and stepped inside anyway. How much worse could things really get?

Two minutes later she stopped in the same sitting room where she'd so recently met up with Luca. The red thread led past this spot, but the orange one diverted straight off sideways.

Maia didn't have to look hard to see where it led. Half-hidden behind furniture, two shoe-clad feet stuck out from under a long, dark skirt. Her gaze travelled over the prostrate body to a too-pale, familiar face she'd seen several times in her attempts to time-travel.

It was Cahlie, and she was clearly dead. There were no marks on her, but by her greyish colouring, Maia would bet she'd been killed by alter-power.

Maia stared at the body, and stared, and stared. Then she

looked down at herself, at the orangey curse thread that still led to Cahlie's body, and noted how it hadn't really faded at all. But curses could last long, long beyond the caster's death. Just look at pharaohs' tombs.

"This feels terribly unfair," she said aloud, feeling numb. At this point she didn't even care why Cahlie was dead, or who'd killed her, although she probably should. It could mean her own life was in danger too. "Why should you avoid me by dying? Why should you not have to face me for what you did?"

"Didn't…she…already?" A hoarse voice broke the silence following her question.

Maia jolted upright, then turned and found the speaker, lying on the floor on the far side of the wide room, near a set of exit doors. It was Luca…no, Luke, because Luca was gorgeous and unlined and vividly coloured. This man was weary, with grey bags under his tired eyes, unkempt dark hair, and an expression of absolute sorrow.

"You!" Maia spat, still full of vivid memories of alternate pasts where this man failed her over and over. "Your Creature abandoned you, did it? You look terrible."

"That's fair." Luke didn't look like he could even manage a shrug. "I feel terrible."

Oh. "I won't feel sorry for you," Maia continued somewhat militantly, although her anger was draining out of her because of his pathetic appearance. "Did you kill Cahlie?"

He just looked at her.

Maia took a step closer. "Cahlie. Did you kill her? Did your Creature kill her?"

"My Creature…" Luke coughed. "Legion. It – he – is called Legion. And yes, he killed her, although I'm surprised you're asking. But he… he…" His face crumpled. "He took my son."

His son…? Did he mean Jay-Jon? But a moment later, the truth hit. "The other son," she said in dawning realisation. "The one you had in Dailan with another hard-to-please girl, Legion said, and she refused you any parental rights."

Her head slowly turned back to the still, dark-clad figure on the other side of the room, and the pieces of the puzzle finally clicked into place. Her broken heart took another crack. "Cahlie? You had a baby with *her*?"

Luke didn't answer, not to agree, disagree, or explain

himself. Was he…was he *crying?*

Brute. Fiend. Faithless…*argh.* "And why in Chaos would Legion take your other boy?" Maia choked out. "What did he have to gain?"

"He used an old soul-drinker to make himself a little kingdom of his own," Luke whispered. "Changed it with alter-power so it could hold any number of souls, plus his own real body. Used that old circlet you used to carry around – you know the one. But he needed something more to get it going. Something pure."

Maia's heart sank. She knew what he was saying. "And you didn't stop him?"

"I couldn't." Luke's voice cracked. "I've been an observer in my own mind for so long. I couldn't- I couldn't stop him. Not for any of it. And now… now he doesn't need me anymore, and he's left me to die as well."

It was obvious Luke could barely move now his Creature had left him. Were all ex-carriers so weak?

Maia pushed aside any pity. She studied his fallen form, shaking her head, then turned back to where Luca's red thread of power led from her chest, further into the mansion. (No, it was Legion's thread, wasn't it? Luca no longer existed.)

There were two time-chain beads left, and she had somewhere to be.

11
Ouch

Maia followed Legion's bright red thread down several hallways and into a large atrium, then stopped when it hit a plain black wall. But it didn't take long to see the faint outline of a doorway, poorly hidden by illusion.

She pushed against it experimentally, and it swung open. A moment later she moved to step through, but too late saw thin dark spikes shoot down from above. A sudden, intense pain took over her right side.

In slow motion, and full of dread, Maia looked down to see she'd been pierced right through her right shoulder and out under her arm with a spear as thick as her little finger, and longer than she was tall. No wonder it hurt.

She swore, then again. "The Chaos-damned door was booby-trapped! No wonder it was so badly hidden!"

And she was stuck! And it *hurt!* Although…

Maia tried to shuffle sideways but found she was fixed in place. This was so-damned-unfair-

Crack. The pain intensified for a moment as the spear broke, then it eased off, and suddenly she was free. But half of the spear was still in her.

She examined it for a moment, then gritting her teeth, set to removing it. She might bleed to death even if she did manage it, but who cared?

Ten very unpleasant minutes later, the spear was out. Maia tossed it on the ground with a clatter, grimacing at the pain of each movement. But the wounds weren't as bad as she'd imagined. They weren't even bleeding anymore. Instead, a shimmer of alter-power puffed out with each movement, and they just…sat there.

Like holes in wet clay instead of living flesh.

Oh, boy. Something was *really* wrong with this world.

Maia puffed out an unhappy breath and moved forward, following the red thread as it disappeared into a cloud of darkness in front of her. The booby-trapped door slammed shut behind her, and then she was in that darkness.

A few moments later, her sight adjusted, and she saw she was still in the same space. And in the centre of what turned out to be another high-roofed atrium was a little pedestal, topped with a familiar object. The Amaranthus circlet, with that odd little safekeeper inside it – the pale one covered in metallic shapes. The whole thing had been hidden inside the booby-trapped inner atrium, disguised by a dark cloud.

"Finally!"

This time, Maia was smart enough to check for signs of another trap, but none emerged. No one around, either – no Legion, not that she wanted to see him in his true form.

She picked up the half of the spear/spike that was still stained dark with her blood, and poked at the circlet with one end, intending to pick it up.

But when the spear touched it, there was a spark of bright alter-power, and then *whoosh!* – she was rushing towards the safekeeper and-

———✴———

"So we can all agree," Tarie said flatly, "that safekeepers don't work on Creatures when you don't know their names."

They were still just as surrounded as they'd been when they first had the bright idea to test out calling Creatures into the safekeepers. Gavriel might be gone from the colosseum – she could almost feel his weight in the safekeeper she held in her jacket – but the tree-ringed structure was also ringed by Creatures great and small.

None of them looked even half as pretty as the images at their temples pretended they were, Tarie thought. In the images, they always appeared fascinating, inhuman and otherworldly – and beautiful. But in real life, they were more like monsters from VR games than anything you'd choose to pledge to.

The horrible Creatures filtered out of the half-ruined city in the distance, now plonked in the middle of the Erusian countryside. Some were coming out of the hills, and even from around the train wreck. Luckily they wouldn't come past the tree line, or even touch it, but it was clear that Tarie and the others wouldn't be passing them easily.

Bets was standing at the very edge of the structure, her hands alight with silvery flame, and a pile of fruit next to her. She made a throwing movement, then looked back over her shoulder. "Heh. The fire does not quite reach them, but the fruit does. See?"

She picked up another fallen reddish fruit and lobbed it at the nearest Creature. It spun, alight with flame, then splattered on the Creature's chest. A moment later the whole thing was alight, and the Creature howled and ran straight into a neighbouring Creature, which was laughing until it too caught fire.

"Oh!" Bets said in surprise. "I vow 'twas not intentional."

They all watched for a while as the crowd of Creatures laughed, howled and completely failed to deal with the alter-power-fueled flames in their midst.

"This feels a little cruel," Max said. "The fire is meant to burn away the Creature presence, right? But they *are* Creatures."

Just then, one larger Creature picked up the nearest flaming one by its foot, swung it in a wide circle, and sent it flying towards the colosseum. For a moment it seemed like the thing would make it inside, but then it caught on the end of a tree branch and went spring-boarding right back the way it had come, knocking over another waiting Creature.

But the others seemed to have the same idea. Next moment, another small Creature came sailing towards them, and actually made it through the barrier of trees. Tarie shrieked and batted it away with a branch, and the four of them exchanged horrified glances.

"I've changed my mind," Max said quickly. "Fire away, Bets!"

Then it was all-out war, with Bets lighting fruit which the others lobbed like grenades, and the Creatures trying to send more of their own over the wall. Tarie got most of those first try, and if she didn't, they couldn't outrun the vines that would come pouring out whenever she spoke, catching them and burying them in a tangle of red and green.

Then the Creatures backed off, showing a hint of the intelligence that had caused them to rule most of the world, and began to gather in groups, well away from the firing line.

"This isn't good," Tarie said. "They're planning something. We've got to get out of here." She looked up the spiralling branches of the nearest tree. What *was* up there? "We have to go south. We have to meet up with our families!"

In the background, the two boys had been doing that weird miming communication again. "Sure, Tarie could run if we flew and carried Bets," Jon said to Max. "But I wouldn't try outrunning a Creature. And what if there are more of those hover-vehicles like Gavriel had? They'll catch us easily."

"Hover-vehicles?" Max echoed. "There's one in that safe-keeper I dropped."

There was a moment of stunned silence, then the four of them scrambled into action. They quickly found the dropped safe-keeper, which had fallen down several steps but was otherwise in good condition, and called out the hover-vehicle. (But not its rider, who by pure luck had been called into the safekeeper along with it.)

"Anyone ever driven one of these?" Tarie asked.

"I did a training course in VR years ago," Max said. Then when the others raised their eyebrows, he shrugged. "What? It was interesting."

Useful, more like. And next thing, Tarie and Bets were on the small hover-platform, which had just enough room for the two of them, while Max fussed over the controls at the front. "I think it's this one," he murmured. "Or was it this one?"

"Just figure it out and tell me," Tarie told him. "I don't think there'll be room for all of us up here." Not with her super-sized as she was.

Jon, who was flying up high above the colosseum as their look-out, called down to them. "Come on! The Creatures are coming back, and I think they have a catapult!"

"Time to go," Max said quickly. "Ah...let's say it's this one."

The vehicle hummed into life and rose up a little shakily, then abruptly shot away, nearly clipping a wide branch of the nearest tree. And then they were heading towards the south and Erus city, leaving the tree-ringed colosseum – and Creatures – behind.

—❋—

Maia was inside a safekeeper. She knew this because firstly, she clearly recalled hurtling towards the safekeeper as it grew alarmingly large, and secondly, she could still see the shape of the thing, complete with metallic implants, just from the internal view. A dim glow that must be the Amaranthus circlet showed faintly through where the 'sky' was.

She now stood on a city street. It was like her hometown of Elsewhise in that the buildings weren't more than two or three storeys high, but there were ten times as many as Elsewhise had. More than that, even, creating a decent-sized city.

Most of the densely packed grey and white buildings reminded her of the vids she'd seen of the neighbouring city-state, Dailan. The buildings followed the curve of the safekeeper, heedless of gravity, until they stood out at a ninety-degree angle. From here Maia could see people moving around on the distant sideways streets, as though gravity didn't apply to them either.

Maia recalled asking her mother what it was like inside a safekeeper. Davinia, who'd been making one in that moment, had replied 'small and dark, I imagine'.

Well, she'd been wrong. It wasn't at all dark – more like a cloudy day, really – and there was enough space in here to fit hundreds of thousands of people. Millions, even, had the buildings been densely built up like in Erus city. Maia would never have imagined a safekeeper could be so spacious.

And Legion was somewhere in here. Luke had said so, but Maia knew it was true. She could still see the red thread wrapping around her and leading from her chest.

Maia followed the thread along narrow city streets, turning corners and dodging pedestrians as she went. The people in here looked ordinary, not like those outside in the wrong-feeling Erus full of Creatures. There weren't any vehicles, but there were people of all ages, just as she'd normally see in any city, and more so as the thread led her deeper into the city centre.

She passed busy restaurants full of laughing patrons – although didn't see or smell any food – and at least three party-hubs, the music pumping out of the open doors along with flashing lights sparkling with alter-power.

Hmm. Maia paused and studied the lights with narrowed eyes. Those were different. Like what was happening outside the safekeeper, but without the ominous air out there. Just power;

high-intensity power. She glanced at the nearest reveller as they fell against their companion, laughing. Their eyes were glazed and held a slight shimmer of power as though they weren't in their right mind.

Maia put her head down and followed the thread deeper into the city. The buildings grew more luxurious and ornate, reminding her of some old, beautifully kept structures she'd seen in VR. And then the thread led to the largest, most majestic building of them all.

It was raised above the others, built with stone columns beautifully melded with glass, curved roundels topping the roof and its many spires. It looked like a cross between an old fairytale castle and a temple.

"Of course he'd be in the grandest building," Maia scoffed under her breath. She stomped up the many wide steps leading to the massive front door, and just as she went in, a man came hurrying out with a small child in his arms.

"Don't go in there," he warned. "Things happen to people in there."

Maia studied his eyes, noting that they held a faint shimmer of power, but less than the reveller she'd seen earlier. "What sort of things?"

He just shook his head. "Bad things. There's…*something* in there." And he hurried away down the steps.

But the little boy in his arms looked over his shoulder, back at Maia, and for a moment his young face changed. His eyes became larger, almost bulging, and glowing white, and his small mouth curved in an unnatural smirk.

Maia stared, her heart sinking, until suddenly the child blinked, and his eyes were normal-sized and a regular dark brown. He tucked his head against the man's chest as they moved out of sight.

'Something' in there. Some*one*, more like. Maia felt heavy with dread at the thought of confronting Legion, but knew she had to keep going. She had no other choice.

Inside, the building matched its outsides. It was as grand as she'd ever seen – more so than in real life, if this could be called real. She stood in a wide carpeted lobby with three curved staircases leading up to the next level. Looking up, she could see another nine or ten levels and then the high ceiling with a colossal shimmering chandelier.

Stairs. How archaic. But the red thread led her further in, further up, so Maia sighed and began to climb.

There were people in here too, she found as she moved through the building's winding hallways and many rooms. Most of them seemed curious and even happy, more like the revellers outside than that one worried man. And there was a buzz in the air along with the alter-power tingle, something that pushed at her and made her want to be happy too, and not worry about anything. She scowled and pushed the temptation aside. There was nothing to be happy about, not here or out there.

Here and there, people would watch her as she passed, their eyes briefly changing to that bulbous glowing white before returning to normal. They never seemed to notice the change.

And the red thread tying her to Legion seemed to grow stronger. She could *feel* him nearby; feel the mix of anxiety and anger he brought about in her. *Intimidation.* That was his strength. Maia scratched at her chest anxiously as if she could pull off the threads of power he'd covered her in. She'd find him soon…

But then, when she was deep in the centre of the building, that anxious/fearful feeling faded away… and she realised the red thread had gone too. The power covering her unravelled even as she watched in dismay. But the orange rejection curse remained, along with the duller red one underneath that had come from her mother. "What…"

A teenage girl passing in the hallway turned to watch Maia with glowing white eyes. "Maybe I don't want to be found," the girl said in a light voice that was clearly not her own. "There you go, Maia. You're set free."

"Set free of your power, not of the curse I came to you for in the first place!" Maia shouted. "I just need to talk to you!"

But the girl's glowing eyes had changed to an ordinary grey-blue, and she hurried away, an expression of confusion on her face.

Legion was somewhere around here. Maia knew it! She turned around, looking angrily as though he'd suddenly appear in the walls. She stomped down the hall, checking in on each room as she passed by. Each was empty except for a bed, and on each bed was a sleeping form. No Creature anywhere; just humans.

But in the third room, Maia realised the bed's occupant was

a child. A little boy of no more than three or four years old. He was tucked in under a thick blanket, and its ornate pattern seemed to extend to his sleeping face.

She took a step in and realised it *did* extend to his face, and it looked a lot like the metallic patterns covering the safekeeper as a whole. Dismayed, she reached down to gently touch the boy's skin, and she could feel the faint tingle of power coming off him. This thing was leaching life from him.

Luke had said that something had to power this unique version of a safekeeper, didn't he? And that Legion had stolen Luke's own young son. Could this be him?

Maia gripped onto the edge of the pattern and pulled. She could almost feel it, like it was somewhere between gas and solid, but she focused and pulled until it tugged away from the boy's face and moved back down to the blanket.

And then the boy's eyes opened, and for a moment they were hazel, like baby Jay-Jon's. Then they lit up white.

"I told you, Maia," the boy said in a high, lilting voice. "I told you not to come whining to me if things didn't work out how you wanted. I told you to go away. But perhaps you need help leaving."

And then the pattern lifted off the blanket and stuck to her. Suddenly it was pulling the breath from *her!* She gasped, tugging away, and the pattern/power-trap pulled back. They tugged back and forth, Maia stuck in the strangest trap yet, until finally she yanked herself free with a gasp.

The pattern fell back to the blanket, and the boy's eyes closed again.

Maia stood panting, staring at the blanket with its innocuous pattern as though it was covered in snakes. "Fine," she managed to say. "I'll leave. I don't want to be in here anyway. But I need to talk to you about how the time-chain works; the one you gave me. Won't you just give me a minute to discuss it?"

There was movement at the corner of her eye, and then a man stepped out of the ludicrously ornate wallpaper. Had he been there the whole time?

For a moment Maia thought it was Luca, since he had the same tall, slim build and dark hair, and he wore a sleek, fashionable suit. But then she saw that his eyes glowed, like all the others she'd seen here, and as he moved, his skin flashed dark blue.

"A minute?" The man cocked his head on the side. "Time doesn't really apply in the Kingdom of Legion, haven't you noticed?"

"Legion?" Maia tried to hide how shaken she felt. "I thought you'd look…less like Luca."

Legion shrugged, and for a moment his figure blurred and warped into something much larger before returning to its original form. "I choose. It doesn't matter, since this is just a projection. Now what problem do you have that's caused you to break into my home like this?"

His home. A palace within a city within a safekeeper… "The time-chain you gave me doesn't work. I've checked three different alternate pasts, and all of them end in my death."

Legion stared at her. "And that's my problem, how?"

"You said Cahlie put a rejection curse on me!" Maia cried. "And then you killed her before she could take it off! But it's a death curse, isn't it? Why do I keep dying in all these different realities?"

"The better question is, why are you still alive in this one?" He shook his head. "The death curse has nothing to do with me. It's older. Stronger."

He must mean the underlying curse she kept seeing. The one with those dull red strands that she'd traced back to her own mother. But that couldn't be true! Davinia had been so proud of Maia, right up till she'd got pregnant and Cahlie had cursed her. Surely Davinia wouldn't have cursed her own precious daughter with death.

"But… but I've only got two attempts left," Maia whispered. "Can't you give me some direction on the right detour to take? The right time to turn back?"

Legion let out a long, put-upon sigh. "How in Hades should I know? I didn't get involved with your miserable little life until I met Luke DeMannard three years ago – and by met, I mean I got hold of him when he accidentally deviated into the borderlands on one of his long trips. *You* have to pick. You made the trade for the circlet, and that's that."

He'd so casually admitted to forcing his carrier link with Luke, but Maia was so shaken that she couldn't take it in. "Why did you want the circlet so much? How does it help power this little kingdom you've set up?"

Legion leaned back against the wall and smiled a wide, satisfied smile. "It doesn't power my kingdom, Maia. It protects it."

When she didn't respond, he said slowly, as if to a child, "Creatures cannot touch the circlet, not with the name it bears. Creatures therefore cannot enter this place. So no matter what happens out *there*, in here, I'll be safe. See?"

She didn't, not really. He was saying so much, yet explaining so little. The word on the circlet was a *name*? And... "What's happening out there?"

He raised an eyebrow and for a moment looked just like Luca again. "The Other realm merging with the normal?" he said in a faux-polite tone. "The end of time, and so forth? Did you not notice?"

Maia shook her head numbly. "I was...busy."

"Yes, well, so was I. I was aiming for one-point-two million people with the bombs I set in Dailan, but I had to make do with a paltry five-hundred-thousand. Everyone else had gone in to pledge to the Tiger statue," he continued as if he wasn't just admitting to mass-murder. "Inconvenient, but it will have to do. I can't exactly go back out and try again."

"So...all this," Maia said, gesturing around them. "This is...a soul-drinker? Everyone in here is *dead*?"

"Everyone in here is *alive*," Legion snapped. "Quite alive, and that took some doing. And they're happy too, did you notice? The only ones who are any different are you and me." His glowing eyes narrowed. "I'm surprised you got in at all. You're halfway through your transition, by the look of you. My spear trap clearly got you on your way in."

"Transition...?"

Suddenly Legion was behind her, and hard fingers on her shoulders turned her sharply sideways. Then she could see her reflection in a window, a reflection that hadn't been there before, one that was grey-skinned and red-eyed and looked nothing like what she knew of herself. Black veins spread from the wound exposed in her shoulder.

"Creatures can't cross the barrier of the circlet," he said again in that slow, faux-patient voice. "And with the Other and the normal merged, what happens to mortals that die out there? There's nowhere for their spirits to go now, nowhere except to stay in their warping, decaying bodies. And so what do they become?"

Dread filled her, sharp and painful, at what he was implying. But...her shoulder didn't hurt anymore... "You're wrong," she choked out. "You're a liar. You're a Creature yourself!"

"Not technically a Creature," Legion shot back, "and that's all that matters, in this case. But you, Maia DeDavinia, are a trespasser." He vanished from behind her, and then his voice echoed throughout the room, without any clear source. *"And you won't be coming back."*

Then a tremendous force pushed at her chest, at her whole body. There was an intense tingle of alter-power from every angle, and then *pop!* She was ejected from the safekeeper just as abruptly as she'd entered.

With the hover-vehicle's weight limit exceeded, Max had no choice but to fly. Now, Elspeth was flying a vehicle for the first time ever – and one would hope, not also the last.

'Twas rather more challenging than she'd imagined.

"Left! No, *other* left!" Tarie commanded.

Elspeth swung the hover-vehicle's controller in the other direction, and the vehicle swung with it, narrowly dodging a large missile that might have been half a vehicle. They sped on past the Creature that had thrown it, not looking back.

"The good thing about all of this," Elspeth mused, "is that with the Other and normal realms merged, the Creatures seem to have very little of their usual powers against us. While there are more of them than I expected, and very few humans, they appear to rely on brute force-"

"*Turn!*" Tarie lunged forward and grabbed hold of the controller right over Elspeth's hand, forcing the hover-vehicle to shoot upwards. They barely missed the pointed roof of a structure below.

"By the rood," Elspeth said cheerfully. "That building seemed to come out of nowhere, did it not?"

"That's it," Tarie said in exasperation. "Buildings don't come out of nowhere. I'm driving!"

Tarie pushed her aside – mayhap not quite as gently as she'd intended – and took the front steering spot, which was precisely what Elspeth had wanted her to do. Elspeth happily moved to the back of the rapidly moving vehicle and focused on the scenery.

Ooh, there was Jon, flying just above and behind them, and Max flanked them on the other side. Elspeth had never envied their ability to fly – in truth, when she'd been offered the chance to have any supernatural gift, she'd chosen to speak any language over flying about like a bird. But they did appear to be enjoying themselves so. After what had happened earlier, she wondered if her abilities had grown, and she herself could now fly…?

Why not try it? Max thought at her. *What's the worst that could happen?*

I'll catch you, Jon added from the other side. Elspeth could sense his dry humour, but still…

A sudden blow to her stomach caught her entirely by surprise. What might've been an old tyre hit her full force and sent her tumbling right over the side of the vehicle. In the half-second that passed, she thought, *Oh! I can attempt to fly!* And then a few moments later when she was still plummeting towards the ground: *Nope. Most certainly not.*

She landed solidly and unharmed in a pair of white-clad arms, and Max grinned down at her. *No flying skills yet?*

Elspeth sighed. *It appears not.*

Hey, Jon said jokingly from nearby. *I said I'd catch her.*

Sorry. And then Max dropped her.

Hmm. They really were very high, were they not…? But incredibly, Elspeth felt not a jot of fear.

But Jon was quick to catch her again, and she laughed aloud, putting her arms around his neck. "What a lively game!" They swerved sideways to dodge a low-hanging branch from a solitary Word tree, and she ducked just in time. "Once this is all over, we ought to do this again!"

Well above them and ahead, Tarie looked down from the hover-vehicle with wide, alarmed eyes. "BETS!" she hollered. "WHAT ARE YOU DOING?"

Sigh. "Mayhap you should return me to the vehicle," Elspeth murmured to Jon. "Tarie does not have such a sense of humour at this time, does she?"

But then Tarie had not come so close to death like the other three had today. Elspeth knew not why, but it seemed to have changed them beyond just their sudden ability to share thoughts.

Back on the vehicle, Tarie looked at Elspeth accusingly. "Please tell me you didn't just jump off for fun."

"Most certainly not. I wouldn't do something so foolish." But Elspeth had certainly been tempted.

Tarie muttered something that sounded like 'Are you sure?' but Elspeth decided to ignore it. Now, they were reaching the farthest outskirts of Erus city, and something on the ground caught her attention. Far below, a tiny figure dodged between small, widely spaced houses, seemingly pursued by slightly less *human*-looking figures. But from up here, Elspeth could see the person was about to be hemmed in.

On it, Jon sent, and a moment later he was diving down like a hawk swooping in on a mouse. And that comparison was apt, for Elspeth heard a distant "Hey!" and then Jon had grabbed the person under the arms and lifted them onto the third level of a nearby building.

"What in Chaos are you doing?" the man demanded of Jon. He was thin, red-eyed and weary-looking, but his irritation came through clearly.

"Helping you," Jon said, feeling a little irritated himself. He'd expected some gratitude, at least. "You were being chased by Creatures, and about to hit a dead-end."

The man gave him a deeply unattractive bug-eyed look that didn't seem to fit on a human face. "I wasn't being chased!" he snarled, so vehement that his skin turned red and spit flew out of his mouth. "I was running after my daughter!"

"Why…were you running after your daughter?"

"So she wouldn't get away!"

Jon was getting a bad feeling about this. The man hadn't lost that bug-eyed look; in fact, it was becoming more pronounced. As was the red skin, and the Tiger pledge mark that sat too deeply on his now-creased forehead. There was something terribly, terribly wrong here…

"Ah…sorry to have disturbed you," Jon began.

Just then another man pulled himself up over the balcony,

the protective forcefields presumably having failed due to all the alter-power around. This second man was distinctly grey-skinned, like a dead kind of grey, or a from a fantasy VR programme Jon had once used. His pledge mark was creased deeply into his forehead, like cracks in drought-ridden soil. He was also far too thin, his clothing hanging off him, and his ears sitting oddly loose from his head.

"Hurry up, Syth," the grey man said. He glanced narrow-eyed at Jon, and his eyes were like yellow slits against that grey skin. "You'll miss it." Flashes of sharp yellow teeth showed as he spoke.

Jon briefly wondered if the man was a Halfling, but dismissed the thought. Darkness emanated from him, something Jon had only ever come across in the few Creatures he'd had the misfortune to meet. And those at least *tried* to look impressive.

"Didn't mean to," Syth replied sulkily. "This one grabbed me." He shuddered, and his bulging eyes popped out to distinctly inhuman proportions. "I don't like how he feels."

Well, Jon didn't like how Syth felt, either! "Right," he said, taking a step back. "Goodbye." And then he shot up into the air, leaving the two well below him.

A moment later, Max pulled up beside him. *What was that about?*

I don't know, Jon replied. *But we probably should look out for some girl down below. That bug-eyed man was chasing her, apparently.*

Max glanced down. *Bug-eyed man? That's a Creature.*

Jon looked again, and sure enough, it was. Syth the ungrateful rescuee (who in fact hadn't been rescued at all) was now the spitting image of a skinny, red-skinned, bulging-eyed Creature – one that just happened to be wearing human clothing. He was climbing back down the side of the building along with the grey-skinned man, and down below, a small cluster of other sort-of Creatures were amassed in an alleyway. More were coming from every direction. Jon caught a glimpse of a wide-eyed, frightened human face backed into a doorway, and then suddenly the whole gathering went up in silvery flame.

"Coming through!" he heard Bets holler as sort-of Creatures scattered, shrieking. "Out the way, you reeking villains!"

The hover-vehicle charged through, and Tarie dropped from it like a concrete block, the ground vibrating as she landed. "Do a circuit!" she shouted upwards.

Oh, for goodness… *Bets* was driving? "I thought we decided that was a bad idea," Jon muttered to Max.

But Max had already taken a swan-dive downwards to join the fray. Jon sighed, following, but by the time he reached the ground, there was nothing much to do. The sort-of Creatures had scattered, and Max was putting his hand out to a preteen girl, who was looking up at him with wide, frightened eyes.

I shall talk to her, Bets called from above. *Max, you look thoroughly disreputable.*

Jon pushed back a smile. Besides being a tall, strongly built man, Max was currently battered, bloodied and ragged. *You do look like a bandit*, Jon told him.

Looking slightly miffed, Max pulled back. Then next thing, Bets was down there, chatting to the frightened girl who – while surely much younger – stood about eye-level to her. Unlike the others, her pledge mark seemed to sit lightly on her sallow forehead, like it was printed on and might wear off at any time.

"I don't know what's happening," the girl was saying in a small voice. "Everyone was acting crazy. They all chased me." She sniffed back tears. "I don't know what to do."

"Come with us!" Bets offered.

"I can carry you," Max offered, clearly trying to redeem himself.

But the girl leaned away.

Right, Max muttered. *Hover-vehicle it is.*

Tarie huffed out a sigh from where she was getting back on the hover-vehicle. "Good thing I've shrunk from that battle, right? Or we wouldn't all fit."

The girl got up, her shoulders hunched, and she scrubbed a hand over her forehead. The pledge mark sloughed off like a dead leaf from a tree and floated to the ground. They all watched its slow movement in silence as it landed gently on the pavement then disappeared into a shimmer of alter-power.

"Was that…fake?" Tarie asked disbelievingly.

The girl shook her head. "It was real. I just…I didn't want it. They said we had to take it, though, so I did."

"And now it's gone," Jon finished. "And so should we be." Those around them were definitely getting back to their feet again – still Creatures, unfortunately, and not looking any friendlier.

"Onwards and upwards," Bets said cheerfully. She sprayed silvery fire once more around them as if in afterthought, then helped the girl onto the hover-vehicle, which seemed a lot smaller with three people in it.

Off we go.

Back in the darkened atrium, Maia huddled in the faint light from the Amaranthus circlet. Within it, the unique safekeeper sat gleaming and buzzing with alter-power.

She felt brittle, despairing, and twisted inside with anger. Her shoulder and arm ached dully from the spear wound, and the rest of her body felt similar. She felt like if she let herself, she'd attack the first person she saw, just to get rid of this dreadful feeling.

She looked down at her hand where it rested in her lap. In this light, it looked grey, and the veins on the back of her hand bulged horribly.

She got up and made her way out of the atrium until she reached the nearest wall. It was clear, showing a view of the garden, but she recognised the material as a smart-wall, most likely voice-activated. "Reflect," she ordered it.

The smart-wall flickered and fizzed, showing that the technology was failing, but soon enough it displayed a faint image of a slim, wan-faced girl. Shadows under the eyes; hollow cheeks; a gleam of red in her pupils…

That same bitter, twisted feeling welled up inside Maia, and she pushed it down with a touch of panic. But with that came acceptance. She'd been badly wounded, and somehow she was changing. Could Legion have been telling the truth?

"But I don't want to be a Creature," she murmured. "I want… I want…"

Nothing she could get. She couldn't change her situation one jot, and it seemed to grow worse and worse by the hour.

She made her way back to the atrium where the Amaranthus circlet still sat. Had Legion really said it was someone's name? A Creature of sorts, no doubt, because no one with that kind of power could be human.

Maia sat down again, her back against the wall, and stared

at the circlet. She used to say the 'word of power' over and over, day by day, feeling a gentle hum of *something* each time she spoke it out. It had felt so valuable, and Legion said the Creatures couldn't touch it. That soon, she wouldn't be able to either.

And he was surely right. Even now, the thought of even voicing that word – or name, if it was one – made that bitterness well up again.

The bad feeling. The Creature feeling that seemed to be killing her bit by bit…

Argh! Now she wanted to smash the circlet! To bury it, to cover its light so she never had to look at it and-

"Am-a-ran-thus," she choked out, feeling like she was throwing up a brick. The word didn't want to come out of her mouth. *"I don't want to be like this!"*

And then, like feeling the sun's warmth on her back even when she couldn't see it, she realised she was no longer alone.

12

The Name on the Circlet

Tarie skimmed along in the hover-vehicle with Bets and their young hitch-hiker. She flew the vehicle as high as possible without touching the silvery barrier above, while still being mostly out of reach of Creature missiles. Jon and Max flanked them, flying on either side, or above and below when the path became too narrow.

One or two mysterious objects had skimmed past close enough to be noticed; lit up with alter-power or simply weapons. One of them even hit the silvery barrier and exploded in a puff of light.

Ouch. They wouldn't be going up *there.*

But it was a challenging journey. The dark landscape was scattered with colossal Word trees whose tops pierced that barrier, plus the wreckage of twisted buildings, much of Erus city having vanished along with the countryside's transformation.

The centre of the city was still whole from what she could see to the west, but the Tiger statue was now clearly visible, as though the surrounding levels had disappeared, or it had grown much larger. It seemed to glow orangey-red with the occasional flash of green light.

If Tarie squinted, she thought she could make out other lights in every direction, as though the other city-states also had their own Tiger statues.

She shuddered and looked away. They had enough problems without worrying about what Dailan or Memrys were doing.

Now they were moving into the city proper, where the outer suburbs made up two or three levels, each of which housed forty or fifty floors of buildings. Gaps between buildings created ravines that plunged into darkness far below, from which an unpleasant smell emanated.

"Ugh," Bets muttered from behind Tarie. "Whatever is that stench?"

"Rubbish?" Tarie suggested without taking her eyes off the path ahead. She'd never driven a vehicle manually for so long, since auto-drive was generally perfect. But this vehicle's auto-drive was dead or switched off, and as a council vehicle, it wouldn't have taken them where they wanted to go anyway.

"Creatures," Jon called from their left.

Tarie's eyebrows shot up. "You can smell them from up here?"

"No, ahead! Look!"

Following the most direct route to their destination, they'd turned between two massive old housing blocks, not too far from where Tarie had briefly lived as Jon's neighbour. They were flying down the narrow gully created with that darkness well below, but up ahead was a dead end.

A barrier covered the gap between the building blocks entirely – made of vehicles and mangled materials that Tarie couldn't even name, and all lit up with bright patches of alter-power. Twisted pillars of rock reached upwards, bracing it, and the whole thing swarmed with tiny figures that Tarie could see weren't human even from this distance.

"By the Rood," Bets said, sounding interested rather than frightened. "I do believe we are trapped."

"Try not to sound like you're having fun!" Tarie shot back, although the other girl's calmness was helping her not to panic. "Should we turn around?"

Bets turned and looked behind them silently.

"Well?" Tarie said several long moments later. "Are we turning or not?"

"Ah…I shall say not."

"Why?" But Tarie turned to look too, and behind them was a roiling mass of black cloud. It stretched from the ground to the silvery sky barrier, and it was rushing towards them, filling up the entire horizon. She could smell its stench even from here.

"Uh…"

"Let's go up!" Bets suggested.

"But we don't know what's up there!"

"It looks better than what lies behind, does it not?"

Tarie gave the roiling darkness behind them one last wide-eyed glance and shuddered. The odd silvery ceiling above them would be a better option than getting caught in *that*...right? "I guess we're going up."

"I know you're there," Maia said hoarsely to the empty room. Or at least, it looked empty, but she was well used to people hiding themselves through technology or alter-power. There was a certain *feeling* about being in company, even unseen, and she was most definitely in company. "You may as well come out."

No one came into sight, but the sense of presence became more intense, and the whole room seemed to light up several shades. A thought came into her head: *I've been here the whole time.*

Maia paused. That thought...felt like her thought...but it wasn't, because it came with a faint pulse of alter-power, and a slight warmth. "Who are you?"

You said my name.

"Amaranthus?" she whispered. This time, the name came a little more easily, although something inside her still twisted as she shaped the syllables.

And then the light in the room coalesced into a man's figure and became solid. He was short and balding and ordinary in appearance, but instead of a shadow behind him, a light was cast, and it marked the outline of a much, much larger figure. *Here I am.*

He *was* a person! Maia realised in amazement. Or something like a Creature...a projection of some much vaster being...whatever he was! He wasn't just a word of power after all! Maia's gaze dropped to the floor as her mind filled with memories of the many times she'd spoken his name – and had surely drawn on his power for herself and for her child.

But he'd never complained. He'd never tried to stop her...

He tilted his head to the side, and his dark eyes were filled with remarkable kindness. *You never took anything I wasn't willing to freely give. And when someone uses my name with good motives, I will* always *freely give.*

She'd tried to use his power to make a better life, and what had it brought her? Nothing.

"My life has turned to ashes!" she cried. "What has your power led me to except pain?"

She knew even as she spoke that it wasn't true, that it was unfair and that she was blaming the wrong person, but she was so hurt and angry and she *wanted* it to be true so she had someone she could blame.

And she felt so low and disgusting compared to this being of alter-power, that lashing out seemed preferable to throwing herself to the ground and begging for help and mercy, which she wanted more than anything, and that made her hate him a little.

Then Amaranthus stepped closer to her where she sat on the floor of the now-bright atrium, and leaned down. He reached out with one hand and his presence moved wider, touched her face even though his hand didn't, and memories came rushing in.

No, more than memories. Pictures, and scenes, and knowledge that she'd never had.

Maia saw her mother Davinia, young and bound in chains of dark power that she couldn't see, eagerly creating curses and weapons of subjugation and death to be used against her enemies and against innocents.

And each time she did, each time Davinia casually spoke death into being, a tiny thread of it would come back against her. Dull red, fine and permanent, it lashed around the thing she valued the most. Her future.

Maia.

Davinia hadn't meant to curse her favourite child with an early death, Maia realised. No, it had been the result of the life she'd chosen to live.

Then Maia saw herself, much younger and bound in those fine, dull red death curse threads, going mindlessly through life and dodging near-miss after near-miss, and not even knowing it. But the threads grew thicker and bolder until Maia knew her death must be a certainty; must be incredibly close…

And then an unseen hand carefully placed the circlet just where Maia would see it, lighting it up so she'd see its value even if no one else did. Maia saw how each time she'd used it, each time she'd spoken out *Amaranthus*, life power was released and the death curse grew just a touch weaker.

There were more visions of averted deaths. Ties of light, of promise, wrapping around her son before he was even the size of a fingernail, giving him a mighty future that would change history.

Because she'd asked. Because she'd used Amaranthus's name to speak it into being.

"But...I've lost it all," Maia whispered, tears coming into her eyes. "If you were doing all of this for me, why am I here now?"

You still made your own choices, dear child, and consequences come from any choice. But your future is far greater than your past.

And then Maia saw herself on the day everything had first gone so dreadfully wrong, grimly deciding to visit a Creature. To beg for freedom from the rejection curse that had been placed over her. The circlet glinted on her wrist but seemed to go unseen; massively undervalued as only just an encourager, not a power in itself.

And there she went, into the lair of something that she now realised would have killed her in an instant. She went in, and the White Prince appeared thin and white and vicious, and promised to free her if only she'd put down the circlet.

So she'd done it. In the darkness of the White Prince's temple, with the red threads of her death curse seeming thick and vibrant, she'd taken off the only thing protecting her and had placed it on the ground.

Then faster than she could focus – too fast for her memory to recall at all – the Creature had lunged at her. And in the moment before she'd been caught, another hand had reached out and...

...pulled her away. Pulled her outside of time, where she'd waited with a ghostly echo of the circlet around her forehead, and her eyes blank with sleep, until the White Prince had been destroyed and its temple along with it.

Seventeen years, and she remembered none of it.

"But how did I escape?" Maia murmured, not understanding what she'd seen. "Where was that place I was taken to? Did you...?"

Amaranthus smiled gently. *There are infinite potential realities, Maia. But only one exists.*

Did that mean...she *couldn't* change her past?

Try the time-chain again. And this time, use it with the circlet. I give it to you freely.

Tears pricked Maia's eyes, but this time they were tears of

hope, and maybe relief. She glanced across to the circlet where it lay with Legion's safekeeper at its centre, and the name inscribed seemed to gleam as if in invitation. But when she glanced back, Amaranthus was gone. Although, she could still feel his warm presence…

The ugly feelings of bitterness and despair eased inside her, and she sat fully upright. Her shoulder twinged sharply, and she looked to see that the wound was now red and bleeding slightly, not blackened like it had been before.

She'd changed. She'd changed *back*.

But ow, her arm hurt worse now!

Maia shook her head. Still not her worst problem today. But she fumbled in her jacket for the last two beads of the time-chain, then reached for the circlet with the other, placing just one finger on it. And this time, she wasn't pulled inside.

She closed her eyes in relief, then squeezed a hand around one of the last beads, crushing it. "Amaranthus," she said aloud. "Show me where to go."

Let's go up, Tarie had said.

Barricade ahead of them, massive buildings on either side, roiling black cloud rushing up behind them, and silvery-prismatic sky barrier above. Not too much of a choice.

As if synchronised, Jon and Max shot upwards alongside the hover-vehicle, all of them moving together towards the low, reflective sky barrier in an attempt to jump the Creatures' blockade.

As they approached, Jon could feel the alter-power coming off that waterlike barrier; could see the myriad colours reflected. They must be coming from inside the barrier itself, because down here, everything was growing increasingly dark.

And while Jon was wondering if the sky barrier would be too powerful to touch, would shock them and send them flying, he found himself filled with anticipation. Would they need to touch it? Could they somehow get past this blockade without seeing what the sky-water-silver barrier was made of…?

Then they hit the barrier. It caught him by surprise, like getting a pillow to the head without warning. Soft, but still startling. There was the briefest sense of moving through power, much like when he'd moved through a remnant gateway across time, and then he was inside another realm.

Breathless. Blasted with power. Everything happening at once…

Jon saw a version of himself standing in a garden, talking with a little old man. And there he was walking away after that conversation… and there he was talking to Bets, and there he was talking to people he'd never met before, then flying happily in a game that didn't exist…

Dozens of Jons rushed around in the brightest light he'd ever seen yet still been able to take in. A few of them met his eyes and either smiled or waved before vanishing from sight.

It was absolute chaos, and his mind seemed on the edge of implosion, yet somehow, he could take it all in. All of its detail and glory and unending nature.

This is my future, a thought came in to the middle of that beautiful chaos. *In a space free from time, I can do anything. See anyone. Relive any moment, anytime. And it's easy.*

Then Jon dragged his eyes upwards, into the brightest light. And there he saw what might have been the Mountain of Glass, if that place went on to infinity. It was as pure as glass and backlit by fire in every colour imaginable, with water running all over it, and surrounded by verdant growth. Every living plant was equally as bright and vivid and full of alter-power, like they were pumped full of the Water of Life. So were the people – *so* many people, all vibrant and brighter than any human could ever be.

Of course they were. Because this, Jon thought in amazement, was where the Water of Life came from…

He blinked for the first time, and the light around the whole scene seemed to form a shape like a human being. Like all of this was held inside one single *mind*, perhaps? Or like it was being powered by just one being…?

And then he saw the light reflected in on itself, getting smaller and more intense until it formed just one solid little figure, the size of an ordinary, rather short human man with a bald head.

Amaranthus smiled at Jon…then winked.

Jon gasped, flailing as he reached out towards him. But suddenly he was moving downwards again through what felt like a gateway, away from the glorious, brilliant Mountain with its infinite possibilities. His wonderfully opened mind seemed to shut down until it was small and dark and simple again… normal.

They were going back down through the barrier, Jon realised. They might've only moved above it for mere seconds, even just a minute. And now they'd fallen back down below it.

Damn.

But as he looked down, he caught a glimpse of the strangest view. The earth below now looked as thin and temporary as a piece of paper that was on fire at both ends. Darkened, covered in a moving black cloud that absorbed everything it touched, barring the Word trees that stood out like glowing pillars, especially where they touched the barrier. Tiger statues dotted the landscape, the darkness spilling from them until they were almost covered themselves.

I don't want to be back down here, Jon thought for just a second before he was fully through. Then the world around him was once again darkened city with the light world above him, behinds its silvery barrier. He was back amongst battered-looking building levels melded with twisting rock spires, with the occasional Word tree breaking up the gloom. But he couldn't forget what he'd seen up there.

Wow.

Wow.

Woooooooww.

And how disappointing to be back. But somehow, he knew it wouldn't be long till he returned to that place.

Right, he thought at the others. *Let's reach the meeting point, then head straight up, OK?* There didn't seem much point being down here anymore, not when the alternative was so…fantastic.

Except…where were they? *Hello…?*

A faint response came in his head of Bets' voice, almost too quiet to hear, then a brief image of the city outskirts. *Down south. Where…you?*

Jon finally recognised his surroundings as the very area he'd grown up in, not far from his and Anni's apartment. In fact, the location of his apartment appeared to have been swallowed up by a Word tree that had sprung from the depths of their level.

But of course, Tarie had lived there too. Jon barely spared it a glance. *I'll cut across the city,* he told the others, sending the thought as clearly as he could. *Keep going.*

A hint of approval came back from several sources, which he took as agreement.

"Good," Jon murmured to himself. Now the next step…was to find out *how* to get across the city, because it didn't look a thing like he was used to.

Just then he saw a figure far below, its movements frightened and tense. As if his eyesight zoomed in, suddenly he could clearly see the older man who looked to be trying to make his way…somewhere.

Not a Creature this time. So far, so good.

Perking up, Jon prepared to assist.

Maia had crushed the second-to-last bead of the time-chain, giving Amaranthus free rein to direct her. The amber/golden bubble sprang up around her, blocking out the atrium in Luca/Legion's house, and then images began to play outside of it.

There was her real past self, walking cluelessly through the darkened gateway of the White Prince's temple, with the circlet around her wrist. Damn it, present-Maia thought, the place even *looked* ominous! But that had really happened, because she remembered it.

And there was the White Prince again, tempting past-Maia to put down the circlet. And like that last time, present-Maia watched as her past self did the same thing – the same idiotic, dangerous, monumentally stupid thing of putting down the circlet and then the White Prince lunged and…

…And then the scene seemed to pause.

Go on, someone seemed to whisper. Not a voice; more a feeling. *What happens next?*

Present-Maia watched, perplexed. Well, someone had rescued Maia and pulled her out of time…

OH. Right.

There was only one reality, Amaranthus had told her. And that was the one that had happened.

Maia looked down at the final bead in her hand. She'd thought it was a final chance to relive her past; but that wasn't possible, was it? The other alternate pasts were only ever what-ifs.

She sighed, reached through the golden bubble's tacky

surface until she felt the cloth of past-Maia's clothing, then yanked her past self through. The White Prince's claws clutched at nothing, and he sprang forward, looking about as if baffled – and furious.

Maia sat inside the bubble, her eyes wide. In front of her, her past self sat still and quiet, not even moving to take a breath. She didn't turn; she didn't seem to register anything.

That, Maia thought, was because she *hadn't* registered anything. And technically, wasn't she herself sitting outside of time right now?

"Amaranthus," present-Maia whispered as if afraid to wake her past self, "please protect me."

And then she let go of her past self, and the amber bubble shrank and pulled away until it only covered past-Maia, leaving present-Maia out in the darkened atrium. A faint outline of light marked past-Maia's forehead, complete with the scrolling word *Amaranthus*, before the entire thing blinked out of sight.

"Well," Maia said aloud, "I suppose that's that." There was a lump in her throat, but she pushed it back. This was it. She wasn't a Creature, and she didn't know what came next, but she couldn't dwell on what she'd lost.

This was her life now, and there were no other chances-

What about the final bead?

Maia looked down at the gleaming outline of the last time-chain bead. Luca/Legion had told her that although there had been five beads, she could only choose one past to interact with. She'd viewed three, rejected them, and interacted with the fourth…

And when have you known him to be right?

She paused thoughtfully. Good point. And what harm would it do to try?

Maia took the last bead in one hand, still touching the Amaranthus circlet in the other, and thought of the only possible location where she might be effective.

"That was marvellous!" Tarie heard Bets shout over the roaring sound in her ears. "Might we do it again?"

Tarie's hands shook where they clenched the steering pillar.

She blinked, trying to remove the image of searingly bright lights that had imprinted on the back of her eyes so she could take in their surroundings. They'd missed the Creatures' blockade, right? "You want to do that *again*? I'm still recovering from the first time!"

She felt Bets come up behind her and lay a hand over the steering pillar. "Ooh. You do not appear so well, Tarie. Let me steer for a bit."

It was a sign of how confused Tarie felt that she actually let the other girl drive. For a few moments she just braced herself against the sides of the open-roofed vehicle, blinking and waiting for the tingling to subside across her skin. "So that's what it feels like to be immersed in alter-power, huh? I guess you've had more practice, what with your time-travelling."

"Immersed in alter-power?" Bets barely looked up. "I did not notice. 'Twas quite an interesting hour I spent up there, though. So much to see."

"Hour?" Tarie exclaimed.

Bets glanced back over her shoulder. "Was it not for you?"

"No! It was barely a few seconds – and that was enough for me! That bright light…"

Bets' eyes widened. "And what else did you see?"

"Nothing!" Tarie paused. "Why, what did you see?"

"Er…this and that." Bets turned back to focus on the path ahead of them, which was much clearer than before, although they still flew around the occasional tall building or random Word tree (which Tarie was sure she hadn't planted).

She caught sight of Max flying nearby, and he gave them a wave. But that reminded her… "Hey, where's Jon?"

"He came out in the centre of the city." Bets sounded unconcerned. "He will follow us here, never fear."

Tarie frowned. That had happened more than once. But something else was missing…there was more space on the vehicle than there'd been before. "Ah, chaos! Where's that girl we rescued?"

"She stayed up above, remember?"

"No!" Tarie stared at her friend's back. "Are you saying we lost her?"

"No, I'm saying she chose to stay above."

"Stay above where?!"

There was a long silence. Bets looked back over her shoulder, and her lips curved slightly. "I see you do not remember. Will you trust me if I say the girl is well, and that we can discuss this later, at a safer time?"

Tarie's mouth opened and closed again silently. "I…I suppose so," she said finally.

Bets beamed. "Now, would you like to drive?"

Tarie took control again silently, still too stunned to speak. It seemed Bets's experience above the barrier was poles apart from Tarie's, and Tarie didn't like that. What had Bets seen that Tarie had missed?

But she did trust Bets. They would discuss it later, and that had to be enough, because right now they had bigger problems to deal with. "We need to meet Da and Lydia," she murmured to herself. She'd find the two of them, and then they'd decide what to do in this mad world they'd found themselves in.

Tarie steered on, checking around them anxiously for any sign of more organised Creature walls, or strange black clouds that might be chasing them, but there was nothing out of the ordinary. (Not that anything was ordinary.)

She did manage to recognise some of the roads, including the wall marking the south border of Erus city proper up ahead.

"We're coming to the meeting point," she said in relief. "Look out for a purple multi-seater, OK? One that almost matches mine." For once she was glad to have such a hideously distinctive family vehicle. She spotted the occasional vehicle on the roads spread spaghetti-like around them, but nothing stood out.

There was a long silence.

"Like that one?" Bets said, pointing.

Tarie looked. A twisted spire of grey rock stood out incongruously from the landscape, with multiple branches coming off it, almost like a poor version of the Word tree that sat so close to it. Several vehicles hung off its stony branches, clearly empty and with their doors open. About halfway up, well above ground level, was a familiar purple multi-seater.

It was empty.

But you already spoke to Cahlie, Luke had said when Maia had seen him half-dead in the other room. And Maia had known that was nonsense, because of course she hadn't spoken to Cahlie, not in years! But…what if she *had,* and she just hadn't known it yet?

Her hand hovered over the last bead of the time-chain. Then she crushed it, and thought of a time and place she'd never visited.

The final golden bubble sprang up around her. Outside it, a small multi-seater vehicle came into view. It ran along an urban road, heading higher and deeper into the city. Then it stopped briefly in an elevator between levels, rose up to the next level highest to the sun, and then drove into what Maia recognised as this very neighbourhood.

The vehicle's mirrored sides reflected the surrounding city in early stages of the current chaos, but Maia wasn't surprised when it stopped at Luca's property, the doors opened and out stepped Cahlie. She looked so similar to how Maia had last seen her – a bit sharper around the edges, perhaps, with less of a glow to her skin? But attractive and well-dressed, and minus the silly pointed hat she'd been wearing that last time in Elsewhise.

A small boy clambered out of the vehicle behind her, his eyes wide at the luxury around them. Maia's heart stuttered at the familiar shape and colour of his dark eyes, so much like her baby's. He could have been Jay-Jon's brother…

He *was* Jay-Jon's brother, from the woman that had ruined Maia's life.

"Hurry up, Kyel," Cahlie ordered, her tone just as sharp as Maia recalled. "We're late enough as it is."

Perfect timing. Maia leaned into the bubble's wall, intending to push through it as she had earlier, but the surface wouldn't give an inch.

A moment later, outside the bubble, Luca stepped out of the house's front door with a welcoming smile on his face.

Maia scowled, pausing with one hand against the surface. Should she try to go through anyway, or to wait until Luca was looking away? Luke *had* said something about her speaking to Cahlie…

But her choice was taken away from her when the golden barrier still refused to give. Instead, the scene moved along and she watched as Cahlie and the child went inside and were offered drinks and small talk in the same place where she'd so recently spoken with Luca. The small talk devolved into accusations – where it became *very* clear that Luca had drugged or poisoned

Cahlie – and as she collapsed, her son ran towards her. Luca snagged him with one arm, and the boy went still as if paralysed.

Chaos.

Maia tried to force her way out of the bubble, driven by the fear in the little boy's face, but it wouldn't give. Was it getting thinner? "Amaranthus!" she shouted in desperation. "You wouldn't tell me to use the last bead, knowing it didn't work?"

Then she could only watch as Luca sauntered over to the fallen Cahlie, checked her briefly, then using his free arm, pulled something out of one pocket. It was a safekeeper; a different one than Maia had seen earlier. He held it over Cahlie's face, and a gleam of shimmering gold emitted from her nose and mouth, briefly making the shell-shaped object glow before it dulled to brown again.

Not a safekeeper, Maia realised. Those only held objects, or occasionally, people. This was a soul-drinker – a bastardised safekeeper that stole the alter-power, the very life, from people, leaving a husk behind.

"No!" Maia shouted, digging her fingers into the bubble's surface. It seemed so close to breaking – but it held as Luca pulled away from Cahlie, smirking, then stalked away in the direction of the atrium, the stiff child still held under one arm.

There was a visible burst of alter-power as he left the room, and Maia caught a glimpse of a colossal, distorted shape for a moment before Luca came tumbling back into the room.

No, not Luca, not any more than the safekeeper was safe. This was just Luke, weary and lined and older, appearing half-unconscious as he rolled across the floor and came to a halt by hitting his head against the wall.

Legion *really* didn't need his carrier any longer.

Finally the time-chain's golden barrier gave, and Maia burst through it into the scene, catching herself as she landed several hours in the past. She didn't stop for the two prone adults, instead running after Legion where he'd disappeared with the child.

But ahead was only the atrium where she'd been impaled. The door was as well-disguised as it had been before, but she went straight for it. This time she was ready for spikes to shoot down at her – but she didn't expect the intense jolt of electricity that sent her flying backwards.

She skidded to a halt, her whole body fizzing with pain and

residual power. *"Ow..."*

So the spikes were the *second* trap.

Maia climbed to her feet, stretching to shake off the lingering pain, and studied the door. She could see the orange and red lines of alter-power stretching over it, creating a barrier that would make any intruder regret their actions. Strange that she could see it so clearly now when usually she'd only catch glimpses, but this was no ordinary time.

She'd chased after Legion and the boy on instinct, and it made her sick to think of any child being vulnerable and afraid as he must be.

But...if there was only one reality, then she *hadn't* saved the boy. He was still in there, sleeping alongside so many others, when she'd gone into the safekeeper – would go into the safe-keeper – a mere few hours into the future.

Maia paused a moment longer, then whirled around and dashed back to the parlour where she'd come from. She went straight to Cahlie's prone body, which was sprawled on the floor where she'd fallen. Her face was deathly pale, but Maia could see faint sparks of gold light mixed with wisps of black cloud around her mouth and nose.

The gold was life-force, Maia knew that much. Legion hadn't taken all of it. But what was the black cloud?

Maia cupped her hands over Cahlie's nose and mouth, willing the alter-power to return to where it had come from. Sometimes this would work, because alter-power was suggestible...

This time she was in luck. She lifted her hands to see the faint gold sparks had mostly vanished, along with the black cloud, but Cahlie was lying so still. Maia tried once more, intently willing the alter-power to return *inside* the woman's body. Then finally there was nothing left showing, and perhaps Cahlie's colour was just a little better, but she certainly wasn't awake.

"Amaranthus, heal her!" Maia said in frustration, forgetting she wasn't holding the circlet – and that her usual use of the word of power now sounded more like a request.

There was a faint light, maybe a touch more gold, but nothing noticeable. Maia watched the woman's chest move ever so slightly, then a faint groan from behind her caught her attention.

She turned her attention to Luke. The man's colour was almost as pale as Cahlie's, which ill-suited his olive skin tone, but at least he was clearly alive. But far more gold came from his nose and mouth, along with other parts of his body. Unlike Cahlie, there was no black mist.

Maia set herself to forcing the alter-power back into Luke's body too, until it seemed to all rest inside and nothing more escaped. "You're not dead," she told him coolly. "I already spoke to you. Will speak to you."

But the probably-unconscious Luke didn't respond.

Maia was well aware that in this room were two of the people who'd most wronged her. Cahlie had done so by maliciousness, but Luke had by intentional neglect. And then the last person – the one who'd misshaped Maia's life as a bounce-back from her own misused power and then intentional neglect – lay long-dead in the back of this house.

A tear trickled down Maia's face. She knew why they'd done it; or enough, anyway. Now she was here with them, she didn't want to know more.

Except then she looked across at Cahlie and saw the woman's eyes were slightly open. Maia stared at her, and Cahlie stared back. Maia found one question springing to mind. "Are you sorry?"

Cahlie blinked a long, slow blink, and her response was soft but clear. "Sorry...for a youthful...mistake? I make a point of never...regretting...any of my choices. Life's...too short...for that."

No, Cahlie wasn't sorry, even at death's door. Maia didn't think she would be, but hearing it still hurt. She looked away, disappointed in spite of herself. "I lost my baby," she said. "My sister raised him. He's grown up and doesn't know who I am."

Cahlie raised a hand and let it flop on the ground. "Chaos...happens."

For a moment, Maia was angry enough that she could have kicked the other woman. "It does. Luke's Creature just took your little boy away, and I couldn't stop him. Irony, huh?"

Cahlie sucked in a breath, then when she exhaled, a puff of black cloud came out once more. "Kyel...?"

"If that's the child who was here with you and Luca a few minutes ago, yes." Maia turned away, ashamed of herself.

A wordless, anguished groan came out of Cahlie's mouth, then silence. When that persisted several seconds longer, Maia turned back to see Cahlie had gone still. A few sparks of gold dissipated into the air around her mouth, but another small cloud of black puffed out, hovered in the air briefly, then disappeared.

Cahlie looked dead.

She *was* dead, Maia realised. It didn't take a genius to work that out.

"I thought you said people couldn't die right now," Maia said to no one in particular, Luke still being unconscious, and the horrendous Legion being inside that booby-trapped room with that poor little boy. (Poorer for being Cahlie's.) "But look at Cahlie."

No one looked, although Maia did one more time. She felt numb again, standing in front of the person who'd actively ruined her life, and knowing that resolution was impossible now.

Chaos happens. Yeah, it sure did. And now Maia had used up all of the time-chain, and had gained only a few hours for all her trouble.

But she'd spoken to Cahlie, and maybe had saved Luke's life. She'd also seen Legion take Kyel.

"Kyel was asleep when I saw him in the safekeeper," Maia thought aloud. "And that won't happen for a couple of hours. So I don't get him out, do I?"

But there must be *something* she could do. Anything.

Maia turned and walked back to the booby-trapped atrium. She touched the door lightly, and this time, the jolt was weaker. It sent her reeling back rather than knocking her over.

"And this trap," she mused, "wasn't working at all. So someone broke it – *will* break it. I wonder if it's me?"

And the Amaranthus circlet must be in there right now. It would still be there when Maia arrived (would arrive) later, so Maia knew she wouldn't take it away now. But even if she couldn't get inside the safekeeper, maybe she could use the circlet anyway.

"Plan sorted," she said decisively.

Now, how many attempts would it take to get through that door?

13
The Real Legion

Elspeth's heart sank as she recognised the purplish vehicle as a match to Tarie's own. Along with other vehicles, it hung off the rocky spire high in the air, much like a poorly decorated Ecksmas tree from centuries past.

Even from here, she could clearly see the damage to its body and blackened paint. It was also clearly empty.

"Nooo," Tarie moaned from next to her. "Da…Lydia! Where are they?"

And Anni too, Elspeth thought grimly. "Let's have a look, shall we?"

Tarie drew as close to the spire as she could manage, then leapt off the hover-vehicle, leaving Elspeth to scramble for the controls. Tarie landed lower down on the spire, grabbed at it, then fell further as chunks of it came off in her hands. "Argh!"

But it seemed to be a scream of frustration, not pain, and with a set expression she began to climb upwards, using the soft spires as handholds.

Elspeth focused on getting the hover-vehicle safely to the ground. It kept shuddering underneath her, the tremors and irregularities that affected technology now very much in play, and she drew it to a halt before stepping off and looking up. The ground underfoot seemed strange: sticky and almost tar-like. *Do you see any sign of Tarren, Lydia or Anni from up there?* she asked Max.

He was high above them, closer to the low silvery barrier, and he looked around before shaking his head. *Not a sign of them or anyone else.*

Oh, collywobbles! They should have been so lucky.

A few moments later Tarie reached the battered purple vehicle. 'Twas clear to Elspeth that whatever she saw, 'twas not

"

what she'd wished to see. A few moments after ducking her head inside the vehicle, Tarie pulled away and began to climb down.

As she reached Elspeth, she said grimly, "We never should have separated from them. Now we don't know where they are, and anything could have happened! And we left for what, a feeling?"

It had been a certainty more than a feeling, and beyond that, Elspeth had much the same certainty now. "There were no signs of injury?"

"No sign of them, either. Not a hint."

"Then they are around here somewhere," Elspeth said optimistically. "Where would you go if you suddenly found yourself without a working vehicle?"

"Nowhere, because we agreed to meet them here." But Tarie's expression lightened a little. "With all these Creatures about, surely they've hidden somewhere. We just need to find them."

They looked around. To Elspeth, it seemed as though the landscape had darkened significantly, any light being dimmed by the oddly moving rock and strange spires that now seemed to be everywhere.

The buildings out here were sparser and lower, not reaching the exceptional heights and structures of the city centre, but they too seemed to have changed even in the last few minutes. The idea of finding anyone who didn't want to be found seemed ludicrous.

But in the distance, a smudge of red and green stood out against the grey and black surroundings. "Look, a Word tree!" Elspeth pointed out triumphantly. "I'd vow they've gone there!"

"It's a bit of a walk," Tarie argued, but without energy. "Do you really think they went there?"

"I would, should I have found myself here." Elspeth looked up once more at the vehicle where it hung so bizarrely. How had it got all the way up there?

They could've been captured by the Creatures, Max suggested. *That would explain the vehicle, and when's the last time you saw a single regular human?*

The rescued girl, less than an hour earlier. But nobody since, and for a city with more people than had lived in Elspeth's own country in her birth era, that was most unnatural.

"More to the point," Elspeth mused aloud. "When is the last

time you saw *any* living being, human or Creature?"

Tarie gave her an odd look. "Did I miss something?"

"Nothing of import," Elspeth replied lightly. "We should get back on the hover-vehicle, yes? And see what we can find. Except..." She looked above them again, frowning. The bright silvery reflection of the sky-barrier was dimmed, or rather, partially blocked by more of that odd, light-swallowing rocky substance. It looked rather like tar. "Was that there before?"

It's growing, Max told her, his mental voice sounding fainter. She couldn't see him any longer. *It's blocking you off!*

"Get back on the vehicle!" Elspeth told Tarie urgently. "We're in a trap!"

But Tarie's eyes widened, and next thing, she yanked Elspeth off the vehicle by one arm, tossing her to the ground. A wave of heat and alter-power blasted her from behind as light filled her vision.

"Not this again," Elspeth muttered as she pushed herself up off the sticky, rough ground. Behind her, the hover-vehicle was alight with purple and green flames interspersed with what looked like lightning, but Elspeth knew was alter-power. Frowning, she blasted it with silvery flame. The purple and green flames died back, but the ground shuddered and a new spire shot upwards, taking the battered and burned vehicle with it. A few moments later, the hover-vehicle hung next to all the others, hooked by its broken windows and high in the air.

"Mystery solved," Tarie muttered. "But what now?"

Elspeth looked around warily. Her impression that the roof was closing over them seemed to be confirmed as the odd rock moved by the second. But worse than that, was the way the same tarlike substance seemed to be alive as it crawled over every building and bit of ground space...

It's not as bad as that, Max's voice came faintly. *It's just Creatures. Lots and lots of Creatures. Er...you might want to get out of there.*

As if her vision came into focus, Elspeth saw that the moving walls were actually dozens of tar-coloured figures, each rough-hewn and stringy-skinned as though they'd been formed quickly as an afterthought. But their eyes shone distinctly one yellow, one blue, and the Tiger's pledge mark glowed orange-red on their foreheads, like cracks in hardening lava.

And in the last few seconds, the spacious gaps around Elspeth and Tarie had narrowed to nothing.

Lots of Creatures, indeed. But get out of there...how, exactly?!

——— ✷ ———

It didn't take long at all to get into the atrium once Maia stopped using the actual door. Instead she walked around the side of it, found a substantial break in the soft wall presumably caused by the chaos around them, and slipped through. The wall fell back into place after her.

Huh. Lucky.

Inside, the circlet sat on its pedestal, glowing faintly against the artificial light, with the enhanced safekeeper sitting in its centre. Maia moved as close as she could without touching anything, then cupped her hands close enough to the circlet that she thought she could feel the tingle of power coming off it.

"Amaranthus," she said quietly, and this time she knew she was speaking to a person, not just a power source. "Keep the boy – Kyel – safe. Don't let him die. Don't let Legion steal more than Kyel can afford to give up."

The circlet seemed to hum with agreement, so Maia took a deep breath, then continued. "Amaranthus. May Legion's plans fail. Whatever they are, if they're selfish, let them fail. Don't let him take another life, not even one. Let the safekeeper be truly safe for everyone inside until it's time for them all to come out. But protect the boy. Especially the boy."

And that sent Maia's mind straight to her own boy, who had been stolen from her by the passage of time, and then who her own choices had led her to harm earlier that day. "Amaranthus," she said, and this time her voice was small. "Please...make that right. Please...give me another chance, and keep my boy safe. May he be strong, and smart, and lucky..."

Then Maia fell automatically into the same speech patterns as she had through the last few years of her waking life. Speaking blessing over her son, no matter how old he might be. Begging...asking so carefully for another chance at relationship and motherhood and *life*, even though it felt so farfetched and even stupid to ask. But she still asked.

She spoke out requests and statements until the room was

saturated with alter-power and reflected with gold lights from the shining circlet, and the safekeeper shone like a diamond within it. And then she was jolted back to attention by sounds from outside the atrium.

Maia immediately recognised the sound of her earlier self. Angry. Bitter. Had those hours passed already? Quickly, she jumped up and slipped out of the atrium the same way she'd come in.

The next stretch of time was bizarre. She stood silently at the crack in the wall, watching as her recent past self was stabbed in the shoulder by one of those traps – ouch! – then tried to pick up the circlet and was pulled into the safekeeper. Not long later, she came flying out again, and her skin was much greyer and somehow wrong-looking compared to how it had been.

Then came the anger, ugh, which went on forever, and then came the talk with Amaranthus. Oddly enough, as Maia watched her own past self, it was as if she was having the whole conversation again too, as if Amaranthus was speaking to *this* her as well.

And then finally past-Maia was cleansed of all the negative alter-power. This Maia saw it happen; saw the greyness wash off, replaced with healthy skin and a kind of glow that was surprisingly similar to the circlet.

Did Maia really look like that?

But present-Maia managed to keep silent and remain an observer until her past self went through the process of using the last two beads of the time-chain, and finally, disappeared into the last one.

Present-Maia stood silently even after her past self had gone, uncertain if it was safe to come out, and where her past self was now. She dithered for a few moments longer, then realised that she'd caught up with herself, and the only Maia around in this moment was in fact her.

Shaking her head partly in amusement, she went back into the atrium the same way she'd left it. The circlet was still there, of course, but it seemed to glow so much more, and carried the same welcoming brightness that Amaranthus himself had.

It looked like it wanted to be picked up. To be held and used for its intended purpose.

So Maia held out a hand to it, and then without thinking further, snatched it up.

A red-orange ring of power exploded from the safekeeper, throughout the room and dissipated into the walls.

Uh oh.

For a moment nothing happened. Then something huge and greyish white seemed to rush out of the safekeeper, going from tiny to enormous in mere moments. It smashed through the atrium wall and even the *house's* wall, then settled as a sizeable, crystalline-walled building where the north wall of Luca's house had been.

Maia just stared. Then remembering the city's worth of buildings inside the safekeeper, she threw herself to the ground.

It turned out to be a good move. Mere minutes later, the massive rush of buildings exiting the safekeeper had come to a halt. With them had come people: figures Maia glimpsed only briefly before they disappeared into either a gold light that vanished upwards or a dark vapour that seemed to absorb into the ground.

Then finally, when she dared lift her head, she saw the fine mansion around her had been obliterated. In its place was a narrow city street, filled with buildings upon buildings in what was surely the architectural style of neighbouring Dailan. They were packed tightly together, sitting awkwardly as though they'd been carelessly placed by a giant child. Deep shadows sat dark in the hollows created by the evening weather.

Evening? When had it been evening?

Maia climbed to her feet, shaking herself off, but still gripping the circlet like the treasure it was. She looked up. Instead of the light greyish sky she was certain she'd last seen, the sky revealed by the mansion's destruction was…odd. Light patches shimmered silvery and almost rainbow-coloured amongst pitch black, like clouds made of tar. But the darkness was growing and covering the light moment by moment, like an auto-roof drawing shut.

She shuddered and wrapped the circlet twice around her wrist, afraid she'd lose it. But it didn't seem like enough, so she took it off and shoved it onto her head. She'd been aiming to wear it around her neck, but the thing seemed to stick at forehead level and refuse to move. It felt good there, warm and powerful, so she left it.

The safekeeper caught her eye. It had fallen off the pedestal (which was now presumably pulp) and it gleamed silver where it lay partially hidden by the doorstep of a new Dailanese building.

Maia blinked, and for a moment seemed to see a tiny figure superimposed over the safekeeper's form. A little boy, curled up with his knees against his chest. And wrapped around him was a…big, squishy-looking blob.

The boy was Kyel. Maia had only seen him briefly through the time-chain, and before that within Legion's safekeeper city, but she wouldn't forget those eyes that were so much like Jay-Jon's.

Maia opened her mouth to call him out of the safekeeper, but then halted, remembering what had happened to the others. As all the other people had come out of the safekeeper, they'd rapidly vanished into bursts of alter-power, which had gone…somewhere. She didn't want Kyel to suffer the same fate, whatever that fate might be.

And what had happened to Legion? Maia tensed, looking around her anxiously as she suddenly recalled that she hadn't seen the Creature out here. He'd have been turned into mist too, if she was lucky enough. Otherwise, he'd be somewhere in that tangle of buildings…

The circlet pulsed on Maia's head again, and again her vision briefly changed. The image of the little boy reappeared along with his squishy wrap, then vanished.

Maia made a decision. She couldn't leave him in there, even knowing what he risked on coming out. She bent down to the safekeeper and touched her hand to it. "Ky-"

Something *exploded* from the safekeeper, hitting her full force and sending her tumbling backwards, skidding along the ground until she came to a stop at the base of the nearest building.

Then she was blinking upwards at the…thing…that was on top of her. It was like a bag of jelly the size of a room, gleaming royal blue and shimmering pink and gold with every gelatinous movement. She lay for a moment, mesmerised by the play of what looked like pure alter-power held by a thin membrane. And was that a *spine* inside? But then the power-jelly-bag rippled and moved, and tentacles formed out of it, shaping into a dozen little heads with glowing white eyes. A central head formed: dark blue, handsome and human.

But Maia recognised it, and swallowed.

She hadn't thought the real Legion would look like *this.* She'd tried to call for Kyel!

"What," the heads all hissed in unison, lowering down to press against hers, *"have you done, Maia deDavinia?"*

She couldn't even take in a breath. She gasped for air, hiccupped, then spat out a stream of words she didn't recognise, but which glowed with alter-power. A thick red and green vine shot out of nowhere, slapping Legion like a whip, and he reared back, heads vanishing back into his gleaming mass and reappearing from the other side.

Maia scrambled to her feet, snatched up the safekeeper with its single occupant, and fled into the maze of buildings.

Tarie spun in circles, trying to keep everything in view, but it really was as bad as she'd thought. They were surrounded. How in Hades had they got surrounded?

Literally, literally just moments ago they'd been in a darkened cityscape, and now they appeared to be in a rapidly shrinking cavern, surrounded by dozens of pairs of eyes in the darkness.

She was speaking the Words in a steady stream – she couldn't have stopped if she'd wanted to – and red and green vines sprang up from the strange black stuff surrounding, only to be swallowed up moments later by the ever-moving darkness.

"Do not panic," Bets said from somewhere to her left, "but we appear to be in a trap. We shall have to fight our way out."

Oh, *good.* When were they not in a trap?! Tarie stopped rattling off Words just long enough to hiss, "Why do these sorts of things always happen around *you?!*"

"Indeed, I'd vow they always happen around *you,*" Bets' voice came back, but it was almost inaudible. "I merely happen to be in your company."

Rude!

One of the nearest tar figures lunged at Tarie, faster than she'd expected, and she batted it away almost carelessly. It sailed across the space and vanished into the nearest wall. But they were everywhere, and it felt like at any moment she'd be attacked full-force with no place to go and no way to stop these things.

Just then, a bright, silvery light exploded in the side of Tarie's vision, and an opening appeared. For a moment, Bets stood in it, ringed by light, then stepped through. Her hands were alight with flame in a steady stream, and the darkness around them lurched back as she neared. The tar creatures hissed.

"By the rood," Bets breathed, sounding a little rattled. "'Tis a mercy that they respond to the flame, yes? When I was separated from you, I thought I mightn't see you again!"

Tarie's eyes widened and she took a big step towards the other girl, until they were side by side. She hadn't actually realised they'd been separated. If she had, no doubt she would've panicked for real. "Any chance this is all in our heads?" she asked hopefully.

Bets shook her head. "If only 'twere. No, regrettably this is quite real. But you need not panic-"

"Stop saying that!"

Another tar figure lunged at them, eyes glowing, then another, then a whole swarm. Suddenly they were all Tarie could see, coming at her from every angle even as she rattled off the Words and punched wildly and called up saplings that seemed to be swallowed up in darkness even as they appeared. Flashes of silver punctuated the edges of her vision, but beyond that, she couldn't see Bets any longer.

A sticky dark-grey hand grasped her exposed wrist where her smart sleeves had failed, and a jolt of lightning shot through her. Actually, it felt like something had been taken from her, like she'd grown weaker.

She shook it off, hissing in pain, and punched at the figure even as others mobbed her from all around. For a moment her hand seemed to go *inside* the figure, and it burned just the same. She tried to pull away, but the tar people had got her from every angle, and it was in her mouth; blocking her eyes; filling her ears; holding down her arms…

Master, a voice whispered. *Here is the safekeeper.*

And Tarie didn't know how she felt it with everything holding her in place, making her blind; but she felt the safe-keeper's removal from her jacket.

Gavriel. That was the one with Gavriel inside.

Oh, sch-

Jon managed to find seven people in the strange depths of this Erus city, helping six of them to reach the safety of Word trees even as Creatures pursued.

The seventh person reached the base of the Word tree then bailed, deciding the natural staircase was a worse option than the darkness and danger outside of it. They turned into a Creature before his eyes.

Jon leapt away into the air before the new Creature could attack him, but his eyes were wide with horror from what he'd seen yet again.

Humans should not become Creatures. For his entire life, his understanding of existence, Creatures were one thing; humans were another. And now, somehow, that had changed along with the two realms merging into one.

And yet, he wasn't surprised. It was like when he'd seen Max descend from the tree stairway with Tarie, earlier when they'd thought he'd died. And seeing him again, Jon had been happy, but not surprised. It had seemed…obvious.

And in the same way, seeing this human turn away from the Word tree then turn into something entirely new, seemed obvious too. They'd made their choice, and here was the consequence. He had to accept it and move on.

Jon sailed around the highest points of the city once again, listening for cries that would indicate anyone else needing help, but the usual sounds had been replaced by a strange whispering, like everything had been coated in sponge and there was no room for normal sounds. It was growing darker by the moment.

I've been helping a few people, he sent across to Bets and Max, who he hadn't seen since their brief trip through the silvery water-ceiling. *Call out to me, and I'll come to you.*

But there was just silence, even in his mind. He paused mid-air. *BETS! MAAAX! WHERE ARE YOU?*

We-…in…ksh…

The response was so quiet that Jon almost didn't hear it. *I'LL COME TO YOU,* he thought as strongly as he could. Because what else could he do?

He tried to orient himself amongst the remains of what had

been an impressive neighbourhood, and realised he wasn't far from the palatial home Luca had taken as chairman. Then-

Well. An entire new city block appeared.

A building rushed up in front of him, as fast as the Word trees had grown after the flood, although thankfully not hitting him this time. It was as big as his apartment block had been, forty or fifty floors of shining crystalline surface, and in an unfamiliar style. As it shot up, he saw shimmers of gold come off it along with wafting black mist.

"What on earth...?"

On such a strange day, this still managed to surprise him. So Jon flew backwards in the air until he was safely in a gap between two buildings, and watched incredulously as the landscape sprouted a new neighbourhood.

It took less than a minute, and when the deluge of buildings finally stopped, they sat there in the darkness shining like glass. They were too close for comfort, clearly sharing far less space than they'd been designed for, and somehow he'd been caught up in their reforming. He looked up to see an entire building set sideways across two others, above his head. As he watched, patches of sticky black appeared on the shining sides of the new building, then began to spread.

Huh.

He looked down to see the same thing happening to the levels below him. Some kind of toxic alter-power, he guessed? Strange that everything was so different, but with the glimpse he'd had of the world beyond the silvery barrier, he didn't care that this one was so quickly being covered up.

"GIVE ME THAT SAFEKEEPER!"

The voice was a roar that seemed to echo from every plane of the buildings around him. But the tone sounded oddly familiar...

Far below him, a girl ran through what passed as narrow streets, sprinting as though for her life. Her reddish hair sailed behind her, and her skin shone in the semi-darkness. He could hear the panting of her startled breaths. She leapt over a fallen vehicle, paused and looked back behind her, and he'd swear a Word vine came out of her mouth, blocking the path behind even as she turned and ran again.

And then her pursuer came into sight. Jon blinked at it, then just stared.

The thing was the size of a train car. Its shuffled along on stumpy legs that seemed to appear as they were needed, and dozens of heads on long necks moved in and out of its shining blue sides.

It was almost beautiful, Jon thought, considering it resembled a squishy pet toy he'd had once as a child. It didn't have the foul feeling that other Creatures had; the sense that they ought to have been buried some weeks before, but were somehow still walking.

"STOP, OR YOU'LL BE SORRY!" a central head roared, and was echoed by a dozen smaller heads. A whip-like tendril came out of the Creature's side and slashed at the girl ahead, barely missing her and striking the hard surface of the building instead. A burst of gold alter-power emitted, and the tendril pulled back into the main bulk of its body as if injured.

He probably ought to help the girl, Jon thought. Here was hoping he could carry her.

Jon dove for the ground, calling out, "Hold up your arms!"

Her head lifted, her eyes meeting his for the barest moment before he grabbed her outstretched arms. Her hands wrapped around his forearms, and his around hers, and he shot back up to the top of the nearest building.

Mere seconds later, they came to land, and Jon let her go. In those few moments, he'd recognised her. But unlike the last time he'd seen her and taken her as an imposter, this time he *recognised* her.

"Ma...*aia*?" He'd almost said 'Ma', but had caught himself at the last moment.

His birth mother watched him with owlishly wide eyes. She swallowed audibly and gave a short nod.

Maia DeDavinia looked just like the pictures Anni had shown him. But somehow she seemed smaller; shorter; younger. And her skin had a glow of alter-power that was echoed by the thin silver line around her forehead. Scrolling text moved along its surface as he watched.

Huh. Jon looked down at his own wrist to where he still wore the circlet he'd borrowed from his younger self, then back at the girl in front of him.

Yep. Somehow, she wore the same circlet around her

forehead – surely the one she'd stolen from him earlier. *Nice job, Ma.*

Maia licked her lips and pointed at his wrist. "How…do you still have that?"

"I stepped outside of time and stole a version from my younger self." *Like mother, like son.*

"Oh…" Her head dipped at his unfriendly tone. "Well…you'd be better wearing it around your forehead. It helps you see differently, and…I think it's what it's made for." There was a silence, and she added in a small voice, "If you want to."

"Thanks." But Jon didn't move to adjust the circlet.

Several more moments passed where he couldn't look away from that oddly familiar face. Maybe once he would have blasted her: told her all the ways she'd failed him. But today, he just saw her face and knew she was sorry, and sad, and in pain, and most definitely his birth mother.

"I thought you were working with Luca," Jon said. "I saw you getting into his vehicle the day you came to my- to Anni's apartment."

"I thought it was a hire-vech. I thought…I thought all of this was a trick." Maia gestured around her in a way that echoed his own movement. "The years passing. I didn't believe it. I…I left you with my sister in the morning, intending to be back in the afternoon. But…it all went wrong." Her voice broke. "All those lost years. I want them back, but I can't get them, can I?"

He believed her. It was as if in this strange atmosphere, in this broken version of Earth, she couldn't lie to him. He would have seen it. And he didn't think to lie to her. "No."

Maia's head dropped.

"But," Jon found himself saying, "there's something new, something different, up there." He pointed upwards to where the silvery sky barrier had been blocked by buildings. "If we can get to a Word tree, you can climb up there yourself."

"A what?"

"A- you know, one of those?" Jon pointed.

Maia saw it, nodded once, then stilled.

This was the most awkward conversation he'd ever had. *His mother was alive and hadn't meant to leave him.*

Also, the world appeared to be ending.

Talk about bad timing.

The grown-up Jay-Jon stood across from Maia, his face glowing slightly in the semi-darkness and displaying a distinct lack of judgment or hatred.

It felt like if Amaranthus was a perfume, he'd be wearing it.

Being so close to him, with everything that had happened and *who he was*, made Maia want to cry. But she swallowed it back and blurted out, "I love you. And I'm sorry I left you, but I had a rejection curse that made everyone leave me, then it turned out to actually be a death curse and it was only- well, *me* that kept me alive but asleep all these years.

"Luca said I could take it all back and start again. He gave me a time-travel device if only I'd get him the circlet you were- are wearing, and that was why I took it from you, and I'm sorry! But Amaranthus…well, Amaranthus explained that I couldn't change the past. What's happened, happened. I couldn't undo the time I lost, only…work with it. So I did. And here I am, but I don't know what to do."

It all came out in a rush, and when she finished, Maia felt so confused and hopeful and ashamed that she couldn't meet her son's eyes.

And then she felt a light touch on her hand. She looked up to see Jay-Jon with his cheeks a little flushed, but his expression intent. "This is so incredibly important, all of what you're telling me now. And for whatever you did or didn't do, I forgive you, alright? And we'll have time to sort through all of this. But…"

Maia raised her eyebrows expectantly.

He grimaced, then continued. "Firstly, I think the world is ending, or something like it. I need to find my friends, and we need to get ourselves up above that silver barrier, assuming we don't see anyone who needs our help." And while she came to grips with that, he continued, "Also, the Creature-thing that was following you has climbed up the side of the building. We should probably move now."

"Oh!" Maia stepped aside just as one of Legion's shining tendrils shot over the building's edge, barely missing her, then fell back. She could hear the *suck, suck, suck* sound of his weird foot-things attaching themselves to the building's hard sides. Chaos.

She hadn't realised he could climb so well. "Can you fly us away?!"

Jay-Jon took her arms again, and this time she let herself float as he carried them across the short distance to the nearest building opposite. They touched down just as Legion's gelatinous mass *flumped* his way into view on the building they'd just been on. He sagged with what was surely disappointment, and the shimmering blue of his bulk briefly turned dark. He let out a roar.

Jay-Jon watched him with a frown, then said in an aside to Maia, "You can fly a little? I didn't feel your weight just then."

She shrugged, a little embarrassed. She'd lived this way her whole life, but it felt strange telling her suddenly-grown-up son. "I replicate the gifts of people I'm in contact with, but in a weaker way. So I have all sorts of weird abilities that come and go. But the flying one will be nice while it lasts."

"That explains the vine," he murmured. "You borrowed it from Tarie."

Just across from them, Legion was stretching himself into spaghetti-like strands and reaching carefully out over the gap between buildings. It didn't look like he'd make it, not by a long-shot. After a few moments he seemed to have the same conclusion, and with a noticeable mutter, began to suction his way back down the first building.

"Lucky that Creatures can't fly," Maia said without thinking. "I wonder why that is?"

"Long story that I'll tell you when I get a chance," Jon replied. "But why is that thing following you? Something about a safekeeper?"

"Oh!" Maia pulled out Kyel's safekeeper from inside her jacket. "Well, it's Luke."

"In there?!"

"No, no! I meant, the thing chasing me is a sort-of Creature, but somehow it's not, I don't understand how. No, Luke was his carrier and went by…Luca, that's right. But the Creature's real name is Legion. He didn't need Luke anymore. Got rid of him today."

Jay-Jon went very still. "Is Luke…dead?'"

Maia looked at the Dailanese buildings packing the space where Luca's mansion had been, and grimaced. "He wasn't…"

The boy's whole body slumped. "Luke changed so much

when he became a carrier," he murmured. "I never understood why he chose to when he hated Creatures so much."

"Luke didn't choose it. Legion said he forced it on him." That had been just one more shocker to deal with – that Creatures *could* force a human to become a carrier – but it hadn't been the worst thing she'd had to deal with.

Jay-Jon swore under his breath. "I can't believe that thing is Luca. It doesn't look like any Creature I've seen."

Maia shrugged. She couldn't disagree. Legion was…unique.

Jay-Jon began, "Do you-"

Suddenly a shining tendril shot out of nowhere and snatched the safekeeper right from Maia's loose grasp, pulling it back to where Legion now sat at the edge of this building. He'd managed to climb down the last building and up this one far faster than she'd expected, coming from the side with the greatest drop. She gasped and lunged for it even as Legion's central head hissed at her, and a silvery flame seemed to shoot out of her hands.

She'd been aiming for Legion, but the silver rushed out of her and covered her instead. For a moment it burned like fire, but the pain passed and was replaced with a cool pleasant feeling. And everywhere it touched, she saw the fine threads of her ancient curse burn up and fall off. Seconds later, the flame disappeared.

Maia stood with her hands outspread and just about wept. All this effort to remove a curse, and now she'd just done it by accident?!

A scream caught her attention. Across the rooftop, Legion was thrashing in a mist of silvery flame – she'd caught him with it after all. A moment later, the safekeeper tumbled from his grasp. It fell over the side of the building, hit the paved space below that was all that remained of that high city level, then bounced. She saw the tiny pale shape bounce to the edge of that level, then tumble down into the darkness.

Maia and Legion wailed in unison.

"What was in there?" Jay-Jon asked in a too-calm tone.

"Your brother!"

"My what?!"

They both dove over the side of the building.

Elspeth sent her fire gift everywhere, slashing and burning and shouting at the tar-people-Creatures that were coming at them from every direction, pressing in so very close. Now she could barely see Tarie at all, although she could still hear her occasionally, but no matter how hard she fought, the tar-Creatures kept coming. The very *walls* appeared to be working with them and working against her.

She wasn't afraid, but she was angry indeed. With a frustrated scream, she sent a rush of flame in every direction around her – shooting out from her entire body rather than just her hands. She forced it out with all the energy she had in her (which was quite a lot, it turned out), and when the light faded, she saw she'd cleared a sizeable space in the darkness down here.

Then Elspeth saw a woman. She was pale white against the surrounding darkness; pale of skin and with hair the same shade; the only thing that seemed to be almost human down here, and her back was to Elspeth. She stood over a pile of red/green vines that was surely Tarie, which was also surrounded by a crush of tar-Creatures.

One Creature blinked blue and yellow eyes and held up a hand with something small in it. *"Master,"* it whispered in a tone that reverberated from the very walls. *"Here is the safekeeper."*

The woman took the object in one dead-white hand, holding it up in front of her. "Gavriel, come out," she ordered in a smooth, pleasant voice.

A cloud of grey and yellow billowed out from the safekeeper. Then there was Gavriel, just as Elspeth had last seen him before Tarie had ordered him into the safekeeper. But he looked worse for wear. His golden hair was flattened and irregular, and his previously handsome features were now thin to the point of gauntness. "My master," he began. "I–"

"Enough." The woman stretched out a hand and gripped Gavriel's neck. His eyes closed as if 'twas a caress – then suddenly a rush of shimmering light came out of his nose and mouth, going straight into the woman. Gavriel shuddered, then like an apple core withering, dried and changed into darkest grey, stringy form. He blinked newly bright eyes; one yellow, one blue; and his Tiger pledge mark stood out against his forehead like wounds or cracks.

He had turned into just one more tar-man.

Then the woman turned, and her profile came into view, revealing a pug nose and a severe underbite. Taken along with her lamp-yellow eyes and white colouring, Elspeth recognised her instantly, and 'twas as if she came awake with that realisation.

Lilith! 'Twas the pox-riddled, cankerous Halfling wretch who Elspeth had faced so recently – it seemed like mere weeks ago to Elspeth, but to Lilith, it must have been centuries.

See this, *this* was why one ought to dispose of their enemies promptly rather than leave them be, for it could cause no end of trouble in years to come. And how did the witch never age?!

"Lilith!" Elspeth roared, lifting a hand. Silver flame shot out in a steady stream, straight across the distance. But at the last moment, the woman sprang aside, and a trio of tar-men were in her place. The flame caught them instead, and they fell in a shining puddle to the ground, which seemed to absorb them.

A pillar of black sponge-rock shot up in front of Elspeth, but she darted around it, flame full-ahead. She had naught in mind but to reach Tarie, but there were so many obstacles in her way. Why were there so many?

But she had a full view of a new pillar that came tumbling down, as big as an apartment building, and landed squarely on Tarie and her pile of vines. The sound of it landing was as loud as a cannon blast, and the ground shook from its impact.

Elspeth was stunned into silence. No human would survive such a strike, not even indomitable Tarie with her special abilities.

Across from her, Lilith met her eyes and laughed. "I don't know who you are," she called, "but I've met others with that silver flame. They all died, and so will you."

"They did *not* all die!" Elspeth shot back. "I am here, am I not?" She held up both hands, each alight with silver flame that burned like a torch, sending flickering shadows all around. "How do you intend to defeat-"

SMACK. She was hit full-force by another falling pillar. She got the barest sense of *size* and a crushing blow, and then – nothing.

14
Made of Magick

The safekeeper, Jon thought as he shot downwards into the darkness, towards where he'd last seen that tiny object. *My brother's in the safekeeper. (What's he doing in there? And oh! That's right – I have a brother!)*

From right behind him he could hear: *Faster. How do I fall faster? Oh, how could I have dropped it?* Then, *Oh, there's the ground. I hope I can stop-*

Jon reached back and grabbed hold of Maia just as they reached a platform several levels down, pulling them both to a halt right before they hit the dark concrete. Down here, only the faintest rays of light reached, leaving everything in shades of grey. Over the platform's edge was pitch darkness – what he'd guess were several levels more, and then the rarely seen ground level.

How had the safekeeper managed to fall this far? But Jon knew it had.

No one ever went to the ground levels of Erus city. They'd been built more than fifteen hundred years before, and rather than demolish them, the city had just kept going up, and up, and up.

And pooh, they *smelled.* He'd come close to this the day before when they'd headed north to Elsewhise, but hadn't gone so deep. But he'd smelled it then too; rank and rotten and chemical all at the same time. *Wrong.*

"It's Creature," Maia whispered from beside him. She still wore the glowing Amaranthus circlet around her forehead, and her eyes reflected some of its golden glow. "Down there. Can't you see it?"

"Ah…*a* Creature?"

She shook her head. "No. No…it's all Creature. I can sense where the safekeeper is, but I'm afraid to go get it. I don't think I'll be able to fly up in time."

Jon could. This might be an elaborate trap, but he was willing to risk it. "Where is it exactly?"

Maia gave him an exasperated look. "Put your circlet on properly, and you'll see it yourself."

Jon returned the look, but took off the circlet, still gripping it tightly, and held it in front of him. As before, looking through its centre gave him a sharp, bright view, and he moved it carefully around, trying to spot anything on the ground far below.

Huh. The ground wasn't as far as he'd thought it was…and what *was* that? It was all black…spongy…something…?

Creature, Maia had said. But that was no Creature he'd ever seen before.

Just then, a shining blue shape shot across his vision, heading right downwards. Jon caught a glimpse of it through the circlet's centre, then it was gone. He swore. "The Creature thing has gone down there. I have to go after it."

Then with the barest pause, he leapt over the edge. He just heard Maia's voice call after him, *"His name is Legion!"*

Legion, was it? Well, a Creature was a Creature, and this one had taken over Jon's own father. He had a score to settle…and he still had a working safekeeper of his own.

Maia watched her grown-up son leap off the platform and disappear into the near-darkness. Through the odd clarity the circlet gave her, she could see the incredible danger below, even though she didn't understand it.

And there was Legion, looking rather like a shiny blue slug against the dark background from this far away, and the even brighter safekeeper with its holographic image of the little boy curled up inside. Could Jay-Jon reach it in time?

She clenched her fists, shifting from foot to foot as she watched. She so wanted to help, but she kept seeing a vision of herself unable to fly back up this height. Her borrowed abilities didn't seem to extend that far.

A sudden sound behind Maia made her turn. And like a leaf falling to the ground, a large black hover-vehicle drifted its way from the upper levels, almost silently, then with a clank, landed on the far side of the platform she stood on.

The vehicle's windows were solid black and its chassis was dented and scraped, but she recognised it immediately. It was the same one she'd mistaken for a hire-vehicle, but which had actually taken her to Luca/Legion's home. It was well worse for wear, though, even before falling this far.

The battered door slid open, and Luke fell out, head first, one arm on the paved surface. Gold and black alter-power spilled out of his mouth and nose, and his skin was nearly grey. "H'lo, Maia."

Relief washed over Maia, because she really had thought he'd died when a city's worth of buildings had appeared in his home. It seemed she hadn't given up on him entirely. But she felt irritation too, mostly caused by fear, because he was dying. *Again.*

Two minutes later, she'd coaxed the alter-power back into his body enough that he could almost sit up. But it was still leaking out the moment she stopped, and a certainty set in her that he didn't have long left. He'd been too injured when Legion had left him, like the exit had torn his soul.

"Why on earth did you come down here?" she murmured to him. "Where were you trying to go?"

"Looking for you," Luke said, then coughed up some gold/black. "Saw my boys go down here. M'vehicle still works – thought it could help you get back up out of here."

Just then, the vehicle's engine made a shrieking noise, then died. Maia sympathised. "Really?"

Luke slumped. "And didn't want to be left alone. You see what's out there."

That was true. The first part was too, she could tell, but it seemed that often for Luke, his fear overrode his desires. "Stay here," she told him. "I'll check on Jay-Jon."

He waved a hand. "As if I could go anywhere."

He was right, Maia knew as she hurried away towards the platform's edge.

Luke wasn't going anywhere without help. In fact, without help, he didn't have much time left at all.

Oof. Darkness to the left; darkness to the right. And above and below, to round things out.

But not ahead, Elspeth thought with satisfaction as she sent another puff of silver flame shooting forward. As before, the odd, almost spongy rocklike substance that surrounded her cleared back as though avoiding the flame. And even though she was enveloped by the stuff, swaddled as thoroughly as a newborn babe, she was not afraid.

She could feel Tarie's mind nearby; almost hear it like the girl was speaking her thoughts aloud. There was a hint of anxiety, but mostly irritation at being *'squashed under this mountain of what-in-Hades-is-this-stuff and how am I supposed to get out?!'*

Tarie, Elspeth sent to her, then sent another puff of flame in that direction too, digging her way underground like a mole person. *Tarie.*

And I'm not big anymore. I can tell. I mean, I still feel strong enough, I suppose, but ugh *I'm half-choking on these stupid vines and I can't see anyone or even dig-*

TARIE!

There was a pause. Then from much closer, Tarie's mental voice continued, *That almost sounds like Bets.*

There she was, Elspeth thought in satisfaction. She sent another extra-long blast of flame that cleared a tunnel ahead of her, and then she was looking at Tarie's wide-eyed face, all wrapped around with red and green leaves, and almost smothered in the rocklike substance.

"You were calling me!" Tarie blurted out. "I could hear you!"

Indeed, but she had not been speaking *aloud.* Tarie seemed to be yet unaware of this fact. But was this a conversation she truly wished to have at this time? Elspeth thought not. "The black stuff moves away from the flame," she announced instead. "Follow me and I shall take us to the nearest Word tree."

"I can't believe you found me," Tarie murmured, but she obediently began to crawl towards Elspeth. "Ugh, I thought I'd be more bothered by this small space, but I'm doing well, right?"

"Indeed."

"And I thought I was dead for sure," Tarie continued. "But apparently not. There was just this bright flash of light, and sound, and for a moment I felt like I broke into a thousand tiny pieces. And then I was fine."

Heh.

"Why is that funny?"

"My apologies," Elspeth said over her shoulder. "I am most relieved that you are well. Er…can you sense the location of the nearest Word tree? Mayhap 'tis connected to your vines?"

Tarie frowned. "Aren't you leading us there?"

"Er…not quite. I thought I could find it," Elspeth said apologetically, "but I was wrong."

"Oh. Well, it's…that way." Tarie gestured ahead of them and slightly to the right, and Elspeth obediently began to flame them a passageway in that direction. "I don't think it's very far."

'Twas not far at all, as it turned out. Soon enough, a blast of flame revealed a hole in the horrible black stuff. There were massive twisting roots and a touch of natural light, and a hint of delicious fruity smell wafted through the hole. "Excellent!" Elspeth cheered, and crawled through.

Tarie followed her, and they both stood up in the small space directly around the massive tree trunk. To one side, the huge, stair-like branches wound their way upwards in a natural staircase. But just ahead, the stuff they'd just been crawling through filled their vision entirely. Elspeth kept one hand afire so they could see anything at all.

"What," Tarie said tightly, "is that?"

Bets didn't know, but surely there'd be a better view from up higher. And 'twas not as though there was any other place to go.

"I agree," Tarie said, seeming not to notice that Bets hadn't spoken aloud. "Up we go." And then without waiting another moment, she turned and began climbing the natural stairway.

Jon plunged down into the darkness, his circlet held outstretched in front of him, and through its centre, a noticeably different view. Through it, he could see the safekeeper so far below him, but shining like a light, with a clear image of the precious child inside. It sat on a bed of what looked like tar but was mostly hard except where it was *moving,* and stunk to high heaven…

Creature, said the image through the circlet. But that didn't make sense. The black stuff covered everything down here, and was surely the source of the terrible smell Jon had noticed previously. Was this something the Creatures were making? But regardless, he'd be on the lookout.

Still, Jon reached the safekeeper without hearing or seeing anything else. He paused a few metres above it, not wanting to risk touching the stuff, and for the first time he saw the glowing blue form just on his right. It was Legion, looking shapeless as he clung to the remnants of a building, except for one tendril/arm reaching out to the safekeeper below. Legion didn't seem to have seen him, but for Jon to reach the safekeeper, he'd need to move directly underneath the Creature.

Jon frowned and reached for his own safekeeper – one of those he'd taken from his grandmother's house. "Legion," he declared, "get into this safekeeper!"

The luminescent blob glowed a little brighter, and a humanlike face appeared in the side nearest him, seeing him for the first time. It sneered. "Safekeepers don't work on me, idiot."

"Why not?" That seemed terribly unfair. Or was it that Jon didn't have his real name?

"I'm a being of pure magick, of alter-power. I can't be controlled by alter-power unless I will it." And then it flung a tendril of blue at him, fast as a whip.

Jon dodged to one side, then held out the circlet. "Amaranthus!"

A blinding white glow shot out of the circlet, like an enormous weapon, and a perfectly round hole appeared in Legion's side. For a moment he looked utterly startled, then the hole filled right back in. "Like I said, pure alter-power." Several new tendrils appeared, fanning around Legion's central head like multiple snakes ready to strike.

That was a problem. Jon moved away a little, but his gaze never left the other safekeeper. Strange that it hadn't been covered by the black stuff, but maybe it couldn't be. An unusual idea came to mind.

May as well try it, he decided. "Safekeeper, get into this safekeeper!"

The second, more precious safekeeper didn't move from its spot on the pulsating tarry ground, and Legion laughed obnoxiously. "Don't you know anything? You can't put a safekeeper inside a safekeeper!"

Jon scowled, then shot power through the circlet again. This time, he hit his target of the wall just below where Legion rested. As hoped, the sort-of-Creature began to tumble down, towards the stinking black stuff.

Legion's side just brushed the black before he was able to grip back onto the building sticking out from it. There was a *hiss* and his bulk shrank as a shimmer of dark mist and gold sparks vanished into the tarry surface. Legion let out a sound of distress.

Jon would almost, *almost* feel sorry for him if he wasn't an unrepentant murderer. And now Jon knew he had a weakness. Whatever that tarry stuff was… well, Jon certainly wouldn't be touching it. But to get to it, he'd have to move right underneath Legion and risk those whiplike tendrils. "Why do you need it so badly, anyway?"

"Long story," Legion said as he stretched down towards the safekeeper again. "It starts with me not wanting to be subjugated to the Tiger, and ends with me not wanting to be absorbed into the Tiger's empire." Legion sneered again, but Jon could still sense the fear shown earlier. "Didn't expect the empire to look like this, did we?"

Absorbed into the empire…? Jon didn't understand the comment. "Like…?"

Legion didn't answer. Instead he stretched out several tendrils for the safekeeper. But as he reached down, the tarry black seemed to reach *up* in much the same way, and he pulled back.

Jon watched it all warily. He didn't want Legion to get the safekeeper, but neither did he want to be caught by that stuff himself. Clearly the circlet could burn away the stuff too, but that would just make Legion's job easier.

And while he knew he could fly to the safekeeper, could he get there faster than Legion without being injured?

Better just to risk it, Jon thought, because this cautious stand-off would only last so long.

Legion must've had the same thought, because as Jon dove towards the safekeeper, Legion also lunged for it. And then…

THWACK. A battered black vehicle fell out of the sky and squashed Legion flat, right into the tarry stuff. There was an explosion of gold sparks and black mist, which was all quickly absorbed into the stuff below. For a moment it seemed to have a smear of glittery blue on its surface around the sinking vehicle, but then that too was gone.

Legion hadn't even had time to make a sound.

Wide-eyed and holding the circlet in front of him, Jon reached down carefully and plucked up the safekeeper where it still sat quietly on the black surface right next to the vehicle. Then with one careful glance around him, he shot back upwards, away from the crawling, moving *stuff*.

Minutes earlier

"Can you see anything?" Luke called hoarsely from his position next to the vehicle. He'd somehow managed to haul himself out – Hades knew why he'd bothered – and now lay on the building's hard roof, looking an inch from death. So, basically the same.

Maia squinted over the edge of the building, down towards where Jay-Jon had gone. With the circlet on, she could see hints of his movements far below, the bright light of the safekeeper, and a glowing blue that she knew was Legion. "They're close. They seem to be...talking? Oh! Now Jay-Jon's shot Legion, but he doesn't seem to be injured."

"Won't be able to."

"What?" She turned her head sharply back to look at him over her shoulder. "Why not?"

"He's...not physical. Not really."

Now that deserved her full attention. Maia turned completely away from the stand-off below – which somehow hadn't turned to complete violence – and back to Luke. "You mean like how Creatures shouldn't be able to come into the normal realm? That kind of physical?"

"No. Like, he's not a normal Creature. He was...a sort of experiment by the Tiger and a Halfling, Lilith. An attempt to create a powerful body that the Tiger could borrow and use to enter the normal realm. But it failed, and instead of an empty, powerful body, there was just this...bag of alter-power with a spine and an attitude." He scoffed. "Lilith was an evil witch, and she should have unmade him then, but she seemed to think of him as her...child." He paused. "*Legion* thought of himself as her child. Called her Mother."

To Maia, if this Lilith had recognised Legion as a person,

then she couldn't be entirely evil. Because where there was a consciousness, there was a spirit – although from what Maia could see, Legion would end up absorbed into that black mass too, if he wasn't careful. It would be safer all round. While he'd been created with all kinds of potential, he'd clearly chosen to follow his 'parents' in behaviour.

Luke coughed weakly, and a rush of gold/black came out of his mouth and nose, more than the last time. Gritting her teeth, Maia rushed over and set herself to pushing that alter-power back inside him. Keeping him alive.

But it was no good. She'd lost some of it to the atmosphere, and he looked even grayer than before. The mark on his forehead deepened.

"No!" Maia wouldn't lose him. So he wasn't a good man – his weakness had allowed all kinds of evil – but she wouldn't let him go till things had been made right. You couldn't argue things out with a corpse, as she well knew from Cahlie earlier today.

She pushed again, grabbing for whatever alter-power she could find, then forcibly dragging particles out of the air. She hadn't done *that* before. Finally the mark seemed shallow again, and his colouring just this side of 'alive', and she collapsed over him in relief.

Maia didn't know what happened next. But there was a creaking sound, and Luke groaned something like 'oops'… and then the vehicle lurched towards her, its hover function seeming to give one last burst of power. It went directly over Luke where he lay on the ground, and she barely flattened herself too before it moved overhead. Its underside scraped her nose. She looked up to see it in slow motion, tipping over the side of the building, and-

Maia leapt up and ran for it with a scream, but she was too slow. "JAY-JON!" she called down. "WATCH OUT!"

But his tiny figure far below didn't hear her, and she could only watch as the battered, oversized vehicle bumped its way down the building's irregular side. It spun once, then again, until it was as small as a children's toy.

And then it soundlessly hit the small, glowing blue shape that was Legion. And the blue light went out.

Maia watched wordlessly as Jay-Jon grabbed the shining safekeeper and shot upwards. She slumped to the ground, slack with relief, and she was still sitting there when he reached her level again. *I was so scared,* she thought as she saw him. *I thought you would be crushed.*

And somehow, her son seemed to understand. His face softened. "That was close, but I got the safekeeper."

Maia nodded silently, then pointed back at the fallen Luke. Jay-Jon's eyes widened.

Jon had wondered for half a second if Maia had something to do with the falling vehicle, which could have just as easily crushed him as it had Legion. But he knew…he could *sense* that wasn't the case even before he saw her relief.

And then he saw the man slumped behind her. Luke.

Oh, Hades.

Shortly afterwards, the two of them were huddled around the fallen form. The precious safekeeper was almost forgotten.

"I thought he was dead," Jon murmured. Maia had said something about Luca's house and a fallen building, hadn't she? "Or…is he?"

The girl swept her hand over Luke's slack face, and a shimmer of gold alter-power pushed from the air, into his nose. "I've been keeping him alive, but I can't leave him alone for long. He doesn't have much time left."

Jon stared down at his father. His real father, not the carrier Luca, who'd been more like Legion operating Luke like a puppet. "I haven't seen the real him in years," he murmured. "Not since he became a carrier."

Just then, Luke opened his eyes. They were pink and watery, but the hazel irises were bright as they locked onto Jon. He blinked. "Did I get him?"

"Who?"

"Legion. The vehicle."

"You did that?" Maia exclaimed.

"Brake. Locked on to power signal. Was meant to have…weapon, but not working."

Jon looked between his parents, as odd as that felt. Was Luke saying that *he'd* dropped the vehicle that had nearly crushed Jon? He was tempted to say something sharp, but considering the man was near death, it didn't seem the best time. Instead he turned to Maia. "How much do you know about safekeepers?"

"Some. What do you want to know?"

Jon gestured to Luke's prone form. "Will they always keep a human in the same physical form, without deteriorating?"

She arched an eyebrow, for a moment looking just like her sister Anni. "I believe so."

"Huh." Jon looked at Luke, then at the safekeeper that held little Kyel – unbelievably, his own brother.

Luke could do with some quality time with at least one son, right?

Luke had heard just enough to know what was going to happen, but still, he was startled to find himself inside a small space with a small boy. They were surrounded by grey mist, and he could feel something solid underneath his backside, but it seemed to vanish if he focused on it. He decided not to focus on it.

He felt better though. No longer on death's door, more like-…exhausted to near immobility. But his tongue still worked.

So Luke turned to the boy, who he hadn't seen in more than eighteen months – longer, if he counted when he last had full control of his body. And even then, Cahlie had barely let them interact. "Er...hi, Kyel."

Kyel wore a startled expression, probably much the same as Luke's own. At the question, he turned wary. "Who are you?"

Huh. Not the best start. But better late than never. "Well..."

"Is it just me," Tarie mused, "or does this tree look like it's dying?"

They were making their way up the endless branch/staircase that ran tightly up against the massive trunk of the Word tree, but patches of sticky black were appearing along the narrower side branches. She'd been trying to ignore them, but...well, how could she?

She looked back to where Bets trotted right behind her. The other girl wore an expression of dismay. "I was hoping you would not notice."

Tarie had noticed, alright. She'd never seen a Word tree show even a hint of decay – although of course, she'd never seen a Word tree get larger than a small shrub, before the last few days. She set her jaw and kept climbing.

Bets! Tarie!

Max's voice echoed somewhere around the tree, but she couldn't see where he was. "Max?" What a relief. At least *one* of the others was alright.

I'm just...oof. Just below the silver barrier. Keep coming, and you'll find me soon enough.

What about Jon? Bets' voice came.

I've been watching him. He's way down below along with someone else, but they're coming up this way.

"Excellent!" Bets exclaimed, and Tarie realised with a start that the earlier conversation hadn't taken place...well, out loud.

But how...?

"Now's hardly the time," Bets told her earnestly, as though responding to her thought. "We shall discuss it at length as soon as we are all safe, yes?"

Tarie supposed so.

"Excellent. Now, let us reach Max... Ah, there he is."

They came around the curve of the tree, and there was the silver barrier, shining like the surface of still water under bright morning light, except upside down. Max was halfway through it, head and shoulders sticking out towards them, and his face bathed in a similar light that made him look otherworldly handsome.

He was also upside down, but oddly, his hair didn't seem to respond to gravity...

"Come on!" he told them briskly. "The rot is following, and you don't want to get caught in that again. It's only going to get worse."

Tarie didn't know what he meant by that, but his words rang true. And the fact that she recognised the truth of those words, while they seemed like nonsense, was an entirely new experience. Closing her eyes and mouth tightly, she followed Max and Bets through the silver barrier.

"It's no good," Maia told Jon. "I won't be able to fly that far. I can only hover, see?" And she took a little jump off the ground, enough to soar a body-length or two, then came down to the ground. "Unless you think you can pull me up?"

Jon looked up at their destination; the tiny patch of silver high above that wasn't obscured by the tarry mess around them. It seemed to be shrinking. "Maybe..." He'd pulled her around before, but not so far. And he'd carry her, but she wasn't small like Bets...

He looked down at the safekeeper that held two souls – bodies still attached, fortunately. Maia going into that was an option, but would she trust him that much?

Maia took in a slow breath through her nostrils. *Yes.*

"Yes?" he echoed. He had to hear it aloud.

"Yes. Now, let's do it before we lose our chance, because I don't know what happens when we can't access that silver barrier." And in her thoughts, Jon heard, *I don't know what happens when we DO access that silver, but I'm sure it's the right way to go.*

Jon had to agree with that. He shrugged one shoulder, relieved yet a little nervous. "Alright."

And if the safekeeper felt just a little heavier afterwards, it was just because he knew it now held three precious souls.

Deep in the darkness, with spongy or sticky tar in every direction, Lilith waited for her master. She stood patiently, her hands folded in front of her body, but her eyes felt a little too wide.

This...this was more than she'd expected. There had to be sacrifices, she'd known that, but not so widespread. Everything had been absorbed. Every last living thing, from grass stalks to insects to humans bearing the mark.

It was a big world out there. She couldn't be the last one, she hoped desperately, because why would the Tiger want to rule a world without anyone in it? But she couldn't see, or hear, or even sense another living soul.

And then a bright spot appeared in the darkness. Brilliant blue, and almost too bright to look at, it emerged smoothly from the nearest wall. Lilith's jaw dropped. She'd felt his disappearance earlier, along with the rest of her bonded servants, but could

Legion really have made it?

More to the point, would the Tiger have *allowed* Legion to remain whole?

The brilliant blue light reshaped until it was distinctly four-legged: long-bodied and sinuous, with a feline head and a curving tail. Shimmering points like gems studded its sides, interspersed with faint stripes, and a silvery spine was just visible through that gorgeous hide. A sharp ridge of pointed scales ran down the peak of its back. All of it sparkled with alter-power, making it the most beautiful immortal Creature Lilith had ever seen.

But she waited, holding her breath. And when that feline head turned towards her, one bright eye was yellow, the other blue.

Legion was gone after all. And it seemed that his body was finally getting its intended use.

Lilith swallowed and knelt, bowing her head. *Master.*

In the Old Tongue of the Creatures and their former king, the word held far more weight. It meant one you'd pledged your whole being to; one who owned your every breath. One who you'd die for, because you were nothing apart from them.

Servant. The blue form padded towards her, feet seeming to stick to the black surface with every step. *I need just one more thing from you.*

Anything. She didn't dare refuse. She never had dared.

But as Lilith felt her own alter-power rush out of her, felt her body disintegrate and become part of the stinking mass around them, she had just enough presence of mind to think: *Anything but THAT-*

⁎

The Tiger spared the briefest thought for his final servant. That one had been obedient because it was afraid, just like all the others, and it hadn't wanted to turn to his enemy. But in the end, it didn't matter.

Nothing mattered except the end goal.

And the others, they gave *everything* to that goal.

15

Up

Elspeth stepped through the silver barrier into a bright, beautiful garden. A gentle breeze barely ruffled the lush trees around them, and the unseen sun shone upon a massive, gleaming city in the garden's centre. 'Twas brighter still than her last visit – she could not even look upwards.

The faint babble of moving water came from the stream nearby, one of many that ran through this place she'd visited many a time. But something was amiss…

The garden was empty. She could see not even one single solitary being besides themselves. And the water…the water was going *upwards*…

Elspeth looked back to see Max's feet go floating past her head. His gaze was set upwards, lit golden from a source too bright to see. "What…?"

Going home.

Of course he was, she thought with some surprise. It seemed the most obvious thing in the world that he'd be going…there. And that the previously unknown place was, in fact, Home.

Oh, and now Tarie was passing her too. And when Elspeth looked up, looked properly at the light, it did not seem so blinding after all. Instead, she could see 'twas a pathway leading up to a place different yet so familiar…

A small-statured girl with fiery orange hair waved down at Elspeth. *When are you coming, slowcoach?*

Elspeth leapt with joy at seeing her sister again. And the leap took her one step into the air; she, who'd never flown in her life. Then another, then another, until she reached a second barrier she hadn't even noticed till this moment. The barrier that would take her from the Mountain of Glass, through to a new place that the Mountain seemed to be based on-

Bets.

Jon's voice rang in her head, small but distinct. She paused mid-air and looked downwards to see Jon emerging through the silver barrier that divided the Mountain of Glass from the hellscape below. His face shone bright with joy, and also determination, and he held out a small pale safekeeper-

...from which three people exploded. One moment there was just Jon, and the next there was a tall, slender girl with a slightly anxious expression, a very small boy, and a tall, skinny man who looked an inch away from expiring.

Jon's expression of horror was almost comical, and Elspeth felt his shock even from up here. She twisted mid-air, enjoying the sensation, and took one last glance at the light world above. *Soon,* she promised Anne, who just shrugged and laughed.

Then Elspeth turned on her heel, forced herself away from the light, and went down to help Jon.

At the same time

Tarie saw the garden and the pretty lights. She saw the water going straight upwards like a reverse waterfall, and when her gaze followed it up, she saw a light so intense it should have burned her eyeballs. But it didn't. Instead it felt...pleasant.

And then, in the light, she saw shapes. Figures. A city, a landscape, something vaster and more beautiful than she could have imagined, and resounding with a musical chord that seemed to go through her very soul.

Home, Tarie thought, and reached for it.

And in that moment, several thoughts occurred. Firstly, that she'd never really belonged anywhere else. Secondly, that something significant had occurred when she was crushed by that falling pillar earlier, and thirdly, that...

Oh. Everyone was here already. There was Da, and Lydia, looking well and beautiful along with Anni and several people from back home in Memrys city-state.

And there was… *Mother.*
Tarie ran.

Also at the same time

Unlike Maia's previous experience inside Legion's safekeeper city, this safekeeper was tiny and misty and a little bit cold. She got the sense of space, or perhaps *potential* space, but all there really was, was her. And Luke. And a little boy who'd she'd seen so briefly before.

"It was the only way to get us all out of there safely," she told the two of them apologetically. "Jay-Jon will look after us."

"That's your brother, Kyel," Luke told the little boy, who took that into his stride. To Maia he said, "How do you know he won't take revenge for everything we did to him?"

We? Excuse her! Maia would have responded sharply, but then suddenly she was hurled out of the safekeeper as fast as she'd been drawn in. She caught a glimpse of Jay-Jon's shocked expression, then she was face-first in lush green grass.

"Oh," she heard Jay-Jon say. "That wasn't meant to happen."

Maia climbed to a sitting position just as the petite brunette from earlier seemed to appear out of nowhere. The girl gave Jay-Jon a quick hug. "It appears safekeepers do not work here on the Mountain of Glass."

The Mountain of *What?* Maia studied her surroundings with new interest. Garden of exceptional beauty, big enough to feed a city; an *actual* city, apparently made of some reflective material; an excessively bright light above them that she dared not look into…

But Jon seemed to brighten at the girl's comment. "Hey, we made it! But where is everybody?"

Maia looked around but didn't see anyone except the four of them. Even the little boy, Kyel, looked confused. But then she saw an expression of the most intense awe and happiness come over his face. She watched wide-eyed and open-mouthed as he began to rise up into the air, as if he was walking on an unseen staircase, until he vanished into the brightness.

But where had he gone?!

Maia squinted upwards for just a moment longer, just until she felt the tug of something warm and beautiful latch onto her, something that would call her up there too.

But she intentionally turned away. *Not yet,* she told it. *Not without Jay-Jon.* Adult or child, she wouldn't let him down again.

Ma.

The childish voice came from up above her. She looked up again, towards the light, and saw something she never could have imagined but had wanted so desperately.

And this time, she let herself be pulled upwards.

Jon hadn't meant to let Luke out of the safekeeper. Not because he was annoyed with his father and keeping him in such a controlled, tiny environment felt like a worthy punishment – although it did – but because Luke seemed an inch away from death.

Up here amongst the lovely surroundings on the Mountain, Luke's illness seemed even more apparent. The spidery Tiger's pledge mark still sat on his greyish forehead, but now it seemed too light, like it sat over the skin rather than on it. He blinked reddish eyes and tried to sit up. "What is this place?"

"Perfect for you," Jon said triumphantly. "Let's get you a drink of water and you'll feel so much better." And then they could all go upwards…because *everything* in him wanted to go there.

Bets clapped her hands. "Oh, what a marvellous idea!"

But when Jon went looking for the nearest stream, the bed appeared to have dried up.

Dried up. The water of life.

Um…

"Er," Bets said, her tone reflecting Jon's mood. "Shall we go to the Hall of Treasures? I recall my sister speaking of a healing liniment that can be found there."

Jon looked at the city, whose nearest wall was really quite close. It didn't seem to shine as it usually did, though a single door stood open. "The Tapestry Room has a fountain at its centre," he said thoughtfully. "Amaranthus showed me once."

They half-walked, half-dragged the other man up to the city

wall and through the door. Once through, Jon found they were inside a vast room, well away from anywhere they logically should have been. A massively long greyish shape lined the room's edges – what Jon knew was actually a very fine black and white tapestry of sorts.

The Tapestry Room, as requested. Excellent.

"Phew," he said. "I half wondered if all the Mountain's functions were turned off, if the water's not working."

"Where's this fountain?" Bets asked.

"It's…"

It *should* have been in the middle of the room. Mostly it was hidden from sight, but ever since Jon had seen it once, he'd seen it each time. A big shape that appeared to be black but was actually every colour of the rainbow, and from which water gushed. But today, he couldn't see it.

"I'm going to die, aren't I?" Luke asked matter-of-factly.

Yes, Jon wanted to say. He felt it in every part of his being, like Luke's death was mere moments away. Or on his timeline, fractions of an inch, and whatever time he had now was being unnaturally extended.

Amaranthus, Jon thought intently. *What's going on here? What do we do?*

He looked down at the circlet in his hand. He'd been carrying it so consistently and carefully, treating it like his greatest treasure ever since he'd used it to destroy the White Prince. Its sides were inscribed with Amaranthus's name, over and over, and it held power too.

Then he lifted it up so he saw through its centre. His view changed, and Luke's awful pallor became much worse, like an actual dead person's, or one of those Creature people right before they changed. But it only covered half of him. Luke seemed to be one half dead, one half alive, and who knew which would win?

Jon's mouth tightened into a straight line, and he lowered the circlet. Then he deliberately held it out to Luke. "Put this on. It'll help."

Luke's watery eyes fixed on the circlet. He paused, and did he lift a hand?

But then into the room came something new. Something bright. Something terrible.

Something that did not belong.

Just before

The mass of darkness grew and twisted to fill every space, pushing ever upwards until it covered even the atmosphere. Then, riding the wave of darkness as casually as an expert surfer, the bright and glorious Tiger reached the silver barrier, felt the slight resistance caused by the alter-power, and…stepped cleanly through.

Into the Mountain of Glass for the first time in many ages.

The Tapestry Room

It was a cat, of sorts. Or more like a cat, if a cat was twice the size of a Siberyian tiger and spangled blue like it was clothed with the night sky.

Like a cat, if a cat had been crossed with some wonderful, terrible alien being.

Like a cat, if a cat could be made of pure alter-power, with a visible silver spine through its gem-studded sides.

(Huh. So *that* was what happened to Legion…)

Jon swallowed. He couldn't take his gaze off that shining, stunning, terrible Creature that was surely the Tiger. But he also had the strongest sense that they shouldn't be in its presence. It was as lovely as… as… as a *god,* but it also felt as wrong as brushing your teeth with a grater.

"We shouldn't be here," he whispered.

Bets nodded mutely.

It didn't seem to have seen them, or if it had, it was ignoring them. It began to pace around the circumference of the tapestry, seeming to study the fine black and white pattern as it went.

Then the Tiger spoke. Its voice rang through the room and vibrated through Jon's very bones. If a mountain had a voice, it'd sound like that. **What an exercise in futility. He shut me out at the start, yet here I am. The story was always mine.**

And then it batted at the tapestry with one paw. There was a ripping sound, a flash of gold and grey, and the vast tapestry began to tip over, falling off its invisible perch from the edges of the round room in one long pile. Where it fell, it revealed just greyness beyond: a mist, nothing of substance.

Then the Tiger turned and began to saunter towards them. And suddenly, the room felt far too small.

Jon couldn't move. He wasn't frightened, precisely, but he felt the wrongness of this moment right to his very soul. At his side, Bets reached up and took his hand. He gripped hers tightly.

But near their feet, Luke's face wore an expression of awe. He reached out a hand towards the rapidly approaching being. *Glorious*, his mouth shaped. *Bright.*

Jon's heart sank as he realised Luke was only seeing the beauty and power of this thing, entirely missing the danger. *Oh, no.*

"The circlet!" Bets said urgently.

Jon was already moving to force it over Luke's head. If it would burn away that Creature tar and destroy Creatures themselves, surely it would keep Luke safe now.

But Luke abruptly began struggling, and he slapped at the circlet, sending it flying. Then he began crawling towards the Tiger – and suddenly, the Tiger was standing right over him. So close to Jon and Bets. So enormous, and emanating such terrible power.

"Amaranthus," Jon choked out, and the Tiger's head turned slowly towards him. It didn't blink; those bicoloured eyes like shining gems in its luminescent head.

Then suddenly it was enveloped in a cloud of silver flame. Fierce, brave little Bets was blasting it with everything she had.

It went on and on, and then finally the flame died back to reveal the Tiger standing there in the exact same condition and position. If anything, it shone brighter.

That wasn't supposed to happen! Bets' voice came plaintively in Jon's mind. *'Tis a Creature, is it not?!*

It *was* a Creature, Jon knew. But it was also wearing Legion's beautiful, magical body somehow. And that body hadn't followed the usual Creature rules…

You two, the Tiger said. **You slaves of the old master. You are not needed here; this one is mine.** And it put its massive paw over

Luke's shaking shoulder, covering it entirely.

Like Hades Luke belonged to the Tiger! "We're not slaves," Jon managed to say, but his voice seemed small and weak to his own ears. "We're...friends. And you can't have him. He's my father!"

The Tiger's powerful gaze fixed on Jon. ***And who will stop me? You? Your master? He is not here. He has fled.***

That wasn't true. Jon didn't know where Amaranthus was, but he wouldn't have run. He'd gone elsewhere, that was all.

But where was he?

Very well, Bets told Jon. *I shall distract it; you grab the circlet then Luke. Carry him up, if you will. I do not think 'twill follow us.*

As Jon was thinking what a terrible plan that was, the ground underneath them lurched. The walls of the Tapestry Room shook, and half of them crumbled and fell away. But rather than revealing the Garden outside, instead there was just open space, with the silvery, waterlike barrier below.

From this side, it truly did look like water. And Jon could see the earth far below that too, covered in a solid darkness that was surely the tarry substance they'd escaped from. As he watched, the tar began to move, and a vast shape emerged. It was a hand the size of a city, attached to an arm the length of Erus city-state, and it was reaching up towards them.

Jon had enough time to think, *Surely that thing can't get through the barrier,* when suddenly the Tiger kicked Luke. He went flying: skidding across the ground and over to the broken floor, then tumbling into the open air.

Elspeth hastily revised her plan as the floor fell away. Time seemed to slow down, and she had a moment of complete bafflement at how truly disastrous this all was. How did one deal with such a situation?

Go back a bit, to when things were better.

That thought occurred as she saw Luke get tossed casually off the broken floor, to what was clearly his doom. Foolish man – he should have taken the circlet.

But how did one go back to when things were better? Did that mean a week ago? A *year* ago?

How about mere moments ago?

Still feeling as though 'twas all happening too slowly, Elspeth moved and found herself tripping over the end of the fallen tapestry. She landed hard on the unfinished end, sending up a flurry of images as she touched myriad threads all at once, each symbolising myriad lives. And then right in front of her face popped up once particular figure, who was currently mid-fall and thinking *WHAAAAAAAT...?*

Luke!

Thank you, Amaranthus!

Elspeth grabbed at the thread and imagined herself within the moment. A golden tunnel popped up around her, misty-sided and moving and oddly musical. And outside of it, she could see a close-up of Luke with a horrified expression on his face, moments away from being absorbed by that *thing.*

He was not moving. Had time stopped? Elspeth mused. The tunnel continued infinitely on her right, going backwards down Luke's life thread. But to her left, there was nothing.

Remembering her and Jon's earlier experience in a similar tunnel, she slowly began moving down the tunnel, into the past. And outside the tunnel, she saw everything take place again, but in reverse.

Now Luke was moving slowly backwards – flying back across the floor as the broken pieces filled back in.

Then the Tiger was lifting its paw off his back.

Then Luke was crawling *away* from the Creature as it appeared.

Then he was shuffling back across the empty room, until the scene changed around him and he was abruptly in a garden.

And then-

That would do, Elspeth decided. She went back to the end of the tunnel, to the end of Luke's life thread, and reached through. She grabbed the much larger man by his collar, yanked him inside the tunnel, then marched a few steps to her right. She shoved him out again at the spot right when he would have appeared in the room originally.

Elspeth knew not what she was doing. But surely this was better than doing nothing at all?

—✦—

Jon watched in horror as his father tumbled towards the colossal tarry hand reaching up to him. But just before Luke would have hit its surface, he vanished from sight.

Then he reappeared on the other side of the Tapestry Room, well away from the broken point. He was blinking and grey-faced, but still appeared to be himself.

There was a horrified, baffled pause – then Jon threw himself at the circlet, and the Tiger lifted its paw again. It slammed down, and another chunk of the floor fell away.

Time seemed to slow down as Jon grabbed the circlet, but the Tiger had already got to Luke. Then Luke was tumbling out into open air again-

…Until once again he vanished, and reappeared in yet another part of the room where they'd first emerged. This time, with the circlet Jon could see Luke hadn't just vanished. Instead there'd been a flash of gold *something*. It reminded him of those time tunnels…

Jon looked sharply across at Bets, who gave him a thumbs up. She had one hand pressed against the fallen cloth. How had she even reached the tapestry?

I do not know, she told him cheerfully. *And I do not care. I'm keeping Luke alive for now. Get the circlet to him.*

Right.

Then the next while was like a game with the most horrific high stakes as the floor crumbled away and Luke went skidding around like he was the ball, with Jon the player trying to catch him. It was getting harder and harder because there was less and less floor, and he couldn't reach his father before he'd fall and then reappear on the increasingly small spaces. And when he *did* reach Luke, the circlet seemed to skid away rather than touch the man.

But Bets was clearly doing *something*, and the Tiger was a hideous bright patch in the corner of Jon's vision, and-

…By pure luck, or perhaps Amaranthus *finally* assisting, Jon found himself in the same place as Luke. He leapt on his father, grabbing his hand, and held out the circlet. "Take it," he begged, because it was clear by now that the circlet couldn't be forced on anyone. "It'll save you! That darkness can't go near it!"

But Luke just stared at him, and his expression when he looked at the circlet was revulsion. He shook his head just the smallest bit.

This wasn't working. Dismayed, Jon looked up across the room at Bets. She was hanging off the end of the tapestry, which now hovered in open air, but didn't seem bothered by this. *He won't take it,* he told her.

Can't, most likely, Bets returned. *There is something about the name Amaranthus – people cannot help but to reject it wholeheartedly, if they cannot accept it. I wonder why?*

They didn't have time for this!

We do, if you will but come and find it.

The tapestry, Jon realised. The tapestry was a picture of how infinite lives interacted, but it was also a literal path through time.

Dropping Luke's hand, he leapt up and flew towards the tapestry, landing right next to Bets. Gold light sprang up around him.

Show me what to do.

"I'm not truly certain," Elspeth said apologetically, "but would it be possible to find a moment in Luke's life in which he *would* accept the circlet? Then drag that Luke to this moment here? Would that work, do you think?"

That is a…WONDERFUL idea, Jon thought at her enthusiastically. He leapt into action, running down the time-tunnel that marked every moment of Luke's life, and leaving a startled Elspeth behind.

She called after him, *You need not run! We have all the time in the world.*

But do we? he shot back over his shoulder. *We're reusing the same moments over and over, coming out in the same spot. Sooner or later, we'll run out of space!*

Would they? What a dreadful idea. Elspeth mentally shrugged and took off after Jon. *How are you going to do it?*

Keep offering him the circlet. He'll take it sooner or later. Jon paused. *Earlier or later, I mean.*

But would he?

Searching through every moment of a person's life was a harrowing prospect, Elspeth quickly decided. One saw the most dreadful things, from one's worst sins (murder) to the worst moments of their life (being made a carrier) through to everyday embarrassments (overuse of the privy).

Eventually Elspeth steeled herself to it, following Jon as they moved through year after year of Luke's life, trying to find quiet moments where they could casually thrust the circlet in his face and see his response.

But mostly, 'twas as though Luke did not even see it. He'd turn away, over and over, even as Jon waved the item right in his face.

After a dozen such moments and a dozen casual dismissals, Elspeth became disheartened. They'd gone well back into the past, long enough that Luke was a youth of mayhap only twelve or thirteen. An unhappy soul even then, for sure.

What if he cannot see it? she asked quietly. *What if because we are back within time, so to speak, that these tunnels do not work in the same way?* 'Twas not as if they'd had time to ask questions.

You can't change the past, Jon told her. *So if it works, it will always have worked, we just won't know about it till it does.*

...Pardon?

We just have to try, Jon said. *We'll try until we don't have any other options.*

Sadly, he was right about that. But Elspeth couldn't help but wonder if the idea was indeed nonsense, and mayhap never would have worked. They were merely fumbling their way along, and had been the whole time, she thought as she followed Jon back down the tunnel of Luke's life thread.

Here!

Elspeth's head snapped up, and she saw Jon leaning partway out of the tunnel. He was face to face – well, face to chest with a small boy of about six years old. Luke was almost unrecognisable at this age, but there was something about his eyes, posture and floppy hair that reminded her of both Jon and the other boy, Kyel.

"And see this name here?" Jon was saying urgently as he showed the boy the circlet. "This will save your life one day. *Amaranthus.* See?"

Young Luke studied the circlet with wide-eyed solemnity. Then he took it and set it on his head. Surprisingly, it fit perfectly. "It's a crown," he explained. "You've got to wear it properly."

Jon's jaw dropped a little, then he caught himself. "Oh. Yes.

It's…a crown." *How come I didn't know that?*

Elspeth shrugged, more focused on their plan, which amazingly, seemed to be working! *'Tis a circlet, which I suppose is a form of crown. Circlets are usually worn on the head.*

You didn't tell me that! But Jon sent a flash of an image, of the auburn-haired girl from earlier, wearing an identical circlet the correct way. On her head.

You did not ask! Elspeth shot back in surprise.

Jon shook his head a little and focused on the young version of his father. "Ah…will you come talk to your future self, please? He's not listening, and he's in trouble."

And then, incredibly, Young Luke nodded and followed Jon right into the tunnel.

Elspeth cheered, beaming, and let them pass her.

Jon began to lead Young Luke back down towards the moment they'd left, and as his eyes met Elspeth's, he said, *I can't believe we're doing this!*

What were the consequences of allowing someone to see their future? "Mayhap do not look outside the tunnel walls," Elspeth called. But she followed them back nonetheless.

Jon felt like they were breaking reality. They'd gone back through someone's life – his *father's* life – and had interacted with his very past self. Hard to believe Luke DeMannard had ever been so small.

But even this size, his expression held a reserve unusual in a six-year-old. But Jon knew that if his own childhood had had challenges, it would have been even harder being raised by a miserable brute like Mannard.

Really, Jon *knew*. He'd seen it through the tunnel walls, along with everything else. And that was why he did try to keep Young Luke from seeing any of his own future, the poor kid.

And really really, they probably *were* breaking reality. But it seemed already thoroughly broken to the point he couldn't take it in, so what was one more minor mishap?

Then they reached the end of the thread, and without even meaning to, they popped right out into the shattered remains of the Tapestry Room. Jon had a moment of complete horror – he'd brought a child *here?* – but then the boy's eyes locked on to Adult Luke's. He was lying on a patch of ground that seemed to float on its own, not an arm's length from where they stood.

Adult Luke's expression changed. "I…I remember this," he murmured in amazement. "I thought I'd imagined it…"

Child Luke looked at his older self solemnly. Then he stepped away from the tunnel, heading towards Adult Luke, and as he did, his form turned transparent. By the time he'd reached Adult Luke, he was a mere mist, but the circlet was visible as he took it off his head and handed it to the older version.

Adult Luke took the faint, misty circlet, which dissolved even as the child version did. Then he looked across at Jon. "I…-"

He never got to finish his sentence, because the ground under him collapsed, and he plummeted down into darkness. And this time, the fingers of the giant hand closed around him before he had a chance to even scream.

Jon did scream. *Noooo!*

And before he could think about it, he leapt off the ledge, through the faint silver barrier, and onto the mound of tarry Creature.

16

The Value of One

Jon!

Argh, he'd jumped without the circlet! Elspeth thought miserably from her place inside the time-tunnel of Luke's life. Now how was Jon supposed to fetch Luke?! Assuming the man hadn't been immediately absorbed into the tarry mess of Creature…stuff.

Immediately she began searching for Jon's life's thread. She noticed a faint blue light in the corner of her eye, through the side of the time-tunnel, which she took to be the Tiger. A problem indeed, although not her greatest one at the moment.

'Twas easy enough to find Jon's life's thread where it crossed over Luke's on multiple occasions. Elspeth stepped through from Luke's time-tunnel into Jon's by sheer will, ignoring the oddness of such a situation, and began searching for a moment to re-steal the circlet. After all, had Jon not done that himself after he'd lost the circlet to that woman, Maia?

Maia. Elspeth perked up at the thought. *She'd* had the circlet, had she not?

She quickly found an intersecting thread of Maia's and stepped into a third time-tunnel. She'd prefer to think there was no need for haste, as she now stood outside time, yet she could not shake the urge to hurry nonetheless.

But once inside Maia's life's thread, Elspeth came across a startling discovery. Maia herself stood right inside the time tunnel, face to face – well, face to chest with Elspeth. She was glowing golden from the reflected tunnel light, and she held out a circlet. *Here.*

What…how…?

Maia smiled and moved a little. *I'm reliving the good bits.*

Elspeth stared at her, baffled. But her movement had revealed a figure behind her, small enough to be a child. Elspeth caught the slightest glimpse before they were hidden from sight. Kyel, she wondered? But why would he be here with Maia, who he barely knew?

Maia thrust the circlet at her. *For Luke.*

Ah…indeed. My thanks to you. Elspeth took the circlet, glancing down at it as if to ensure 'twas the right one. And when she looked up, the other woman had vanished, along with her mysterious companion.

She frowned, then shook her head. There'd be time to solve that mystery later.

Now, Jon needed her.

Jon landed hard on the black surface, and was absorbed knee-deep before it seemed to reject him and push him back out so that he was resting softly on it, somewhere around where Luke had fallen.

Somewhere. But how could he identify Luke's location in a surface the size of a city-state? He couldn't overstate the vastness of the thing. And the whole of it was moving, trembling like it was alive, and giving off the worst, rank yet chemical stench.

Ugh. If Jon could've thrown up, he might have done it on principle.

A moment later he realised he didn't have the circlet with him, and horror really did make him almost throw up. He'd given the circlet to Child Luke…and he'd jumped after Adult Luke too soon.

He froze for half a moment in that precarious position on top of the black surface. Did he have time to go back up to what was left of the Tapestry Room, go into the tunnel of his own life, and snatch a version of the circlet from his earlier self? He didn't *remember* that happening more than once…

Catch!

Bets' voice came from above, and Jon looked up just in time to see a shining circle tumbling down towards him. He stuck out his hand, and it fell right over his wrist, spinning a little with the force of its landing. Up above, Bets' face looked small and bright

The very beginning. A world freshly torn in two – a mostly physical realm filled with confused humans relying on sticks and stones to protect them, and a separate realm entirely of alter-power, empty of life, with the sun just rising on the one single day that would pass...

The Tiger howled and pulled away from that memory, a cold recording of what had begun all of this, right after his failed coup. When the world had been split into the normal and the Other, with the new Creatures banished to only one small portion of that new realm.

And there was his enemy again, in that same small form. He didn't seem to be gloating – his stupid mortal face wore a solemn expression – but he pulled up a new piece of tapestry even as the Tiger leapt again. Another piece of history sprang up.

Human cities cover the normal realm, with humans crawling on them like ants on an anthill. But although the Creatures are tied to their own little piece of the Other, they rule and influence the normal realm. It's a land of pain, mourning and death, and the continued interventions of the light king still can't make it anything else. It's broken to the core, and so are the mortals. And for the vast majority of them, as their short lives end, their physical bodies return to dust. Their spirits go into the Other, fuel for the colossal Creature cities that have developed since the Rift between realms.

Had the enemy intended it to go so badly for its little mortals? The Tiger doubted it, but his fury was maddening because it. Knew. What. Came. Next. It tried to pull away from the tapestry, but its paw was already skidding across the fabric until it hit a starburst of white threads-

The light king has taken mortal form. A poor, weak form even by mortal standards, in a dusty, war-torn little corner of a much vaster human empire. Yeshua of Nazareth is baffling to the conquering Remans, despised by the established religious groups, and loved by the many poor, weak mortals that otherwise have no place in the society of the time. But then he's captured, and killed, and-

Something happens. Three days later, the world is filled with the same refrain, echoing over and over and over throughout both the past and future.

Yeshua paid my passage. Yeshua paid my passage. Yeshua paid my passage...

And in the bloated Creature cities, the alter-power spirits of innumerable mortals flood out of the walls and floors, heading straight upwards. Straight to the original light world, to a destiny they never could have deserved.

Because Amaranthus, as Yeshua, had paid for their passage in his blood.

The Creatures lose the rule of death. The death crown is stolen, taken to sit on the hand of the light-king. And the world is never the same again.

The Tiger was flung backwards, right off the tapestry. He skidded across the cracking floor, burning from the alter-power that flooded even the memory of that moment. And when he finally managed to get back to all four feet, shaking with anger and pain, the old enemy was standing in front of him. Still in that weak mortal form. Still wearing those scars from its single but significant death. But somehow, full of all the power and glory that the light king had ever held.

HHAAATE, the Tiger managed to spit out. ***HATE you.***

I know. Now say what you've come to say, One-Who-Was-Beraht.

The enemy knew that the Tiger had come to bargain. Of *course* he did. That reminder of his omniscience just made the Tiger more furious, and it had to force it down before it was even able to speak. And when it did, the carefully planned speech was forgotten.

You always seem to know what's coming, it spat. ***But that's worthless when you cannot stop it. You could not stop me from tearing the light kingdom in two, even though you punished me for it. And you cannot stop me now, when I have everything you truly value.***

I have your mortals. Every last one of them, and they're entirely my creatures now. They're so covered in filth that you'll never touch them. It doesn't matter that you have the death crown, or that you've offered free passage to the light world for any who choose it. They have to choose, and they won't. Their minds are full of darkness, and their wills are mine.

Now here was the speech he'd planned. *I can release their wills. I can give you all those filthy creatures, whichever ones you want. But in return, you must surrender these lands to me. Surrender this place. Surrender your crown here, leave, and give me this earth and this entire universe, right to the gate to the light world.*

There was silence.

*I know I cannot **take** the Heart of your power,* the Tiger continued. ***But you can surrender it. Give it to me, or I will destroy Every. Last. Mortal.***

Every?

The Tiger abruptly remembered the last, tiny human, unmarked by Amaranthus, and somehow yet to be taken. But oh, so close. ***It is just one. I have so many-***

You never understood, Amaranthus said gently. *It is never* just one.

With the circlet over his head, Jon could see right through the tarry bulk of the Creature stuff covering the earth, and to the tiny, fragile form of Luke curled up deep below the surface. His arms were tucked into his chest, his knees pulled up as if in foetal pose, and his eyes scrunched tight shut. The faintest sheen of what might've been a circlet gleamed over his hands.

Not absorbed yet. Still there, Jon saw in relief.

"Amaranthus!" he shouted. A light shot out from around him – not from his hands, like when he'd last held the circlet against the White Prince. It struck the black stuff, which recoiled, revealing a chasm big enough to fit an apartment building.

But through his new vision, he saw that Luke was moved aside, deeper still, and was just as solidly surrounded as before. The light of the circlet Luke held seemed to flicker and for a moment, almost die.

No!

"You need to put the circlet on!" Jon shouted, trying to send the same message mentally too. But could Luke even hear? "Put it on! Say Amaranthus!"

Luke was cold. So cold. And it was darker than anything he'd ever experienced. And this stuff was pressing all around him, leaching every drop of warmth from where it touched him.

He tried to pull away, but his sleeve caught and ripped, then disappeared. He sucked in a breath, and with it came a thick stench, like being in a fog of chemicals and rotten eggs. He choked a little before managing to calm his breathing.

How *could* he even breathe? Hades, he was so alone…

Not quite, a little thought came in.

Luke looked down slowly at the faint warmth in his hands. He could only just turn his head, because the darkness pressed against him, sticky and sucking at his hair, his skin. But he could just make out a circular shape, like a big ring made of the faintest light.

As he studied it, it solidified. Then he could read the text on the outside: AMARANTHUS.

Seeing that word made something inside Luke feel strange and vulnerable, like he wanted to either reach out or recoil. Nothing in the middle. But when he remembered that moment in his childhood, the moment someone had taken him on what he'd thought of till now as a strange dream, the desire to recoil faded back, and the wistful desire to reach out grew stronger. And as it did, the circlet in his hand grew more defined.

Luke opened his mouth a little as if to speak out the name, even in the bare little air he had left, but choked. Like the word was just too big, or too awkward to form.

Jay-Jon had said the circlet would save his life one day, Luke knew. But if it was so essential – and it was obviously *sooo* essential – why was it so hard for him to look at? To accept? To even say that name?

He turned the circlet again, seeing the same name repeated over and over all around the outside.

But then he saw something on the inside. What he'd taken for a smudge was in fact more scrolling text.

Yeshua paid my passage.

Passage to where?

An image flashed to mind of the light he'd seen so briefly above them in the garden place; the light that had enveloped both Maia and Kyel. They'd gone somewhere, obviously. And that somewhere must be better than here, although that was a low bar to set.

Yeshua paid my passage, he read again. But that wouldn't apply to him. He hadn't done anything special to particularly deserve help, although he preferred to think he hadn't done anything truly awful either.

Just…a series of mediocre or bad choices, neglectful

behaviour when he wasn't giving in to fear, and of course…the horrendous things his body had done while Legion was in charge. Huh. Those would surely exclude him from this paid passage thing.

A thought came clearly into his head. *No, they don't.*

How do you know? he argued back, then paused. He'd spent enough time sharing a head with Legion to know what an external voice sounded like. That thought wasn't him. *Who is this?*

In his hands, the circlet's glow intensified. *The one who paid your passage.*

Luke almost choked on a breath, something in his chest tightening to extreme pain – then just as suddenly, relaxing. *But…why?*

Because I see you. I see what you are, what you could have been, and what you will be if you come with me.

For a moment, those thoughts solidified into a clear presence, like someone was curled up right there with Luke. Someone big, and tremendously strong, and *safe.* And even though this was the least comforting situation in his existence, he somehow still felt comforted.

He forced himself to look down at the circlet. Saying 'Amaranthus' still felt like too much, but he could probably manage the text inside. *If you say you paid for me to get out of here, I'll believe you. I'll accept it.*

And then the circlet snapped into full, shining clarity, and the darkness exploded.

Jon squinted down at the tarry mass below him. He could just make out the curled-up shape of Luke, deep in there, but with a faintly glowing shape in his hands. *Say Amaranthus,* Jon sent to him urgently. *Say it! It'll save you.*

There was no warning for what happened next. One moment, Jon hovered over the endless bulk of the Creature…stuff. The next moment, a cavern opened up underneath him, underneath Luke. And Luke fell.

Jon swore and dove after him, but even as he did, the cavern opened more, and grew deeper, as though it didn't want Luke to touch it any longer. And Luke fell deeper and deeper until finally he came to a sudden halt, hooked by his ragged clothing on a post sticking off a high-level building wall.

Jon ground to a halt in the air just as the clothing ripped, grabbing his father's arm before he could fall further. And in the intensity of the moment, Luke felt weightless.

Not stopping to think, Jon grabbed him by both wrists and shot upwards, urgency driving him to reach the platform above as soon as he could. He caught a glimpse of Luke's wide-eyed face, pale and lined, but shining with a faint light that must've been reflected off the Mountain of Glass above. Luke's own circlet gleamed in his clenched fist.

Thank you, Luke mouthed.

It didn't need to be said. As if Jon would risk losing his own father – someone he now could see he cared about tremendously, although he mourned their distance over the years, and the resentment he'd felt over Luke's apparent decision to become a carrier. But if only Luke could live, then they could make it right.

Yes. Yes, we can make it right, Luke's mental voice came across, light with relief. *We have time?*

Yes! Luke must've said the name, Jon thought. Luke must've said Amaranthus, because how else could he have been freed from that fate that had taken so many others? How else could Jon now hear him in his mind?

Didn't.

What?

And then they finally reached the silvery barrier that marked the line between the ragged Earth and the Mountain, and shot right through it. Jon found a solid piece of land and came to rest before taking in what Luke had said.

"What do you mean, you didn't?" he asked aloud.

Elspeth had not argued when Amaranthus moved her away from the Tapestry Room. Instead, she'd waited on another chunk of the Garden which was separated from the Tapestry Room area by a series of chasms.

She still had an excellent view of Jon down below as he sought his father. She also had an excellent view as the Tiger stormed back into the Tapestry Room shortly after she left it and began shredding the tapestry itself.

A very good thing that she hadn't stayed in the tapestry! Then there seemed to be some kind of conversation between the glowing blue Creature and Amaranthus – she caught only snatches of it, and flashing lights, so instead gave her attention to Jon.

And finally he reappeared from within the tarry stuff far below, dragging ragged, filthy Luke along with him. Jon flew as fast as she'd ever seen him, coming to land within seconds on a clear space of Garden nearby. Now he wore the circlet on his head, and it shone like a lamp. But Luke gripped one in his fist as though 'twas a lifeline.

At last, Elspeth thought. At long last! She ran towards them, pausing only to make her way carefully around breaks in the ground. But as she reached them, the men were mid-conversation.

"What do you mean, you didn't?" Jon was asking Luke.

Luke brushed a hand over his stringy hair, trembling a little from the effort. "Didn't say the name on the circlet. Couldn't. But saw the inside."

Elspeth and Jon exchanged startled glances. *Inside?* she queried.

But he got free of the darkness, Bets. How could he if he hadn't said the name? It's basically the password!

Luke held up the circlet, and as he did, his trembling eased. "Inside. See. Yesh…ua…paid my passage. I told him I'd believe it, even if I couldn't say the name. And then I was free."

For the first time, Elspeth realised there was text inside the circlet too. Plain, clear words that spelled out a phrase she didn't quite understand, but which sat quite right with her. "Oh! See if it's on yours too, Jon."

He gave her an amused look. *Mine is his, right?* But still, he took it off his head and held it out. And indeed, inside were inscribed the same words. *Yeshua paid my passage.*

How did you fail to see these earlier? Elspeth queried, eyebrows raised. *You made a habit of looking through the circlet rather than wearing it!*

Jon shrugged a shoulder sheepishly. *I saw them; I just didn't read them. My mistake.* "I think I heard about this when I was back in Frencia in the seventeen hundreds," he said aloud. "Something about a sacrifice?"

"I know the answer!" Elspeth blurted out. The information had fit together in her head along with something she'd heard in childhood – on one of the few occasions Mass had been in Anglish rather than Laten as was the custom. And she'd put it together with her own experiences of Amaranthus, for who else could he be but the one they'd called the Eternal One?

"'Tis like this," she continued. "It takes incredible power to take humans such as we are, low mortals, and make us...*other*. More like the People. And for the power to do such a thing, for the balance to change our very natures, it took a tremendous sacrifice."

Now she had the attention of the other two, and she continued, emboldened. She'd pondered this idea briefly as a child, had accepted it, then moved on with her life. But now, it made so much sense. "Amaranthus, who is immortal, took mortal form as one of us. As a man named Yeshua. And then although he lived a flawless life, he was executed as a criminal." She held out her hands, both palms upwards. "An undeserved but willing death for an immortal meant enough power to give *life* to all of us who were meant to die. To give us passage to Amaranthus's home, if we would but accept the sacrifice, and be transformed."

Both men were staring at her, and Luke's expression held a glow of hope and expectation. *Yes,* he thought clearly, but she heard him all the same. Then aloud, "Yes. I accept that."

And then...and then 'twas as though the heavens opened up. The light had been above them the whole time, but now it intensified, and Luke was caught up in its glow. And when it faded a little, he was gone.

But where he'd been was a...a tunnel? Like the time tunnels they'd already used, but one that headed directly upwards, and its sides were covered in moving text and symbols, lovely shapes, only a few of which she recognised as words. There was the most beautiful sound, like whale song mixed with string instruments and the sound of the wind in the trees, but somehow just perfect. And across from her, Jon held out his hand. *Shall we go?*

And because there was no reason to stay, and quite a few to leave, Elspeth took his hand, grinning. Then the light enveloped them, the sound filled her senses, and the battered Mountain of Glass was gone.

The Tiger felt the loss of the last one: the former host of Legion, that failed experiment; and the last filthy mortal for whom Amaranthus had come to this place. But it was a miniscule loss, and he tossed it aside, instead focusing on what really mattered.

You'll give me the Mountain. You'll give me back full access to all realms and your crown in this place, and I shall rule it all, all this world below. And in return, you may have your mortals back.

He sent a pulse of energy through the roiling mass on the planet below, and it writhed and twisted in agreement. The other Creatures were mixed in with the life forces of what had been innumerable humans, but they didn't matter. All that mattered was here in this place.

But Amaranthus cared about those humans. Such a weakness – and one the Tiger would now exploit.

No.

No?! The Tiger jolted in shock, and the extended mass jolted with him. *But I have your humans! All of them – or many, anyway. Are they not the ones you freely died for? That you debased yourself for?*

The other being looked at him solemnly from that tiny form, eyes deep and fathomless as always. *Yes. I gave everything for them.*

Then why will you not give just a little more? The Tiger found himself pleading, and despised himself for it. *You claim to have given everything, why not take the small step that will reclaim these many souls?*

There was silence, then… *No.*

The Tiger snarled, lashing out with one paw, and a series of trees fell on the other side of the Garden. Chaos, this place was pathetically small. *THEN I WILL DESTROY THEM!*

He exerted his will over every lifeforce connected with him – but they were impossible to distinguish, instead being a mass of fear, anger and general hatred. It suited him well, because he felt the very same. And below, the black mass began to climb upwards. Up from the darkened earth, up until it reached the broken barrier between the Mountain. And right in front of Amaranthus's pathetic, tiny form, the Tiger began to shred the black substance, sending it into the atmosphere in a shower of dust.

Time passed, or it didn't, and then all the blackness was gone. In its place was a haze, thick, almost impossible to see through, covering everything around them.

And in its midst, the small form of Amaranthus.

Then the mist began to reduce, and coalesce, and shrink into its original form. Then smaller still, and denser. It shrunk and shrunk until it was exceptionally tiny: only the size of a human fist. But its darkness was intense. The Tiger could feel it emanating even from where he stood watching in speechless fury.

All those mortal souls. All the other Creatures. What had been enough mass to cover a planet was now small enough to be held in a human hand.

Then Amaranthus bent down amongst the rubble of his shattered Mountain, and picked up the new dark stone. It hovered between his small hands, seeming to thrash about, but not touching his skin.

I cannot have them back, Amaranthus said quietly, *for they will not come back. They have chosen.*

Amaranthus cupped in his hands the remnants of innumerable lives, the immortal fragments of what could have and should have been lovely and eternal. But a simple rejection meant he could not touch them, could not bring them in to himself.

That was the problem with free will. A choice freely made could not – would not – be overridden. And these ones would not return, for they refused to.

He looked up at the one who had been Beraht, the Bright One. Once so dear, with tremendous potential, but who'd chosen the same as these.

You may not have my crown, Amaranthus told the Tiger. *But you may have what you have demanded. And with it, I speak your true name.*

The name this 'Tiger' held close, but refused to accept or to speak out. For to accept it would mean that all of this, all this war and hate, was for nothing.

Amaranthus spoke it out in a single breath, and the former

Beraht cowered. With it, the remnants of the Mountain of Glass shook and collapsed.

The name Amaranthus spoke could not be repeated by human lips, or even by most Creatures. But it meant one who was always reaching for the unattainable – always hungry, never satisfied. Always empty, never filled.

The one who strove and sought and fought fruitlessly, for it was all for the wrong things. And the right things had been those he'd already had, and had turned his back on.

That one shrieked, and his borrowed form exploded into ash, dissolving into the thinning atmosphere.

But he'd be back, Amaranthus knew. And when he was back, he'd have exactly what he'd asked for.

Epilogue:
The City of Light

Once, as a very small child, Jon had tried to fill a drinking glass all on his own for the very first time. The beverage had come out drip, drip from the dispenser, and he'd waited patiently, thinking this was how it worked. He'd even paused to take a tiny sip, then had put the glass back, although he'd been so thirsty.

Then along had come Anni, who'd said, 'Oh, it's not turned on properly'. She'd touched the tap, and a tremendous gush of liquid had come out. Jon's drink had been ready in an instant, and had overflowed onto the bench.

That was in a very small way what this felt like. Freedom from time, in comparison to his use of the Eternity Stone, the remnant gateways, and the time tunnels. They'd been just a tiny drop, a delicious taste of what *true* freedom felt like. It was like he'd been a tiny piece of glitter, and now he was a disco ball, with each facet reflecting a thousand new facets as he looked closer-

That's my comparison, an old friend told him from somewhere across this timeless place. *You don't even know what a disco ball is.*

Jon did now, because he was sharing in the memory. So seventies, but fun, right? And they'd all dressed up in bell-bottomed jeans and practiced dancing Night Fever, or something that was fun but looked terrible. Jon felt it as strongly as if he'd done it himself.

And then his old friend – Ashlea, from his earliest time travels – laughed. Jon laughed with her.

Not a disco ball then, he decided. A colossal gem with infinite faces – where each sparkle of light represented a moment, a place, where he could be fully immersed and experience every-thing going on around him, and join in the fun of people and places he'd never even imagined could exist.

And it was always changing, yet somehow he could find anything whenever he wanted. And every touch, every experience, felt fuller and more intense and perfect than his old self could have handled.

Jon stretched out his mind and focused on a single timeless moment, a beautiful one where he sat in the branches of a fruiting tree with Bets at his side. The scent of fruit and flowers filled the air. Her arms were wound around his waist, and her mind overlapped with his, bright and shining and joyful. And he caught a glimpse of her truest self, and her truest name that couldn't be pinpointed to one single word. *Elspeth-Bets-Bethie-Sweet One-Eager One-Bright One-Sister-Friend-Love-*

And then he pulled away from that moment, instead focusing on another beauty, another mind he'd been separated from in life, but now had the freedom to access at any time. Here, his birth mother moved through glowing time tunnels, something like those he'd used earlier. A connection shone with Anni, although Anni wasn't fully present, and Jon could hear the ongoing chatter between the two sisters. But when he allowed himself to fully join Maia in the tunnels, she turned to beam at him, even though the chatter didn't stop.

Eternity really did allow for multi-tasking.

Then they walked together along the time tunnel, fully absorbing all the scenes that flashed by around them. And as they walked, Jon felt himself change and shrink into his childlike self in line with the scenes around them. For they were walking along his own life's thread – reliving the memories which Maia had missed. Reliving them along with his mother, in such a beautiful way, without any pain.

Some way into the journey, a small figure popped through the wall. It was Elspeth, from their last day in their old life. Jon moved behind Maia as he'd done infinite times, and he saw Maia hand over a version of the Amaranthus circlet. The old version of Elspeth took it and dashed away, back into a past that now only existed in this time tunnel.

The time tunnel was his life's thread, for although the old Mountain of Glass had been destroyed along with its tapestry, the same tapestry existed here. Bigger. Better. *Real.*

But unlike in the old Mountain, here, in the City of Light, they could see its true design. And every single thread fit together to build a beautiful image. A story of pain, and suffering, and redemption that covered over all of the pain.

Jon smiled.

When Amaranthus withdrew from the Mountain to return Home, he also withdrew the Water of Life. It disappeared from every fragment of that place, taking the light with it. And what was left behind wasn't even solid enough to be called a wasteland – instead, it was the shadow of what had once been.

And when the one who'd been called Tiger and Beraht regained his form from the dust, it was to see that he had everything, and nothing.

All yours.

For Amaranthus, returning in full to the City of Light felt like taking in a deep breath. Relaxing. Allowing himself to take up all the space he truly ought, without the restrictions forced by the nature of the place he'd been visiting.

And with him came all his new people, the former mortals who'd been trapped in time, but who were now like him. Free. Everlasting. Exactly what he'd first come to that realm for, even knowing the outcome.

But the tiny dead coal came too: all that remained of those who had denied him. Amaranthus drew it into his deepest self, into the Heart of his power and identity. And there it would stay, separate from the beauty around it. Alone, hidden, but never to be forgotten.

Always in his heart. But now, in nobody else's.

And across the Light Realm, Amaranthus felt the smiles of myriad children – his earlier people, and the newest ones.

And he smiled too.

Dear Reader,

OH MY GOSH this felt like the world's longest novel. (It's not even the longest in this series – that's Mountain of Glass.) But I was finishing off a seven-book series that I wrote over thirteen years (!!!) and trying to tie up all loose ends, make the heroes win and the villains lose in a satisfying way, and – yes – end the fantasy world I'd created.

It was a big job, and so serious in some places. I made a joke in a previous afterword, something about killing all my characters. And I actually did that, too. Of course, in this series death can just be a pathway to immortality, so it wasn't so bad.

For those who've been with me through this entire journey, I hope you enjoyed it. I hope you found it fun, and interesting, and surprising, and maybe even thought-provoking. I also hope you go and read another one of my books! Try *Tyger* or *Take Me Home* or *Breaking the Glass Slipper*, or just have a nice big break from reading.

Will I ever come back to the world of Across Time and Space? I have no plans to extend this series, what with the world ending and so forth. But there is room for a book 5.5. Ash and George's children, growing up between three time periods with the social challenges that raises, and running into all sorts of supernatural shenanigans in Erastus in the twenty-fourth century.

Maybe. Just maybe…

If you enjoyed this book, or at least didn't hate it, feel free to leave a rating or a review wherever you bought it. Reviews in particular really help books get seen by readers (rather than languishing for years at the bottom of the algorithm or however it works).

That's all.